Annie Marks was born in Twickenham and developed her taste for history at an early age by being lucky enough to attend primary school within Hampton Court Palace, where history lessons were simply walking in the corridors and State apartments. In 1970 she moved to the Isle of Wight, but her spiritual home is the West Country, particularly the moors of Devon and Cornwall, where she plans to retire. She is married and has two grown-up sons. Her previous novel was *Daughter of Tremar*.

AN ENCHANTED PLACE

Sequel to DAUGHTER OF TREMAR.

It is 1942. Four years after Julia's return to normal life from almost twenty-four years in the county asylum, Tremar has become a convalescent home for officers for the duration of the war. In the beginning, everything is fine: Julia has both her beloved husband Matt and the beautiful Annie, for whom she and Matt committed murder. But Annie has taken a shine to a heavily disfigured young airman, and Julia harbours grave suspicions about his family. Meanwhile, there is the arrival of the dreadfully injured Oliver Crompton who loved Julia so destructively in 1938 . . .

Books by Annie Marks
Published by The House of Ulverscroft:

DAUGHTER OF TREMAR

ANNIE MARKS

AN ENCHANTED PLACE

Complete and Unabridged

ULVERSCROFT
Leicester

First published in Great Britain in 2002 by
Robert Hale Limited
London

First Large Print Edition
published 2004
by arrangement with
Robert Hale Limited
London

British Library CIP Data

Marks, Annie
    An enchanted place.—Large print ed.—
    Ulverscroft large print series: general fiction
    1. Ex-mental patients—England—Cornwall—Fiction
    2. Hospitals, Convalescent—England—Cornwall—
    Fiction 3. Large type books
    I. Title
    813.5′4 [F]

    ISBN 1-84395-149-5

Published by
F. A. Thorpe (Publishing)
Anstey, Leicestershire

Set by Words & Graphics Ltd.
Anstey, Leicestershire
Printed and bound in Great Britain by
T. J. International Ltd., Padstow, Cornwall

This book is printed on acid-free paper

1

1941

Tremar was beautiful, basking in May sunshine. Gulls called in the clear, blue sky and across the formal lawns, towards the old grey manor, the wind blew salty from the sea. Blossom snowed on to a carpet of bluebells in the orchard, and the rhododendron walk bloomed in a riot of glorious colour.

May had brought blossom, spring and the promise of fruitfulness more than three hundred times to Tremar, and as the centuries had passed little had changed. The manor had grown older and weathered, the dower house and the terrace had been added much later, but were perfectly blended now; apple trees had been born, grown old and died in the orchard, and great oaks and beeches had grown up on the fringes of the formal grounds, enclosing the generations of Drakes who had lived their varied lives within its bounds.

They had been a happy and prosperous family, the Drakes of Tremar; supporters of the King in the days of the Civil War and well rewarded for their loyalty after the restoration of the monarchy. They had borne healthy children and been careful with the family fortune through the centuries, and in 1900 the 12th baronet, Sir George, and his wife, Lady Florence, had been the parents of a fine son and daughter. Another generation to uphold the proud name of Tremar.

And then they had spoiled it.

Alexander, their handsome son, had died in the mud in France in 1917, like hundreds of thousands of others; a glorious hero. To his memory they had raised a full-sized, marble monument, exquisitely carved and placed in the north aisle of the village church, where it would probably lie for hundreds of years to come.

Julia, their beautiful daughter, however, they had committed without pity or compassion to the county asylum, for being guilty of nothing more than the sin of desire; and they had left her to rot there for twenty three and a half years. A terrified 17-year-old girl abandoned to give birth alone to her poor little dead baby, and subsequently starved, raped, beaten and bullied as Tremar crumbled with its guilt.

But in 1938 Julia had been rescued, and had come home to Tremar in triumph; and there she had found, to her fury, the man who had fathered her child all those years ago. Not dead, as she had always believed, but living in squalor, with his downtrodden wife and cruelly ill-treated daughter; consumed by his guilt and reduced to a life of alcohol and bitterness. Killing him had been in her mind from the beginning; it had simply been a matter of choosing her time.

Annie, exhausted by her father's cruelty, Matt, the man she loved, and Julia herself, had conspired to murder Arthur in the middle of one of the worst storms in history, and had left him tossing in the surf. It had been a new beginning. Now, after almost a quarter of a century, Julia had a loving, gentle husband and a daughter to replace the one born dead in the pitiless cold of Blackridge asylum; a beautiful girl to love and cherish, to watch over with overwhelming pride and to dream blissfully for.

Now Tremar flourished again under the last in its line, and gave generously to reward the kind hands that cared for it. Now it enveloped the final Drake in its tranquillity and, in the three years since her return, there had been numerous changes, but Tremar had always rewarded love with love, and did so now with great generosity.

There were no formal gardens to speak of any more; this new war had revamped the views from the windows considerably, and Tremar now looked upon very different lives, many of them heavy with broken dreams and promises, but it offered what it had always offered: peace and security.

Below the terrace, where three years ago there had been an old summerhouse gently rotting with the passing years, badly mutilated young officers tended vegetable beds. All of them were either severely disfigured or had missing limbs; all had been in the front line, and for all of them their war was over.

Captain Guy Taylor, who wore his army uniform proudly — with the legs of the trousers neatly pinned out of the way — had learned to manoeuvre his wheelchair quite skilfully now, and collected the eggs from the old stables every morning, before getting himself down into the vegetable patch to do his bit. Nobody made him do it; nobody made any of them do anything. They chose to work under the grey terrace, in the warmth of the spring air, and chatted peacefully as they worked.

Guy would never go to war again; when he was discharged he would go home to his wife and small son, and hope to find something to give a legless ex-army officer a purpose in life. Guy had warm brown eyes and a quick wit. He also had great courage where his artificial legs were concerned, for he struggled with them painfully, but his courage was there for everybody to see, and no one knew how he felt inside.

Leaving the basket of eggs on the terrace as was his routine, he swung the wheels of his chair sideways to go down the gentle slope to the gardens, and found, as Julia came up towards him, that he was jammed against the wall.

'Hullo, Guy,' she said, smiling. 'You're a bit stuck, would you like a hand?'

'Oh thanks, Julia,' replied the ever cheerful Guy. 'Where's our lovely Minnie this morning, by the way?'

Julia freed the wheelchair and pointed it in the right direction.

'She's up in the housekeeper's room,' she replied, 'with Mrs Collins. They're doing some running repairs to sheets and blankets. I'll send her out to you later, if you promise to make her giggle.'

The bright-eyed, brown-haired Guy grinned. He was a lot younger than Minnie; a lot younger than Julia, too. He'd been a very keen sportsman before the war, an exceptional cricketer, but he never talked about that.

'My wife doesn't believe me, you know?' he said as he started down the slope towards the

5

vegetables, and glanced back at Julia, 'She says I can't be growing vegetables, I've never grown anything in my life, I'm a townie!' He uttered a peal of laughter. 'Just goes to show, doesn't it? I suppose one day the docs'll tell me I'm well enough to go home, but I shan't half miss Tremar when I do. I could get used to this gracious living, you know?'

'I think I could, too,' Julia replied with a chuckle, 'but I never seem to be able to snatch enough time to find out. Anyway, you enjoy it, I don't think you're going anywhere for a while yet. And you can tell your wife it's not just vegetables you're good at, either. Minnie thinks the sun rises and sets over you!' Blowing him a kiss she watched as he coasted down the slope and began to wheel himself off along the gravel path.

The dower had been a long-stay convalescent home for officers since the beginning of 1940. Julia and Matt had been told it would occupy the whole of the dower and some of the top floor of the manor, but that if they preferred, it would not be allowed to encroach on their lives. To Julia that had seemed a nonsense; she was hardly going to deny the patients free use of the library, half of them had precious little else to do but read, and then she had had the idea for the vegetable beds, and those who could worked in them, whilst everyone benefited from them.

At full stretch there was room for twenty patients who like Guy, had all had their lives shattered. Probably because most of them were there for so long, the merging of life in the dower and life in the manor had happened quite early on, and Julia and Matt regularly ran into people in uniform on the stairs as they came and went from the old house.

Annie's mother, Gladys, had taken on the job of organizing the domestic arrangements for the dower and had recruited five girls from the village, whilst Mrs Collins, Julia's own housekeeper, had recruited another four for the manor, since there were a regular five people in residence now. They were young, sometimes a bit nervous, and worked on a strict rota, and they regularly reminded Julia of how life had been when she was a child, in the days before her parents had betrayed her.

They were dressed differently, of course. There were no girls in black dresses and white aprons being chased about by the housekeeper Mrs Grassick — who had been truly terrifying — no footmen and bootboys scurrying about under the fiercely watchful eye of the butler, Mr Baskin; but Gladys and

Mrs Collins between them could be sufficiently ferocious when required, and Julia happily enjoyed her memories. They were good.

It was spring 1941, and they were two and a half years into the war. Against the odds the Battle of Britain had been won, and the evacuation of Dunkirk had been little short of miraculous, but with France fallen, the bombers came now, flying over Polwean on their way to Plymouth and the South Wales valleys, and the number of civilian casualties was on a scale never before seen in war. It was not nice, this new sort of warfare, and it was all around to be seen, in its full horror.

Julia went along the terrace with the basket of eggs and stepped through the French windows into the drawing-room, turning once more to watch the young officers working beneath the terrace. She saw Guy wheel himself along beside rows of peas that were just blossoming with white flowers and stop beside a young man erecting bean sticks. He was precise in his actions, tying the tops together with string, and he stood with his back to her so that all she could see was his amazing yellow hair. He would turn round in a moment and she would see eyes as blue as the sky, with lips pink and sensitive . . . and an ugly scar across his face that looked as if someone had carelessly swung an axe at him.

Julia had been watching him carefully since his arrival, for he worked amongst the vegetables with fierce determination, but as yet the only person of his own kind he ever seemed to talk to was Guy. He could see only light and dark through those wonderful blue eyes, which was why he was so precise with his fingers, and he was one of the few to whom Winston Churchill had said was owed so much, but the look on his face told her how deep his pain went. He had to go back to hospital in a couple of months' time to have another operation on the shattered bones in his face, and after that he would be back again for another long convalescence: Tremar was to be home to this young man for some time to come.

However, Julia's attention to Squadron Leader Patrick Thornby wasn't quite as altruistic as it might have been, for there was someone else at Tremar who had taken an instant fancy to him, and someone else to whom he spoke whenever he could. Annie had noticed him the morning after his arrival, and had gone immediately to introduce herself. Ever since then Patrick had done nothing much except talk about Annie; and Guy had become Julia's confidant.

In the beginning it had amused him to do a

spot of gentle matchmaking, until he had discovered that Patrick apparently had a fiancée in Ireland. Then a couple of letters from her had arrived which he hadn't even wanted read to him, and he had casually told Guy that the engagement had been engineered by his mother before the war and that he had no feelings towards the girl one way or the other.

For Guy, who did not come from a family that behaved in such an odd fashion, it seemed inexplicable, but it had sent all Julia's defences up immediately, and Guy and Patrick were fast discovering that where Annie was concerned, Julia was a tigress with a precious cub.

Underfed, filthy little Annie with the phenomenal intellect and resilient spirit, who had fallen out of the cedar tree above the terrace on a summer evening in June 1938 into the middle of Julia's life. She was grown up now. She would be eighteen this coming Christmas, she had breasts and long legs, and many of the young officers in the dower watched her with undisguised pleasure.

She had never had much schooling, but she wrote beautifully and had read pretty much every book in the library. Julia had sent her away to school in the January after her fifteenth birthday, but she had hated it and stayed exactly two terms. With the outbreak of war she had donned overalls and gone out on the land, and there she was in her element. She could milk twice as fast as anybody else, she was quick and gentle in the lambing sheds, and she ploughed expertly. She was Matt's second-in-command and he relied on her judgement; Annie never let him down. But there wasn't any doubt that since the arrival of Squadron Leader Thornby, Annie had discovered that there was more to life than earth and animals. She had discovered there were different kinds of men, too. There were drunken, vicious fathers, like her dead one; there were lovely, proud fathers, like Matt; and there were handsome boys who would make excellent fathers — like Patrick!

Patrick turned and stared towards the house as if he sensed that he was being watched. Julia saw Guy speak to him and then reach out a hand to touch him briefly, and at once she saw the confusion of being newly blind on his face. Sad for him, she turned from the window and went down to the kitchens with the basket of eggs.

The beginning of a new season when Tremar must give to the full. There was hardly a field left now that didn't grow food, and the face of the estate had changed drastically, for there were now crops growing on land that hadn't been ploughed for a couple of hundred years. Matt was in overall control, and he — and, to a large extent, the Government — decided what was grown where. The bulk of the work on the estate, however, was done by the Women's Land Army, and they had changed the face of Polwean considerably! They were a joyous bunch of young women, but they were mostly town girls and had blown in amongst the narrow-minded long-term inhabitants of the village like a small explosion. They were loved or loathed, disapproved of or looked upon with kindness, but they were like a breath of fresh air!

In the great, cavernous kitchens of the manor, Julia put the basket on the table and counted the eggs. She kept nineteen chickens and one cockerel in the old stables, and these hens were cared for by the servicemen, who in the main enjoyed the eggs. At Five Elms, one of the estate farms, there were two hundred hens, whose eggs went to the Government.

She put the eggs in the fridge, and took the basket into the scullery. As she came back there was the sound of a stick tapping on the kitchen steps, accompanied by the uneven tread of its owner, and turning she greeted

Rory Nelson as he came down into the kitchen. In his free hand he held a canvas bag which clinked when he lifted it carefully and placed it on the table: six bottles of excellent quality sherry.

'The other six are still at the top of the stairs,' he said. Julia retrieved them for him and stood them on the table beside the first six.

They gazed at them appreciatively for they were a real treat — with a shrouded history. Julia had tried asking him about them, but Rory came up with the drink regularly and never revealed its source. 'Them as asks no questions don't get told no lies,' he had said in the beginning, and now Julia just accepted the sherry run placidly.

'Your 'friend' on his three-monthly visit to Penzance?' she observed, and he chuckled.

Rory Nelson, a man well in his fifties, had taken over the running of the village school when the headmaster had been called up at the beginning of the war. He was very charming, neither particularly handsome nor particularly plain, but his manners were delightful and he was much respected at Tremar.

He referred to himself as a government refugee because his home had been requisitioned by the military at the beginning of the

13

war, and having been offered a home at Tremar he was a most accommodating companion. He had grown up in Polwean, and then left, but had returned to the village in 1938 after a long absence. He was supposed to be retired, for he was extremely lame and not terribly robust as a result of the last war, but his dream of living out his old age at Cliff House, which stood high up on the cliffs on the other side of the harbour, had crumbled somewhat when he had found himself politely invited to find alternative digs for the duration, and the offer of a home at Tremar had seemed like a gift from God.

Rory was determined to pay his way. They drank a sherry most nights before dinner as a matter of course, and it was always provided by him. He bought spirits, too, when he could get his hands on them, and shared them generously.

Julia had accepted the war, she'd had no choice, but she did not compromise with it. Not a single one of the inhabitants of the manor would have dreamed of coming to the dining table wearing working clothes, and when guests were invited from the convalescent home, they always wore their uniforms. Julia, Matt, Rory and Annie dined with guests regularly, and always with the silver cutlery and finest china. It might not have been

appropriate with the world at war, Julia
thought occasionally, but it was absolutely
appropriate for Tremar and its fragile
community of broken and damaged young
men — and if anyone had ever thought to
disapprove, they wouldn't have dared say so
to her!

'No questions then, Rory dear,' she said,
kissing his cheek, 'but you spoil us, you know.
There's all your wine down in the cellar, too,
and we seem to be drinking it at an alarming
rate. I thought you'd only moved it down
here to stop the army guzzling it up at Cliff
House.'

He chuckled.

'Well that was partly the reason, certainly,'
he replied, 'but really I had an enormous
amount and, if I'm honest, I never quite knew
why I bought it. I think someone told me
once that wine was a good investment, but I
can't imagine when I thought I was going to
drink it. When mine's all gone and yours is all
gone, well then we'll do without. Until then
we'll jolly well enjoy it! And I'm off back to
school. See you this evening.'

They went up into the hall together and
then Julia went on up the polished wooden
staircase through the dim coolness of the
house, making her way along to the
housekeeper's room. It was a huge, airy room

with linen cupboards, trestle tables and a sewing machine. The room looked down over the grounds, where Guy and his pals worked on the vegetable garden, and across the orchard towards the pine copse and the sea. Julia remembered the housekeeper's room from childhood — though she had never been welcome in it in those days — but more fondly she remembered making Annie's first little summer dresses up here in 1938, and also the two of them sitting there, making her wedding dress and the bridesmaid dresses Annie and Minnie had worn.

She and Matt had enjoyed two and a half years of married life now, and they couldn't have been happier. Two people plagued by loneliness and solitude who had found everything they were looking for in each other. Matt ran the estate and Julia ran the house, and everything that went on around them was a product of their ingenuity.

As she walked into the room, Minnie looked up at her and then grabbed the repair she had just completed, holding it out like a child for approval. It was the only thing Minnie could still do now, use a sewing machine. She had even lost the co-ordination to feed herself successfully, but provided Mrs Collins set it up for her, she could still turn the handle and feed the material through to sew a seam. A lifetime of such work performed at Blackridge, Julia thought sadly.

Julia walked over to her and bent to kiss her, running a finger along the seam.

'That looks good to me,' she said gently. 'What does Mrs Collins think?'

Mrs Collins smiled at Minnie proudly, and above all else Julia appreciated her housekeeper's care of Minnie.

'She'm proper professional, an' no mistake,' she said. 'It's a fact I wouldn't get 'alf as much done without 'er. She do work like you do, ma dear, neatly and thoroughly an' without complaint.'

'There you are,' Julia murmured, slipping her arms about Minnie's shoulders. 'From one who knows.' Minnie snuggled against her, searing Julia with memories.

Twenty-three years of gazing from barred windows at distant moors that might as well have been the surface of another planet, such was their unattainability, and all through those years, this vulnerable and damaged human being had been all that had kept Julia alive: for frightened little Minnie, robbed of most of the skills of life, had apparently chosen Julia as her protector only days after her arrival at Blackridge, and had loved her with the devotion of a dog from that day onwards.

'Guy's been asking about you this morning,' Julia murmured, kissing the top of her head affectionately. 'He's outside working in the vegetable garden. Would you like to go and sit with him for a while?'

'Guy!' Minnie exclaimed in delight, and Julia helped her up.

Minnie's legs were stiff and crooked as a result of dreadful treatment from her drunken father in her childhood. They grew stiffer each year and walking became more and more difficult. One day, if she lived that long, she would be forced permanently into a wheelchair — but it was unlikely, the doctor had said. Julia had been warned that Minnie's life was growing short.

She needed to be helped on the stairs and then most particularly on the terrace steps, but the moment she saw Guy he held out his arms to her, and she stumbled clumsily towards him like a happy child. He wouldn't leave her, Julia knew that, so she put a rug on the ground beside his wheelchair and sat Minnie on it comfortably. At once Guy began to tease her, and at once she began to giggle.

Julia looked at Patrick; he was tying the bean sticks together with the precision of a watchmaker, concentrating on his task to the exclusion of everything else. She tried to imagine the face without the deep scar that cut across it so obscenely, and she felt sad. When there had been no blemish on that face had there been no pain either, she wondered? When he had been smooth and handsome, had he been brave and fearless? She suspected not, other than when he had been facing enemy aircraft above the Channel. Then, she was certain, he had been a hero. But his face was far too sensitive for him to have been a happy child, she thought, and wondered if she would ever find out.

'Hullo, Patrick,' she said, and he looked up.

She touched one of his hands and he smiled, and then returned her touch with a gentle squeeze of her fingers.

'You're doing a wonderful job there,' she said and went back up to the housekeeper's room.

She picked up at the sewing machine where Minnie had left off, taking the next sheet on the pile. Mrs Collins had already cut it down the centre and, with the speed and skill of years at Blackridge, Julia sewed the two edges together and then began hemming the sides.

Mrs Collins was darning a blanket, working with neat tiny stitches, and with the window open the peaceful sounds of the men working beneath the terrace and the gulls calling in the spring air filled the room.

Almost nightly now, the village heard the

uneven drone of distant enemy aircraft and the boom of anti-aircraft guns. They came in across this corner of the Cornish coast, but so far they hadn't dropped any bombs, not coming in or going out, and they were just a noise, rather than a fear. Closer military noises came from the army training camp five miles away at Cliff House. Cliff House and the camp around it were full of Canadians, and the bombers might not have made a difference to the village, but the Canadians had caused a considerable flutter amongst the village maidens — and amongst the Land Army girls. The war had certainly shaken up Polwean!

From her place at the sewing machine, Julia heard Minnie giggling with Guy in the garden, and looking up, smiled gently at Mrs Collins.

'Any news this morning?' she asked. 'Anything happened anywhere that we should know about?'

It was recognized that Mrs Collins was the voice of Polwean at Tremar, and she regularly brought in all the news. *Gossip* was supplied by the two fearsome spinsters who ran the village shop, and who had a talent for spite and a gift for stirring up trouble. Miss Penrose and Miss Hewlett always knew exactly what was going on, and made up what they didn't know. Everyone in the village was frightened of them; yet everyone, apparently, told them everything, and they could be relied upon to spread the word. Julia listened with interest to what they said and tried to pick out any nuggets of truth that might bob about on the surface of their witches' brew — and Julia was the only person in the village towards whom they showed the slightest deference. Class rearing its ugly head!

Mrs Collins, however, never passed on scandal.

'There's one piece of news should interest you,' she said as she finished her darning and deftly folded the blanket, sorting through a pile for another one. 'Seems that little Mrs Tregennis from up Pinch Street 'as 'eard from Mrs Crompton again. You 'member I told you as 'ow Dr Crompton was pulled from the water ever so badly hurt 'bout two months ago?' Julia nodded. 'Well, seems 'e'm gettin' better, slowly, an' Mrs Crompton thinks 'e'm goin' t'be well enough to leave 'ospital in a few weeks. They'm going to be sendin' him for convalescence somewhere, cos 'e'm badly crippled, an' Mrs Crompton says they mentioned Tremar. Well, you can *imagine* what them ol' witches in the shop 'ad to say about that, can't you?'

Julia got up slowly from her sewing

machine and went to stare out of the window. Down below her, Minnie was giggling with helpless delight as Guy teased her mercilessly, and Patrick, who had finished his bean sticks, was sitting on the grass having a smoke. From the rhododendron walk the pony and cart suddenly appeared driven by Annie, her mass of red hair done up in a jaunty scarf, her arms brown and strong as she held the reins and urged the pony on. In the back of the cart two black and white Border collies sat with their ears cocked and their pink tongues lolling from their mouths.

Julia was transfixed with her memories.

★ ★ ★

Surgeon Commander Oliver Crompton, once an ambitious would be consultant, and now a crippled war hero, lay in his narrow hospital bed and, through his one eye, stared at the ceiling above his head. One eye, one good arm, one good leg. He would walk with a limp for the rest of his life, because half his left foot was missing.

That, were it all, he thought bitterly, he could happily have lived with. Half a foot wouldn't have left him stranded in life. A mangled hand and a missing eye did, though. Not much good would come from a one eyed, one handed doctor, and certainly not from one with such appalling facial scars.

He had only a hazy recollection of the moment when his life had changed so completely. He remembered a bitterly cold night at sea, and one of those occasions during war when boredom, not fear, was the enemy. He knew he had been in his cabin, writing home, trying desperately to think of something to say, and a dull, vibrating explosion that came out of nowhere had caused the destroyer to lurch violently to port as the U-boat torpedo tore half the hull away. He remembered noise and panic and something falling from somewhere and severing half his foot, causing him to land in a terrifying wall of flame. Strangely enough, he remembered the awful smell, the stink of burning oil, but after that there was only a hazy sensation of suffocating pain, and then nothing until he awoke on another ship bound for England, and realized, through the unspeakable agony of his injuries, that he at least was still alive and not a prisoner of war.

In the beginning all that had mattered was relief from the pain. They had told him that they would have to amputate two of his fingers, and a bit of a third, because they were too badly burned to be saved, and they had explained that skin grafts took time and patience, and none of it had mattered unless it was a way out of his agony. Now, though, the pain was reduced to tolerable levels and he was able to see beyond it.

And there was nothing there.

It was a large, one-time private house, this hospital that was now the tight world in which he lived; a regimented world of starched nurses and white-coated doctors. The nurses took his temperature and jollied him along, the doctors explained their treatments — he earned that much because he had once been one of them — but made him no promises.

Somewhere, out in the middle of a freezing ocean, his gung-ho delight of fighting a war lay in ruins on the bottom, along with the destroyer he had very nearly gone down with. Many of his shipboard companions had done just that, including the captain; many more had died in the water, freezing to death and surrounded by burning oil, their injuries so horrific that death had come quickly to their mutilated bodies.

Oliver had yet to decide whether he was glad to be alive, but on the whole he thought not. Only one thing in the world kept him from despair: his two beautiful children. He saw them every Saturday afternoon; they came with their mother, his wife Sophie, and they were the light of his life. He was allowed to go outside in a wheelchair when his children came, for they were not encouraged to come into the ward. They loved him and snuggled up to him — but neither of them had yet seen the full extent of his injuries. They had not seen his hand without bandages — or fingers — and they had not fully seen the burn scars on his face.

He had been told that he would be going to a convalescent home within a few weeks, because all that could be done for him had been done, and now he must learn to live with the way he would look for the rest of his life. He had been told that his wife was taking a particular interest in where they sent him, and Oliver feared that above all else, for his marriage was in shreds; it had broken down before he had ever gone away to fight, and he was terrified that Sophie planned to ship him off to a distant corner of the country somewhere, so that he wouldn't see his children at all any more.

His mother fed him that poison when she came to see him on a Wednesday afternoon. His mother and his wife loathed each other, and he was well aware that right back at the beginning of the war he had forced Sophie to move into his parents' home in Arundel — and he had not done it with any sense of altruism. He had done it as an act of spite. It rebounded on him now, painfully.

The door opened suddenly and there was a rustling sound in the room. A brisk-looking nurse in a starched white cap and apron came to the bed and looked down at him. She was an Irish girl and she had extraordinary red hair and green eyes. She reminded him regularly of a little Cornish lass called Annie Paynter, and every time he thought of Annie he shied away from the memory, because that meant he would have to remember the rest of it. Remember Tremar, and Julia Logan . . . his love for her, his pain, his hate, and his obsession.

He fought hard not to think of Julia Logan. Ever.

'I see we're not asleep,' the nurse observed in her pretty Irish lilt, and not for the first time Oliver savagely thought that if he'd ever been in a position to go back to doctoring, he would never again have been guilty of using the royal 'we'.

'We're not tired,' he retorted edgily. 'What we are, nurse, is bored to death.'

She smiled.

'Well, your mother and father are here,' she said, 'so that should cheer you up a bit. I'll help you into your wheelchair and you can sit outside with them for a little while, it's a beautiful afternoon.'

Oliver sighed heavily and then began to lever himself up. It was hard to remember now when life had not been painful, when getting up and sitting down or taking a little walk had just been something you did without any particular thought. It was all such an effort these days.

'No clothes today?' he asked wryly, and as the nurse steadied him so that he could turn and ease himself into his wheelchair, she laughed softly.

'I think you can receive them in your dressing-gown today,' she replied. 'After all, you've been poorly for a couple of days, and it *is* your mother. You don't have to maintain the stiff upper lip *all* the time, you know.'

Oliver gave her a sour look and uttered an entirely mirthless laugh.

'I'm lucky I've still got an upper lip, so I'm given to understand,' he observed. 'I'd be a lot luckier if I had the fingers on my left hand and the sight in my left eye, of course. I'd be in a position to choose for myself then, wouldn't I? I wouldn't be a captive audience for my mother every Wednesday afternoon, and my wife every Saturday afternoon. Choice is an exquisite luxury that you simply don't recognize until you haven't got it anymore. Did you know that?'

The red haired, Irish nurse chuckled at him gently.

'Ah, get along with you,' she said. 'You'll feel better in a day or two. Your children will be here Saturday, and you know you always enjoy seeing them.'

Oliver held his heavily bandaged, ruined left hand close against him as the nurse negotiated the wheelchair out into the corridor and then along towards the drawing-room and the garden.

It was a large drawing-room, but nothing like the size of the one at Tremar, and nothing like so exquisitely furnished, though there were still touches of a by-gone age: a remarkable gilt mirror above the fireplace and a small gilt clock on the mantelpiece in front of it. The clock bore no comparison to the porcelain and ormolu clock that stood on the marble mantelpiece at Tremar, but it tinkled out the hours and half-hours in exactly the same tone.

As he was wheeled in he saw his solidly built mother and his faintly unkempt, slightly vague father sitting there waiting for him. Harriet Crompton had iron-grey, neatly permed hair and might not have been entirely unattractive had her mean-spiritedness not been so apparent in the lines of her face. She wore a brown costume, despite the fact that

28

the weather was warm, and clutched a no-nonsense handbag on her lap, beneath her full-blown chest. Charles Crompton clutched a rather battered Panama hat, which had long since seen better days, and wore a cardigan with leather patches in the elbows. His trousers needed pressing and his shoes needed cleaning; he looked to have come straight from the garden, which he probably had, and no doubt, Oliver thought with a sinking heart, he had been nagged non-stop from leaving home to arriving here at the hospital.

Abruptly the little clock on the mantelpiece tinkled out the hour of three and Oliver turned to stare out of the window. It didn't look right, so he closed his good eye to shut out sight altogether, and in his heart he saw a warm, grey terrace with a cedar tree bowing its branches above it. In the distance he saw an orchard, blossoming with spring, and beyond that a pine copse that mingled its scents with the wind from the sea. And in his heart he saw a woman, tall and beautiful, with chestnut hair and a lovely smile. A woman with deep, gentle eyes that gazed into his and took the world away . . . *Julia* . . .

Oliver was transfixed with his memories.

2

Sunday morning. Sophie Crompton hated Sundays more than any other day of the week. She rolled on to her back in the big, solid double bed she doubted she would ever again share with Oliver, and stared at the ceiling. It was cracked. Well, that wasn't saying much, most people's ceilings were cracked from the bombing these days; but it was cream, like the walls. Cream paint, dark brown furniture, a brown and cream carpet, and blackout curtains at the window; dull and uninspiring, like its owner.

In a minute Harriet Crompton would bang on her door and announce that she was going to early service, and would Sophie kindly have the children washed and dressed and suitably breakfasted when she returned, so that they could all troop off to church again for the eleven o'clock service.

Every week it was the same. Summer and winter. Year in, year out.

Edward had been three years old when they had come to live here with Oliver's parents in 1939, and Alice almost seven; now he was six and Alice just ten, and the

30

intervening years had done them no favours at all. Edward was an intransigent child; he hated his grandmother fiercely and, when sufficiently pushed, was given to vicious tantrums. He bit her when the rage was upon him, threw things and screeched, and when she punished him, which she was still able to do because she was a lot bigger than him, she simply made him worse.

Alice, on the other hand, had started out life as a quiet, rather nervous little girl, and her appalling grandmother, a life of painful sporadic bullying at school and the months of the blitz when they had spent so many nights in a velvet-black, earthy-smelling underground shelter, had rendered her virtually silent now. She did manage to talk to her daddy on their Saturday afternoon visits to the hospital, but the rest of the time she said very little indeed. She wet the bed on a regular basis, for which her grandmother punished her by refusing to let her have a drink after four in the afternoon and making her go to bed mad with thirst, and she was terrified of the dark.

They had been Sophie's pride and joy, her two lovely children. She had been very young when she had married Oliver; immature and romantic; and he had been wonderfully handsome and touchingly attentive. Neither of the births had been easy: Sophie was a thin, narrow little thing, dainty and fragile and not really designed for childbirth, but she had been so proud to present Oliver with a daughter and a son. She had planned to bring them up in an atmosphere of happiness, to let them learn through play and sharing with each other; she had never bargained for Oliver's betrayal, and worse than that, his punishment of her afterwards, for not understanding.

Abruptly she heard her mother-in-law's footfall outside in the corridor and there was a sharp rap at her door.

'Are you awake?' came the voice, muffled by the wooden door.

Sophie sighed and gazed at the ceiling. When she thought of Harriet Crompton it actually made her feel physically sick, and sometimes it was awfully hard to answer her.

She said flatly, 'Yes, I'm awake. How could I not be?' and the door opened.

This morning, Harriet's costume was grey and she wore a pale blue blouse underneath it with a neat collar. She was a large woman with broad feet, and she was heavy on her shoes, a fact that was obvious nowadays when shoes were not so easy to come by and the rule was make-do-and-mend. Hers were polished, but quite clearly old. Black shoes with a firmly low heel.

'Would you get Daddy's breakfast at the same time as you get yours and the children's, please?' she said, watching Sophie with spiteful eyes in her prim face. 'And be sure to be ready for 10.15, if you don't mind.'

Sophie hauled herself up and her lovely, corn-coloured, silky hair hung untidily about her head. She wore a satin nightgown; it too was old, but she had taken care of it over the years, though she wasn't quite sure what for. There was no one to look pretty for in bed any longer, nor any prospect of such a thing in the foreseeable future.

'I was thinking of keeping Edward home this morning,' she murmured. 'He was fretful and a bit feverish after we came back from seeing Oliver yesterday afternoon.'

Harriet Crompton's mouth tightened and her eyes were snake-like.

'No, Sophie,' she replied. 'You know the rules. When you live in my house, you will attend church on Sundays. All of you. Now get him up and get him dressed, and you tell him from me that if he creates a scene in church this morning, I will give him a sound thrashing, so help me God I will!'

'Oh, I don't think you need God's help, Mother,' Sophie muttered. 'You manage just fine on your own!'

Harriet Crompton pressed her lips together at the jibe. She and Sophie had acknowledged each other as enemies a long time ago, and in fact Harriet would have liked nothing more than to see her and the children leave — except that they had nowhere to go.

She knew there had been some trouble when her son had been the doctor in that village in Cornwall, and though she had never been furnished with the facts, she had seen for herself how cold the relationship had grown. When Oliver had insisted on closing up their London flat at the outbreak of the war, she had been astonished to receive her daughter-in-law and her grandchildren as permanent residents, and further astonished by Oliver's belligerent refusal to let them go up to Fort William to be with Sophie's father, who lived there with his sister now he was widowed.

Harriet didn't know why he had behaved in the way he had, and Sophie didn't really know, either. The difference was that Harriet believed that if it was Oliver's wish, then it was right. Her assumption was that whilst he was away fighting, he wanted her style of unbending discipline for his children, having received it himself as a small boy, and she had therefore immediately set about imposing it. Sophie had just faced up to having been betrayed yet again — and this was far worse than anything Oliver had done to her in Polwean.

She had been on the verge of leaving — to go God knew where — when Oliver had been pulled so horribly injured from the sea. After that, leaving hadn't been an option, since with her in mind the powers that be had put him in hospital only a very short distance away from the house in Arundel. Only now they were talking about convalescence, and in passing someone had mentioned Tremar. It had only been in passing, because the assumption had been that he would want to remain close to where his family was, but the idea had set Sophie's mind racing.

It would be nice, she thought bitterly as she listened to her mother-in-law marching away along the corridor and prepared to drag herself from bed, to throw him back at Julia Logan. Let her see what had become of him, the handsome doctor she had stolen from his wife and children! But more than that, so much more than that, at last here was her chance to get away from Harriet Crompton.

Susan Tregennis had offered them a home in Polwean, on a temporary basis at least, and she was sure it wouldn't be too difficult to find work in the village. At the moment she worked on a voluntary basis with Harriet, doing jobs she was ordered to do, being belittled and humiliated. All the dirty jobs came her way, the ones the other damned women in this bloody voluntary organization — to which she didn't want to belong anyway — didn't want to do. Oh Harriet certainly enjoyed that.

Then there were the children: Alice, who was so frightened of some of the evacuee children from London with whom she went to school that she wept with despair on occasions; Edward, who had been hauled up before the headmistress for biting twice already, and had only been at school a very short time. If they could go back to the little school in Polwean, if they could be removed from anyone who wanted to beat them or punish them, then surely it wasn't too late to create the children she had always dreamed of having?

She went into their room, the one next to hers, to wake them. It was an unimaginative, shabby room, just like her own, but this one had a large piece of bare wall in the corner where the paint and the plaster had been picked away. Edward had done that at four years old, sat up here by himself, with his grandmother and his mother doing their 'war-work', and his vague, slightly absent-minded grandfather pottering in his garden.

Sat here, bored and miserable, full of hate and resentment, picking at the wall.

Harriet had decreed it should stay as it was to teach him a lesson. Whatever that lesson was, it was lost to Edward. He couldn't have cared less what the wall looked like in his bedroom. In fact, when he felt like it, he picked at it some more now and then.

Now, as she woke him, he put his arms around her and buried his blond head in her neck. He was a forthright little boy, certainly, but he was extremely loving. He needed a hero, someone he could admire, but there was no one in this house, and he hadn't found anyone in school either. Sophie noticed how brave he was where his father was concerned, for it would have been easy for him, being so small, to shy away from Oliver's injuries; but he loved his daddy and was generous in that love. It cut no ice with Harriet.

'I don't want to go to church,' he said, and as she looked at him, Sophie saw his eyes were very bright and his cheeks rather pink. Evidently he wasn't feeling all that fit — he was nothing like sick enough to gain any sympathy from his grandmother, though.

'You sit with me,' she replied, kissing him gently. 'We'll play a little game perhaps, when she isn't looking.'

Suddenly they were aware of Alice crawling to the end of her bed, her silky brown hair done up in plaits. She was tall and thin, a very pretty little girl with a faintly ethereal quality inherited from her mother. She was her daddy's pride and joy, and she, too, was brave about his injuries, but neither of them had seen Oliver without his bandages yet, and Sophie desperately longed for them to be in a safe environment before they did.

'I've wet my bed,' she whispered, tears springing up in her eyes.

Sophie screwed up her face wearily. She knew what that would mean.

'Oh *dear*,' she replied. 'How did you manage that, Alice? You didn't have anything to drink before you went to bed last night.'

Alice wiped her face with her hands as the tears trickled down her cheeks.

'I was so thirsty,' she sobbed. 'I had to have something. I drank some water from the bathroom.'

Sophie wrapped her in her arms, holding her tightly. She was so angry, *always* so angry these days. Now there would be recriminations for the wet bed, then church — and it was obvious Edward wasn't very well, so he would almost certainly cause a scene. Then to cap it all, Sunday lunch. Dear God, there couldn't be a worse cook in the *world* than

Harriet Crompton. She cooked the meat until it was dry and crumbling, boiled the vegetables until they were wet and slimy, and smothered it all in a ghastly, fatty gravy that tasted dreadful. And Edward and Alice were made to sit there until they ate it — or spat it, which Edward normally did, earning himself yet another thrashing with the back of a wooden hairbrush.

'Don't drink bathroom water, darling,' Sophie whispered. 'Please don't. It isn't fit to drink, it's nasty tank stuff. You can always call out to me, you know. I'll get you a drink somehow.'

For a moment they clung together, the three of them, like frightened refugees; then Alice broke into sobs and rested her head against her mother's shoulder miserably.

'I wish the war would end!' she wept. 'I don't want to live here any more, I *hate* it here!' Sophie cuddled her fiercely while in her mind she made a bold decision.

'They're talking about sending Daddy to a convalescent home,' she said, 'and they've mentioned Tremar. You won't remember Tremar, Edward, you're too young, but Alice might. Do you remember Tremar, sweetheart?'

Alice nodded. 'That was where Miss Drake lived, the lady Daddy rescued.'

'Yes. Well, she still lives there,' Sophie said, struggling to keep the bitterness out of her voice, 'only she's Mrs Logan now. But anyway, her big manor house is a convalescent home for the duration, and I think it would be really nice if Daddy could go there. We could go back to Polwean then, just the three of us, and you could go to school there again. How would that be?'

'Would that mean we wouldn't have to see *her* any more?' Edward demanded, thrusting out his chin belligerently. 'Well, I want to go *now!*'

Sophie kissed his blond head affectionately. 'Oh that we could,' she replied softly.

★ ★ ★

Edward bit his grandmother in church. It was her own fault: he was leaning sleepily against his mother, for he really wasn't feeling very well, and she reached out roughly to grasp him and pull him upright. So he bit her; hard enough for her to utter an exclamation of pain.

When they got home, she dragged him up to his bedroom, put him across her knee and proceeded to beat him with her hairbrush. When Sophie, sobbing with rage, screamed at her to stop it diverted her attention from her

40

task long enough for Edward to bite her again and this time she threw him into bed and told him he wouldn't be allowed any lunch. Howling with pain and fury, Edward turned his tear-streaked face to his grandmother and stuck out his tongue as far as it would go. Harriet raised her hand menacingly and Sophie shoved her out of the way.

'Don't you *dare* touch him again!' she screamed. 'You horrible woman! No wonder Oliver turned out to be like he is!'

Harriet Crompton stared at her daughter-in-law with glittering eyes.

'And what's that supposed to mean?' she asked softly. 'Oh, I knew there'd been trouble when you came back from Cornwall. I *knew* there had. So what did you do to my son, might I enquire?'

Sophie gaped at her in astonishment.

'What did *I* do to *him*!' she whispered, and for a moment they stared at each other, then she turned away with a sneer. 'You haven't got a clue, have you?' she said and walked away firmly.

As Sophie entered the gloomy, shabby sitting-room downstairs, she found Charles Crompton sitting in an armchair, doing his best to hide behind the newspaper. He couldn't have helped overhearing everything that had gone on. The house was large, but not *that* big. He wouldn't have dreamed of interfering though; he never did, and in the end it had cost him his daughter, because Oliver's sister, Francesca, who was married with two children of her own, had taken after her father, not her mother. She was a quiet, unassuming woman, who had endured the bullying until she simply couldn't take it any more, and in the end had moved away and then used the cost of travelling as an excuse to see her parents as seldom as possible. Charles rarely saw his grandchildren.

He looked up at Sophie and his light blue eyes were frightened. Sophie sighed. She actually liked Oliver's father, as far as she could, but his weakness was despicable sometimes.

'Haven't you *ever* stood up to her, Daddy?' she asked wearily. 'Not once ever told her she couldn't do something?'

He shrugged uncomfortably.

'Got to let the memsahib have her way, you know,' he muttered. Sophie clicked her tongue irritably.

'Until she thinks she's a god and makes everyone else's life a misery! Well, for your information, I'm about to do my best to ship the children and me out of here, because we simply can't take any more, and if I manage to do it, you'll be lucky if you ever see us

42

again. So, if you love your grandchildren, you might be wise to spend a little time with them in the next few weeks. Oh, and don't tell the *memsahib*, please, because she'll go bleating to Oliver, and I'll tell him when I'm good and ready!'

The next morning, Edward was running a temperature. He was sweating and feverish and wailing for his mother. Sophie took him in her arms, cuddling him close to her, and at once he put his thumb in his mouth and mumbled against her as his nose began to run.

Sophie went in search of Harriet.

'I won't be going to work with you today,' she announced. 'I shall be staying here with Edward, he's very poorly.'

'Daddy can look after him,' Harriet said as Sophie watched her gathering papers together in her self-important way. 'I expect it's only a slight cold. He'll be better by this evening.'

'No,' Sophie replied, drawing her lips into a thin line. 'Daddy *can't* look after him. Daddy gets so carried away digging for victory that he forgets Edward is here at all. You do my shift, it won't hurt you. You were quick enough to give me the job in the first place.'

Harriet Crompton sighed, and her face was sharp with disapproval. She was not used to anyone standing up to her, no one had ever done it before. Even before the war she had belonged to numerous committees, many of them from the church, and no one had ever dared defy her. When Oliver had first brought Sophie home she had shown suitable deference, in fact she had been a nervous little shrinking violet, struggling to please all the time. Not any more, though. Now she was rude and arrogant and seemed to think that, despite living there in Arundel with her in-laws, eating at their table and sleeping in their sheets, she had a right to her own opinions. Preposterous!

'Surely I don't have to remind you, Sophie, that there is a war on,' she said slowly, as if she were talking to a backward child. 'We do not do our voluntary work just when we feel like it: we do it all the time, because it's needed.'

Sophie smiled acidly.

'Then you go and do it,' she replied, 'because I'm staying at home with my son.'

It wasn't long before Edward had drifted back to sleep and Sophie went downstairs in search of her father-in-law. He was out amongst his vegetables, hoeing and weeding. Charles Crompton spent most of his life out amongst his flowers and vegetables; it kept him out of the house and away from his wife.

Finding herself alone and at leisure, Sophie

picked up the telephone. She asked for the number of the hospital, and when it was answered she asked to speak to Oliver's doctor.

★ ★ ★

June at Tremar was exquisite; apples formed in the orchard, the hedgerows blossomed, the fields grew thick with corn waiting to ripen, and the new generation of young animals thrived in the warmth and sunshine. The grey stone wall of the terrace seemed always to be warm, and the vegetable garden flourished where once the tennis courts had come into their own at this time of year.

In her mind's eye Julia saw it peopled with those unworldly creatures of long ago in her childhood. Their lives had been so privileged; those exquisite, beautiful women who had lounged about watching their young men play pretty unskilled tennis. They had lived only vaguely aware of the army of servants who moved quietly on the edge of their lives, ensuring that everything was to hand and perfect.

Well, they had found out what suffering was eventually, when their young men had come back, shattered and limbless, from the war — or hadn't come back at all in the majority of cases; and afterwards, in the new order of things, it had been a different life. But no one seemed to have learned many lessons. They were coming back shattered and limbless again now, and surely many of them, like Oliver, had simply not believed it could happen to them.

She remembered Oliver sitting there on the terrace with her, three summers ago; handsome, self-assured Oliver who couldn't wait to go and fight. He was coming back to Tremar now, and his life was in ruins. Whatever he found to do for the rest of his days, his career as a doctor was finished.

They had told her yesterday that he was to become a patient in a couple of weeks, and she was surprised she hadn't heard from Sophie. Then that morning Mrs Collins had told her that Sophie had asked Susan Tregennis for a temporary home, and Julia was more than a little hurt. Pinch Street was well named; the cottages on either side of it were extremely pinched for space, yet knowing perfectly well how much space there was in the manor, Sophie had elected to share a cottage in the village with a family that was already bursting at the seams.

As she sat on the terrace wall in the early evening, listening to the sounds of dinner conversation drifting out of the dower and waiting for Matt and Annie to arrive, she drank a glass of sherry with Rory Nelson and turned her face to the evening sun, letting it warm her skin.

Minnie dozed in an armchair in the drawing-room. She, as usual, had been teased and petted by Guy during the afternoon, and like a child, she was exhausted but blissfully happy.

Julia watched her fondly for a moment, then looking up she said, 'Oh, by the way, Rory, I've got some news for you about the Cromptons. I seem to remember you said you knew Sophie quite well when they were here in '38, didn't you?'

It was the last thing he had expected.

He whispered, 'Sophie . . . ?' as his heart lurched uncomfortably, and he had a great deal of trouble keeping his face expressionless as Julia spoke to him.

Sophie Crompton. He had done his best to forget her since she'd left the village. It had seemed the only honourable thing to do, but it had been very hard to let her go, for though it had thankfully never been common knowledge, he had been very much in love with her.

It had been a hard summer for him that year; one he would never forget. He'd inherited Cliff House from his parents only a

47

couple of years before, and when he and his beloved wife Penny had moved in, they had looked forward to a long, happy retirement. Rory had depended entirely on Penny, she had been the mainstay of his life, and as they grew older his one secret relief was that he confidently expected he would be the first to go, because of his weak chest and crippled leg: his legacy from 1917. To find her dying of liver cancer when they had barely had time to unpack their tea-chests had been shattering, and the agony of watching her become yellow and silent, as her skin became stretched across her bones and pain haunted her eyes, had almost killed him.

At that time, to find pretty Sophie Crompton in his life, walking up to Cliff House at least once a week with her sweet children, bringing tempting little offerings for Penny, sitting out in the garden with them drinking tea and passing on village news, had been like a lifeline, and he had clung desperately to it.

That was how he had found out about the miraculous return of the daughter of Tremar — and been so appalled at her parents' treatment of her. That was also how he had found out about her affair with Oliver Crompton, and had felt bitter and angry at Sophie's humiliation; for by then, despite the fact that Sophie was young enough to be his daughter, he had already begun to fall in love with her. But in the end Penny's death, Julia's marriage and Sophie's departure had all come together, and what he really remembered was the searing loneliness of that Christmas.

He had been greatly touched when the new Mrs Logan had come to visit him early in 1939, and had accepted her offer of friendship gratefully. He knew how bitter Sophie had felt towards her, but Sophie had gone, and though he had loved her very dearly, he had begun to come round to the idea that his love had had as much to do with Penny's suffering as anything else.

And now, suddenly, Julia was talking about her coming back and making his heart turn over in his chest in an almost frightening way.

Julia touched him, abruptly bringing him back to reality.

She said, 'Rory? Are you with us?' and he uttered an uncomfortable chuckle, knowing all his emotions were chasing each other across his face and there was nothing he could do about it.

Licking his lips he replied, 'I'm so sorry, do forgive me. I wasn't expecting . . . ' He broke off. Then he added, 'She was a fine girl, Sophie Crompton. No one could have been kinder to me — or to Penny — that summer, and I suppose hearing her name just brought back so many memories; you understand?'

'Of course I do,' Julia answered fondly, 'and I'm sorry, I didn't mean to dig up the past so abruptly. I just wondered if you had any idea where the Cromptons might have gone when they left Polwean.'

'Well, I did hear that they were living in Arundel, with Oliver's parents,' Rory said. 'Why do you ask?'

Julia sighed and stared broodily across the gardens to the orchard.

'I suppose I just thought that with Oliver coming to stay in the dower, Sophie might have asked us to put her and the children up here for a while, that's all,' she said. 'And now I understand she's asked Susan Tregennis to house them, and let's face it, Rory, you can't *move* in the Tregennises' little cottage. I thought she'd forgiven me, you know? When she came to my wedding, we got on quite well. But I suppose I was wrong — and why *should* she forgive me, of course? What I did was wicked and hurtful, I know, but . . . Well, I wish she'd give me a chance to make amends, that's all.'

Rory reached out and touched her arm gently, and she was warm from the sun on her skin.

'Leave it to me, Julia,' he said. 'Let me speak to Susan Tregennis when she brings the children to school in the morning, and I'll see what I can find out about Sophie. But it's not really so surprising that she hasn't telephoned you, is it? I mean, even if she no longer feels any bitterness towards you, you were hardly best friends. Sophie's not the sort of girl who would presume she has a right to a home here just because Oliver is to become a patient, you know.'

Julia pressed her lips together uncomfortably and stared down into her sherry glass. She suffered awful guilt about Sophie Crompton, and she would have given a great deal to go back to the summer of 1938 and change that wretched affair she had had with Oliver.

'Thanks, Rory,' she replied eventually. 'I'd like to offer them a home, I really would, and there's so much room here. She and the children could have half a floor to themselves if they wanted it.'

Rory gazed at her, realizing, not for the first time, how naïve she really was. Almost twenty-four years of sensory deprivation had left her a peculiar legacy, and often it raised its head when it was least expected. It shouldn't *occur* to her to want Sophie living at the manor. True, Sophie had staged a very brave defence of her one memorable afternoon on the green, but the only reason she had attended the Logans' wedding was to have the satisfaction of watching her husband's obsession being married to somebody else. Time might well have healed a lot of things, he thought, but he doubted whether it had healed Sophie's animosity towards the beautiful Julia.

Nevertheless, if Julia wanted her there, then he knew he would do what he could to oblige her.

Abruptly there was movement within the drawing-room and Annie came through the French windows, out on to the terrace. She wore a soft, summery dinner dress, and had tamed her unruly mane of hair and pinked her lips. Her face glowed and her skin was gloriously bronzed.

Julia stared at her for a moment in a kind of wonder and then grinned.

'My word, you look splendid!' she observed. 'I can't believe you got dressed up like that for *us*, did you?'

Annie blushed, and her green eyes were very bright.

'As a matter of fact I'm goin' out for a walk after dinner,' she replied. 'Patrick an' me's goin' t'push Guy to Home Farm and Five Elms. I couldn't think of nowhere else where we could sensibly 'andle the chair — and anyway I 'as to lock up the chicken shed at dusk.' Suddenly she bit her lip and Julia recognized the excited longing in her eyes; recognized it because so many years ago, her own eyes had looked back at her from the mirror with that look in them . . . for Annie's father. 'Guy said it was Patrick's idea,' she whispered. 'He wanted to ask me to take a walk, but 'e didn't 'ave the courage, so this time Guy says he'm goin' to go with us, but only the once, 'e says!'

Julia felt a jolt in her chest. Annie was falling for Patrick, and the idea filled her with dismay; for having discovered that Patrick came from the same drawer in life as she did, she had done a little private digging — and quickly discovered that if she hadn't been missing from life for so long, she wouldn't have needed to. Patrick was the second son and fourth child of Lord and Lady Thornby of Chawston Hall in Warwickshire. They were a fabulously wealthy, ancient family, with vast estates in Ireland and considerable property in Belgravia, as well as Chawston Hall, and Isobel Thornby had a reputation for being monstrous. In the circles through which she moved, she was famous for her snobbery and her ruthlessness — and she was not *at all* popular!

How, Julia wondered bitterly, could she explain to Annie that a woman such as Patrick's mother would be appalled at the idea of her son spending time with someone like her, even if it was no more than a mild flirtation, which quite evidently from Annie's point of view it wasn't? Annie was young and modern — and the heir to Tremar — but she had no pedigree and could never grow one. It didn't matter a jot to her, nor did it matter to Julia, because Julia's painful life had raised her above things like that, but it would matter greatly to the Thornbys, particularly Isobel Thornby.

Added to that, Guy had told her that he found Lady Thornby's letters to her son cold and uncompromising. In fact, he'd asked Julia if it was normal for people from Patrick's elevated background to be so lacking in compassion. This reminded Julia of her own oddly cold mother and the letters she had received at school, which had mostly been like a prolonged weather forecast.

And then, of course, there was the fiancée.

The letters from Mona Baines-Morton, according to Guy, were ungrammatical, badly spelt and written in the language of a hearty schoolgirl. So far Patrick had only written back once, and it had certainly not been a letter from a beau to his beloved. He never called her his fiancée, and certainly kept no picture of her beside his bed. He didn't even know her very well, apparently, but all the same the engagement was official; it had been announced in *The Times* just before the outbreak of war. And official engagements in Patrick's world, when organized by a woman like Lady Thornby, had a way of being binding, Julia knew.

Kissing Annie softly on the cheek, she said, 'Well, I hope Patrick's nice and strong, darling, because that's quite a bumpy path along the rhododendron walk to Home Farm. Still, you've got a wonderful evening for it anyway. Ah, here comes Matt, so we might as well go in to dinner then.'

A short while later, in a genial atmosphere, the inhabitants of Tremar ate dinner together in the formal dining-room, served by two of Mrs Collins's girls; and afterwards Annie excused herself and ran off to find Patrick and Guy.

Julia watched her go with a worried look on her face.

'Should I do something about that?' she asked and Matt shook his head.

'Not for the moment,' he replied calmly. 'Don't interfere.'

She glanced at him wretchedly. She loved Matt more than anything in the world, but theirs was destined to be a childless union because of her enforced sterilization at the hands of officials at Blackridge asylum. Her life had been thrown away then; wasted; and not just by her parents, but by her callous lover as well. Now, though she envied Annie the thrill of it, that moment of waking and knowing you are in love, she could not escape from the fact that Annie was a trusting, generous farmer's daughter with a Cornish accent. If Patrick broke her heart, Julia thought, she would be beside herself with fury!

One of Matt's hands rested on the table and abruptly she reached out and covered it with her own. She didn't need to say anything, Matt knew what she was feeling; and so, apparently, did Rory. He smiled at her and shook his head very slightly.

'I'm afraid Matt's right, you know,' he said. 'You mustn't interfere; not yet. Give him a chance. You never know, he might be one of the modern generation, too.'

Julia pressed her lips together.

'So he might be,' she retorted sourly, 'but I assure you his damned mother isn't!'

Outside, in the beautiful evening, Annie ran down the slope of the terrace and found Guy and Patrick waiting for her.

'Hullo,' she said shyly, and Guy grinned at her.

'Hullo, gorgeous!' he replied, appraising her appreciatively for a moment and then turning to look at his friend. 'Hey, Patrick, do me a favour and tell her how beautiful she is, will you, because believe me, me old mucker, I'm telling you no tales!'

Patrick turned his bright blue, sightless eyes to Annie and in the warm, heady fragrance of the evening, with gulls calling overhead and drunken bees lurching about amongst the flowers, she didn't even notice the scar across his face. She just saw Patrick, and as her heart leapt she blushed like a rose.

Oh Lord, Guy thought, I'm already playing gooseberry and we haven't even started yet!

'Well then,' he said brightly, as Patrick began to push the chair and Annie put her arm through his to guide him, 'we now need to find a topic of conversation, don't we? So let's start with a bit of background, eh? Since I'm a townie and live by a railway line, you can both tell me lovely stories about what it was like growing up in a stately home in the country, because I've developed quite a liking for this place, you know? Gracious living has a lot going for it, I've decided, and I wouldn't mind some more.'

Annie burst out laughing. 'I didn't grow up in no stately 'ome,' she retorted cheerfully. 'I grew up in a slum farm! An' I was bruised an' starvin' most of the time, an' all, till Julia come along an' rescued me. It 'ent a slum no more, 'course. 'Tis neat as a new pin now, but it were a slum all right when me pa was around, cos he spent all our money on drink. But you knows all that anyway — crikey, you knows my mother well enough! Patrick's the one who can tell you 'bout growing up in a stately 'ome!'

To her surprise, Patrick suddenly stopped pushing the chair and stared off, though he could see nothing. His expression was desolate, as if he was remembering a hurt so deep he would never find the words to share it, and she felt pain deep in her heart for him; then, after an age, he suddenly spoke.

'It was hateful,' he said coldly. 'Chawston was an *awful* place to grow up. Bloody awful! It's always cold and it's full of empty corridors and empty rooms. Empty of people, I mean; *stuffed* with possessions. It's full of cold people, too. My mother seems to think it's her right in life to get her own way over everything, and my father grows prize-winning flowers and loves them more than he's ever loved any of us. Certainly more than he's ever loved me, anyway. In fact, I'm not sure he even *remembers* me any more.'

Annie's beautiful face clouded as he spoke, and taking his hand she pressed it against her cheek. It was the first time they had ever touched, and for a few seconds there was complete stillness between them, then his fingers caressed her warm skin and very softly brushed her lips. It was deeply, touchingly, intimate — and made Guy wish the ground would open and swallow him!

'I think if I could have anything in the world I wanted,' Patrick murmured, 'I'd choose to stay here for the rest of my life. I fear going back to Chawston more than anything I can think of . . . ' He stopped, and then the moment broke and he laughed softly. It was a very bitter little laugh. 'So there you are, Guy,' he observed, 'that's growing up in a stately home. What else would you like to know?'

Quite a lot, Guy thought wryly, but that's enough to be going on with — and don't panic, old man, I saw what you wanted me to see.

'Tell me about the chickens, Annie,' he said, 'since we're going over there to lock them up for the night. How many are there, and do we have to chase them?' He chuckled cheerfully. 'Because I'm pretty damn fast on my wheels nowadays, you know!'

3

Sophie Crompton was tucking her children into bed when the telephone rang. She heard the living-room door open and close, and then heard her mother-in-law's loud bark. Harriet Crompton *always* answered the phone; that way she always knew who was on the other end, even if they didn't want to speak to her.

Edward hugged his mother tightly, his arms wrapped around her neck so that their faces were touching.

'I *hate* Granny,' he whispered, and giggled. Sophie giggled back.

'So do I,' she replied softly.

Alice was lying on top of her bed reading a book. She was quiet, and Sophie guessed she was thirsty. She felt depressingly certain that if Alice was simply given a drink with her evening meal, and no one mentioned anything about wet beds, she would be fine. But it was always the same: Granny's thick finger pointed at her across the table like some wicked magician's wand, and behind the finger the blunt face, scowling as the threats began.

Well, Oliver was going to Tremar in ten days' time. He didn't know it yet, and neither did Charles nor Harriet; Sophie was keeping it for when she was ready. And when she *was* ready, she decided, she was going to get her own back for all the suffering she had endured since the outbreak of war, no matter what!

All of a sudden, and much to Sophie's surprise, her mother-in-law flung open the bedroom door and strode into the room.

'There is a Mr Roderick Nelson on the telephone for you,' she announced, as though Sophie had somehow committed a misdemeanour. 'He says he's phoning from somewhere called Tremar, and that you'll know who he is.'

Sophie untangled herself from Edward's arms and sat up quickly.

'Rory!' she exclaimed. 'Good Lord!' Pushing past Harriet, she ran lightly down the stairs.

As she picked up the receiver, she was aware that her hand was shaking slightly. She remembered Rory with great fondness, both for his devotion to his dying wife and his extraordinary gallant kindness to her, when she had known the entire village was gossiping about Oliver and Julia Drake. She had liked him enormously and missed him when they had left the village, but she had made no effort to keep in touch with him because it had seemed . . . not quite *proper*. She had known, the day she said goodbye to him, that her feelings for him were more than those of just a friend, and the look in his eyes had told her he felt the same; and now, suddenly, he was asking to speak to her.

'Rory?' she said softly and his familiar voice, coming across the telephone wires, made her heartbeat quicken.

'Hullo, Sophie, my dear,' he said. 'How are you?'

They exchanged small talk; lovely, friendly small talk; something that had been sadly lacking in Sophie's life for a long time now. It felt so good to be talking to him that it took her some moments to realize that Harriet Crompton was standing on the stairs unashamedly eavesdropping on her conversation.

Clapping her hand over the mouthpiece she glared at her mother-in-law contemptuously.

'Do you mind?' she snapped. 'This is a private conversation.'

Harriet Crompton pursed her lips and then walked unhurriedly down the rest of the staircase. As she entered the sitting-room, she slammed the door behind her and Sophie promptly burst into tears.

Standing in the hallway of Tremar, with the early evening sun streaming into the drawing-room through the French windows and the general tranquil sounds that accompanied life at the manor, Rory was greatly alarmed to hear Sophie's distress.

'Oh, my dear, it can't be that bad!' he said as he listened to her struggling to control herself. 'Come on, I thought we were going to see each other again soon. That's what I'd heard, anyway, that you were coming back to the village. That's why I've phoned.'

In the gloomy hallway of the Arundel house, Sophie begged him to be patient with her, scrubbing fiercely at her face with a hanky. Control was very hard because suddenly hearing his familiar voice seemed to make her isolated loneliness a hundred times harder to bear, but finally, gaining control of her weeping, she began to tell him about Oliver. She was careful to keep her voice low, for she wasn't wholly certain that Harriet wasn't still eavesdropping, but she talked about the children and a little about herself, and to know he was listening to her was so comforting.

At Tremar, the others enjoyed their pre-dinner sherry whilst Rory was speaking on the phone, happy to wait for him to finish his conversation; and he watched them sitting out on the terrace peacefully chatting as he explained to Sophie about Julia's wish to have her and the children stay at the manor.

Eventually, when they had been talking for more than half an hour, he said, 'So you do see, my dear, don't you, that you cannot possibly stay with the Tregennises? It simply isn't fair! There isn't room to swing a cat in that cottage.'

'But Tremar . . . ' Sophie replied uncertainly. 'How can we stay at Tremar? Surely I'm the *last* person her ladyship would want to keep coming face to face with? Or does she like to be reminded of the way she behaved?'

'That's unfair,' Rory said quietly. 'In fact, you're being unfair to Julia altogether. And if you're honest with me, it isn't Julia you're angry with, is it? It's *Oliver* who condemned you to the life you're living now, not Julia. Come on, you've got nothing to lose by giving it a try. Let me meet you at the station and bring you here just for a few days and if you absolutely hate it, we'll set about finding somewhere in the village, but it would be awfully churlish simply to throw Julia's offer back in her face. And you're *not* churlish, Sophie. One of the things everybody in the village always liked about you was your beautiful manners.'

There was a long pause, and suddenly in the cream and brown hallway of the Arundel house two things happened at once. The sitting-room door opened and Harriet Crompton tapped her watch face irritably with her finger, before announcing that the telephone was not for 'endless, frivolous conversations'; and Alice appeared at the top of the stairs.

'Mummy, Edward's crying,' she said in a frightened voice.

Sophie had to make a decision quickly and when a few moments later she had broken the connection with Rory and gone back upstairs to cuddle Edward, she rocked him in her arms and pressed her chin against his curly head, wondering if she had just made the biggest mistake of her life.

Oh well, she thought, if it's going to be worse than being here, then it's going to have to be pretty bloody awful, that's for sure; and taking both her children on to her lap she murmured, 'We've got a new home, and we're going there to live in a week's time. Shall I tell you all about it?'

Rory came through the drawing-room and out on to the sunny terrace.

'Well?' Julia asked. He smiled at her.

'She says thank you for your invitation, she's happy to accept,' he replied.

Annie and Matt glanced at each other, then Matt, in his quiet way, turned his head and looked out across the estate, narrowing his eyes against the sun.

'I hope you know what you're doing,' he observed, and Julia pressed her lips together slightly uncomfortably.

'Well if you want me to be brutally honest,' she replied, 'I don't think I have any choice.'

★ ★ ★

Oliver looked so vulnerable with his awful injuries, Sophie thought, and no one had actually seen what he was really going to look like yet. He wore his uniform every day when he was well enough to dress, like all the other patients in the hospital, but it sat so incongruously upon him now that he was no longer able to fulfil its purpose.

She knew when she and the children found him in his wheelchair in the garden that he had already been told the news. She saw his look of betrayal when he caught sight of her, and was surprised to find that it did not make her feel the slightest bit guilty. She was quite pleased that she didn't feel triumphant either, but she was not prepared to feel sorry for him.

He didn't even greet them as they

approached, he just made a grab for her arm and hung on to her grimly.

'They tell me I'm going to Tremar,' he said with what sounded almost like panic in his voice. 'And they tell me that you requested it!'

Sophie stood before him. She wore a new summer dress and, because she was so slender, she looked wonderful in the new, sharper fashions that encouraged the use of less material. She had a pert little hat on her head and her hair was styled fashionably, and Oliver was painfully aware that whenever she came to visit him she was the topic of conversation amongst his fellow patients afterwards.

They teased him about her mercilessly, about what a lucky cove he was to have such a tasty morsel to go home to, and as he stared at her he tried to remember when it had all started to go wrong. He thought they had still been happy when they had first gone to Polwean, but perhaps they hadn't. She'd been such a hopeless housekeeper, he remembered, completely unable to cope with two small children, and she hadn't looked like she did now, either. She'd been untidy and colourless then, not red-lipped and smart as paint as she was these days, and she made him feel nervous, for she seemed to have managed to turn the tables on him somehow. The once shrinking violet was full of confidence when she came to visit him now; full of confidence and getting harder by the day.

'Not in front of the children, Oliver,' she said warningly, as Alice and Edward, who had stood before his wheelchair patiently waiting for his attention, moved forward to kiss him. 'Later, if you don't mind.'

They drifted off to play after a little while and normally he would have quietly and contentedly watched them, but this afternoon all he could think about was what he saw as Sophie's betrayal of him.

'How could you do it to me?' he demanded, when they were out of earshot. 'How could you do it, Sophie?'

Sophie pulled up a canvas garden chair to sit beside her husband. The garden was dotted with servicemen in many and varied states of disfigurement. None of them was ever going to fight again, that was for sure, and most of them faced lives very much changed from the ones they had led before the war. Sophie supposed Tremar would be the same, and imagined she would get used to it, with everyone seeming to live side by side, according to Rory.

'I haven't done anything to you, Oliver,' she

said calmly. 'Your doctor said you must go away to convalesce, and Tremar was the obvious place. I thought you'd be happy to be with people you know. Anyway, according to Rory, it's absolutely marvellous; just the place to regain your strength and make plans for the future.'

'Rory?' Oliver turned his head sharply to look at her. She had sat herself on his blind side, something she regularly did because she said if she sat on the other side she restricted even further what limited vision he had. He had never quite trusted that. 'Rory Nelson, you mean?' She nodded. 'When did you speak to Rory Nelson?'

'He phoned a few days ago,' she replied, narrowing her eyes against the sunshine as she watched Edward running about pretending to be a Spitfire, and Alice sitting in the grass, making a daisy-chain. 'The children and I are going to Tremar as well, Mrs Logan has invited us. Nice of her, isn't it?'

There was a long silence between them. Oliver looked down at his still heavily bandaged hand. He was not able to get it into the sleeve of his uniform and wore a sling to support it against his chest. He wondered sometimes what would happen the first time he put his hand out to one of his children, when the bandages were off and they could see for themselves the stumps and shiny scar tissue where his fingers had been. He wondered how they were going to look into his face, too. But he had not expected to face these hurdles in front of Julia, the woman who had turned his life upside down, the woman who had married someone else after he had wrecked his marriage for her. Dear God, how was that fair?

He turned to stare at his wife resentfully.

'You can't,' he said. 'You can't just uproot and take yourself off to Cornwall when you feel like it, for heaven's sake. What about your war work? What about the children's schooling? And, come to that, what about Mother and Daddy? They have looked after you since the outbreak, you know.'

Sophie lifted her face to the sun, and forced down her overwhelming desire to yell at him.

'Oh, I think your mother and father will live quite happily without us,' she observed. 'Especially your mother. You ask her when she comes on Wednesday. Unless I'm much mistaken, she can't wait to see the back of Edward. You see, darling, he's just like her. They both always want their own way, and so every time she punishes him, he bites her or spits at her. As to my war work, well I can get a job anywhere, everyone's needed, and it will make a nice change. If your mother thinks she might find it difficult to manage without me, she can have a go at the work herself, can't she? I'm the one who gets my hands dirty every day, she makes sure of that.'

Oliver sighed. He got very tired of the battle that went on between his mother and his wife, and was tired of hearing them whining about each other. It had never occurred to him, because he simply didn't think like that, that most of it was his own fault.

'Well, I think it's very selfish of you,' he said, 'to just walk away from them after all this time. And anyway, I'm not going to Tremar. I told them I didn't want to go, that they'll have to find me somewhere else.'

'Well if they do,' Sophie replied evenly, 'then you won't see Alice and Edward at all, because, you see, we are going to Tremar. We're going next Thursday.'

★ ★ ★

As the evening shadows lengthened and a breeze blew in from the sea, which added a faintly salty smell to all the other fragrances in the air, Guy and Patrick together with a handful of patients, sat on the dower terrace, greatly enjoying the evening and comfortable

71

with their thoughts. It had been very special, since Annie and Patrick had openly acknowledged their affection for each other, and Patrick had blossomed astonishingly in that time.

Guy watched the corner of the rhododendron walk for Annie; he knew she would come back that way, probably with Matt, and he wanted to be sure and tell his friend when he could see her. They'd been told to expect a new inmate in a few days, a Surgeon Commander Oliver Crompton. Someone had told them he was a friend of the Logans, but Annie had been fairly disparaging about him the previous evening. She had made a strange remark about him 'not being good enough' for Julia, and though Patrick hadn't understood the remark in reference to Julia, it had caused stirrings of unease in his own heart.

Suddenly he raised his face and sniffed the air, breathing in deeply.

'I think it's going to be true what they say, you know,' he observed, 'that when you lose one sense the others sharpen up to compensate. There's a very different smell about this place, a lovely tang of the sea.'

Guy chuckled.

'Don't have too much difficulty spotting the difference between the smell here and the smell in my home,' he replied. 'Mostly smells of trains where I come from.' He grinned, which was lost to Patrick, and then studied his friend for a few seconds. After a while he touched him on the arm and went on, 'D'you know something, my friend? Since Annie started taking the long way home, via the dower terrace of an evening, you've been a different person. Are you aware of that?'

Patrick smiled, and to Guy's amazement he actually blushed. His whole face seemed to light up and it was suddenly as if the awful, disfiguring scar simply wasn't there. His bright blue eyes turned towards Guy and in the breeze from the sea his extraordinary sun-coloured hair blew about his head.

'I didn't know the world had people like Annie in it, you know,' he whispered, and Guy pressed his lips together quickly.

'Then don't you think it's time you wrote to Miss Baines-Morton and told her that your engagement is off, old man?' he said. 'According to her letters, she cut the announcement from *The Times* in 1939 and has it on her dressing table mirror so that she can look at it each day. She's so looking forward to the day when you'll be well enough to travel to Ireland, etc., etc. Not very kind, is it, to let her go on believing in something that isn't going to happen?'

Patrick put a cigarette in his mouth and

offered one to Guy, handing him the matches at the same time. Their smoke drifted upwards and blended with the fragrances of the early evening, and for a moment his blind blue eyes seemed to stare across the estate, as if they were forever searching for something they would never see.

Eventually, blowing out a lungful of smoke he said flatly, 'It isn't that simple, I'm afraid. In fact, it isn't simple at all. Perhaps in your world it might be acceptable to break off an engagement, but it's not in mine. Mother put the announcement in *The Times*, Mona started accepting gifts, and provided I lived, it was an arrangement written in stone. If I write and tell her now that I don't want to marry her, I'll be out of here so fast my feet won't touch the ground, and my mother can arrange things like that, believe me. She can arrange anything if she wants it badly enough.'

Guy stared at him in astonishment. He came from a good family and had benefited from an above average education, but the likes of the drawer from which Patrick and Julia came were beyond his understanding, and there were times when he was extremely grateful for that. Playing by the rules of the aristocracy seemed to be full of ghastly pitfalls as far as he could see.

'So are you stringing Annie along then?' he asked quietly. 'Using her as a bit of light relief? Because if you are, old man, you're being very unkind; she looks at you as if the sun rises and sets over you. And I should watch out for Julia, too. I sometimes have the idea that she'd kill for Annie if the situation warranted it.'

He broke off, realizing he'd said too much, and Patrick's head shot round towards him.

'You've been talking to Julia about me, haven't you?' he snapped. 'Well, you shouldn't. I'm sorry, Guy, but it's none of your damned business, frankly!'

'No, you're right, it isn't,' Guy replied, feeling slightly wounded, 'but it *is* Julia's. Everything that concerns Annie is Julia's business, I'm afraid, and you might as well know that she's extremely concerned.'

Patrick took a deep draw on his cigarette and closed his eyes, blowing smoke in a long stream from his lips. Guy wondered, oddly, if Patrick had ever known he was handsome when he could see, or whether his very obvious insecurities had always hidden that from him. He gave off an aura of grave uncertainty, like a small boy struggling to stay afloat in the deep end of the swimming bath, as if one bold plunge would take him to the bottom, not the side.

'If only you'd all be patient,' he said wearily. 'Give me time. I'm not trying to hurt Annie; if you want to know I think she's the most splendid girl in the world, but I'm being carted out of here next month for another operation and I promise you if Mother gets so much as a sniff of my feelings, I'll never come back. She'll make certain I go to Ireland for convalescence next time, and like you, my friend, I have no control over my destiny just at the moment.'

Guy raised his eyebrows quickly.

'Point taken, old man,' he observed, then he saw Annie and Matt come around the edge of the walk and start across the lawns together, with the dogs at their heels. Annie waved immediately and Guy waved back. 'Wave!' he said and Patrick obeyed.

Annie turned to look at Matt and he marvelled at her bright eyes. She was in every way his much-loved daughter now, and he watched over her with great affection. He was perfectly at peace with her obvious yen for Patrick; Matt liked the boy immensely and would have been happy to see their romance flourish, but he nevertheless understood Julia's misgivings, and was as protective of Annie as she was. He never wanted to see her unhappy, but equally he didn't feel the time was right yet to jump in and start trying to lay down ground rules. Annie and Patrick must be given time to discover and acknowledge their feelings for each other, and if they truly wanted to be together then what needed to be done would be.

'He's a good wee lad, that Guy,' he said in his gentle Scottish lilt, as he gazed at the dower terrace. 'And he doesnae miss a trick where you and Patrick are concerned, I've noticed. In fact, he seems to have a talent for bringing pleasure into people's lives. Minnie absolutely adores him. And what about you, Annie? Do your bright eyes tell the truth about your feelings for young Patrick?'

Annie grinned rather sheepishly and Matt offered her his arm, so that they could walk close together towards the formal lawns.

'You know that Julia once had the idea you might go to university?' he said. 'Mebbe become a doctor, or something.'

Annie nodded.

'Mmm. I had that idea once, an'all,' she replied, 'till I went to St Margaret's. They was bleddy horrible to me at that school, you know. I mean, I never told Julia all of it, 'cos I didn't want to 'urt 'er feelings none, but they made me feel ashamed of my Cornish accent — an' no one 'as the right to do that. That's why I come 'ome when I did; an' then Julia told me she'd made me her heir . . . an' after that, well, I didn't 'ave to make no decisions any longer, did I?'

Matt kissed her briefly, and his lovely, sandy beard tickled her face in the familiar way that made her feel so safe.

'Yes, you'll certainly be a fine mistress of Tremar,' he observed. 'She'll no' go neglected and unloved all the while you're here to care for her, that's for sure. Only ... well, supposing you and Patrick decided you wanted to be together? Supposing he was to ask you to marry him — what then?'

Tremar was warm and welcoming in the early evening sun, and Annie had known it all her life, even when it had been a place of tight secrets, crumbling in its pain, as its heir rotted in the asylum. She had liked it even then; felt sorry for it as its roof began to collapse and its walls were stained with lichen; now she loved it dearly. Like Julia, her life revolved around the welfare of Tremar. It was an enchanted place.

'It won't be a problem,' she replied simply. 'We shall stay 'ere. It's what Patrick wants anyway. 'E don't never want to go back to Chawston; 'e said so.'

Oh, that life were that simple, Matt thought.

As they came closer to the house they saw Julia and Rory emerge on to the terrace, and

78

waved to them cheerfully.

Annie said, 'What 'bout this business with the Cromptons, Matt? D'you think Julia should've asked that Sophie and them children to come and live here — after what happened, I mean?'

Matt blew out a little sigh.

'No,' he answered bluntly. 'And if she wasnae as naïve as Rory says she is, she wouldnae have done it. But we have to make allowances for the fact that Julia has a tendency to think along the lines of a pleasing child sometimes, and that's what she's doing now. If the little Sophie abuses her, I shall soon have something to say about it; although from what I remember of Sophie, she'd nae say boo to a goose.'

'An' the doctor?' Annie asked.

Matt chuckled.

'I've nae worries about the doctor,' he said. 'After all, in the end it was me she chose.'

'So it was,' Annie muttered cynically. 'But Dr Crompton weren't known for bein' a good loser. I'm told he's been ever so badly hurt that he won't never be a doctor no more. One of the nurses told me that. I wonder if it's true?'

'Quite true, so I understand,' Matt answered, 'and it's going to be a hard ride for him. Mebbe Guy and Patrick would offer the hand of friendship, if you were to ask them?'

Annie smiled. She had a very sunny smile; Matt remembered it from when she had been a half-starved, brutalized 14-year-old and had captured his heart with such remarkable sleight of hand. In fact, both the women in his life had worked a remarkable magic on him in the beginning, at a time when he had lived a nomadic existence for more years than he could remember and, never, ever expected to become a family man. As he looked at Annie he felt sorry that Patrick would never see her smile, for there was something quite breathtaking about her when she was filled with joy.

They were nearing the house now, and Annie would go briefly to the dower terrace first; she always did. Then, after dinner, she and Patrick would stroll together in the evening sunshine whilst Matt sat comfortably with Julia and Rory.

Changing the subject from Oliver, he said, 'We're haymaking at Five Elms next week by the way, so you'd better tell your young men you'll no be around quite so much for a while. Still, if it keeps fine and everyone puts in a full day's work, you can have a couple of hours off next Sunday. I might even give you the whole evening — if the blisters on your hands are big enough!'

Annie grinned at him and pulled a face.

'You'll work me to death one day, you will!' she declared, and Matt chuckled.

'Aye, but you'd no have it any other way, and you know you wouldn't!' They had reached the terrace steps and were at the parting of the ways. 'And think on, lassie,' he added, as she turned to go up to the dower, 'I'm starving for my dinner, so don't you be keeping me waiting, or I'll have you out at five tomorrow morning!'

He went up the steps to his own terrace with the dogs behind him and the sound of Annie's laughter ringing in his ears. She turned and ran along beside the vegetable beds towards the slope that would take her up to the dower, and as she jogged comfortably up the warm gravel path, she could see Guy watching her. She could see Patrick looking in her direction, too, with his blue eyes. It was hard to believe Patrick was blind, particularly as she could read his emotions in his eyes so clearly.

'Hullo,' she said as she came to the top.

There were half a dozen officers smoking on the terrace, and one, whose arms ended suddenly where his hands should have been, blew her a kiss with a bandaged stump, receiving a cheerful grin for his pains. Annie was very popular amongst the patients, as were the Land Army girls. They brought smiling faces and different news with them when they came, and pretty well everyone had a favourite. Often the girls would come for social evenings with the lads, and though there wasn't a lot of running about or dancing, singing and playing board games were popular pastimes.

Annie and Patrick's romance, however, was deemed to be a bit more serious nowadays, and Patrick's fellow patients were beginning to take bets on the likelihood of a wedding.

Patrick put out his hand to touch her as she came to stand beside him, and looking up to her face he drew a long, deep breath.

'You smell of the fields,' he said appreciatively.

Annie laughed.

'I smell of the cowshed,' she replied cheerfully. 'I must do, I've just come from doin' the milkin'. Are we'm 'avin' a walk after dinner?'

'I'm up for it if you are,' he answered and for a moment they held hands.

'Are you comin' with us, Guy?' she asked. Guy smiled ruefully.

'I don't think so, beautiful,' he replied, stretching his arms comfortably above his head. 'I'm going to write to Pam and Edwin this evening, and then I'm going to have another go with my tin legs. When I can master them inside, then I shall bully you to take me for walks so often you'll think me the worst kind of gooseberry!'

'Then I'll go and 'ave me dinner and come back as soon as I can,' Annie said, reluctantly breaking her intimacy with Patrick. 'Wait for me 'ere, won't you?'

He'll wait for you there till he turns into a pumpkin at midnight, Guy thought with a silent chuckle to himself as he watched her dart into the house.

Annie arrived for dinner half an hour later smelling fresh and delightful. After dinner, which was always a pleasantly unhurried meal and a time everyone looked forward to each day, she immediately offered to help with the clearing up, which was touchingly generous when she worked so hard anyway, and everyone knew how desperate she was to be off. It didn't take a great deal of time, it was only a matter of moving the dirty crocks down to the kitchen and stacking them by the sink for Mrs Collins's girls to wash in the morning, but each moment was precious to Annie.

'Not tonight, my dear,' Rory replied at once. 'It's my turn to do it tonight.'

Annie smiled.

'May I go then, please?' she asked, and

Julia nodded. Happily, she ran off along the terrace.

'She is head-over-heels in love with that boy,' Julia observed sourly as she, Rory and Matt continued to sit at the table amongst the dirty dishes and Minnie dozed in her chair.

Matt nodded placidly and searched around in his pockets for his pipe. He and Rory always smoked a pipe apiece on the terrace after dinner, but Julia wouldn't have either of them smoke in the house, mostly because it seemed to make Minnie cough.

'Aye,' he replied, knocking out ash into a glass ashtray and then beginning to fill the pipe with fresh, spicy-smelling tobacco. 'And blossoming like a rose because of it.'

'But she's only seventeen,' Julia complained. Matt gazed at her steadily.

'Which is a year older than you were, when you fell in love for the first time.'

She snorted triumphantly.

'Absolutely, and look what happened to me! Besides, the damn boy is engaged to be married to someone else — or have you forgotten that?'

Matt smiled and pushed back his chair, indicating that it was time to settle Minnie into the swing seat on the terrace whilst they enjoyed the last of the sunshine.

'The way Patrick behaves when Annie's

around, I don't think you have to worry about anybody else,' he said in his tranquil way. 'And as for the rest of it, well we're hardly likely to do to her what was done to you, are we?'

'No, but he can still hurt her,' she snarled softly, and received no answer.

They went through to the drawing-room and Matt laid Minnie with great care into the swing seat, rocking it gently to settle her. In half an hour Julia would put her to bed, knowing Rory would clear the table, and probably lay it for breakfast whilst he was about it. Rory was a most accommodating house guest.

As she emerged into the sunshine, Julia glanced at the little fountain that stood at the head of the terrace steps. It had been dead when she had returned from Blackridge, and repairing it had been of vital importance. Now she played it every day without fail, for it represented her freedom and always would. In its centre stood a fat, lead boy clutching a fish in his plump arms, and she remembered the darkness of him invading her dreams at Blackridge, when existence had been a constant living death without hope of reprieve. He laughed at his glittering fish and he made her feel safe.

'I don't want Annie to have her heart

broken; I can't bear it,' she whispered broodily as Matt and Rory settled themselves comfortably on the grey stone wall and lit their pipes, adding the fragrance of their rich tobacco to the fresh smells of the summer evening. 'It frightens me to think of her being unhappy, because I love her so much.'

'She's bound to be unhappy occasionally, my dear,' Rory said quietly. 'Everyone is, no matter what. She's not unhappy at the moment, though. Look!' He tipped his head towards the orchard, where Annie and Patrick strolled together between the apple trees. Beautiful Annie and her handsome prince.

Well, he'd been a handsome prince once, anyway, which reminded Julia that her 'handsome prince', the man who had rescued her from Blackridge and then fallen so selfishly in love with her, would be making his not-so-triumphant return to Tremar soon.

'I hate war,' she whispered bleakly. 'I hate what it does.'

Nobody answered her, there wasn't any need to. Both Matt and Rory had nightmare memories of their own; of what they'd seen and smelled and heard. And both men still occasionally awoke sweat-soaked from dreams of horror. Julia's memories were vastly different . . . and they had gone on for

86

a great deal longer.

Oh, please God, don't let this one destroy Annie like the last one destroyed me, she prayed as she watched their progress through the orchard. Please, God.

4

Charles Crompton drove his daughter-in-law and his grandchildren to the station on the morning they were leaving for Tremar. The car was an old Rover with worn-out seats that dipped in the middle and lots of faulty dials on the walnut dashboard. He had intended to put it up for the duration with the difficulty of getting petrol, but there had never seemed a right time, what with the demands of his wife and then his son being so long in hospital. It was early in the morning, but his wife declined to accompany them, pleading pressure of work.

'A great many people are relying on the service I provide,' she observed, with a pointed look at Sophie. 'And *I* don't believe in letting them down.'

'Whereas *I* feel that my husband's needs should come first,' Sophie replied sweetly. 'You know, war hero and all that. I thought we were supposed to be supporting the brave men who are out there in the thick of it; the more so when they come home injured.'

'What we're *supposed* to be doing is our bit!' Harriet Crompton retorted, and she and her daughter-in-law didn't even say goodbye to each other.

With any luck, Sophie thought venomously, I'll never see you again!

On the station platform they stood in a tight little huddle, for there were many people all waiting to catch trains to different places; maybe to do wartime things that would change their lives forever, Sophie thought fancifully.

'I hope you have a safe journey, my dear,' Charles said, wishing the train would hurry up and come, because he didn't know how to handle situations like this. 'And I do hope you'll be happy in . . . er . . . wherever it is.'

'Polwean, Daddy,' Sophie replied gently. 'Where Oliver had his practice before he joined up. I shall be staying at Tremar. You remember — Julia — Oliver told you about her? She was the poor, unfortunate woman he rescued from an asylum.'

Yes, his son had told him about it, and Charles felt certain that there had been a rumble of trouble over this woman from Tremar. He wished that he hadn't taught himself to be so absent-minded. It had taken him years to cultivate the 'vague professor' persona he had chosen for himself, but he had been doing it for so long now that the edges had become blurred and he truly didn't remember very well any more. He remembered Oliver talking about Julia, and he remembered the sharp pain on Sophie's face, but he didn't remember if he had ever been furnished with the facts. Still, whatever they were, he thought sadly, they couldn't have been *that* bad: Sophie seemed almost frantic to get back there.

Or was it frantic to get away from here? He thought that was much more likely.

'Sophie,' he said quietly, 'I'm sorry Mother wouldn't say goodbye, but it's her funny way, you understand. She really felt — well, *we* did — that you would stay with us for the duration. It never occurred to us that when Oliver was well enough to convalesce they would send him hundreds of miles away. I — I mean I know they must do what they think best, but his mother will miss him . . . You know? You *do* know, don't you, my dear?'

Sophie cringed with embarrassment, and wished like mad that the train would arrive. Gritting her teeth, she forced herself to look at her father-in-law and was suddenly aware of his wispy grey hair and his weak face. He was vulnerable and she felt guilty, but it was going to be a seriously long time before she would ever go back to that house in Arundel, she knew. She yearned for Polwean.

'I'm sorry, too, Daddy,' she replied. 'And I suppose I could have asked them at the hospital to find somewhere closer for Oliver to go, but, you know, Tremar is the most exquisitely beautiful place, so peaceful and restful. And Oliver has got a lot of decisions to make about the rest of his life. Much the best that he should do it amongst his own, those who have been seriously disfigured like he has. Please try to understand. Besides, one good turn deserves another . . . ' Her voice had become bitter though she tried very hard to hide it. 'He rescued Julia Logan in the beginning, so now she can help to rescue him.'

He looked at her. She wore a smart, figure-hugging summer dress of sharp lines, with neat, short sleeves, and she had put on her stockings that morning so that she could wear her best brown high-heeled shoes. Even standing there with her two children, she was inviting approving glances from the surrounding servicemen, and he knew quite well that in the beginning Oliver had not even attempted to look beyond her prettiness. Charles had a good idea, too, that the marriage was on the rocks, and had been for some time. He would have liked to know, as much as his wife would, why Oliver had been so intransigent about the London flat before he went away, and he certainly knew the last months of Harriet's company had not done Sophie any favours. Hearing the distant whistle of the train, Charles gazed at her and then put his hand out and touched hers fondly.

He suddenly had an idea that he might never see her or his grandchildren again, and his elderly heart was very heavy. More of his family driven away by Harriet.

'Godspeed, my dear,' he told her, 'and think of me occasionally.'

Sophie kissed him warmly.

'Oh Daddy, I will,' she promised and began to move forward with the children towards the slowing train.

A naval officer stepped forward instantly. He held the carriage door for her as she helped Alice and Edward on board, and then he collected her hand baggage — her three suitcases having been deposited in the luggage van — and began to hand it her on board. She gave him a delightful smile and then turned and waved a white-gloved hand to her father-in-law. As he stood on the platform and watched, she went into the body of the train with her children and her new-found Sir Galahad.

Charles Crompton walked away slowly. The house would feel very empty tonight, and his wife would be in a foul mood; he had felt that coming on since breakfast time. He thought, as he climbed back into his old Rover and could smell Sophie's scent, that he would put some work in on his dahlias that afternoon — and to hell with the vegetables, for once.

★ ★ ★

It was late in the afternoon, and the day had been a perfect one, when the train drew into the nearest station to Polwean and Sophie prepared to get out. Alice climbed down first then helped Edward and they waited whilst the officer who had helped them board that morning handed down their assorted luggage. Matt was collecting the cases from the guard's van. Rory Nelson was waiting on the platform to greet them.

Sophie turned and smiled fondly at her Sir Galahad. He was going on to Penzance and he was actually quite sad to lose the little family. He had found the mother a charming and delicate little thing.

'Thank you so much,' she said. 'It's been such a lovely day, and you've been so kind. Edward, say goodbye to your new friend.'

Edward snapped to attention and saluted, and the officer returned the salute.

'You just mind you take care of your

mother and sister, young man,' he called out. 'You're the man of the house now, remember, until your father gets better. Goodbye then.'

Rory watched as Sophie and the children waved to the train and his heart beat quickly in his chest with delight. She was in every way as beautiful as the picture of her he had kept in his mind, delicate and touchingly vulnerable.

Matt, who was trundling up the platform with the cases on a luggage trolley, watched as well. He saw how the officer gazed at her and he could see perfectly well that the man felt protective towards her in her fragility. But Matt was an unusually perceptive and observant man, and he remembered Sophie when he had first known her. Then, he thought, she *had* been delicate and vulnerable. Then she had been insignificant with untidy hair and a pale face free of makeup. Not any more. Unless he was much mistaken, during the ensuing years Sophie Crompton had learned some valuable lessons. For a start, she had learned to use her waif-like prettiness to its best advantage. Evidently she could smile and most men would respond in exactly the way she wanted. He wondered briefly what Julia would make of her.

'Sophie, my dear! How nice to see you!' Rory exclaimed, taking her in his arms and

94

kissing her on both cheeks. 'And looking so splendid, too.'

Sophie smiled and was just in time to grab Edward and pull him back sharply as she saw him raise his fists towards Rory's bad leg in a flash of jealousy.

'Stop it!' she hissed and his chin shot out furiously.

'She's *my* mummy!' he declared.

'Of course she's your mummy,' Rory replied, 'but I'm only saying hullo. We were friends a long time ago, when you were just a baby.'

'Well *I* don't remember,' Edward retorted menacingly. Without warning, Matt came into view.

Sophie took an involuntary step backwards: Matt had that effect on most people because of his enormous height and huge, broad shoulders. There wasn't a poacher left in Polwean who hadn't learned to be wary and respectful of Matt!

'Mr Logan,' she said softly and he smiled.

'I think it's time to drop the formalities, lass,' he replied. 'How are you, Sophie? You're looking very fine.' He turned his attention to Alice who was staring up at him in terrified silence, and he remembered that he'd only ever seen her once, when she had been on the beach with Annie. He put a huge hand on her silky dark head and then briefly cupped her pretty face. 'You've grown up, lassie,' he observed, 'but then so's Annie. I reckon you'll no be recognizing each other.'

Finally he turned his attention to Edward. The 6-year-old was gazing up at him fiercely, and Matt's dark-blue eyes twinkled merrily at him. He remembered Annie the first time he had seen her, shaking with rage and staring indignantly at him; Edward was very reminiscent of her suddenly.

Edward studied him in silence for a few seconds, then he thrust his hands behind his back and cocked his head. 'As a matter of fac', I can make fings, you know,' he stated seriously.

'Is that so?' Matt replied just as seriously. 'What things would they be?'

Edward frowned.

'I made a Spitfire in school. It was really good, *and* it flew. Well, a bit, anyway.'

Matt nodded.

'And what did you make it out of?'

Edward pursed his lips thoughtfully.

'Car'board.'

'And did you bring it with you?'

'No, I had to leave it behind. Mummy said it would get spoiled.'

Matt inclined his head. He made no attempt to ingratiate himself, nor to patronize the child by talking down to him. He looked genuinely interested and nodded thoughtfully as he began to gather the luggage together to go out to the car.

'Would you care to make one out of wood?' he asked, as they all strolled out of the station into the late afternoon sunshine. 'I have a workshop at Tremar, and I could probably help you if you fancied it. Only thing is, no one does anything for nothing at Tremar. If I help you make a Spitfire, you've got to help me on the farms. D'you think you'd care to do that?'

Edward gazed at the waiting Lagonda and his eyes gleamed. It was very rarely that Matt got the car out, but there had not been room for everyone in Rory's battered old Ford, and the pony and trap had not seemed an option with the distance from the station and the amount of luggage he knew Sophie would be bringing. It stood, blue and beautiful in the station forecourt, reminding Sophie of those days in 1938, when Matt had been seen driving Julia about in it so regularly, of the day Minnie had come home to Tremar for the first time, and of Matt and Julia driving away together, on their honeymoon.

'Can I go in front with you, please?' Edward asked astonishingly politely. Matt nodded.

'Aye, lad,' he replied, beginning to pack the suitcases in to the boot. 'Would you see the others into the back for me first, please?'

They had to sit close on the back seat, the three of them. Rory found himself touching Sophie. Alice seemed to creep in beside her mother and Sophie put her arm round the child very protectively. It had not gone unnoticed, either by Rory or by Matt, that so far Alice hadn't opened her mouth. Evidently the little girl was quite disturbed, and Matt decided it was time to bring her into the conversation.

'So,' he said, as the engine of the Lagonda purred into life and the diminutive, blonde child sat proudly beside him in the deep, leather seat. 'D'you think there's jobs that you and your sister could do at Tremar, to help out, now you're coming to live? I mean, we're running a *big* business there and there's not one of us doesnae have his or her job to do, is that not so, Mr Nelson?'

Rory was touched that Matt thought to include him in this conversation with the little boy.

He replied, 'Absolutely. Even those of us who have to go to school as well, like me.'

'Does Annie work at Tremar?' Alice suddenly asked, very timidly. Matt remembered that Alice had had quite a crush on

Annie, back in the summer of 1938. That was good.

'Annie?' he echoed. 'Annie's ma second in command! There's no' a thing she doesnae know about farming, but there are plenty of jobs she's responsible for that I know she'd be grateful for some help with. I can think of one straight away. There's two hundred hens at Five Elms have to be fed and watered twice a day, and all those eggs collected. There's a fine wee Land Girl called Doreen doing the job at the moment, but she'd be right glad of some help; it's hard work for one person.'

'And,' said Edward slowly, wriggling his toes in his shoes, 'if we was to say we'd do that job, you'd help me make a Spitfire out of wood, wiv a propeller that really turned, and wheels and fings?'

Matt glanced down at him, and Sophie watched from the back seat in fascination. Matt was reeling him in, like a fish on a line. This intransigent child, who had spent the last eighteen months of his life being angry, was suddenly bargaining for what he wanted.

Happily, she let him get on with it.

It was a glorious summer afternoon, full of heady scents that filled her with joy. She remembered very well that Cornwall had smelled delicious; she had enjoyed her time here — well, mostly, anyway — and it was such a pleasure to be back. Sitting close to Rory, she too was aware of their thighs touching as the great Lagonda purred peacefully through the countryside, and she made no effort to do anything about it. They could feel each other's body heat so close together, and both were conscious of it, but whilst Rory was struggling to squash the alarming feelings within him, Sophie pressed tighter.

Sophie had learned a great many bitter lessons since the summer of 1938, and one of those lessons was that life is a two-way track. She had wanted Rory just before she had left the village, and wondered at the time if it was because she was so hurt by Oliver's rejection of her. Half an hour in his company now, after two and a half years apart, had convinced her that she still wanted him.

And she intended to have him.

As they turned in through the gateposts of Tremar, Sophie remembered with a little rush of pleasure how tranquil and beautiful the old house had been. Huge old cedar trees shaded the drive, throwing down big fir cones that burned brightly in the wartime winter fires, and the ancient stonework of the building was warm and grey.

Sophie had only ever been to Tremar twice. The first time, she hadn't gone inside at all;

she and Julia and the children had walked down through the gorgeous formal grounds to the bay. The second time had been for Julia's wedding reception, and she had seen very few of the rooms. Now she was to *live* here: ordinary little middleclass Sophie, living in the huge, centuries-old, exquisite Tremar. If she didn't remember Julia with such pain, she thought, she might have felt as if it were all a fairy tale.

As the car slid to a halt on the drive, Julia emerged from the front door. Sophie recognized immediately the familiar thick chestnut hair and classically beautiful face of which she had been so jealous, but this Julia was not impeccably clothed in fine creations from the most expensive dress shops in Truro: she wore gardening clothes. In fact, she looked exactly like a country farmer's wife!

'Oh welcome, welcome!' she said cheerfully, reaching out to open the car doors. 'How good to see you.'

Alice was the first one to climb down. She gazed up at Julia wide-eyed, but as Alice had taken to looking at most people like that since her life had become so persistently unhappy, Sophie was not inclined to judge Alice's feelings by her looks.

Julia touched her softly.

'My, how you've grown!' she whispered, smiling down at the child. 'Annie won't believe how big you are.' Her attention was then grabbed by a fist yanking at her trousers and she turned to admire the 'little Oliver'. 'Edward!' she exclaimed. 'Good Lord, aren't you a big boy?'

'Him,' Edward said, pointing at Matt. 'The big man. He says he'll help me make a Spitfire out of *real* wood if I c'lect eggs and fings for him. Good, isn't it?'

Julia only just stopped herself from bursting out laughing. Sophie was just amazed at Edward's remarkably civilized behaviour. It was almost as if she had left Arundel with one child and arrived in Cornwall with a different one.

'The big man has a name, Edward,' she observed, as she stepped down from the car, holding Rory's hand to steady herself. 'He's called Mr Logan, and people like to be called by their names.'

'Oh! Couldn't they call him Uncle Matt?' Julia cried before she could stop herself. Blushing uncomfortably, she added, 'I — I mean, it's just that Mr Logan is — well — so formal, and since you're going to be living here . . . Oh, *please*, I don't mean to interfere.'

Sophie stared at Julia in astonishment. She

could only remember her as the formal lady of the manor. Brisk and sharp in her dealings with the two old 'cats' in the village shop and Annie's appalling father; Oliver's Rhine maiden, his Valkyrie. Now, standing here in her old gardening trousers, her face and arms brown from the sun and — Sophie noticed quickly — her hands and nails showing signs of hard work, she seemed so different, so keen to be welcoming and friendly. So perhaps her preconceptions of Julia Logan had been all wrong?

'Would you really like them to call you aunt and uncle?' she asked. 'I'm sure they'd be delighted if you would. They've had a pretty grim time living with their grandmother for the last couple of years, and after the weekend their daddy will be living here as well, which will be very strange for them.'

'I'd *love* them to,' Julia replied with a warm smile. 'It would be lovely for us. We don't have any nephews or nieces and, as you know, we will never have any children of our own. I mean, we've got Annie of course, but we share Annie with Gladys. I just like the thought of . . . sharing lots of children, and having a huge family to fill Tremar.'

Sophie stared broodily at Edward who was regarding Matt respectfully.

'Would you like to call the big man Uncle

Matt?' she enquired and Edward looked enchanted.

'Cor, yes!' he declared, and tucked his tiny hand into one of Matt's huge ones. 'C'mon, Uncle Matt, let's go.'

'Well, mebbe when we've taken the luggage in then, if you like,' Matt agreed. 'Mebbe then we could all go across and see if we can find Annie. I'm thinking your sister would like to see her. But you've to help me in with the luggage first. We have a strict rule here: always jobs first.'

'OK,' replied Edward cheerfully. He grabbed the handle of the biggest suitcase with both hands. He had not a chance of moving it, but he struggled with it happily. Sophie and Julia picked up some of the hand luggage between them and stepped carefully around him.

Sophie had forgotten the beautiful drawing-room. As Rory and Julia stood in the doorway, they watched her walk very slowly to the French windows and stand, looking out across the terrace, towards the gardens. On the terrace, the fountain was playing in the warm summer air, and below them, between the rows of vegetables, disabled servicemen hoed and weeded. Amongst them were Guy and Patrick, together as always. Guy in his wheelchair and Patrick … like a reflection in a cracked mirror.

'This was what Oliver wanted, you know, all of this.' Sophie spoke quietly. 'The presumed status that went with your remarkable home; the idea of an army of yokels respectfully doffing their caps. He thought he could have it, with you.'

'I'm afraid he's thirty years too late,' Julia replied simply. 'No one doffs their cap to me, and I don't expect them to. I grow vegetables, sew sheets, make beds and bottle fruit. I've even plucked pheasant. The only thing I haven't tried is skinning a rabbit — and I expect I could do that if I had to. Poor Oliver. Perhaps it's just as well he's coming back here then, so that he can see for himself I'm no different from anybody else, and neither is Tremar. It's just bigger than most places, that's all.'

Sophie continued to stare out at the busy estate that had once been Julia's alone. Digging for Victory! They'd taken it to its absolute extreme here.

'Somehow,' she whispered, almost to herself, 'I just wasn't expecting it to be like this. I don't quite know what I *did* expect, but it certainly wasn't this.'

Chuckling, Julia said, 'Did you think to find me ensconced in my old manor bemoaning the unfairness of life? My mother might have done that, I suppose. I have no idea how the last war touched her, if at all, except that I assume she grieved for my brother. Whether she was obliged to turn to and do things for herself, suddenly finding herself without an army of servants, I can't say, but from my point of view I worked every day at Blackridge, so I'm quite used to it. What we have here is a commodity to be used to its best advantage. My father saw it as his right, and as an excuse to condemn his daughter to a life of suffering — and, frankly, if it's not too flowery a thing to say, I don't think Tremar approved of that.'

Sophie turned from the window and, for a moment, she stared at Julia, then she glanced at Rory who stood quietly in the doorway, and she pressed her lips together quickly.

'I told you that you'd misjudged Julia, didn't I?' he said. 'We all live a different life now. If you remember, my dear, I'd not seen Julia since she was a child before you left Polwean in 1938, and I'd severely judged her. But I wouldn't be living here now if my judgement hadn't been entirely wrong.'

'No, I know you wouldn't,' she replied, smiling at him. 'That's what convinced me to come.'

'And you are most welcome,' Julia said as

Matt appeared in the doorway with a Crompton child on each hand.

'We've put the luggage upstairs, and we're away to find Annie,' he announced. 'Will you be wanting us for anything for a while?'

Julia shrugged and smiled.

'I don't think so, will we?' she enquired and Sophie shook her head, touching each of her children fondly.

'You do as you're told now, won't you?' she said, watching as Matt went out on to the terrace with them and disappeared down towards the vegetable garden. 'Is he always like that with children?' she asked in wonder.

Julia laughed.

'Well, he won Annie's heart in about two minutes flat,' she replied. 'He won Minnie's in even less time, and let's face it, Minnie *is* a child. A permanent child. Come on, let's go and see your rooms and at the same time you can see Minnie and Mrs Collins. They're upstairs in the housekeeper's room.'

They went back into the panelled hallway where the grandfather clock still ticked away the ages, and climbed the great wooden staircase to the first floor.

Matron passed them on the landing heading for the dower, and Julia introduced her to Sophie. She was a large-bosomed woman in a starched uniform that crackled as

107

she walked, and she had an air of jollity that Sophie suspected was kept strictly for the patients.

When she had passed through the door into the dower, Sophie said, 'Scary!' and Julia burst out laughing.

'Terrifying, so I've heard!' she replied. They turned and went along to the other end of the house. 'I've put you next to Rory, and the children have the room next to yours. It's one of the biggest bedrooms in the house. I thought it would double as a decent playroom for them — although they won't need one much in the summer.' She threw open the door, presenting Sophie with a huge, light, airy and beautifully appointed bedroom. 'Oh, and by the way,' she went on, opening the door to Sophie's room, which was almost as big and just as beautifully appointed, 'the children are quite safe on the estate. It's possible to roam for miles, but there's always somebody about. We've got heaps of Land Girls,' she turned from the door, carefully ignoring Sophie's half-open mouth; the last thing she wanted to do was to seem to be patronizing her, 'so please don't worry about them. They'll be starting school in September, of course, but you have plenty of time to talk to Rory about that. Let's go along to the housekeeper's room. Mrs Collins will be so pleased to see you again.'

Mrs Collins was exactly that, and almost immediately they became involved in a long conversation whilst Julia took Minnie to the window to see Guy. As usual he flirted with her, and as usual she asked to go down, so Julia took her.

'It's fast becoming a ritual,' she said to Rory on her return, as they stood by the window for a while. 'Lord knows how she'll react when Guy finally goes home.' She watched as he touched Minnie gently and made sure she was comfortable on the grass beside his chair. 'She's a lucky girl, his wife,' she observed. 'He's got a heart of gold, that young man.'

Rory smiled.

'As has Patrick,' he declared. 'Or at least Annie thinks so.'

'Oh, please,' Julia snapped. 'Don't let's get on to the subject of Patrick at the moment. One thing at a time, Rory, I beg you.'

Rory stared at her for a moment and then began to chuckle softly.

'You're nervous!' he exclaimed. 'The cool and collected, unflappable Julia Logan. Well! Chalk that up as a victory!'

Julia gave him a sideways scowl.

'If you tease me, I'm likely to blow up in your face,' she warned him, and then grinned somewhat sheepishly. 'I'm sorry, Rory, but yes, I *am* nervous. I haven't seen Oliver since my wedding day and we didn't part the best of friends. It took you more than half an hour on the phone to talk Sophie into coming here with the children, so she wasn't exactly straining for my company, and now we're destined to live here all together. If we need a peacemaker, the role may very well fall to you, you know, so don't crow at your successes just yet.'

'Well, you were warned, but I'll do my best,' he replied, touching her arm fondly. 'And the first thing I think you should do is find out from Sophie exactly what are the circumstances of Oliver's transfer to here. It seems a little strange to me, and I'm beginning to wonder if this isn't an escape route.'

Julia gazed broodily across the room. Sophie was willowy and attractive and smart-as-paint standing chatting to Mrs Collins. For a moment Julia remembered the sight of her with Edward pressed against her hip when she had been thin and pale and noticeably untidy; the harassed mother of two small children, with an unsympathetic husband.

'Why don't we all go down and have some tea?' she suggested.

Sophie turned. As she did so, her eyes settled on Rory and at once they softened as her red lips spread in a gentle smile.

Oh good grief! Julia thought. What have we here?

She wasn't going to have to wait long to find out.

★ ★ ★

They dined at 7.30, after Edward and Alice had eaten a tasty supper laid on for them by Mrs Collins and were playing in their room before bed. Julia had found some wonderful old toys, left over from her childhood, during a foray through the attics a few days previously, and the small Cromptons couldn't believe their good fortune. She had gone through the library, too, collecting all the children's books, and Alice, who was a voracious reader, was already curled up in her new bed, deeply engrossed.

It was unlikely, Sophie thought wryly, that Edward would peel the paint off the walls here!

Before dinner, Sophie had learned about what Julia called her 'absurd rule of dressing for dinner', and had panicked at her lack of dinner dresses, but Julia had cheerfully offered her spare materials and the use of the sewing machine. Sophie wondered briefly if there would be a price to pay for all this generosity, but she was already beginning to think probably not. Julia's motives appeared to be wholly altruistic.

I might have liked you if you hadn't ruined my marriage, she thought with a flash of resentment, but however nice you are to me, you've caused me a great deal of suffering, and I'm going to find it really hard to forgive you.

The dining-room at Tremar was warm and tranquil. Minnie sat between Matt and Julia, and though Annie didn't make a point of hurrying her meal, everyone knew she wanted to be off to spend a couple of hours with Patrick. Sophie sat next to Rory. She wore pale blue, which highlighted her delicacy, and she watched the quiet table feeling as if she was in a dream. Either Matt or Julia fed Minnie, but no one made a show of it, and when, after she had finished eating, she drifted off to sleep, Matt gently lifted her backwards into her chair so that she wouldn't fall into her plate. She snored comfortably as the others talked around her.

Annie excused herself. She kissed Matt and Julia before she left the dining-room and, as she went, she left a fragrant smell behind her. Sophie found it hard to believe she was the same girl as the dirty, half-starved urchin who had roamed the village when they had first come to Polwean in 1937. 'Annie Paynter; she'm 'levenpencehap'ny in the shilling.' Well, the village had certainly got *that* wrong.

Matt watched her affectionately as she ran lightly out into the hall, and Sophie thought that almost certainly a solitary being like Matt would not give his love lightly. Julia and Annie had earned his love; he would not have looked at either of them and not seen the whole person beneath.

Oh, that Oliver might have behaved with the same amount of care and perception, she thought sourly as they left to go out on to the terrace, to sit in the sunshine and enjoy a small cup of something that called itself coffee, but had long since ceased to taste like it.

Sitting on the wall, Sophie watched Annie and Patrick strolling down towards the orchard, and heard the murmur of quiet, male voices from the dower terrace — and she decided it was time to be honest.

Looking steadily at Julia for a moment, she squared her shoulders. Might as well confess boldly, as a confession seemed to be on the cards.

'I think I ought to warn you,' she began slowly, 'that when Oliver arrives at the weekend, you might find him ... not altogether pleased to be here. I didn't quite know how to tell you. In fact, I wasn't even sure I was going to, but you've been so kind since we arrived, made us feel so welcome, that I feel I must be honest.'

Matt smoked his pipe and seemed to gaze away across the estate as though he weren't listening. It was his way; to detach himself. This was Julia's problem, and she had to deal with it in her own way.

'So he hasn't been *sent* here then?' Julia asked. 'Not in the way that, say, Patrick and Guy were sent here?'

Sophie shook her head.

'When the hospital said they wanted to send him for convalescence, Tremar was only mentioned in passing,' she replied. 'I think because someone knew we had once lived in Polwean. To be frank, he could have gone somewhere much closer to Arundel; it was certainly what the hospital staff expected me to ask for. Oliver won't be a doctor again, and he might find cutting up his food quite difficult until he adjusts to having only one and a half fingers and a thumb on his left hand, but he didn't need to come here, specifically, to do his adjusting. It was me who pushed for Tremar.'

'So what made you, my dear?' Rory asked

as they watched her, and her corn-coloured hair caught the sun and made Matt think of the coming harvest.

Sophie looked a strange mixture of sheepish and bitter.

'I needed to escape,' she replied. 'We all did. I won't go on about what it was like living with Oliver's mother, I'm sure you don't want to hear it, but if I tell you that Alice was wetting the bed almost every night and Edward was biting anyone who made the mistake of getting close enough, you'll begin to get the idea.' She stopped and licked her lips, then she looked away. 'There was something else, too,' she added quietly.

Julia fixed her eyes on her. 'Me?' she suggested.

Sophie looked miserable.

'He's never got over you,' she said bitterly. 'He's never even tried, and for some reason he seems to think that the children and I should be punished for your rejection of him. I suppose I wanted to redress the balance in some way. I wanted him to face you, and for you to show your shock at his appearance, and I wanted him to be forced to see you with your husband every day. Quite evidently you've moved on with your life, and you've built a happy family for yourself. He didn't make any effort to do that after we left here, and now he's just feeling sorry for himself.'

Julia felt the stillness around her. In the silence Rory and Matt were carefully not looking at her, and she could hear *precisely* what they were thinking.

'Well, thank you for being honest, anyway,' she said at last. 'For all that I'm *still* glad you're here; you and the children. I'm sorry. I'm *very* sorry for what I did to you, and any way I can make it up to you, I will. I promise.'

'Oh, please,' Sophie muttered. 'You make me feel awful!' Suddenly Rory smiled brightly and climbed to his feet.

'Right, I've got an immediate recipe for that then,' he announced. 'You and I can go and clear the table. That should calm things down for a little while, and I think you'll find the rest will take care of itself in due course.'

He knocked out his pipe and offered Sophie his hand. Gratefully, she went with him into the drawing-room, leaving Julia and her husband sitting on the terrace.

After a moment, Matt said calmly, 'You got yourself into this.' He glanced up at the sky, watching the clouds with a practised eye. 'Should be fine for the rest of haymaking by the looks of it.'

'Absolutely,' Julia agreed, just as calmly. 'And I'm glad about the weather. I'm a bit suspicious of those two though. Have you seen the way they look at each other?'

'Only a *bit*?' Matt queried. 'I'd say it was a racing certainty. In fact, I'd say that's the main reason she's come back here, heaven help us all!'

5

Matt and Julia went to bed early as usual, leaving Sophie and Rory together in the drawing-room. Julia explained that Matt had to be up with the dawn and told them to make themselves comfortable, then she wished them goodnight and went into the dim hallway.

They sat on together for a few moments, Rory watching as she cast her eyes around the room, slowly taking in all its splendid, understated opulence. On the marble mantelpiece above the fireplace stood two exquisite bronzes; lively, delicate pieces depicting slender, naked dancing girls, one holding a tiny monkey in her hand and the other, a laurel wreath. Sophie admired them for a long time, then she smiled and looked at Rory.

'I think they're the most beautiful things I've ever seen, those bronzes,' she said. 'I bet they're worth a fortune.'

He smiled back at her.

'Probably,' he replied, 'but it's what they represent that matters to Julia. Alexander Drake bought them when he was at Oxford, in the autumn of 1913, and brought them home in great secrecy to share with his sister. They gave their mother one each for Christmas that year. When Julia came home from Blackridge she found that they were the only items left on display anywhere in the house that had any relevance to her. She supposed her father must have forgotten that she gave her mother the one with the monkey — either that, or he didn't want to break them up because they were a pair. She loves them because Alexander chose them himself.'

Sophie pressed her lips together in silence for a moment, then she stood up and walked towards the French windows.

'Is it too late to go out on to the terrace?' she asked. Rory climbed to his feet, taking up his ebony walking cane.

'Not if we switch the lights out first,' he answered. 'I'll do that and then you can pull back the curtains. Take care though, it's extremely dark out there.'

It was not extremely dark on the terrace at all, for the moon was bright and full. It was a brilliant white circle in the black velvet, diamond-studded sky, and it threw a cold ethereal light across the grounds, contrasting with the inky black shadows.

'A bomber's moon,' Rory said quietly as he came to stand beside her in the warm, June air, aware of the lush, intoxicating scents of the night. 'They aren't coming so often now though, I'm happy to say. Was it bad for you in Arundel?'

'The bombing itself wasn't bad,' she answered truthfully, going to sit on the grey stone parapet above the vegetable garden, 'but the nights we spent in the shelter were truly dreadful. It smelled earthy and there were always things scratching about down there, but the delightful Harriet said it was wasting resources to have a light of any sort, so we were obliged to spend the night in the dark. Edward used to whimper sometimes, especially if we could hear the thump of explosions in the distance, but her sympathy extended exactly as far as suggesting he shut up and go to sleep. They're petrified of the dark now, both of them. I had to leave a night-light burning for them upstairs tonight.'

'Julia won't mind that,' Rory observed, coming to sit beside her and then feeling his pulse quicken as she very deliberately leaned against him. 'You'll find she really is a most accommodating landlady, you know. I hope you'll come to like her eventually, I truly do. I know she didn't exactly invite your affection in the beginning, but she *is* worth a second chance.'

Her hair brushed against his face and he

noticed that it smelled fragrant. He could feel the warmth of her body and in slight panic he felt his own body sharpening up in response. Rory had lived a severely monkish existence for some years now, and whilst it wasn't something that particularly bothered him, it was not possible to ignore the fact that Sophie was throwing herself at him.

The sounds of the night were soft in the air. Above them, the branches of the old cedar tree moved in a gentle breeze.

'Do you understand obsession, Rory?' she asked suddenly, tipping her head back to gaze up at the myriad of stars.

Rory watched her, aware of the deep shadows on her face created by the moonlight. Hers was a finely proportioned, intelligent face; not beautiful, like Julia's, but Julia's Amazon beauty didn't appeal to Rory. He preferred women with a certain vulnerability. Julia was not vulnerable; she had no need to be. Julia had survived some of the worst that life could throw at her, and had come through it calm, strong and efficient. Sophie was vulnerable, though she had learned not to show it since he had last seen her.

'Obsession?' he repeated. 'No, I suppose I don't, not really.' He heard her utter a tiny noise of disgust in her throat.

'Oliver is completely obsessed with Julia,' she said. 'So much so that what he planned to do with her when Arthur Paynter died was nightmarish.'

'Good God!' Rory exclaimed in some surprise. 'What *did* he plan to do, for goodness' sake?'

Sophie leaned back against his chest, letting her head drop back on to his shoulder. He loosely encircled her with his arms with some vague idea of keeping her warm, and immediately she rested her hands on his comfortably. It was astonishingly intimate: he could have kissed her, he realized, and wondered, briefly, what she might do if he did.

'To be honest,' she said after a while, 'whether he ever consciously acknowledged his wildest dreams to himself, I don't know, but they were transparently clear to me. If Annie hadn't been as convincing as she was, and the police had arrested Matt and Julia, their futures were written in stone as far as Oliver was concerned. He was going to get Matt hanged, and let's face it, Matt would have been the first to admit that it was he who actually broke Paynter's neck; he'd have done anything to protect Julia. He wouldn't have saved her, though, not from Oliver. Oliver intended that once it all came out, about how Arthur was the father of her child and everything, she would be slung back into Blackridge and there she would stay.'

'But — I thought you said Oliver loved her.' Rory said.

Sophie uttered a bitter, mirthless laugh.

'Oh, he does,' she replied savagely, 'and he would have worshipped her for the rest of his life. He would never have given up his practice, not once she was back in Blackridge. He would have stayed here forever, until he grew old and died — or she did. And, believe me, she would have had everything in the world she wanted: new clothes, plenty of books, plenty to eat. He would have visited her at least once a week, even taken her out occasionally, if he could. She would have been his personal zoo animal; caged and tamed and completely dependent on him, and in time he would have even slept with her again, if the opportunity presented itself.'

Rory listened to the damning words and felt faintly bewildered. He had never particularly liked Oliver Crompton, but if he truly was guilty as charged, then this was the stuff of nightmares. Rory knew nothing about obsession. He had dearly loved his Penny and been a most loyal and devoted husband, but he was not made up of the right material to be obsessional about *anything*. And yet it never occurred to him to doubt what Sophie was saying. He tightened his grip on her slightly.

'I don't think you'll find Ilona Vincent would have gone along with *that*,' he observed primly. 'She's a very highly principled lady, you know.'

'She would never have known,' Sophie said simply. 'Believe me, when you're as obsessional as Oliver, you're extremely resourceful to boot. He would have found a way of getting what he wanted from Julia, you can count on it. I know it all sounds fairly theatrical, and thankfully he will never get a chance to put it to the test, but I'd bet my children's lives on it that if Oliver had succeeded in getting Julia put away for Arthur's murder, he wouldn't be minus a hand and an eye now and wondering what to do with the rest of his life. Oliver went to war to cope with his rage at losing her.'

Rory turned his head to look at her. She was peering into the moonlight, and her eyes were wretched.

He said, 'If what you say is true, my dear, then are you sure you should have pushed for him to come here as a patient? Who are you punishing, him or Julia?' She pulled herself up at once, turning to face him.

'Both of them,' she replied bluntly. 'It isn't

Julia's fault he feels the way he does, but it *was* her damn fault she let him have what he wanted from her in the beginning. True, she made her position quite clear when she married Matt, but that cut no ice with Oliver, I assure you. I just want him to see her happy with someone else, and at the same time I want my children to have some happiness as well, which they will here, because they don't understand all the grown-up business. They had precious little happiness with his horrible mother.' Their faces were very close and suddenly she put her palm against his cheek. 'Kiss me, Rory,' she whispered, and he did.

He held her in his arms and then he couldn't stop kissing her, and it seemed to go on for ages.

'I wanted this before I left, you know,' she murmured, rubbing her cheek against his as they stood together on the terrace. They might have been anywhere in the world, so absorbed in each other were they. 'But I knew it wasn't right then. Penny had been dead for only such a short time.'

'I wanted it, too,' he replied, finding himself astounded at his frankness, 'but I wouldn't have considered telling you. You've changed, Sophie.'

'I've grown up,' she said bitterly. 'I've had to. It's hard enough when your husband doesn't want you. It's twice as hard when he punishes you for not being the person he *does* want. Perhaps *we* could make each other happy, Rory?'

'Not in Julia's house . . . ' he replied immediately, and then laughed uncomfortably, gazing at her, wanting her more than anything in the world. 'Well, not until I've squared it with myself, anyway,' he added. 'Just now I feel it would be . . . unforgivable.'

Sophie smiled at him serenely and broke from his arms.

'I wasn't thinking about tonight, Rory,' she said. 'We have all the time in the world and I don't want to rush a single thing. Come on, you'd better show me to my room, it's going to take me ages to find my way about in a house this size.'

They closed the French windows behind them, and when the curtains were properly adjusted, Rory switched on the lights. The room basked in its beauty, quietly confident of its flawless quality. 'Little, ordinary, middle-class Sophie Crompton,' she remarked. 'Living in a stately home. I can't believe it.'

'I wouldn't call Tremar a stately home,' he replied, 'just a larger than normal happy house. I wouldn't call it a stately home within Julia's earshot, either; you're likely to get an old-fashioned look. And you're not little and ordinary, my lovely Sophie. You're very special and splendid.'

Sophie chuckled and kissed his cheek softly.

'And you are *so* gallant, Rory,' she observed. 'Come on, we must go to bed.'

Outside her bedroom in the dimly lit corridor he kissed her once more and he wanted to make love to her more than anything in the world.

'Sleep well, my dear,' he said. 'I'll see you at breakfast.'

'And every morning at breakfast for who knows how long,' she replied cheerfully. 'Life is looking up, Rory, it really is.'

Except that your husband, mangled and disfigured and surely an object of pity, will be arriving on Sunday afternoon, he thought. Oh Sophie! What road are we looking down, for heaven's sake, and where is it leading us?

Sophie checked on Alice and Edward and found them sleeping peacefully in their beautiful room as their small night-light, glowing inside a glorious pink, Venetian glass tulip, flickered, about to burn out.

She kissed them and neither of them stirred, so she blew out the remains of the candle and opened their curtains to let the moonlight stream in. Even if they woke, she thought, they would feel quite safe in this room, and she crept away to her own bed.

And in her huge double bed she thought of Rory Nelson.

In his room next door, Rory was thinking of her, too, but he was wracked with guilt and doubt. It was not in Rory's nature to steal other men's wives, and it was not in his nature to be a pawn in someone else's game, either. He had been quick enough to notice how much Sophie had changed since he had seen her last, and she had the power to hurt him now, which made him feel extremely vulnerable. But he couldn't hide from himself how much he wanted her, however hard he tried.

As he turned restlessly in his bed and struggled to go to sleep, he greatly feared that he was destined to break a considerable number of his own rules of conduct over the next few months.

★　★　★

The next morning, Rory bathed and dressed at his usual time and then went along to the children's bedroom and quietly knocked at the door. Sophie was just finishing helping Edward, and as he waited to take the little family down to breakfast, he looked at some of the toys Julia had put there for them to play with. Her beautiful dolls' house, fully furnished and peopled, and Alexander's fort, with its cannon and soldiers.

What, he wondered, had life meant to Julia when she was a child, in that extraordinary world in which she had grown up? As he gazed at the toys he thought about the village as it had been before the last war, and he was suddenly visited by a sharp memory of the child Julia, with her long, thick, chestnut hair flowing out from beneath her straw hat, and her long, skinny legs encased in white stockings, hauling the little, plump Gladys Penhaligan across the green from the shop as they clutched their bags of sweets.

He had stopped to speak to them, for though he was much older than Julia, he had always known the manor children, and finding her path blocked Julia had looked up at him with that touch of imperiousness that singled her out as Florence Drake's daughter. She had been a beautiful girl even at eleven, he remembered, and exquisitely mannered. She had addressed him as Mr Nelson, for he had been in his early twenties then, and had politely asked about his mother and father.

A few moments later she had smiled at him in a way that had somehow made him feel he had been granted an audience, rather than just stopped to pass the time, and taking hold of the silent Gladys again she had said with extraordinary grandeur, 'Well, thank you so much, Mr Nelson, for taking the trouble to ask after us. We won't hold you up any longer, Mama says grown-ups are always very busy. Good day to you.' And so saying she had dragged small Gladys away briskly.

Rory thought about the memory and it gradually became replaced by a picture of his hostess as she was now. The generous, cheerful Julia. He realized for perhaps the first time that Blackridge hadn't really changed her at all. She had spent more than half her life in the place and yet its grip upon her was no more than an occasional finger mark. Was it the tightly laced, disciplined childhood, he wondered, or was it remarkable strength of character? Or both, perhaps?

When they got downstairs they found Julia in the dining-room, feeding Minnie her breakfast. She waved as they trooped in, offering a bright smile.

'Welcome,' she said. 'I do hope you all slept well.' She patted a chair beside her. 'Come on Alice, Edward, you come and sit next to me. Mummy and Mr Nelson can sit the other side of Minnie. Now then, there's some wonderfully creamy porridge if you'd like

130

some, and some of Annie's mother's black-berry jam to have on toast.' She suddenly twisted her mouth into a wry grin. 'Of course, not so very long ago there would have been a sideboard full of scrumptious cooked dishes to choose from, but other than for Annie and Matt I'm afraid we only have cooked breakfasts in the winter during war time. I hope you don't mind.'

Sophie watched her in fascination. She had been fully expecting breakfast in the imposing dining-room to be intimidating, and had wondered if Alice would become hunched and frightened surrounded by such austere grandeur. Instead, though the room was hung with portraits of ferocious-looking ancestors, the atmosphere was pleasant and friendly.

'I suppose,' asked Sophie, 'that your parents always ate breakfast in the dining-room?'

'When Mama deigned to come down at all,' Julia replied cheerfully. 'There used to be enough food spread along the sideboard to feed an army and Mama ate next to nothing. My father had a reasonable appetite, and of course Sandro ploughed in when he was home, but I sincerely hope what was left was eaten by the staff each morning, because if it wasn't then we were guilty of criminal waste!'

Sophie blinked. She said, 'How can you be

so — ' abruptly stopping in mid-sentence, blushing hotly.

Julia grinned at her.

'Cheerful about it?' she asked. 'I've no reason not to be any longer. I've got Tremar back, it's all mine. I've got Matt and Annie, and as a bonus, I've got Minnie. Now I've got all of you, so I can't possibly be lonely, can I? I was thinking that you and I might walk down to the village this morning, so that you can reintroduce yourself, if you know what I mean? Mrs Collins looks after Minnie when I need to go out, and Matt tells me that Doreen would be delighted to see Alice and Edward at Five Elms again this morning.'

Sophie gazed broodily at her children. They were looking at her bright-eyed with anticipation.

'I don't want them to get in anyone's way,' she said and Julia laughed softly.

'My dear, Sophie,' she replied, 'no one gets in anyone's way out there. If you're there, you do a job. It's as simple as that.'

'And might we get another glass of warm milk?' Alice asked timidly. 'It was the loveliest milk I've ever tasted, what we had yesterday.'

'Warm milk?' Julia queried, then the penny dropped. 'Oh, you mean straight from the cow. Yes, you're quite right, it's the tastiest milk in the world; gorgeous stuff. I'm sure

Annie'll be happy to give you a glass each. However,' she gave each child a mildly baleful look, 'no one works on a farm without a good breakfast inside them, it's the rule. And this is the same milk, it's just been in the fridge first.'

They didn't so much eat up as *stuff* themselves in delight. Sophie had never seen either of them eat like that before. When they had finished, they asked to leave the table and a moment later could be heard crashing through the hall towards the kitchen staircase and the back door.

'They know their way around already,' she observed in mild surprise. Julia smiled.

'It is nice to hear them tearing about,' she remarked wistfully. 'Tremar hasn't had any children since ... There was Annie, of course, but she was fourteen before she came here and she creeps about; always has done. The legacy of her bloody father. Rory?' She turned her attention to the schoolmaster. 'Would you care to walk into the village with us, or are you driving to school?' She looked at Sophie. 'I assume you and Rory have discussed when Alice and Edward should start school, but with only a couple of weeks to the end of term, I imagine you'll be waiting until September?'

Rory kept his eyes firmly away

Sophie, though he hadn't failed to notice every detail about her this morning, her neatly styled hair and red lips, her smart summer dress.

'I'll let you two go to the village on your own, if you don't mind,' he said. 'I don't walk quite as fast as you do and I don't want to hold you up. Perhaps Sophie would care to come into school on her way back and register the children?'

'I'd love to, thank you,' she replied immediately and, unable to help themselves, they looked at each other, and then kept on looking for far too long.

Julia wore a carefully non-committal expression when they finally returned their attention to her.

'Right then, I'll go and find Mrs Collins,' she said, 'and then I'll meet you in the drawing-room in about ten minutes. We'll go out by the terrace. You won't need ration books in the same way here, by the way; apart from sugar and tea, we're pretty much self-sufficient at Tremar. We make our own bread and butter, and produce our own meat and vegetables. Even our own fruit — provided you like apples.'

When she had gone, Rory and Sophie turned to look at each other again. His shoulders were slightly hunched and there was a wretched look in his eyes, but Sophie's intention was not to hurt or humiliate him.

'Don't look so frightened,' she told him. 'I'm not going to say anything out of place in front of Julia, I promise. But I meant what I said last night, Rory. I *do* believe we could make each other happy, and provided we're discreet we won't be hurting anybody.' Briskly she rose from the table and then her voice became very bitter. 'We certainly won't be hurting Oliver, I can assure you. Only *she* has the power to do that.' She very quickly kissed his cheek. 'I'll see you later.'

He watched her leave the dining-room and then sat on for a few moments, as her perfume lingered seductively and held him in its thrall.

★   ★   ★

The narrow winding road from Tremar to the village was hedged on either side, with occasional gateways into fields that had served as passing places — in the days when there had been any cars on the road. Now the only vehicles to use it regularly were Rory's battered old Ford, the farm tractors and the ambulances that came and went from the dower. This morning it was deserted, the hedgerows smelled of early summer and bright red poppies were beginning to show their heads in the cornfields.

Julia carried a wicker basket with her, in which were four new-laid eggs and a bunch of tender, baby carrots. She inspected the hedges as they walked and said, 'It looks as if the blackberries are forming well this year. It's all hands to the pump when we're picking fruit, so I hope you won't mind lending a hand.'

'I'll be delighted,' Sophie replied truthfully. 'Tell me, who are the eggs and the carrots for this morning?'

'The old biddies in the shop,' Julia said. Sophie gaped at her in amazement.

The battle between Julia and the two old spinsters in the village shop was legendary. Sophie had actually witnessed one spat between them in the summer of 1938 and she had been given to understand that they had declared war on each other when Julia was about ten! 'Viper-toothed and vulgar-minded' was the way Lady Florence Drake had described them apparently, and Julia had been happy to pass on that comment. Yet here she was, taking them presents.

'You don't mean to tell me you've succumbed?' she exclaimed. 'I might have expected you to take them a present of deadly nightshade, but not eggs!'

Julia turned and smiled, and was suddenly aware of how the tables had been turned between them since they had first met. The first time they had seen each other, Julia had been immaculately clothed, artfully made-up and consciously beautiful, whilst Sophie had been a tired, thin, untidy young mother. Julia didn't wear make-up any more, other than a touch of lipstick on special occasions, and she didn't wear expensive fashionable clothes, either. Her everyday dress was that of a farmer's wife, though she carried anything she wore splendidly on her tall, lean body. Sophie, on the other hand, had *learned* to be beautiful, and her clothes were the height of fashion — but who, Julia wondered, was she being beautiful for? Not Oliver, it appeared. Could it be that she had come back here not simply to punish Julia, but also to renew an up till now secret liaison with Rory Nelson? Well, she wasn't going to *ask*, that was for sure.

She looked down at the eggs and carrots in the basket and she said, 'Much though it irritates me to confess it, those two old witches are able to get — from God knows where — boxes of crystallized fruits, and Minnie likes crystallized fruits more than anything in the world, mostly because she never had sweets at Blackridge, and like all

137

children, she adores them. So in return for the kindness, I give them whatever we can spare from the Tremar harvest; things that they wouldn't otherwise have, for they don't keep chickens or grow their own vegetables. They're too old and they have no garden. I tell them when the box of fruits is almost empty, and somehow they find me another one. It works very well.'

Sophie listened to the birds singing in the summer air and asked quietly, 'Is there anything you wouldn't do for Minnie?' Julia thought about it for a moment, then shrugged.

'No, I don't think there is. You see, my father threw me into the rubbish bin when he found I was shop-soiled, but luckily for me he didn't decide to smash my bones first. As a result, I am privileged enough to have a beautiful home, a husband I adore, and an heir who is the light of my life. Minnie only has me, and if I'd left her behind in Blackridge she'd be dead by now. She won't see Annie's children — she won't live that long — so anything I can do to make her life complete I will do, and swallow my pride if I have to.'

The hedgerows swung wide as they came down to the green. The Drake Arms with its smart new sign and brass carriage lamps, given by Julia as a wedding present; the warm, grey twelfth-century church, and the familiar six large houses, one of which had once been Sophie's home. There, on the corner, was the little village shop.

'You make me feel very humble,' Sophie told her, and Julia stared at her in some alarm.

'Oh, please don't say that!' she exclaimed. 'I do what I do because I feel like doing it. I don't do it for people to think me gracious. Right then, let's beard the lionesses in their den — and you can be sure they'll have something to say about you being back. Oh, look!' She pointed up Pinch Street to where an old bucket full of colourful flowers stood on a crumbling garden wall. 'Mr Bradbury's lovely blooms from his garden. I'll leave him a promise and have a bunch of those for my brother before we go back, if you don't mind.'

'A promise?' Sophie queried.

Julia chuckled.

'It's how things work here. He doesn't want carrots or eggs, he has them for himself, but a nice big box of blackberries and apples in a little while. He'll be thrilled with that. Everyone shares what they have. Isn't that how rationing works in the towns?'

'Except that everybody grumbles about it,

which they obviously don't do here,' Sophie observed.

Miss Penrose and Miss Hewlett leaned on their wooden counter in their war-depleted little shop, and their small, gimlet eyes gleamed when they saw Julia and Sophie come in together. The bell above the shop door jangled as they entered and Sophie suddenly found herself nervous; she had been extremely frightened of these old girls, and they didn't look to have changed at all in the years since she had last seen them.

Julia took on an air of grandeur; Sophie saw it creep across her face and recognized it. Evidently Julia was unable to come face to face with these two without pushing her superiority; it was all part of the battle, and she was gracious rather than generous when she offered her eggs and carrots.

'I 'as a new box o' fruits for you outside, Julia, ma dear,' Miss Penrose announced. 'My word, they carrots look very tasty, don't they, Miss Hewlett?'

'Very tasty,' agreed Miss Hewlett who worked her mouth strangely across her slightly prominent teeth and looked at Sophie, not the carrots. 'And if it ent little Mrs Crompton, looking as smart as paint. We 'ad 'eard as 'ow you was coming back to the village, ma dear, but you'm staying at the manor, Mrs Tregennis says. Course, we always said you was a very Christian girl, very forgiving and understanding.'

Sophie swallowed uncomfortably and watched Julia's head go up. 'The look' as Annie and Matt called it, crept across her face until in the end she resembled nothing so much as one of the paintings of her own arrogant ancestors. Oh God, she's going to be rude to them, Sophie thought, but instead Julia smiled like a duchess.

'More so than you realize, ladies,' she said smoothly. 'Mrs Crompton has given up a most successful and important job to come here to be at her husband's side. Would that we could all show as much dedication to our duty, don't you agree? Selfless love for our dear ones? From time to time the children will be coming into the shop, by the way. I'm sure you'll recognize them when you see them, they're just the same as they were, just a little bigger now. If they are purchasing for the manor, please be so good as to put it on my account in the usual way.'

'Naturally,' replied the venomous Miss Penrose and she turned her penetrating gaze upon the lesser prey, the one far more likely to lie down and die without a fight. 'Course you was very friendly with our schoolmaster when you was here before, wasn't you, ma dear?' she asked Sophie sweetly. 'Nice for you, then, that he'm living up there at the manor with you all. Such a comfort when you need it. Always good to renew a friendship, we think, don't we, Miss Hewlett?'

'Always,' agreed the echo. Julia gave them both a slightly sardonic smile and then picked up her box of crystallized fruits.

'Well, can't stop and chat all day, ladies, much as we'd love to,' she said briskly. 'Got to get to the post office and then back to the manor for the children's lunch. Thank you for the sweets; I shall have runner beans soon, and then apples and blackberries when the time comes. Good day, then.'

Outside, Sophie looked quite pale, but Julia was mulling over what Miss Penrose — albeit maliciously — had just said.

'I didn't know you were particularly friendly with Rory before,' she said as they walked up Pinch Street towards the galvanized bucket, from which she chose a lovely bunch of flowers. 'I mean, I was aware that you knew him, because Oliver was Penny's doctor, but I didn't know you and he had been particular friends — friends enough for those two to know about it, if you understand my meaning.'

'No, well you had a few other things on your mind that summer, didn't you?' Sophie replied, hearing the words tumbling out of her mouth in horror and feeling herself blush like a rose. 'I — I mean . . . '

Julia smiled and replied quietly. 'Yes, I know what you mean. Come on, come into the church with me whilst I arrange these flowers for my brother.'

The church was cool, with dim corners and colourful stained glass windows. Alexander Drake lay as Sophie remembered him, except that against the wall behind his head there was now a table with a glass vase on it. Julia began to clear the wilting flowers out of it and then took it away to get fresh water. When she came back, Sophie was gazing down at the white, marble face of the statue.

'Is it a good likeness of your brother?' she asked and Julia chuckled.

'Annie asked me that, the first time she brought me in here to see it,' she replied. 'As a matter of fact, yes, it's just like him. So much so that I still don't think I'd be all that surprised if he suddenly sat up and started talking to me. I come and tell him everything; all about what's happening in the village and the world. I dust him and bring him fresh flowers as often as I can, and chat away to him all the time I'm working. How daft is that?'

'Why should it be daft?' Sophie reassured

her. 'He was your brother.'

'True, but *he* sleeps very soundly amid his companions in France,' Julia said. '*This* is a lump of rock. Still, that's good enough for me. I miss him. I loved him very much indeed and he was snatched away from me before we'd had any real time together at all. If there is a Heaven, and if he sits in it looking down on the world, he must be furious that he wasted his life for nothing. Here we all are at it again.' She finished arranging the flowers and then stood back to admire her handiwork. 'I suppose in a way I'm grateful to my parents for leaving me this,' she said. 'I feel I have something of Sandro to remember.' Abruptly she changed the subject. 'Tell me,' she said, glancing at Sophie out of the corners of her eyes, 'if Oliver had died when his ship went down, would you — '

'Would I what?' Sophie enquired, when the sentence remained unfinished. 'Have erected a statue in his honour? Julia, my marriage to Oliver began to crumble before he went away to war and what I'm trying to do now is be a dutiful wife and mother. I told you last night why I asked for him to be sent here, and you'll forgive me if I'm blunt, but I would be most grateful if you would *not* run about trying to make everything all right when he gets here, because it isn't possible to do that.

It's too late. In fact, I'd like you to go and welcome him when he arrives tomorrow afternoon, if you wouldn't mind. Believe me, that will mean a lot more to him than me welcoming him.'

Julia stared at her in astonishment for a moment, then she licked her lips.

'Well, all right, if that's what you want,' she replied. 'But if you had some idea of pushing us at each other, please don't, I beg of you. I made my position clear when I married Matt. I'm happy to offer you and the children the freedom of Tremar, and I'm happy to do the same for Oliver, but I won't be used as a weapon.'

'A *weapon!*' echoed Sophie and for a moment there was a tight silence between them, then she laughed bitterly and turned towards the church door, wanting to get back out into the sunshine. 'Julia, you misunderstand me. I have no desire to fight for Oliver, nor to manipulate him. If you want him, you can have him. If you don't, that's fine. All I ask is that you don't set about thinking up romantic little surprises or the like, in an attempt to patch things up between him and me. I know what I want and it isn't Oliver, but for the moment, anyway, it will be nice for him to have access to his children. And now I'd like to go into school, please, to register the children for the autumn. Are you coming, or will you walk home without me?'

Julia gathered up the bits from her flower arranging and threw them in the bin. Through the church door she saw the thin Sophie standing, warming herself in the sunshine. Gathering up her wicker basket, she went out to join her.

They walked on to the school and after a moment the atmosphere began to thaw between them and they were chatting peacefully by the time they reached the school gates; but Julia was uncomfortable and uneasy — and unlikely to forget the encounter in a hurry.

6

Oliver arrived at Tremar in a Red Cross ambulance. It was Saturday afternoon and, with his small suitcase in his right hand, he was welcomed into the dower by Matron, who showed him to the room she had arranged for him to occupy with two other officers. Neat iron bedsteads, one in each corner of the ground floor room, each with a locker beside it. Two of these lockers sported framed photographs, neatly angled towards their owners' pillows. One was of a very pretty, fashionable-looking young lady with a bright-eyed small child at her knee. The other was of a beautiful girl with radiant eyes and a mass of unruly hair.

It was Annie Paynter.

Oliver stood and looked at it for ages. He couldn't quite believe it: the dirty urchin, taken in by the beautiful Julia, for whom the beautiful Julia and her extraordinary bear of a husband had committed murder. Annie had certainly blossomed into something amazing, and evidently she was enjoying a romance with one of the patients.

He found out who a few moments later,

when a young airman came slowly into the room, carefully feeling his way. He had astonishingly yellow hair, the colour of the sun, and bright-blue, thick-lashed eyes — and a face that looked as if someone had been careless with an axe.

Blind, Oliver thought in amazement, and lovingly in possession of a photograph. Was this Annie's beau, or the young man with the wife and child?

'Hullo,' he said, looking into the centre of the room with his obviously sightless eyes. 'They said you'd arrived. I'm Patrick Thornby.' He held out his hand. 'You're Oliver Crompton.'

Oliver walked over to him and shook the proffered hand.

'Would yours be the bed with the photograph of Annie?' he asked, and Patrick's crooked face seemed to light up with delight.

'Oh, Annie,' he replied happily. 'The most perfect girl in the world! Just the *most* perfect. She says you knew her before the war.'

'Annie was just a child when I knew her,' Oliver said with unusual tact for him. 'The last time I saw her she was a bridesmaid for the Logans. You know the Logans, of course?'

Patrick sat down on his bed and fiddled about in his breast pocket for his cigarettes.

'Oh, absolutely,' he said with much pleasure, offering a cigarette to Oliver. 'Julia's a perfect love. Everyone adores her. She's such a lady, and yet she'll turn her hand to anything: digging vegetables, plucking pheasant. There's no side to her at all. And of course Matt — well, Annie's quite besotted with Matt, she says he's the best father any girl could have.'

Oliver lit the two cigarettes and watched young Patrick with interest. He listened to his accent. This was no ordinary boy. He recognized the type, mostly from so much time spent around Julia three years ago. He was quite evidently madly in love with Annie, but what did he know about her, Oliver wondered, and how much ice would having the daughter of the twelfth baronet of Tremar as a surrogate mother cut with others of Julia's ilk? Precious little, he feared. Julia was cut adrift from her own kind because of her twenty-three years in the country asylum.

'You know Matt isn't her father, don't you?' he asked, and Patrick grinned.

'Oh yes,' he replied cheerfully. 'But as Annie says, you're much more likely to get everything you want in a father if you can choose your own!'

Lord, Oliver thought, do you go on like this all the time about Annie, I wonder? It would be quite wearing if you did.

'Have you met her mother?' he enquired. 'Her real mother?'

'Gladys, you mean?' Patrick answered. 'Oh, rather; a splendid woman. She works here in the convalescent home. She organizes the staff here, and she cooks like a dream. She'll press a uniform wonderfully if you ask her nicely.'

A real family affair then, Oliver thought sourly.

'And my wife?' he said slowly. 'Have you met her yet?'

Now Patrick seemed to pause and he gazed in Oliver's direction. It was quite disconcerting; his eyes were so bright and so blue it seemed impossible that he couldn't see out of them.

'Actually, yes, I have,' he answered. 'She came down to the vegetable garden this morning with the schoolmaster and your little boy. He's a bright little lad, isn't he? He seems terribly anxious to do his bit. Uncle Matt said I was to do this, and Uncle Matt said I was to do that. You must be extremely proud of him.'

'Well, they certainly seem to have settled in, don't they?' Oliver observed, struggling to keep the irony out of his voice. Suddenly there was a sound in the doorway and Guy negotiated his way in with his wheelchair.

'Oh, *here* you are!' he exclaimed to Patrick. 'We were wondering what had happened to you. You must be Oliver, I'm Guy Taylor.' He stuck out his hand. 'We don't bother much with rank here because, let's face it, none of us are going to be back out there again, so welcome to Tremar. We've been detailed to see you comfortably settled in, Patrick and I, and there's tea and cake coming up on the terrace in a minute. Only ever get cake at weekends, so what say you we hop along out and get ourselves a slice? It's a real suntrap on that terrace this afternoon.'

'Could he join you in just a moment, Guy?' called another voice from the doorway and all three men turned their heads quickly in its direction. Guy and Patrick grinned cheerfully. Oliver turned away.

He put his good hand up to shield his face and then he climbed to his feet and deliberately walked away so that he stood looking out of the window, with his back to the room.

Julia looked intently at Guy.

'A minute, please,' she mouthed and, nodding, Guy reached out for Patrick and yanked him gently in the direction of the door. Patrick had learned not to question everything he couldn't see. Obediently, he put

151

his hands on the handles of Guy's chair and helped manoeuvre it out of the room. They closed the door behind them.

'Hullo, Oliver,' she said softly.

Oliver did not turn round. He couldn't. He couldn't bear to see her, and he couldn't bear for her to see him.

After a moment he said, 'Not Sophie then. Did she send you as the welcoming committee, or could she simply not be bothered to come?'

Julia took a few steps towards him, but was careful not to touch him.

'Please look at me,' she said and saw him hunch his shoulders, as if her voice was a piercing wind in his ears.

'Why?' he asked bitterly. 'So that I can see you enjoy my humiliation? I didn't want to come here, Julia. I'm only here because Sophie packed up my children and brought them here, and this was the only way I was going to see them.'

Julia reached out and very gently put her hand on his shoulder.

'You are not humiliated, Oliver.' She spoke quietly. 'You're a hero. Of all the places in the world you could have gone, you could not have been more welcome than you are here at Tremar. Please look at me.'

Finally he turned. There were still dressings

152

on his face, for the burns had been severe and were a long way from being completely healed yet. It was not difficult to see, however, that the scarring would be extensive and very obvious. Almost certainly it would be an angry red, probably for years to come, and she wondered if, under the dressings, it had pulled the corner of his eye down in the same way it had hitched up the corresponding corner of his mouth. His hand was heavily bandaged still, and it was not possible to distinguish yet that most of its fingers were gone, but facing up to that wasn't going to be far away, obviously.

A very long way away, however, and now entirely out of reach, were his dreams of a Harley Street practice.

'Would you have known me, then, if you'd passed me in the street?' he enquired. To her great distress Julia saw that his one good eye was full of tears. 'Would you have recognized this shambling wreck in a uniform as the same conceited fellow who made such a fool of himself in 1938?'

'Of course I would,' she replied truthfully. 'I'd know you anywhere, Oliver, and you were never a conceited fellow who made a fool of himself. You were my saviour, and you know you were. We were friends. We were *such* good friends once. Couldn't we be friends again? I truly am so happy to welcome you to Tremar.'

He sat down on the little iron bedstead that was his allotted sleeping place and, as he stared down at his knees, Julia remembered his sleek, dark head; the lovely shiny hair he had passed on to Alice.

'Friends,' he muttered. 'We were never friends. I was obsessed with you and you rejected me. Shall I tell you something, Julia? When that torpedo hit my ship, when the decks began to writhe because she was going down, and something came out of nowhere above my head and severed half my foot, when I lurched forwards into a wall of fire that melted my face and seared away the fingers of my hand, I thought I was going to die. I don't know how I stumbled up on deck, I have no memory of that, but it was dark and the water was going to be icy cold, and I knew when I hit it I would be lucky if I survived. Do you know who I thought about? In those last seconds, the seconds I really believed would be my last on earth, do you know who I thought about? I thought about you. Not my wife or my children. *You.* I ruined my life for you, Julia, and now my wife has decreed that I should pay the price.'

Julia sat down beside him on the bed and after a few seconds she laid her hand on his good one and stroked it gently.

'I'm sorry,' she whispered. He chuckled mirthlessly.

'Don't be,' he replied. 'It was never your fault. I punished Sophie, I dumped her on my mother and I knew how unhappy she would be. I didn't need to come here, you know. I could have gone somewhere much nearer home. This is Sophie's revenge, and she's going to enjoy it at her leisure — unless they decide to send me away again in a few weeks. They ought to.'

Julia thought about him coming to Blackridge to find her, of him holding her hands so tightly in his when she broke down and wept in front of him. She thought of him bringing her home in triumph to Tremar, and then she regretted, for the hundredth time, the mistakes they had made afterwards. The pain they had caused, for which they were both to blame.

'There will be no question of them sending you away,' she said quietly. 'When they decide you don't need to be here, I hope you'll agree to move in next door, with us. You can't all troop back to London, not with the war raging on, and at least whilst you're here you can have time to think in peace. Dine with us tonight, why don't you? It would be so nice.'

Oliver smiled and turned to look at her and

his heart lurched with a familiar pain in his chest. So, two years into the war, a miraculous escape from death and the prospect of life as a cripple hadn't changed a thing. He was still obsessed with her.

'Are you happy, Julia?' he asked softly. She stared at him. There was no point in being anything other than truthful, no point at all.

'Yes, Oliver,' she replied. 'I am. I'm very happy. Matt is everything I could have wanted in a husband. He loves Tremar as much as I do and he runs my estate for me like clockwork. He loves Annie and Minnie, and he loves me.'

'Not as much as I did,' Oliver murmured and she inclined her head.

'Maybe not, but much less destructively.' They were silent with their memories for a moment, then she said, 'We mustn't have conversations like this, they don't help anyone. I think you should come out on to the terrace now, your children are waiting for you. They're longing to see their daddy.'

He stood up and stumbled slightly, as he often did, because coping with one eye made the world look very different, and it was hard to plant both feet firmly on the ground when one of them was half the size of the other. She caught his arm, it was an instinctive reaction and for a second they were very close to each other. She smelled familiar; not of perfume, but of herself, a smell he had never been able to forget. It made him think of lying beside her naked body, of touching her smooth skin with his tongue and tasting the essence of her.

'My children are waiting for me on the terrace, but not my wife.' He gave a small, bitter laugh. 'That would be about right. Thank you for your invitation to dine, but I don't think I'd better, do you? It wouldn't look very good amongst my new companions, not on my first night. Some other time, perhaps.'

Julia smiled.

'I'm sure you're right,' she replied, 'but you will have to come and dine one night; everybody who can does, I'm afraid. At times when life is a little quieter on the estate we have little soirées and everyone gets an invitation: officers, doctors and nurses, a few at a time. So, you see, you won't be allowed to escape.'

'I'll look forward to it,' he said, hoping she wouldn't spot the irony in his voice. 'Come on then, you'd better show me how to get to the terrace.'

She opened the bedroom door, which Guy and Patrick had thoughtfully closed behind them on their departure, but just before they went out, she laid a hand on his arm very briefly.

'Oliver,' she said quietly, 'I have to ask you something most particularly before you go outside. As you've probably already gathered, Patrick has a very close relation-ship with Annie . . . ' She stopped, because he was staring at her and she was uncomfortably certain he knew what she was going to say, but pushing on firmly she said it anyway. 'You will be careful what you tell him, won't you?' she begged. 'They're young and they're in love, and yes, they have a huge gulf of upbringing and background between them, and all sorts of difficulties to face if their love is to last, but Patrick doesn't need to know . . . you know . . . Well, not at the moment he doesn't, anyway. Do you promise me?'

Oliver touched his bandaged face softly with his fingers and Julia had an idea the look he threw her was touched with contempt, though she chose not to wonder about it.

'I'm not here to make enemies, Julia,' he retorted coldly. 'I don't need them. I've got enough to contend with as it is. Besides, if my wife has anything to do with it, she'll make as many enemies for me as she possibly can, just for the fun of it!' And so saying he walked away from her.

The dower terrace was not as big as the manor terrace, which was a pity since there were rather more people using it on a regular basis these days, but neither was it as high, nor did it have uneven stone steps leading down from it, so it was certainly safer, Julia thought.

As they emerged into the afternoon sunshine, eight or nine of the patients were assembled; some sitting on the walls, one or two in deck chairs, some in wheelchairs, and amongst them were Alice and Edward, who were already becoming very popular. Alice ran immediately to her father and encircled him with her arms, pressing herself against him fiercely.

Oliver touched her shiny dark head with trembling fingers and for a few seconds they gazed at each other.

'Hullo, Daddy,' she whispered at last and he bent to kiss her.

'Hullo, my best girl,' he replied and hugged her to him as he turned his eyes towards his small son with hair like ripe corn, the colour of his mother's.

'Hullo, Edward,' he said.

Edward struck a pose.

'We're doing important war work, me and Alice,' he declared proudly. 'C'lecting eggs an' feedin' all the chickens and fings. Uncle

Matt says we're helping to feed the nation! Good, isn't it?'

There was a gentle ripple of amusement, but if Edward thought he was being laughed at, it didn't appear to worry him.

Julia began to melt away, hoping no one would see her go.

'An' shall I tell you something else?' Edward persisted. 'It's Sunday tomorrow and we haven't got to go to church *once*. Not like at Granny's. I like this place *much* better than Granny's!'

He said the word 'Granny's' as if it were a nasty taste in his mouth. Oliver, who was well aware of his mother and his son's savage dislike of each other, made no attempt to reprimand him, but simply chuckled softly.

'So does that mean you've stopped biting?' he enquired. Alice turned her face up towards him with a grin.

'He only bites people he doesn't like, and he hasn't met anyone he doesn't like here yet,' she replied cheerfully. 'I like it here too. Aunt Julia has given me ever so many books to read, and Annie says there will be all sorts of jobs I can do for her. And besides that I'm going back to the village school in September, which means I shall see my friend Peggy Jackson again. And Uncle Matt's going to make Edward a Spitfire, and . . . '

She chatted on as Oliver stared at her in wonder. Less than two weeks ago she had been virtually silent; now she had said more in one little speech than he had heard her say in two years. He looked up from her pretty face, and coming up the slope to the terrace was Sophie. She was very smartly dressed with her mouth painted in red lipstick — and she caught the eye of every single officer on the terrace.

There was not one, who could see, who didn't look at her.

'Hullo, Oliver,' she said with a meaningless smile. 'Julia says you're comfortably settled.'

He looked around him quickly. Julia had gone. He supposed it would always be like that; she would slip away when she felt like it and not say goodbye. Perhaps she would be with Matt and perhaps he would be touching her. Matt could touch her whenever he liked: she was his wife. Perhaps, Oliver thought bitterly, he should work out just how quickly he could get away from here, because all of this was like a sudden, icy-cold waterfall of pain, and he thought he would have liked to cry at that moment.

'Hullo, Sophie,' he replied with a smile that was equally as meaningless. 'The children were just telling me how much they were enjoying themselves here at Tremar.'

161

And they both knew he was thinking about Julia.

★ ★ ★

Two weeks later, on an exquisite Sunday evening Annie, who had so far barely acknowledged Oliver's arrival at Tremar, held Patrick's hand as they went together through the rhododendron walk and skirted a field of ripening corn at Home Farm to come to a tiny field on the edge of the estate where Matt kept his mare, Judith, and Tallulah, the pony who pulled the cart. Sunday evening was their special time, and in each other's company they were content to do not much more than just lie in the grass, enjoying the summer air.

A good many of the Land Army girls met their Canadian boyfriends in The Smugglers' Inn on a Sunday night, and Patrick and Annie had passed four of them heading for the gate in the wall that would take them over the cliffs to the harbour. Annie never went to The Smugglers', she had not been inside since the night she had lured her father out to his death, and she was not able to think of it other than how it had been back in 1938, when the roughest element in the village had got drunk in there every night. She knew the local poachers still drank in there, huddled disconsolately in a corner watching the Canadians throwing their money about, and she knew that it wasn't just the Land Girls who frequented the pub and the camp now. Most of the village girls headed off up there at weekends, too.

Annie hadn't even taken the trouble to cross the cliffs and see what the camp looked like because Julia had told her quite sharply that she wasn't to, when she had first come home from school. And now she didn't want to anyway, for with each passing day she was becoming more and more sure of her feelings for Patrick, and of his for her. She would lose him again, briefly, when he went for his operation, but after that he would be back, and then surely, if life was even mildly fair, they should be able to stay here together forever?

Patrick thought like that as well, but in the back of his mind his mother, his sisters and his completely meaningless engagement to a girl he hadn't seen for years loomed like an awful threat and regularly doused his optimism in cold water. How was it fair, he wondered bitterly, when for the first time ever life had given him something wonderful, so much of the pain of the past still lingered sourly, threatening to spoil it for him?

Patrick had railed against God when he had first awoken in hospital and found himself smashed and blinded, but still alive. Instead of being a dead hero, which he should have been, he was condemned to be a crippled dependant, and the unfairness of that had seemed impossible to comprehend at the time.

He remembered very clearly that last morning, with the bell ringing on the airfield, and he and his mostly exhausted companions racing for their planes across the uneven grass, bouncing into the air to face the approaching enemy yet again. It was like a moving picture running constantly through his head. The blue sky, the bright sunshine, the Channel glittering below him and the sharp distant horizon. His last really clear memory was of a shouted warning a split-second too late in his headphones, followed by the thud of bullets crunching into his Spitfire and the lurch of the world below him as the plane tipped and dived and he went down towards the water with a dead engine.

He knew he had ejected late, and he had a clear memory of pain, but he couldn't see anything in his head to go with it. Just the sudden shock of something smashing into his face: agonizing, but brief. Since then the world had been light and dark, bright and black, but seen always as if through a heavy veil. And in the beginning . . . dear God, he had been so depressed; until Annie had arrived in his life.

When she had given him her photograph, he had been touched beyond words for it had seemed to indicate that to her he was a normal human being, whatever his handicap. Now he dreaded the thought of being taken away from her, of his life being once again reduced to ashes, but he couldn't get beyond Mona. He knew the sort of woman his mother was, he had seen for himself what she was capable of when she didn't get her own way, and the thought of her filled his heart with dread. But he felt quite unable to talk to Annie about it, because he wouldn't know where to start.

As Annie opened the gate to the field, Judith and Tallulah came immediately to be nuzzled and offered a couple of treats, and Patrick felt their velvet lips against his palm as their strong, horsey smell filled his nostrils. White campion bloomed against the hedge and the field was rich in clover.

Annie had found a patch of lush grass in a sun-drenched corner some time ago, and they always settled down comfortably there when they were alone. It was *their* place. This evening she lay on her back with her head on his chest, watching the mix of colours whilst he breathed in the smell of summer grass mingled with the tang of the sea. There was no sound at all, only the tug of the horses' mouths as they grazed and a couple of herring gulls, floating on the warm air currents and calling mournfully. It reminded her, suddenly, of beautiful evenings during what she always referred to as 'that first summer', and with the memories came the thought of Oliver.

'So,' she asked suddenly, 'what d'you think of your new room-mate, then, now you've 'ad a bit of time to get to know 'im?'

Patrick smiled and caressed her face with his fingers. Her skin was warm with the sun and he was happy, though he had yet to tell her that this would be their last Sunday together for a while.

'He seems a nice chap to me,' he replied truthfully, 'and, like everyone else, I think his children are splendid. However, you obviously don't like him, and I think he knows that, as well.'

'An' I don't trust 'im, neither,' she retorted, suddenly thinking of all the secrets Oliver knew about Julia; all the trouble and pain he could cause if he chose to do so. 'I'd rather you didn't, an' all. Believe me, Patrick,

Dr Crompton 'as the power to 'urt Julia a lot — an' I ent 'aving 'im say things about 'er to you an' Guy that shouldn't be said. She'm a wonderful person, so don't you go listening to anythin' different.'

Patrick frowned and then pulled himself up slightly, leaning on his elbow with his face close to hers.

'Annie, I wouldn't allow anyone to say awful things to me about Julia,' he said firmly. 'I give you my word I wouldn't, and I know jolly well Guy wouldn't either. But I have to say, Oliver hasn't shown any signs of doing such a thing as yet and I'll be the first to tell you if he does.'

'Yeah, well, give 'im time,' she muttered and for a few moments she was quiet with her thoughts. It wasn't just Julia whom Oliver could hurt if he chose to, she realized, thinking suddenly of the night of her father's death. If he opened his mouth he could damage them all.

Pushing away the thought angrily, she turned and pressed herself into Patrick's arms, and as she briefly kissed his lips, because she suddenly felt unsettled, he decided now was the moment to give her his news.

He said quietly, 'Annie, could we stop talking about Oliver for a moment, do you think? I've got something rather important to tell you. I'm being shipped out on Tuesday morning to have my operation. Matron told me this afternoon. She said she knew it was short notice, but she doesn't like giving people too long to brood about things. I'll be gone for about six weeks in all.'

Annie had known it was coming, of course she had, but it didn't make it any easier. Strangely it felt as if he had just told her he was going back to the front line. Fear and loneliness crept into her heart.

'Oh, Patrick . . . ' she whispered desolately, and he held her tightly in his arms.

'It's only six weeks,' he promised. 'I'll be back after that.'

'Or not, according to 'ow your mother feels,' she replied bitterly, clinging to him. 'Patrick, I ent no fool. I know 'ow your family would feel about me. An' your mother wouldn't even employ me as a servant. I'm right, ent I?'

Patrick was silent. What she said was quite true and he feared it so much it made him feel physically sick. His mother couldn't bear anyone who spoke with a local dialect. Never in his life at Chawston, in London or in Ireland had he spoken to a servant, from his nanny downwards, who didn't speak his mother's idea of perfect

168

English. He supposed there might have been kitchen maids and bootboys who didn't, but he'd never been into any of the kitchens.

He began to kiss her, holding her face between his hands as the familiar delights of her mouth filled him with a mixture of panic and determination.

'I damn well *won't* let her spoil this for us!' he declared at last. 'Once I've had my operation, I'm going to write to my brother Robert and tell him everything. I don't quite know how yet, but there's bound to be someone who writes letters for servicemen at this hospital; there was at the last one I was in. I trust Robert — he married against Mother's wishes, so he's got first-hand experience, and . . . and he's a good man, Annie.' He paused and then added, almost shyly, 'You will write to me now and then whilst I'm away, my darling, won't you?'

Annie's eyes filled with tears that pricked quite spitefully. Suddenly she felt certain she was going to lose him, and the hurt was insupportable. She clung to him fiercely, and after a moment he realized she was quietly sobbing.

'Oh, don't,' he whispered, brushing away her tears with his thumbs. 'Please don't. I love you, Annie. I love you more than life itself. I'd ask you to marry me, except that I know you won't accept, because of Mona, but you would give me great courage if you promised you'd consider me once I'm free of any ties.'

Annie was astounded. It was such a formal little speech, and she wondered if it was always like that in his world. Julia could sometimes be oddly formal she'd noticed, so she supposed their privileged lives had been built around sets of rules written in stone. Well, she'd cure him of that, just the same as Matt was gently curing Julia.

'You can ask me, if you like,' she observed, half laughing through her tears. 'I'll say yes, if you do. I'd marry you tomorrow, afore you go, if I didn't want to 'ave a proper Tremar weddin'. An' anyway, I'm a bit busy tomorrow. But yes, Patrick, I accept your proposal. I would very much like to be your wife. Only you will 'ave to do somethin' about Mona, of course. An' as for writin' to you,' she added, 'I was thinkin' of every day rather than now an' then . . . only the letters'll be full of borin' stuff like harvest an' such like, if you can bear that.'

Patrick hugged her as his spirits seemed to take wings and fly.

'You can copy out the phone book, my darling,' he replied, hugging her until he was almost squeezing the breath out of her. 'Just

170

write your name fifty times on the page, I don't care a damn! Oh, thank you, Annie! Thank you so much!'

Annie put her hands against his cheeks and gazed at the accidental asymmetry of his face. It didn't occur to her to wish he wasn't so badly damaged, and she wouldn't have been bothered in the least if he was to stay looking just the way he was. His coming operation was more about stabilizing and strengthening his facial bones than making him look more like he'd been before.

'Just promise to come back, Patrick,' she whispered as the sun, on its progress across the heavens, threw a shadow across them that told them it was time to be making their way home.

There wouldn't be another Sunday evening together for a while now and by the time Patrick came back to Tremar, harvest would be underway and their time would be short and precious; but neither of them for a moment allowed themselves to think he wouldn't come back.

'I *promise*!' he replied.

★ ★ ★

In the drawing-room, Julia came down from tucking Minnie into bed and found Matt and

171

Rory still lingering on the terrace in the last of the evening sunshine. She was reminded, briefly, of her first summer back home from Blackridge, when she had renewed her acquaintance with the subtle smell of evening after almost a quarter of a century without it. She remembered sitting on the terrace with Annie, and then later with both Matt and Annie, and she recalled the desire she had sometimes experienced to weep, not at what she had lost, but at the luck of finding it again.

Inevitably, as they did with Annie, along with those memories came the memories of Oliver.

'Where's Sophie?' she enquired, stepping out through the French windows.

Rory smiled.

'Upstairs, putting the children to bed,' he replied. 'And before you ask, Annie and Patrick went along the rhododendron walk more than an hour ago, looking like the principal players in a love story.'

'The principal players in a tragedy, you mean,' she spat sourly. 'He's going away on Tuesday to have his next operation — and if either of you think his family is going to allow him to come back again, then you're more naïve than I took you for.'

Matt puffed comfortably on his pipe,

narrowing his eyes against the gold of the evening sun as he gazed across the estate.

'He'll be back,' he said. 'I'll lay odds he's a lot more resourceful than you give him credit for, and there cannae be any doubt about his love for her.'

'Love!' Julia snarled. 'What's love got to do with it? Isobel Thornby wouldn't employ Annie as a parlour maid. A kitchen maid possibly, a tweeny, but when she gets wind of what's been going on here — and she will, you can be sure of it — she'll spirit Patrick away as fast as possible . . . ' She broke off, staring grimly at the edge of the rhododendron walk as she thought of Annie's eyes when she looked at Patrick. 'And just where the hell do they go on a Sunday evening, I'd like to know?' she continued irritably. 'And more importantly, what do they get up to? If he leaves her pregnant, and then never comes back . . . '

'Which he won't,' Matt stated firmly. 'I think you'll find he's a particularly honourable young man in that direction as it happens.'

Julia opened her mouth to reply and then Sophie came out on to the terrace. Smiling, she sat herself down next to Rory on the swing seat and looked around her questioningly.

'Who's an honourable young man?' she enquired. Rory touched her hand.

Rory always contrived to touch Sophie whenever she was close to him and the same went for her; a fact that had not been missed by either Julia or Matt. Julia knew that there was nothing she could say, so she would hold her peace unless they made everyone's life uncomfortable with their attraction to each other, but she hadn't much enjoyed being told off to be Oliver's welcoming committee two weeks ago, that was for sure. It had not made things easy at all.

And she damn well *could* have let the Crompton family go to Pinch Street, she thought sourly.

'We were talking about Patrick,' Rory said. Sophie grinned cheerfully.

'Oh, Patrick!' she exclaimed. 'What a *splendid* boy he is, isn't he? I hope my Alice finds someone like Patrick one day. He's so charming, and my word, doesn't he love Annie?' She looked brightly and innocently at Julia. 'You must be delighted,' she added.

Julia stared broodily out across the estate and her lips tightened fiercely.

'I'm sure I would be if the little sod wasn't already engaged to someone else!' she snorted eventually.

'Oh, that,' Sophie said dismissively. 'That

doesn't mean a thing, you know that? Crikey, he told me yesterday that he hasn't even seen this so-called fiancée of his for about five years. I shouldn't let it worry you.'

Julia would have commented, but realized before she opened her mouth that Sophie wouldn't understand. It was not given to people of Sophie's gentle upbringing to understand people like Isobel Thornby. Rather closer to home, however, the mention of the class thing would send up all her defences again, and Julia felt she could do without all that this evening.

The sun began to set, the sky was streaked with a glorious myriad of reds and golds, and the navy blue of night waited to spill in as the great fiery ball sank below the horizon. Patrick and Annie came strolling back across the lawns holding hands and obviously deeply involved in an intimate conversation.

'Oh, damn and blast it!' Julia muttered and then smiled and waved.

'Julia's wavin' at us,' Annie told Patrick, leaning comfortably against him. 'They're all on the terrace watchin' the sunset. Shall we join them?'

Patrick hunched his shoulders slightly.

'Had I better?' he asked. 'I don't want to intrude.' She hugged his arm, bringing their bodies close enough for him to feel the

175

warmth of her body.

'If you really mean to come back 'ere to Tremar an' marry me,' she replied, 'then you'm goin' to 'ave to get used to being with the other people I love.'

Patrick could see the logic in that.

'Yes, I suppose so,' he said. 'Are we going to tell them that we want to marry each other? No, I'd better ask for your hand first, hadn't I, before I presume.'

Annie kissed him, highly amused by his old-fashioned manners and yet oddly comforted that he was so determined to do the right thing. It would have been easy to be modern and let it slide, but if she was honest she *wanted* him to ask for her hand. It made her feel very important to him.

'When you come back,' she said. 'When you'm free to ask. Now's not a good time; not to ask Julia, anyway. She'm still a bit upset 'bout Mona at the moment.'

So he went on to the terrace with her and found himself amongst the entire household. Sophie spoke warmly to him and Rory greeted him with pleasure. Matt invited him to sit on the terrace wall beside him, and then asked him about Tuesday and wished him luck for his operation.

Patrick was compensating rapidly for the loss of his sight as the weeks went by. It was a skill that, once learned, was reasonably easily perfected, and every day he learned better to listen and sense what he could no longer see from the words spoken to him.

And this evening he sensed a distinct chilliness from Julia.

7

Patrick left Tremar in an ambulance early on Tuesday morning. Annie stood on the drive with him, as in the very early freshness of the July morning their kisses were touched with their coming loneliness and they clung to each other, staving off the moment of parting for as long as possible.

Finally Guy joined them in his wheelchair. Matron stored his small suitcase under the seat on which he would sit as he travelled to the hospital in Salisbury where he was to have his operation, and Julia and Matt emerged from the manor to wish him goodbye and good luck.

Annie stared in a terrible sort of isolated silence as the ambulance drove away between the gateposts. Julia put an arm around her shoulder and hugged her close.

'It's only six weeks, you know,' she whispered. 'And it'll be gone in no time, with harvest coming up.'

'Or else it's forever,' Annie replied bleakly, 'if 'is family decide they don't want 'im to come back 'ere.'

Julia pressed her lips together sharply as

she felt Annie's pain. Anger rose in her throat and had to be swallowed down, for it had no place here.

'Is that what he said?' she asked softly. Annie shook her head.

'Well, 'e tried not to,' she answered truthfully. 'He promised 'e'd come back no matter what . . . Only, I ent a fool. I know as well as 'e does that if 'is mother gets wind of our romance, she'll ship 'im off to Ireland as fast as she can.' Suddenly she looked up at the beautiful grey manor, which was beginning to be touched by early morning sun. 'He's asked me to marry him,' she went on desolately, 'an' I've accepted. He's told me 'e's going to ask for 'is brother's 'elp to get 'im out of this absurd engagement, an' I'm sure he will. I just ent sure I trust 'is brother as much as 'e does.'

They turned from the drive and went back into the manor together. Alice and Edward were chasing each other down the stairs to get to breakfast in a rush, and Mrs Collins was coming up from the kitchen with the tray. Annie thought she'd be sick if she ate anything, and yet the familiarity of everything was strangely comforting. Patrick would be alone with his fear in the ambulance.

'Have you ever thought of writing to Patrick's brother yourself?' Julia asked quietly

179

as they stood in the dining-room doorway. She thought that if Annie was going to have her heart broken by these people, now might be a good time; cutting short the agony. 'I don't see you've anything to lose, frankly. If he isn't the man Patrick thinks he is, you're going to lose him anyway, aren't you? But if he is, it'll be a while before Patrick can do anything about it, won't it?'

Annie looked at her gratefully for a moment and then smiled.

'That ent a bad idea!' she declared. 'I'll make a start on it tonight, I think. Thanks, Julia.'

Julia touched her arm and then went to take her place at the breakfast table. Matt was bringing Minnie down, and Sophie and Rory hadn't arrived yet, but would do so within the next couple of minutes. In the meantime Edward had sat himself firmly in the chair next to Matt's and was waiting impatiently for his hero to arrive.

It was all the same as usual, Annie thought, as her heart wrenched in her chest. Except that when she went into the dower, he wouldn't be there.

It was all very different for Patrick, and frightening, too, because he had only fairly recently been blinded and once he was away from familiar territory he was helpless and dependent. It took hours to reach the hospital and then, though the nurse who greeted him was wonderfully kind, once she had sat him on his bed he was a prisoner in the tiny space, for he dared not wander away.

He went to sleep thinking of Annie, and awoke in the morning knowing they would come and collect him quite early. When they did, they put him on a trolley and wheeled him along corridors that were draughty and echoed. These corridors could have been anywhere in the world except that they smelled of disinfectant.

When finally Patrick was stationary and was told he he was in the operating theatre, he felt someone fit a suffocating rubber mask across his nose and mouth and knew that any second now he would be gone into a world of nothing. But what if he died? His heart protested violently at the thought and briefly he was touched by the irony of the situation. Then the drugs, streaming into his system, spun him unsteadily for a few seconds and he sank. But before they took away his senses completely and plunged him deep into the world of unconsciousness, his last thoughts were of Annie.

★ ★ ★

Oliver and Guy found it odd not having Patrick in their room, particularly Guy who had known him longer and had grown very fond of him. They were allotted someone else for the time Patrick was due to be away: a chap with one leg missing from the hip and a head wound that had left him virtually silent because forming words had become desperately difficult. Guy, being Guy, at once offered him kindness and attention, but with Patrick's bed full of someone else, Guy found he didn't see much of Annie, because she couldn't bear to come into the room.

Oliver had discovered quickly in his two weeks at Tremar that Julia spent at least some part of every day working in the vegetable garden with his fellow patients, and it didn't go unnoticed, either by her or by Sophie, that somehow he always managed to be out there at the same time. Julia might have been better to have ignored him; if not all the time then at least enough of it to make her position clear, but being Julia she didn't. Trying to be kind, she made time for him whenever he asked. And so he asked some more, and she gave. Less than three weeks into his stay it wasn't just the vegetable garden any more, but regular walks into the village as well — and that was very quickly pounced upon by the pussycats in the village shop.

'Didn't take *that* long to start again,' Sophie muttered sourly to Rory. 'He follows her around like a whipped dog and she pets and fusses over him all the time. Well, she wants to be careful or Oliver will start making assumptions. He's good at that.'

Rory had wondered if that might not be the case as well, and he pondered whether or not he ought to talk to Julia about it, but in the end he didn't and so Oliver went on picking up the crumbs she dropped for him, spending a lot of the night hours fantasizing about what might have been, or even might be again, if he could get rid of Matt.

And he hated Matt with a passion. Not just because Matt slept beside Julia at night, but because Matt was fast becoming the brightest star in Edward's sky.

★　★　★

Three days after Patrick's operation, Julia decided it was time to telephone the hospital and ask about him. She was prepared for the reaction she knew she would get.

'Are you family?' the faceless voice at the other end of the line enquired when Julia had, somewhat officiously, asked for progress on Squadron Leader Thornby.

'I'm his Aunt Julia,' she snapped, in a tone that was sharp enough not to invite any query.

'Oh, fine,' said the girl cheerfully. 'Well, he's still poorly, of course, but the operation was very successful. It'll probably be four or five days before he's well enough to be taking any real notice, if you understand me, but when I know he's awake I'll tell him you telephoned, Mrs . . . ?'

'Just tell him Aunt Julia,' Julia replied. 'And tell him his favourite cousin Annie is thinking about him all the time. They're absolutely inseparable and she never stops talking about him.'

The girl at the other end chuckled indulgently and Julia ended the phone call. Annie's pretty mouth was spreading into a broad grin, and her eyes sparkled.

'*Aunt* Julia!' she exclaimed. They giggled.

'But at least we know how he is, don't we?' Julia answered. 'Do you have a letter for me to post today?'

'One for Patrick an' one for Sir Robert,' Annie said. 'Oh God, I 'ope I've done the right thing.'

Julia kissed her, hoping so herself, somewhat forlornly.

'Well, you know what they say,' she observed. 'Nothing ventured, nothing gained.'

On the morning Annie Paynter's letter found its way on to the marble table in the hall at Chawston Hall, Sir Robert Thornby happened to be at home, and he gathered it up with the rest of his post, sorting through the letters as he went up the white stone staircase to his family's suite of rooms on the first floor.

Robert Thornby was a rather short, slightly plump, dark-haired man with a pleasant, homely face. That he was Patrick's brother was amazing, for they appeared to have nothing in common at all, except for one thing: they were both very nice men. Robert loved his little brother very much, and it was just as well, because no one else in the family apparently did.

During this period of wartime, when everything was so changed, Robert had moved his family back to Chawston to ensure their safety, as had both his sisters. It meant there were now six youngsters living in the great museum-piece, and during the summer months they were firmly expected to be, for the most part, out of doors. In the winter they had a playroom and a schoolroom, but there were endless rules that had to be obeyed at all times, one of which was that no children were allowed to use the white stone staircase. Robert found living again at Chawston a chore, and longed to move back to Belgravia — but at least while he was forced to spend time here, he could keep an eye on the place.

Today was a beautiful day. Sunshine filled the great park in which the glittering, enormous house proudly stood, and as he entered the corridor that divided the rooms in their suite, he could hear Nanny in the bedroom, brushing hair and giving instructions for shoelace tying, as his two sons wriggled to get away.

Sitting in the window seat of their drawing-room, gazing across the park, was his wife Kate, an exceptionally fine-featured, elegant woman of gentle disposition and enormous patience. Robert Thornby loved his wife dearly, and had fought hard to get her, for his Dragon Empress of a mother had done everything she could to force him into a marriage that suited her and not him. She had succeeded with his sisters: they had rolled over and obediently complied, and if they were unhappy with the couple of idiots she had palmed them off to, they tried hard not to show it, but Lady Thornby and her eldest son had been at odds with each other ever since the day he was born; and he was the heir.

He tore open Annie's letter, read it quickly and then paused and read it again, slowly and carefully this time. When he had finished, he looked up at Kate and raised his eyebrows.

'Patrick has fallen in love,' he remarked in great surprise. 'He's met a girl at Tremar and she has written to tell me that they're madly in love, they want to get married, and will I help them? Well, well, the old dark horse! Fancy that!'

Kate Thornby reached out and took the letter from her husband, perusing it thoughtfully. After a long while she smiled and then folded it neatly between her long, graceful fingers.

'It's beautifully written,' she said, 'if that's anything to go by. And she certainly sounds like a lovely girl. Very honest, too. But it's going to put the cat among the pigeons a bit, isn't it?'

Her husband chuckled complacently.

'Very much so,' he replied. 'And three loud cheers for that! I mean, I know Mother always wants to get her own way, but affiancing Patrick to Mona Baines-Morton — that was pure spite, it's got to be. Good God, the girl looks like Bessie Bunter and smells like an unswept stable. What's more, Patrick has spent the whole of his life struggling to avoid her. She was ghastly when they last met, and to my knowledge they haven't seen each other now for more than five years.'

Their two young sons, Nicholas and James, came tearing into the room at that moment, finally freed from Nanny's fierce grip, and asked if they could go out to play.

'Of course you can,' their father replied, smiling, 'but *don't* use the front staircase, will you? Grandmama is almost certainly in the morning-room, and if she hears you there'll be a fearful row.'

'Daddy,' said 9-year-old Nicholas, who had no conception yet that one day he in turn would be responsible for this cold, expensive mausoleum, 'when Chawston is *your* house, will we be allowed to use the staircase then?'

'When Chawston's mine you can slide down the banisters if you want to,' Robert replied happily and watched the boys dash away.

Kate Thornby looked at her husband for a moment and then stood up, bent to kiss him and handed him Annie's letter. She loved him dearly, which was just as well because the family that came with him was very hard to bear, and living at Chawston was fast becoming a great trial. In her heart she was anxious to see Patrick happy, as much to spite her mother-in-law as for his own sake, for

Lady Thornby and Lady Katherine Thornby disliked each other intensely.

'So what are you going to do about Patrick, then?' she asked as he tucked the letter into his inside breast pocket.

Smiling he answered, 'Well, I'm due a visit in a day or two, and if I find he's as much in love with Miss Paynter as she appears to be with him, then it will be time for me to start using my connections to do a bit of string-pulling here and there, I think. Once he's both medically discharged and a civilian again, and I can ensure he's got his feet firmly nailed to the floor at Tremar, then we can tell Mother, and she can bluster all she wants, there won't be a thing she can do about it. Are you aware that she hasn't been to see him *once* since he was shot down, by the way? Neither have my sisters. It's too bad, it really is.'

'I'm glad you think that,' his wife replied softly, returning to the window and watching her sons come crashing out into the park with two of their cousins, 'because I find it insulting — and very mean. What the hell is it your mother has against Patrick, do you think? There's got to be something. To be honest with you, when the news came through that he'd been shot down and was in hospital, she was quite openly angry with him

189

for not making the ultimate sacrifice. She wanted a dead hero for a son, and Patrick was expected to fill that role.'

Robert Thornby was quiet for a moment, staring at a rather nice landscape painting on the wall.

Eventually he said, 'He's far and away the best looking of all of us, you know. He always was, even as a child. He's gentle, charming and beautifully mannered, and she's never shown him a jot of affection since he was born. In fact, he almost died when he was six; of *neglect*, would you believe? We were in London, and as usual the house was like a fridge because of her objection to fires — just like this bloody place in the winter. Anyway, Nanny wanted to call a doctor, but Mother wasn't interested. She went out and danced the night away as Patrick got worse and worse. It was lunchtime the following day before she finally thought he should perhaps see someone, and by that time he had pneumonia! Very odd, if you ask me. Actually, once I've got things underway for the lovebirds, I might slope off to the glasshouse and talk to Pa about it. Maybe he can shed some light on it.'

Kate shook her head and lit herself a cigarette, throwing the spent match into the fireplace.

'Your father doesn't even remember who he is,' she observed. Her husband inclined his head slightly.

'No,' he replied. 'I think he does. I think he *chooses* not to; but we'll see, won't we?' He stood up and went over to the writing desk in the corner. 'And now I think I'll drop a line to the delightful-sounding Miss Annie Paynter.'

★ ★ ★

It was six days before Patrick truly felt well enough to take any notice of what was going on around him. He was semi-conscious a lot of the time and was aware only of being turned from time to time, but when he was awake, he longed and longed for it to be over. It was a dark, claustrophobic world of pain he inhabited, with no means of escape. All his fingers could locate were heavy bandages; beneath them his face felt shattered and agonized, and absolutely no light whatsoever found its way in to his blind eyes, so life was permanently black.

But in his world of misery, Annie loomed bright and beautiful. She filled the lonely hours with memories and came alive in his dreams. Patrick would never know what Annie looked like, but it didn't matter. He had a picture of her in his mind and that picture manifested itself into reality during his sleeping hours, and for him she would stay like that for the rest of her life.

When on the sixth morning they came and got him out of bed, they sat him in a chair and he was aware that he was by a window for the sunlight warmed his skin. He leaned his head back against a cushion as the pain inside his face screamed its anger at him, and he felt depressed and lonely. He wished he could go back to Tremar, so that he could hear familiar voices. He wished he wasn't so limited, that there was at least *something* he could do to pass the time, and he wished like mad for Annie.

A couple of hours later, hours that dragged extremely slowly, he heard footsteps at the door and turned his head, expecting a nurse. However, it wasn't a nurse, it was someone with a pleasant, cheerful voice who introduced herself as Prunella and told him that she had come to read his letters to him, if he was feeling up to it.

'Letters?' he said. 'I have letters?'

'Oh, heaps,' she replied. 'You have one from your mother, one from someone called Guy, one from an Oliver and one from your brother Robert. Julia and Matt have written and included letters from Rory, Sophie, Alice and Edward. And . . . ' she paused as she counted, 'someone with lovely handwriting, called Annie, has written five times.'

Five times! His heart soared in his breast.

'I'll have Annie's last, please,' he said. 'You might as well read my mother's letter first, so we can get it out of the way.'

Afterwards he sort of wished he hadn't asked for that, for his mother's letters always frightened him, and this one was no exception. She talked authoritatively of him going to Ireland to convalesce after he was discharged from hospital, of them finding some ghastly place close to the Baines-Mortons' estate, which would give Mona unrestricted access to her intended. He thought of himself, helpless and entirely at her mercy. He envisaged her bouncing in to visit him, smelling of sweat and horses, pressing her damp lips against his mouth and touching him with her coarse hands, and he felt pure panic lifting the hairs on the back of his neck.

Prunella, who of course knew nothing of his history, remarked how nice it would be for him to be near his fiancée, and if his terrified silence on the subject bothered her, she certainly didn't say so. He asked urgently if she could read his brother's letter next, and also asked if she would be prepared to write letters for him as well as read to him, and then his world brightened again, for Robert gave a date for his visit, and that date was the following day.

When she finally came to Annie's letters, the pleasant-voiced Prunella had fitted a few pieces of the jigsaw together. Whoever this charming, sunshine-haired young man was engaged to, the love of his life was a girl called Annie; a girl who wrote cheerful, newsy letters, who talked about harvesting and milking and told him she missed him dreadfully; and Prunella, who was a volunteer at the hospital and read to and wrote for many suffering young men, happily spent the rest of the morning writing letters for Patrick.

★ ★ ★

Annie realized that she would never know what Patrick's writing looked like when she received his letter the following morning, but it wasn't Patrick's writing she was interested in, it was his thoughts, his love. He hardly told her how he was at all, as if it didn't really matter. He told her over and over how much he loved her though, and told her of his brother's visit, and Annie went out to work with a spring in her step that was very noticeable.

At the edge of the rhododendron walk, as she turned to go towards Home Farm, Julia saw her give an exultant leap into the air!

'That's one happy girl,' she remarked to Sophie as they watched from the drawing-room windows. 'I just hope it's going to be this easy for them all the way.'

Sophie shook her corn-coloured hair back over her shoulders and pretended not to see Oliver and Guy coming out of the old stables with the egg basket.

'Well, the response from the brother was optimistic enough,' she replied. 'He seems most anxious that Patrick should be happy, and was very friendly in his letter to Annie, I thought.'

'Yes, I thought so too,' Julia said slowly, 'but, of course, he has never heard Annie speak. Oh, I know it all seems ridiculous to you, but believe me, you need to have grown up with the likes of Isobel Thornby to understand their attitudes to correct speech. My parents viewed Sandro's and my friendship with Gladys and the three musketeers as either a lesson in how to be nice to the lower classes, or as a deep embarrassment, depending on whether or not there were guests staying!'

'Oh, for God's sake!' Sophie exclaimed bluntly. 'Well, it all seems rather baffling to me — although I suppose I have to be honest and say my parents thought Oliver was an eminently suitable husband, and how wrong was that?'

Julia glanced at her uncomfortably. Sophie had been at Tremar for almost a month now, and though she was polite, helpful and beautifully mannered, she was not remotely friendly. Underlying everything she said there was a faint but distinct hostility, not as if she wanted to be rude exactly, but as if she had built a wall to protect herself, and wouldn't let Julia in at any price.

'Are you going down to the village?' Sophie enquired, turning from the window then and walking back into the room. 'Because if you are, I was wondering if you'd post a letter for me? Did I tell you, by the way, that Rory has offered me a teaching job next term? I'm rather flattered and I've written to tell my father.'

'Yes, I know about your teaching job,' Julia said. 'I'm pleased for you. Rory must be delighted, too. I know he was most put out when Mrs Johnson said she was leaving at the end of this term. I tell you what, why don't you walk down to the village with me? It's a glorious day for a stroll.'

Sophie struggled hard to control the flash of resentment in her eyes, but it wasn't possible and Julia saw it immediately. They both looked away from each other and Sophie said, 'I don't think so, thanks all the same. The company you usually keep on your little walks to the village won't welcome a third, believe me.'

Julia bit her lip, feeling uncomfortable. She was already getting tired of this, and the war could go on for years. Of course, Oliver would be discharged from the dower in due course, but it was apparent that they had nowhere else to go but back to Arundel, and she doubted Sophie would agree to that even under extreme torture. The thought of stumbling on endlessly through this minefield of hostility filled her with dismay.

'Sophie, there isn't anything going on between Oliver and me, you know,' she said, 'and there isn't ever going to be, either, I promise you. I walk to the village with him because he asks if he can come, but he knows the score. I'm married to Matt and nothing's going to change that. Any of the other patients are welcome to come with us, if they want to.'

'Yes, but none of them do,' Sophie replied acidly. 'No one likes playing gooseberry, Julia — not even me, with my own husband. Oliver has claimed you as his by rights. He knew you first, so therefore he has first choice of your time. But I should be careful if I were you; when Oliver gets really jealous he has a tendency to become about as mean and spiteful as it's possible to get. Once, when we were here before, he slapped me so hard he cut my lip because he was coming to spend time in your bed and I accused him of lying about it.'

Julia turned away from her swiftly as her throat closed with embarrassment, and she couldn't swallow. Her face burned like a sky-sign and she couldn't turn round, but she could feel Sophie's penetrating gaze on her back.

'I'm just warning you,' Sophie said sweetly. 'Well, they say forewarned is forearmed, don't they? I really should be careful how much time and attention you give him, Julia, because he'll invent the rest, to make it all add up to exactly what he wants — and you could be sorry.'

Julia, suddenly annoyed at being bullied, lifted her head and turned to face Sophie with a proud, autocratic look on her face.

'Thank you,' she said in the dismissive tone she had heard her mother use so often in her younger days. 'I'll bear that in mind. And now I'll take your letter please, because I shall be leaving in a few moments.'

She would have given anything to go to the

village on her own that morning, but Oliver had sought her out before she had even had a chance to leave the house, and short of being rude there was no way she could avoid him. So they left together, passing between the ancient stone gateposts out to the lane, and she knew perfectly well that Sophie stood on the landing at the top of the stairs, watching them.

As they started down the lane, Julia clutched her wicker basket, holding it between them because Oliver had a tendency to walk too close if she let him. The sun was glorious in the heavens, the hedgerows ripe with wild flowers and early fruits, and in Long Field, the first gate they came to, a tractor chugged about its business.

They leaned on the gate together, watching it. Amid the ripening corn were poppies like spots of blood. Poppies, the symbol of remembrance. Oliver wanted to remember; not the dead, but what was dead to him. Julia just longed to forget what she couldn't change.

'Oliver,' she said slowly, narrowing her eyes against the sun and struggling to find the right words without causing offence, 'I'm thinking perhaps we should stop doing this for a while, you know, walking down to the village together every day. I mean, I don't mind sometimes, of course I don't, I welcome your company, it's lovely to talk over old times. But I'm afraid it's beginning to annoy Sophie a bit.'

Oliver turned to look at her and for the umpteenth time she was shocked by his injuries. What was left of the skin on his burned face was raw and angry-looking, and the hitched-up mouth so grossly unattractive, after the head-turningly handsome man he had once been.

His eye, his one, bright eye, was full of a mixture of pain and contempt.

'Sophie is annoyed?' he retorted. 'I don't think so. Sophie couldn't care less. The only thing that annoys my wife is the fact that I'm still alive. Anyway, she's far too interested in the charming schoolmaster to be bothered by anything I do. Dear God, and he's old enough to be her *father*. It's pathetic, really. I would have said she could do better for herself, but of course there's only the old and infirm left to choose from in the main now — with the exception of those in a reserved occupation, of course.'

He said the last bit with an underlying tone of savage bitterness and the spectre of Matt hung between them heavily. Julia gazed across Long Field and caught a glimpse of her husband on the tractor. It was ridiculous, but suddenly she would have given anything to run across the field and hug him.

'If that remark was aimed at Matt,' she stated, 'he wouldn't have been away fighting anyway. He's too old. And I meant what I said, Sophie *is* annoyed. She as good as wiped the floor with me less than an hour ago, which might be all right by you, but not by me. I'm beginning to feel most uncomfortable when your wife is around, and it's not fair. All I was trying to do was help when I invited them to come here.'

Oliver stared at her and suddenly his mouth tightened furiously.

'So, because my wife objects, I mustn't walk to the village with you any more?' he asked indignantly. 'If she objects some more should I keep out of the vegetable garden as well? Perhaps she'd rather I remained chained to my bed all day, every day? And perhaps it matters so much to you lest you should offend her, that you think you can walk all over my feelings without a second thought? Fine; message received, loud and clear!'

'Oh, don't be absurd!' Julia snorted and they went on to the village in uncomfortable silence. Then the two old girls in the shop made pointed reference to the fact that they were together again, and Julia was boiling with rage.

They went to the Post Office and then to run an errand for Matt, and all the while she kept silent as her resentment bubbled away inside her. It was not fair, Sophie and Oliver were using her as a weapon and she didn't deserve to be treated that way.

When they finally began the walk back up the lane to Tremar, she realized that her silence did not appear to have deterred him in the slightest. He didn't ask her about it, nor did he walk any further away from her. He was going to be deliberately obtuse if she gave him half a chance, push for what he wanted and to hell with her feelings on the subject. She would *have* to say something.

As they were approaching the gateposts she suddenly stopped and put her hand on his arm, to stay his progress for a moment.

'Oliver,' she said, and looked directly at him, holding his gaze firmly and gritting her teeth against the urge to look away. 'I meant what I said. I'm sorry, but we have to call a halt to this daily walk. I don't want to hurt your feelings, believe me I don't, but I don't want to be talked about in the village, either, and I simply can't put up with all this growing hostility from Sophie. So please, give me a smile, and I'll see you in the garden later, and then we'll have a little walk occasionally, all right? I'm not trying to reject you, honestly I'm not, I'm just trying to find some middle ground somewhere.'

She saw him draw back. It was as if she had struck him.

'Sophie must be *loving* this,' he snarled furiously, as his eye became bright with tears and Julia simply couldn't look at him any more. 'She's got the lot, hasn't she? She can bed down with Nelson whenever she feels like it and at the same time amuse herself with a spot of emotional blackmail to ensure no crumbs from the cake come my way. No doubt she'll be rationing my time with my children before long — unless, of course, your grizzly bear is already doing it for her!'

Julia closed her eyes tightly and swallowed as her heart sank with despair. Oh God, *why* had she been so stupid?

'So this is really about Matt?' she said softly. 'I had a feeling it might be. Well, for your information, Sophie isn't having an affair with Rory, and Matt wouldn't dream of stealing your children from you. You really must stop this, Oliver, it's completely pointless. Building up hatred and resentment against everybody will just make you feel worse.'

'Which is *my* business, is it not?' he retorted, and turning on his heels, marched away from her towards the dower, leaving her staring after him in despair.

'And I dinnae think the little Sophie *is* sleeping with Rory yet,' Matt observed, as Julia lay disconsolately in his arms in bed that night. 'But I'm afraid it's only a matter of time. Poor Julia, it's no' turning out to be quite the heaven on earth you were hoping for, is it?'

She pouted at him crossly.

'Don't mock me,' she complained, 'it's not fair. When I was at Blackridge all I had was Minnie. She loved me with a single-minded devotion, and I protected her from staff or patients who wanted to bully her because she was timid. It was as simple as that. And on those terms I thought that if Oliver had his wife and children here during his convalescence, everybody would be happy.'

'Which was why,' Matt pointed out, touching her face with his fingers, 'Rory said you were naïve. I'll hold my peace for now, but if I find they're going to heap all their problems on to you instead of facing up to them themselves, I shall have a few words to say, and you won't stop me.' Suddenly he leaned forward and kissed her where his fingers had touched. 'Because I love you,' he whispered, 'and I won't have you abused.'

Julia sighed. Life with Matt was so easy. He

never made unrealistic demands. He never wished for things he couldn't have or encouraged her to make plans for things she didn't want. He never demanded more than she was prepared to give or lay in the aftermath of spent passion painting absurd castles in the air. That was why she could never have truly loved Oliver, because his love had come with strings attached. He had wanted her to change, to want what he wanted, be the person he desired her to be, and that was going to go on and on, she realized.

Oliver wasn't going to come to terms with what had happened to him and try and find ways round it, he was simply going to be angry and resentful as he punished those around him for his pain.

She closed her eyes and thought about him, and her heart ached. She promised herself that she would do her best to help him, because she owed him that, but she might as well not have wasted her time. For Oliver was thinking about her, too, as he lay in his little bed in the dower; and his thoughts were not remotely kind or generous.

8

It was about ten days before Patrick was due
to be discharged from hospital and returned
to Tremar that his mother, Lady Thornby,
picked up the telephone one morning at
Chawston and began to make private,
alternative arrangements for her son. She told
no one what she planned, not because she
desired it kept secret, but because since she
always got her own way when she wanted it,
she saw no reason to doubt that she would
get it now. People, lesser mortals, were not
expected to question her requirements,
simply adhere to them. And that included her
family.

Isobel Thornby had most unfortunately
been born beautiful. It had not been a good
thing. She had been the only child of an
extremely wealthy, aristocratic father, and
from the very beginning she had been
indulged. There had been discipline of
course; it was an important part of placing
oneself apart from the common herd; but her
nanny or her mother had seen to all that. Her
father had simply adored her and allowed her
to see her own exceptional beauty reflected in

his eyes every time he looked at her. He had made her feel not just special, but unique, and then reinforced those feelings at every turn.

And he had created a monster.

She had been granted the first pick of a stable of rich, well-bred young men when she had been looking for a husband and had chosen Gerald Thornby, because Chawston had been the biggest of the glittering prizes. The fact that Gerald Thornby had been neither very handsome nor particularly sociable hadn't mattered to her in the least. She hadn't been looking for someone to compete with. She had moved in to Chawston and taken it over, slowly driving its rather gentle heir into a life of flowers and glasshouses, and over the years she had borne four children — as much as anything because she hadn't been able to help it, she just had happened to be remarkably fecund.

Robert, her first-born and heir to the fortune, had been difficult from the beginning. She hadn't understood that he was actually in many ways like her, forceful and pushy — but thankfully blessed with a conscience and a firm sense of right and wrong. Her daughters, neither of them anywhere near as beautiful as she was, and both of them comfortably malleable, had fallen into line quite quickly and been easy to handle from childhood. They had married the men she had set up for them and borne the children she had expected from them — but *Patrick*! Patrick had simply been a ghastly mistake.

She had resented him from the moment his presence had become known in her womb. She couldn't remember ever wanting to give him a hug or a kiss, and the more beautiful he had grown, the more sensitive of face and graceful of stature, the more bitter she had felt towards him.

She had not laid eyes on him for over a year now, nor made any attempt to do so, and to get him safely to Ireland, where — other than at the wedding — she would probably never have to see him again, was keenly important. She knew just how much he disliked Mona, for she had seen him being bullied by her when they were both children, but that had not been a factor when she had been arranging the engagement. There was something much more important than that: by the time Lord Thornby died, Patrick and Mona would, with any luck, have an army of children — and as Mona was one of only two children, both girls, she would get half her father's estate. Which would mean that quite possibly nobody would ever notice the glaring absence of Patrick's name from any Thornby bequests.

It was the only way she could keep her secret safe. How much easier it would have been had he only had the grace to die when he was shot down. She might have raised an enormous marble memorial to him, as she had heard the Drake family from Tremar had done for their son in the last war, and she might have encouraged the absent-minded Gerald to name a new species of orchid after him. Instead, he was still alive, and all the while he lived, Gerald was sure to be reminded of him from time to time.

When she had finally done her telephoning and achieved what she wanted, she told the plan to her eldest son. Patrick, she announced, was to leave Salisbury in a week and travel to Ireland where she had found a very good nursing home for him, close to the Baines-Mortons' estate. He wouldn't go by ambulance, the family chauffeur would take him. But, she added, it might be nice for him if Robert could find the time to go as well.

Robert Thornby gulped. He was not used to his mother making arrangements; normally she left it to everyone else, and then complained if they didn't exactly suit. This time she had stolen a march on him, and he had very little time to put things right again.

He said, 'You know, Mother, you have no

right to make plans for Patrick. He's not a civilian. Some obscure nursing home in southern Ireland might not be at all what his superiors want for him.'

'Stuff and nonsense!' she retorted haughtily. 'He's hardly a fighting man anymore, is he? Once it is explained to them that he wants to be close to his fiancée, there won't be any objections, I'm sure.'

He looked at her hatefully then. There was something about this exqusitie, fading, cold-hearted beauty that repelled him and made it hard for him to accept that she was his mother. It was as if her mind was almost reptilian in its coldness, as if she viewed her issue as legitimate prey and had no understanding of succour at all.

'But he *doesn't* want to be close to his fiancée, does he?' he observed softly. 'As well you know. He doesn't want to be engaged to her at all, because he's never been able to bear the sight of her.'

Lady Thornby's eyes took on a cold gleam of triumph and her son knew she was going to say something awful. He waited, and she smiled.

'Well, that's all right then, isn't it?' she said callously, 'It's been resolved. He can't see her any more, can he, so he doesn't *have* to bear the sight of her.'

Robert Thornby stared at her in disbelief

210

for a few seconds, then turned on his heels and left her company. One day, he thought grimly, he might just kill her for the cruel, heartless bitch she was!

It took him a day to put things right again, then he announced to his mother that Patrick was returning to Tremar.

'It's what his doctors want,' he stated. 'He was doing very well there before this operation, and they specifically want him to go back. It's all about confidence, so I'm told.'

She glared at him, certain he wasn't telling the truth and convinced he had done this merely to thwart her.

'Well, since he won't be spending the rest of his life at Tremar, I can't see the benefit, frankly,' she answered. 'I think I might ring and speak to his doctors myself.'

Her son smiled sweetly.

'I wouldn't if I were you,' he said, 'because one of the things they might want to know is why you never go and visit him.'

★ ★ ★

Two days later, Robert travelled to Salisbury for the last time and found Patrick counting the hours until he could be with Annie again. Harvest was underway early, apparently, and

211

all was being safely gathered in, so when he came home to Tremar, he and Annie would have plenty of time together. She had written at length on the subject and he found it fascinating, so he said — though Robert couldn't help thinking that Patrick would find it fascinating if Annie simply copied out a shopping list!

Matt had promised Annie three days off when Patrick came home, and in her last couple of letters she had been making endless plans for them. Robert read the letters, enjoying their simple cheerfulness. He longed to meet this girl Annie, who made Patrick's bruised and battered face light up so brightly, and determined that he would do just that, as soon as their engagement was official.

In the meantime he told his brother what their mother had been up to and then pressed his hand reassuringly, for even with heavy bandages still obscuring most of the top part of his face, Patrick managed to look terrified by the news.

'Don't worry, old man,' Robert said. 'You're going back to Tremar. Next week, without fail. However, what I do need to know is that if, by any chance, Mother should get really stupid and send Barrington to fetch you like a naughty schoolboy or something, there is someone there who has the courage to thwart her demands.'

Patrick compressed his lips nervously. He couldn't imagine *anyone* being able to stand up to his mother, not with any success anyway, and yet there was no doubt that Julia Logan was a force to be reckoned with.

He told this to his brother, tentatively, and heard him chuckle softly.

'And this lady is to be your mother-in-law?' he asked. 'Well, one of them, anyway. Lord, Patrick, two mothers-in-law — are you sure this is what you want, old man?'

Patrick appreciated the gentle teasing, and he suddenly thought of Tremar with a sharp longing in his soul. He thought of the smell and the sounds, of herring gulls, and salt on the wind. He thought of how safe he felt there, how he could allow himself the pleasure of undisturbed sleep . . . and he thought of touching Annie, of the fresh taste of her mouth, the smell of lavender soap on her warm skin. Only a week now, maybe ten days . . .

Robert continued to touch his brother's hand, but found it faintly odd, for they were not a tactile family. He realized it was something he was going to have to get used to.

'It won't be easy, Pat, you know?' he said slowly. 'Being blind and everything. You won't resent Annie for what she can do that you can't, will you? Won't come to resent the time she spends on the land — because, quite obviously, she is very much an outdoor girl?'

'I shall *never* mind what Annie does,' Patrick replied firmly. 'As long as she stays true to me.'

And Robert knew he meant it. Marrying Annie mattered as much to Patrick as marrying Kate had meant to Robert. Fortunately for Annie, the difference was that she would *never* be invited to Chawston, would never have to endure the humiliations Kate had been subjected to. Robert suddenly appreciated that, albeit disgracefully late in the day, he was finally doing something truly worthwhile for his neglected little brother, and he was delighted.

He returned to Chawston and Patrick counted down the days. It was the beginning of September: time to bring the straw into the barns and begin to pick the blackberries in the hedgerows, time for the apple harvest at Tremar, as the days grew shorter, and time to go home, Patrick thought happily.

★ ★ ★

His journey from Tremar to Salisbury had seemed extremely long and frustrating almost

214

seven weeks ago, but his journey back to Tremar felt as if it were going to take forever! He did his best to doze in the back of the ambulance, and tried to talk to his companions as well, but he achieved neither with any great success. Cornwall, he decided, must be halfway around the world, it seemed to take so long to get there. There was lunch to eat and there were comfort stops to be taken, and all of them postponed his eventual reunion with Annie, frustrating him deeply.

In the end, the others sharing his ambulance decided to leave Patrick alone and let him be silent, so he leaned his head back, closing his eyes beneath the dark bandages, and willed the time to pass.

Annie had worked all day knowing he was on his way home, and Matt was actually impressed by how much concentration she had put into her labours. He let her finish early, so that she could bathe and change, and when she came downstairs just after five o'clock, Julia was touched to see how much trouble she had gone to. She looked beautiful: there was a rosy blush on her cheeks and a brilliant, excited longing in her eyes.

She went through the library into the dower sitting-room and Guy, who was looking forward to having Patrick back almost as much as Annie was, grinned at her in delight.

'Got yourself all dolled up for something special, have you, beautiful?' he enquired absently as she came to sit with him to wait for Patrick's arrival.

She shrugged, aware of a dozen pairs of eyes on her, knowing everyone had been talking about her before she arrived.

'Nothin' that I can think of,' she replied boldly, and then seemed to shrink and stare at him in panic. 'D'you think it'll still be the same, when 'e comes, Guy?' she whispered. 'I mean d'you think he'll still ... You know ... '

'What, love you?' Guy exclaimed, chuckling. 'Good heavens, girl, don't you read his letters? He's probably pacing up and down in the ambulance right now, bumping into everything and generally getting on everyone's nerves. Much the same as you're doing, as it happens!'

Annie glared at him indignantly.

'I ent bumping into things!' she protested. 'Bleddy cheek!'

'Neither am I any more,' said a voice from the doorway, and everyone looked up.

Patrick stood with a nurse behind him, steadying himself against the door jamb. His bandages were thick across his face and his yellow curls spilled out over the top of them like sunshine above the clouds. He wore his

216

air force uniform, which was neatly pressed, and in his hand he carried his small suitcase.

Annie cried, '*Oh!*' and flew across the room towards him, and a second later, in front of everyone in the dower sitting-room, they were in each other's arms and kissing as though their lives depended on it.

Their reception was much as would be expected from a room full of servicemen. There were cheers and catcalls and then a burst of applause. Annie thought briefly that she ought to be embarrassed, behaving like this in front of all these men, but her delight at being with Patrick overcame everything else.

'It's *so* good to see you,' she whispered at last, pressing close to him, locking her fingers in his. 'Welcome 'ome, Patrick.' She led him into the room, to Guy's wheelchair first and then to the other patients, who all shook his hand and welcomed him back.

Sitting at the table, close to Guy but on his own, Oliver watched what was going on. He greeted Patrick when it was his turn and then sank back into his chair, watching them go through the door into the library. They were going to see Matt and Julia, and Julia would kiss him and be pleased to see him. So would Sophie, of course; Sophie, who was never pleased to see *him*, and had almost certainly

217

been behind Julia's withdrawal from him.

He hardly saw her any more these days, except from a distance when she would wave briefly and then disappear from view. In the vegetable garden she was always close to someone else, never on her own, and when they did pass the time of day now it was on a very superficial level. Miserably he chewed over his bitterness in silence, as the atmosphere around him became increasingly upbeat, with everyone talking about Patrick and Annie. Somehow, *somehow* he knew all this was Matt's fault. Matt, who was brazenly stealing his little son right out from under his nose, who was allowing his wife to behave disgracefully, when at the beginning he had been so bloody moral! It had to be Matt's fault, and there had to be a way he could take revenge.

In fact as yet Sophie had not felt able to take the final step into an affair with Rory. She needed a push, to make her overcome all those sharp, uncomfortable lessons in morality she had endured as a child. That it was Oliver who was about to give her that final push was cruelly ironic.

★ ★ ★

In the last week of September, with autumn well established, the smell of log fires

218

heralding the beginning of winter and the manor filling up with spiders, it was Guy's birthday.

Julia decided to throw a party for him, partly to say thank you to him for all his kindness to Minnie and partly to welcome Patrick back to Tremar after his operation. During the summer there had been very little socializing, but now that it was dark much earlier, autumn things like hops and games evenings were starting up again in the village, and the Land Girls wanted a bit of a break from earth and tractors.

To her little party Julia invited Oliver, since he was Guy and Patrick's room-mate — and realized it was the first time since his arrival that he had graced their table. She thought she would have liked to ask Sophie to be nice to him, but even with her new job Sophie had not entirely lost her brittleness; it was just that she wasn't around to inflict it so often nowadays. Julia settled for sitting her as far away from him as she could.

She lit the dining-room softly with candles and sat Minnie next to Guy, but was quick to assure him that she didn't expect him to feed her. The third mouthful in, however, when she was chattering nonstop and Julia was just beginning to wonder if she should intervene, Guy lifted a spoon to her lips and popped in a mouthful of food.

'Pause to eat, sweetheart,' he said. 'Otherwise we'll get left behind and they'll all hate us for making them wait.'

Matt's eyes sparkled appreciatively at the tact and Julia saw a smile quiver at the corners of his mouth. She saw, too, a look of great tenderness in Annie's eyes and wished like mad that Patrick could see it.

Guy was enjoying himself enormously, and was extremely grateful for his little party. A year ago he had been whole, and losing his legs had made him feel that people somehow expected him to have a crippled brain now, as well. These people treated him like a close and dear friend, and no one ever patronized him.

As the meal progressed, the conversation was unhurried and fairly general, and no one really noticed that Oliver was, for the most part, silent. He was eating his dinner and drinking his wine, but seemed to stay outside the conversation, and that wasn't immediately evident either, because the conversation was mostly about Patrick's time in hospital, and Guy's wife and son.

At length, and for no particular reason, somebody changed the subject by making a casual remark about Tremar's fairly ancient plumbing making spooky noises in the night, and everyone laughed. It had been intended to be amusing and it was; and it seemed impossible that it could have set off such a rapid chain of events, but everyone had bargained without Oliver.

Guy looked up at Julia and offered her his boyish grin. He said, 'I say, Julia, talking of noises in the night, may I ask you a frightfully personal question? I mean, you won't have me shot at dawn or anything, will you?'

Julia found herself highly amused by the idea.

'Probably not,' she replied, chuckling. 'But it depends on how personal it is, really. We haven't had a good execution for ages, so be careful.'

For a moment he was silent, as if he was plucking up courage, then he glanced at her out of the corners of his eyes, and bit his lip comically.

'Right then,' he said boldly. 'OK, here goes. I woke at two in the morning a few nights ago. You know, the darkest hours before the dawn and all that? Anyway, I heard this strange barking noise under the window. Very harsh, single barks. Very spooky. You don't, by any chance, have some ghastly family horror who wanders the grounds barking at the full moon, do you? I mean, we've all heard the stories about ancient families and their mad and deformed heirs carefully tucked away for none to see. *Please* tell me you've got one, it would be such fun!'

Julia burst out laughing, enjoying the idea enormously, then she crossed her eyes and poked her tongue out, earning herself a giggle. Patrick, who couldn't see the exchange had begun to laugh too, and turned his head in Guy's direction.

'City boy!' he jeered. 'Don't you know anything? Mad heir indeed! I heard it too, and it was a vixen barking for a mate, you fool!'

'A *vixen?*' Guy echoed. 'You mean as in fox? Good heavens, I'd expect my girl to make a more appealing noise than that if she was after a spot of romance. Are you serious?'

'Very serious,' Matt joined in, 'and if I catch her, with or without her mate, I shall see her off with ma shotgun, I'm afraid. Foxes are vermin and they go after the chickens. I can't allow that.'

All of a sudden Oliver raised his head very quickly and it was the first time he had looked directly at anyone since he had been forced to permit his dinner to be cut up for him. Now, as Julia saw the gleam in his eye, she knew he was going to say something awful. Holding her breath, she waited in fear.

'Vermin?' he sneered. Immediately everyone fell silent. 'As in drunken local farmers, you mean? Yes, of course. Mind you, it's easier to kill them, isn't it, because they don't move as fast as foxes, do they? Don't need to waste a shotgun cartridge on a farmer when he'll obligingly stand still on the beach and wait to get his neck broken!'

'Oliver, *no* . . . ' Julia breathed.

There was a deadly little pause. It was only a few seconds and yet it seemed as if it went on for hours, then Annie dropped her fork on her plate and stared at him hatefully.

'If you'm talking 'bout my pa, Dr Crompton,' she said, with an extraordinary calmness that forced Julia to look at her. 'It was *me* killed 'im, not Matt, as well you know; an' it's time you gimme the credit for it, too, 'cos like I told you at the time, after what he done to me it were my right.'

Julia saw a look of total bafflement on Patrick's face and silently begged Annie to be quiet, but it was quite obvious that Oliver wasn't going to give up.

'Annie, I'm a doctor,' he observed pompously. 'You might be able to fool a couple of lumbering country policemen, but you can't fool me. There is no conceivable way you gave your father a little push off a three-foot wall and he happened to break his neck when he hit the stones. Matt killed your father, and for some reason you felt you had to lie to protect him.'

Annie's nostrils flared and Julia wished she was sitting closer to her, though she doubted even a warning kick under the table would have stopped her. Her face was pale but for a couple of pink spots on her cheeks. She was beside herself with fury, and she had never liked Oliver.

'If I'd 'ave needed a reason to lie for Matt, I wouldn't 'ave 'ad no trouble finding one, I can assure you of that!' she snarled dangerously softly. 'And I can assure you of something else an' all, I wouldn't never have lied for *you*. You did everything you could to stop me and Julia being friends. You didn't care what 'appened to me, so long as you got your own way. You just wanted Julia, an' you thought you had a right to tell her what she could and couldn't do, and who she could and couldn't see. Well, you didn't get your way in the end, did you? But you wouldn't 'ave cared 'ow many people you'd 'ave 'urt, if you had!'

'Annie, no more, please,' Julia began softly. 'It's all in the past and it doesn't matter any more . . . ' But Annie wasn't ready to stop.

'Well I think it *does*!' she shouted, her eyes suddenly bright with tears of rage. 'You've took him in and you've bin kind to him; he'm sittin' here at *your* table, eating *your* food, and he don't 'ave no right to be sayin' the things he'm sayin'!'

Patrick and Guy had faded into an embarrassed silence and Julia found herself squirming with discomfort. She was desperate to defuse the situation, though it was not Annie she was angry with. Annie hadn't started it. She gazed at Oliver, silently begging him to let it be, but saw him open his mouth to speak. He wasn't given the chance however.

Flaring her nostrils furiously, Sophie suddenly snapped with extreme venom, 'For Christ's sake, *shut up*, Oliver!' and the silence which followed was ear-splitting.

Oliver glared at his wife resentfully and as she stared back at him her mouth was drawn into a thin, uncompromising line. Annie was staring at her half-eaten meal with tears running down her cheeks, and Julia simply couldn't think of anything to say at all. Then, without having any idea of what she was doing, Minnie broke the tension.

'Julia, what comes after autumn?' she asked.

Julia hugged her, pressing her face close to Minnie's withered cheek.

'Winter, darling,' she whispered gratefully. 'You know, Christmas, and your birthday.'

'*My* birthday?' Minnie's dull face had

brightened. 'It's *Guy's* birthday,' she declared confidently. 'It is, it's Guy's birthday.'

'That's right, my lovely girl,' Guy agreed, leaning across to kiss her, 'and we're still four or five mouthfuls behind the clock. Got to eat it all up, so we can have our pud.'

'And there's a cake,' Julia announced, forcing cheerfulness into her voice. 'A poor offering, but not bad for wartime. There should be just enough for one slice each.'

She looked up then and her eyes settled on Matt. He had said nothing since his threat to shoot the vixen and his face looked as if it was cut from stone. Julia knew it was not because of Oliver's accusations: Matt was furious with him for what he had done to Annie, so angry that he had become stock still. Matt didn't lose his temper very often, but when he did he was formidable. Their eyes met and she begged him silently to let it pass. He acknowledged her with a gentle nod, but the blunt fact remained that it had been said, and could never be unsaid.

They did their best to pick up the mood again, but it didn't really work. They sang 'Happy Birthday' to Guy and he claimed a kiss from Minnie, and then they all enjoyed coffee and cake before it was time for the three men to return to the dower. Oliver hadn't uttered another word, but rather more worryingly, Patrick had barely spoken either and the pain in Annie's eyes was there for all to see. Julia thought she would have liked to slap Oliver and she was bracing herself for the agony of tears she expected after the guests had gone, when Patrick suddenly felt for Annie's hand and squeezed it softly.

'Will you walk along the terrace with me?' he asked.

Annie's face flooded with colour.

'Of course I will,' she replied and Julia gave a silent prayer of thanks.

'You two go then,' she said gently, 'but don't stay out there till you catch cold. All right?'

Patrick said his goodbyes and Julia let them out through the French windows into the September night. The moon was full, but tossed on building clouds. Almost certainly it would be wet the next day; the air blew the promise of winter on its breath.

'I'm sorry,' Annie whispered as they stood together and hot, angry tears flooded down her cheeks. 'I'm so sorry . . . ' It was too much. Moving away from him she sat on the terrace wall and began to weep as if her heart was broken. 'I couldn't tell you . . . I couldn't. I'm so sorry.'

Standing in the darkness of the drawing-room shamelessly watching them, Julia saw

Annie's despair and put her hands up to her mouth as her own heart tore in her chest. Then, as she watched, Patrick stumbled forward, snatched Annie into his arms and pressed her tightly against him. She couldn't hear what he said, nor what Annie was saying either, but she saw him find her lips with his own and kiss her hungrily, and then she saw them both sit on the edge of the terrace wall, holding hands as they talked. At that point she silently crept away.

It didn't matter how much of the truth Annie told him, she told herself firmly as she returned to the dining-room. It was just important that he understood what was behind Oliver's cruel outburst. He would have to know one day about Blackridge and about Arthur's betrayal, and Julia's need for revenge. So let him know everything now, it didn't matter a jot, so long as he understood that no blame for anything lay at Annie's door.

The atmosphere in the subtly lit, glittering dining-room was subdued and quite obviously the party was well and truly over. Minnie was sleeping in her chair, exhausted by the fun and the lateness of the hour, and for a few seconds Julia envied her. Minnie's life was so simple and straightforward: she had been fed by Guy and she had eaten cake.

The rest was unimportant. Squaring her shoulders then she turned her attention to the others, smiling what she hoped was a confident, cheerful smile.

Guy, the peacemaker, returned her smile and winked at her cheerfully.

'It's been a *lovely* party,' he said. 'Thanks ever so much, Julia. It was been just like being with family, and the food was positively scrumptious. Oliver, old man, I wonder if you'd be good enough to give me a push through the library into the dower; I've an idea young Patrick is a bit tied up just at the moment.'

'Yes, of course I will,' Oliver replied and stood up, automatically guarding his damaged and still heavily bandaged left hand.

'I'd better push the other side then,' Julia offered. 'Just till you've negotiated the shelves in the library. You can manage after that, I'm sure.'

Oliver said goodnight to his wife, but she pointedly ignored him. He said goodnight to Rory and Matt and then he and Julia pushed the chair between them through the library and into the sitting-room beyond it. It was full of servicemen and smelled of cigarettes. The men were listening to the radio and when Guy came in they looked up, greeting all three of the newcomers brightly.

Guy pushed himself away from Oliver and Julia immediately. It was done with the greatest of tact and made Julia hope desperately, not for the first time, that legs or no legs someone would one day see Guy for the treasure he was.

Oliver turned to look at her and she stepped back into the library to stand beside him. She did not fully close the door and they could still hear the drone of mild conversation going on in the room beyond, but they were alone.

Furiously, almost hatefully, she stared at him.

'How could you have done that?' she demanded. 'When I *begged* you not to? How could you humiliate Annie like that in front of Patrick, when you know what he means to her? That was unspeakably horrible, Oliver, and I could hate you for it!'

'I wasn't talking to Annie,' he retorted sourly. 'She could have kept out of the conversation. I'd just like your damn husband to admit he killed her father, that's all.'

Julia watched him coldly.

'Why?' she enquired. 'What difference is it going to make? I won't feel any different about him, neither will Annie — and nor will anyone else. Tell me, is this because Edward has formed such a close friendship with Matt? It's only a bit of hero worship, you know; it doesn't mean he loves you any less. Matt happens to be good with his hands and he has the patience to make little wooden planes with the child, and in return Edward wants to work on the farms. That's all.'

'I'm a poor substitute though, aren't I? *I* can't make little planes, can I? I can't do *anything* with my hands any more.'

His self-pity seemed to spill out of him pathetically. Julia found it strangely claustrophobic and actually took a small step backwards. She watched him for a moment and clearly in her mind she saw him at Blackridge, confident and handsome as he stood before the sad creature in asylum blue that had been her. Couldn't he see the parallel at all, she wondered? All right, so now, effectively, the boot was on the other foot, but why couldn't he even try and see the wider picture?

'Well, if you want my honest opinion,' she snapped, 'wallowing in self-pity won't make it any better. At least you're still alive; be grateful for that. I wanted to help you, that's why I was glad you came to Tremar, but I don't see what I can do if you won't make any effort to help yourself.'

To her astonishment a cruel gleam suddenly flashed in his eyes, and his mouth twisted in an unpleasant sneer.

'If you want to help me,' he said softly, 'then make that husband of yours tell the truth about what he did. He should have paid the price, Julia. We've all paid a price, those of us in there,' he inclined his head towards the dower, 'and we weren't guilty of anything. Your husband got away with murder. He should have been hanged!'

Julia stared at him, genuinely alarmed. Surely this was obsession of the most dangerous kind? Such festering hatred couldn't do anybody any good; and what on earth did he hope to gain by it, she wondered.

'Even if you had managed to get Matt hanged, Oliver,' she said very quietly, 'I would never have married you, you know. Nothing on God's earth would have made me marry you.'

'You would have done as you were bloody well told!' he snarled and went into the dower, slamming the door behind him, leaving her staring after him.

Eventually she took herself back to the drawing-room and found that Matt had gathered up Minnie and taken her to bed. She thought about what Oliver had said and felt a knot like a fist in her stomach. She was angry, and suddenly she was frightened of him, frightened of what was in his mind.

Sophie was in the drawing-room with Rory.

They were sitting together on the sofa and she knew they were talking about her, because they stopped abruptly when she came into the room.

Julia looked at them sharply and suddenly pursed her lips.

'Tell me something, Sophie,' she demanded. 'If Oliver *had* managed to get Matt hanged for Arthur's murder as he planned, what did he then intend should happen to me, do you know?' She saw Sophie's eyes flicker with alarm and knew she didn't need an answer. 'Don't bother, I can guess,' she muttered, and threw herself down into an armchair. 'Dear God, how did I ever get myself into this? You know, if he's spoiled things for Annie I shall be very, *very* angry!'

'He won't have,' Sophie replied quietly. 'Not unless Patrick wastes his time listening, and I don't think you'll find he will. Patrick is far too much in love with Annie to care what Oliver has to say, thank God. I'm sorry, Julia, I knew he was full of bitterness, but I didn't realize it was quite this bad. In fact, I thought he was feeling better. He sees you and his children every day, what more can he want?'

Julia glared at her briefly, then her mouth lifted in a sneer of disgust.

'An awful lot, apparently,' she retorted and closed her eyes to blot them out.

The room fell silent. Julia quite obviously had nothing further to say, and Rory and Sophie weren't sure what to do. Then, all of a sudden and accompanied by a gust of cold air, Annie burst in. Everyone turned to look at her, and though her cheeks were flushed with the cold and her eyes bright, she wasn't crying.

'Is everything all right?' Julia asked earnestly, holding out her hand to her.

Annie nodded and then sat on the arm of the chair. She was tense and silent and suddenly her eyes filled with angry tears at the thought of what she had done. She hated Oliver! Hated him for even living!

'I told Patrick everythin',' she whispered through trembling lips. 'I couldn't stop. I told 'im the whole thing. The whole bleddy lot. I didn't mean to, but I didn't know what else to do. I'm so sorry. Oh God, I'm *so sorry!*'

Julia touched her gently, as her heart squeezed with pain.

'Well, he had to know sometime,' she replied with forced lightness.

'But he didn't have to know at Oliver's bloody convenience!' Sophie snorted. 'Ungrateful, self-pitying idiot! I think I might just find him tomorrow and tell him exactly what I think of his foul manners!'

Julia sighed and pulled herself to her feet.

She was tired and she wanted to escape, to crawl into bed beside Matt and comfort herself with his solid presence.

'Well, you'd better be quick if you want to get in first,' she observed quietly, 'because after what he did this evening, I think you might find yourself standing in line. And on the strength of that I'm going to bed. Goodnight.'

But she was destined to get very little sleep.

9

Julia lay on her back in bed, staring up at the dark as sleep spitefully eluded her. Surely it didn't matter, did it, that Annie had told Patrick all her darkest secrets? Blackridge was a fact of life she couldn't change, and her incarceration had been a wicked act of revenge; her sanity had never been in question.

She turned restlessly on to her side as outside in the darkness the vixen prowled and barked at the cloud-tossed moon. She was early tonight, anxious for a mate. Julia listened to her harsh barks and closed her eyes, thinking about what Oliver had done.

He had betrayed her because she hadn't done what he wanted, and now he would expect her to forgive him. Rather bleakly she reflected that it wasn't really all that difficult to understand why Sophie was as bitter as she was. What frightened her most was that it would only go on getting worse; she could see no end to it. Oliver was quite evidently not made of the stuff that struggled to make the best of things, and would not see himself mirrored in Patrick and Guy and all the others in the dower. He would only ever see his misfortunes as someone else's fault.

Tired, but without hope of sleep, she yawned irritably and pressed herself against the comfort of Matt. Tomorrow she would have to speak to Patrick — and, dear God, please let Guy and Patrick be the only ones to find out! She dreaded the thought of being talked about and gawped at by everyone in the dower. It would be too much if Oliver decided to start loudly accusing Matt of murder purely as an act of spite.

Julia was not the only one who was having trouble sleeping. In her bed, Annie tossed and turned as her brain refused to slow down enough to let her sleep, and though occasionally she would flirt with it briefly, her eyes would always suddenly fly open again and she would find herself blinking in the dark, as one awful scenario after another thrust itself up at her. She concentrated on Patrick, to try and give herself some peace, and in his little bed in the dower he was thinking of her and was just as wide awake.

All three of the men, unbeknown to each other, were lying there picking through the events of the evening. All three of them heard the vixen right under the window as she briefly scavenged on the terrace, and Guy silently wished her luck. Their thoughts were very different as they huddled in their little beds, and they would never share them; but Guy's birthday dinner had changed a great many perceptions.

The vixen began to move away, further into the night. She called repeatedly, obviously anxious to find a male who would fulfil her desires, and she wasn't the only female awake and hungry for comfort in the cool autumnal darkness.

Sophie had gone to bed in a mixture of rage and despair, and lay alone, sobbing, as the pain of rejection ate into her psyche. She heard the grandfather clock in the hall chime out the hour of twelve as she lay curled in her loneliness. She turned angrily, searching for relief from her pain, and through the wall she heard Rory moving about in his room.

She was surprised he was still awake and at first she slipped from her bed with some vague idea that she might find a little comfort from him for a few minutes. But even before she opened her bedroom door she had changed her mind; and to that end she brushed her hair, so that it hung smooth and silky about her shoulders.

She was finished with Oliver. Perhaps at last she truly hated him. She wanted revenge. She yearned to be touched, to be loved, and as she knocked on Rory's door, she boldly took the first steps towards the final destruction of her marriage.

Rory had got up to open his bedroom curtains once his light was switched off and then climbed back into bed without hope of sleep, his mind full of Sophie's misery.

They had stayed downstairs, straightening cushions and things after Annie and Julia's departure, but only when Sophie had looked at him with eyes bright with tears had he realized she was so deeply upset, but she had refused to tell him exactly why. They had parted on the landing outside their rooms. He wondered if she was crying now, and felt unsettled and miserable. He would have liked to knock on her door, although he wouldn't have dreamed of actually doing such a thing, and so he turned restlessly, finding himself cold and lonely.

When he heard a knock on his door he lay rigid and silent for a few seconds, then assuming it must be Julia, climbed out of bed and limped across to open it. Sophie stood on the threshold in a small triangle of weak light. She wore only a satin nightgown, her hair hung loosely about her shoulders, and though she had tried to clean up her face, it was perfectly obvious that she had been crying.

'There's just one thing I want to know,' she snapped, drawing a sobbing breath as she leaned against the door jamb, looking both painfully vulnerable and astonishingly desirable. 'I meant to ask you downstairs, but I didn't have the damn guts! Do *you* think she's the most wonderful thing in the world, Rory? Do *you* want her more than anything you can think of?'

Rory blinked in surprise.

'Who? Julia?' he asked and saw Sophie sneer furiously.

'Yes, Julia. Julia bloody Logan!' she snarled. 'Oh, all right, I'm furious with Oliver for what he did this evening, but for God's sake she's like some majestic Madonna sitting there at the table with her beautiful face and her beautiful hair! He doesn't even *see* me any more, you know, it's as if I don't bloody exist. So, how about you then, Rory? Do you *yearn* for her, like he does?'

'Good Lord, no,' he replied truthfully. 'I *like* her very much indeed, but I don't *want* her. She doesn't appeal to me. To be honest she frightens me a bit, I suppose. She makes me aware of my limitations and that makes me feel inadequate, but she's very subtle about it all the same.'

'So do you want *me*, then?' Sophie whispered miserably, and he pulled her into the room, closing the door softly behind them. The *last* thing he wanted was anyone hearing any of this.

'As it happens, I do,' he replied, folding her in his arms and feeling the dampness of her tears on his cheek as his heart squeezed in his chest. 'I love you, Sophie. I loved you before you ever left the village, and now you're back I'm never happier than when I'm in your company. Frankly, you've filled my life with a joy I never expected to experience again after Penny died.'

'Then show me, Rory,' she murmured. 'Take me to bed and make love to me. Please.'

He released her as if she had burned him, but the look in her eyes was so forlorn that at once he relented and cupped her face in his hands, gazing at her gently.

'Are you sure that's what you want?' he asked. 'I won't be an act of revenge, Sophie, no matter how much I love you.'

'And I don't want you as an act of revenge,' she replied sadly. 'I want you because you *do* love me. I'm lonely, Rory. I want to be loved and cherished. No one has cherished me for a long time now.'

'I would be happy to cherish you,' he said with a smile.

With great consideration she allowed him a moment's privacy to take off his pyjamas, for she knew that his delicacy and his lameness

241

embarrassed him. Then, as the moon fitfully peeped in through the windows from behind the ever-gathering rainclouds, she stripped for him and let him gaze at her naked body for a moment before she slid into bed beside him.

She knew he worried that he could not be the great lover he wanted to be for her, could not offer her the protection of a strong, handsome body. But with wry bitterness she wondered how he might feel if she told him that strong and handsome were the last bloody things she wanted. Oliver had been strong and handsome when he had taken her to bed on their wedding night; he had promised her that he would love her forever as he held her in his arms, and he had lied through his teeth!

Together in the warmth of his bed they touched intimately; a little shyly at first, then they surprised themselves. Rory had not been intimate with anybody since Penny had died, and before that she had been the only woman in his life. Sophie had never been intimate with anybody except Oliver either, but the fear that they would be clumsy in their inexperience vanished very quickly.

Her body was firm and beautiful, with surprisingly voluptuous breasts for such a little, willowy woman, and Rory found himself heady with excitement as he explored her with his hands. The only thing that troubled him slightly was his leg. It was weak, and Penny had always known he could not support himself on it. He wondered if, at this most intimate moment, he would have to confess it to Sophie, and felt embarrassed and suddenly inadequate. Then, to his astonishment and enormous gratitude, she quietly took the initiative.

She knelt astride him and was glorious as for a moment the moon broke free of its tossing waves of clouds and hung full and bright in the sky. Rory reached up with his hands to cup her breasts, and her hair rippled like silk about her face. She accommodated him with gentle ease, gasping with pleasure as he slid into her, and as she made love to him he was lost. He cried out with excitement and knew, even then, that he had fallen prey to her. For ever more he would want her every damn time he saw her, and suddenly she had the awful power to hurt him, to break his heart.

He also knew that she was an extremely unhappy married woman, many years his junior, with her children — and her husband — asleep in the same house. Surely, with the passion spent, she would want to distance herself from him very quickly?

Steeling himself against the pain, he waited

for her to rush away, but she made no attempt to leave him. She snuggled warmly against him, asking for him to put his arms about her, and for more than an hour she lay with him, relaxed and comfortable, their naked bodies warm together while the moon played tricks with the shadows in the corners of the room. She was aware that he didn't talk to her much, but she had no idea of the fear growing in his mind and would have happily stayed all night, had she dared. When eventually she found herself dozing, and moved unwillingly, knowing she must creep back to her own bed which would be cold and empty, she was surprised that he relinquished his hold on her so readily.

'I have to go,' she whispered, kissing him. 'I wish I didn't, but I don't think we ought to stay here like this until morning; one never knows who might find us.'

She wriggled away and at once cool air crept into the bed where she had been. Rory felt wretched.

'Sophie,' he began, needing to get his little speech in first but finding himself obliged to clear his throat because he was humiliated. 'I'm sure in the cold light of day you're going to be really very cross about this, but I give you my word, my dear, that I shall never mention it to a living soul. What's more, I shall never embarrass you by mentioning it between ourselves either. You have honoured me in the most remarkable way and I couldn't *bear* for you to hate me because of it.'

To his amazement she stared at him for a moment and then burst out laughing. She leapt on to the bed, throwing her arms about him.

'Rory, for God's sake stop being so pukka-sahib!' she exclaimed. 'This is your bed, remember? You didn't thrust your way into mine, ignoring my pleas for mercy; you didn't take me against my will, and more to the point, I didn't do this to get my own back on Oliver — or Julia, come to that. I thought we made love with each other because we love each other. I know perfectly well you won't talk about it in front of anyone else — you're far too much of a gentleman for that — but I sincerely hope you *will* mention it between ourselves. I shall be most upset it you don't!'

'Do you mean that?' he asked uncertainly, and she searched for his mouth with her own and kissed him hungrily.

'If you think you can bear your agony for twenty-four hours,' she replied, 'you'll find out, because tomorrow night I'm coming back for more. Goodnight, darling Rory, sleep well.'

Sleep well! he thought. I doubt I shall sleep at all.

★ ★ ★

The rain was drumming down the next morning, just as Annie had predicted it would. She and Matt had gone out early as usual; cold and rain didn't seem to worry them much. Julia was thankful for the girl who did the fires — even though Mrs Collins swore she was on Hitler's side, the amount of crockery she regularly broke washing up — and couldn't wait to snuggle up near the blaze in the drawing-room. She felt the cold a lot more than she let on, and knowing why, this morning, didn't help.

Rory had driven Sophie and the children to school. They had all gone off straight after breakfast, and unless Sophie was possessed of an extraordinary knack of moving on from something she didn't like so seamlessly that she could give no indication of it less than twelve hours later, then Julia knew exactly how she and Rory had comforted each other the night before.

Oh well, it had been going to happen sooner or later; but for all that she would be furious with them, she thought sourly, if they weren't careful.

When Minnie was safely ensconced by the fire, Julia knew she would have to speak to Patrick. It was easy to think she could leave it, that he would almost certainly never mention it, but he couldn't see her, and that seemed to put her at a disadvantage. She was not remotely angry with Annie for doing what she'd done, but at the same time she was grossly humiliated.

Eventually she poked her head into the dower sitting-room and was lucky enough to find him there. She was luckier still to find that Oliver wasn't; for she had no intention of making anything easy for *him*. She wanted an apology, and when he finally offered one, she would make him crawl.

She said, 'Patrick, could I have a quick word, do you think?' and watched him climb to his feet, feeling about to get some direction as his bandaged face turned towards her.

His companions helped him as far as the library door and she took him from there into the drawing-room, sitting him close to the fire as rain pelted against the windows.

'Would you like a cup of tea?' she asked him.

'Well . . . if you're having one,' he hesitated. Julia rang the bell.

The girl came quickly and Julia asked her for tea. 'And one for Minnie, please, with extra sugar.' Julia watched the girl close the door behind her, then she touched Minnie softly and gazed across at Annie's sensitive young man. It had to be now.

'Patrick, I need you to know that I'm not mad,' she blurted out. 'And I'm not immoral, either!'

Patrick seemed startled. He looked appalled, what little of his face she could see, and his fingers twisted together uncomfortably.

'I never thought you were mad or immoral, Julia,' he replied nervously. 'Good God, the idea never entered my head. When Annie told me everything last night I felt humble, to be honest. I mean, heavens, I've got nothing to grumble about, have I? I've hardly suffered like you or Annie have.'

Julia turned and smiled at him, then realized that was useless so touched him gently instead.

'You have your cross to bear, believe me,' she told him. 'Don't denigrate it because of something that happened to someone else, you're not being fair to yourself. Life is easy for Annie and me now, and we're blessed enough to have each other.' She moved away from him, glancing out at the rain-lashed gardens for a moment, then she turned back. 'Love and hate can be two sides of the same coin I discovered when I came home from

Blackridge,' she said. 'I bore a daughter to Annie's father in 1915, a sadly premature little girl whom I suppose they wrapped in rags and tossed into a hole in the ground when she was found to be dead. Then when I came back to Tremar I discovered that Arthur had fathered another daughter, one whom he actually took *pleasure* in hurting — it was for Annie that Matt and I killed him, not for me.'

'And I don't condemn you!' he assured her anxiously. 'I don't, Julia. In fact, if you really want to know, I've never felt so comfortable with anyone in my life. I love Annie, and you seem to have accepted that, which I hope means you've accepted me.'

Julia cupped his bandaged face in her hands and bent to kiss the top of his head.

'I do accept you, Patrick,' she replied. 'I was wary in the beginning, I admit, but you have more than adequately proved your love for Annie now, I promise you. However, I'm not so stupid as to think your mother would ever accept her, and let's face it, when she finds out the truth about me — which she will — it could make things worse. It might even give your brother doubts, perhaps?'

He shook his head.

'Robert knows I'm happier now than I've ever been in my life,' he answered with conviction, 'and he's good, truly he is. He'll do everything he can for me. In fact, he says he's underway already, poking about in government departments, as he puts it. He seems to think that quite soon I'll be a civilian again, and — well — if it's all right with you and Matt, Annie and I would like to get engaged on her birthday. Officially, I mean.'

The tea came and, having handed Patrick his, Julia began to help Minnie with hers. It was thick with sugar. Julia knew she would have been sick if she'd been obliged to drink it herself, but to Minnie it was intensely satisfying and she drank it greedily. She had all of Julia's sugar ration, most of Matt's and Annie's, the majority of Rory's and some of Mrs Collins's too, such was Minnie's importance in the house. Julia had been touched to discover that Minnie was polishing off most of Guy's sweet ration every week as well. He was sneaking them to her in ones and twos.

Looking across at Patrick, who managed his tea with a sort of easy grace that didn't surprise her but gladdened her in as much as it indicated that his apparently miserable upbringing had at least left him with some benefits now he had lost his sight, Julia thought about him always being at Tremar, and found herself pleased at the idea.

'From my point of view I shall be delighted to make Annie's birthday party an engagement party as well,' she said, 'but there is one thing you have to do first, and prove to me that you've done it. You have to make it quite clear to Miss Baines-Morton that you will not be marrying her, that your engagement is broken. I want no misunderstanding and no equivocation, is that clear?'

'Quite clear,' he promised. 'It's all in hand, really it is. You know, I never asked her to marry me. I haven't even seen her for the better part of five years. I'm only telling you because I don't want you to think I might treat Annie in such a cavalier fashion.'

Suddenly Julia laughed.

'Oh, Patrick,' she said fondly. 'I think hell would freeze over before you'd treat anyone in a cavalier fashion, if you really want to know.'

They were companionable then and enjoyed a second cup of tea together, after which Patrick said he should go and promised to ask Guy to come through and have his daily chat with Minnie. When they got as far as the library, however, Julia felt him pause and saw him put out his hand and run his fingers along a line of books, books he would never read.

'Julia,' he whispered. 'What was it like?' He paused, and when she didn't answer he continued, 'When I was a little boy I remember finding a book in the library at Chawston, full of Victorian engravings of what they called the Lunatic Asylum. It was awful . . . people chained to walls and bound in straitjackets, people with their eyes bulging and their tongues hanging out. They haunted me, those pictures.'

Julia took him in her arms and held him close to her.

'People didn't pay to come and poke at us through the bars,' she replied softly. 'Nor did they chain us to walls, but there were straitjackets, certainly. I've seen those engravings myself, and it wasn't like that. But it was no picnic, either. In twenty-three-and-a-half years the only visitor I ever had was my mother, and she came to see me *once*, and then . . . well, then Oliver came. Oliver rescued me from Blackridge — and I know Annie won't have told you that. Unfortunately, having rescued me he seemed to get frightfully jealous of anyone I wanted to make friends with. That's what last night was all about. I had already begged him to keep it to himself, but I knew it would only be a matter of time before he came out with it.'

Patrick hugged her warmly.

'I won't tell anyone,' he promised, and she kissed him.

'I would be very happy if you'd be good enough to tell Guy,' she said. 'It was his party, and I think he has a right to know. Besides, if you don't tell him, Oliver certainly will, and Oliver's view of it isn't quite the same as Annie's, as you've discovered. But it would be nice if no one else ever found out, certainly. I'm not proud of what was done to me.'

'Then Guy will be the only person to hear it from my lips,' he assured her.

He felt his way cautiously through the door into the dower sitting-room. Oliver was there and looked up as he heard them, but Julia pointedly ignored him. Turning swiftly, she closed the door and walked away. She wasn't done with his suffering by a long chalk yet.

* * *

Oliver did finally come and apologize some days later, for he knew that if he didn't Julia would go on punishing him at her leisure, and he could no longer bear the pain of it. It made him even more resentful that she had such power, but inevitably he saw it all as Sophie's fault, and not Julia's.

As far as Julia was concerned, power didn't enter into it; she just wanted Oliver to know how much he had upset Annie, and she wanted him to apologize to Matt as well, but he made it very clear he wasn't going to do that. So she let it ride. Oliver needed patience and understanding, not bitterness and resentment — and she owed him that. However, she made him promise not to tell anyone else at all, for she wouldn't forgive him next time. In fact, she would make him sorry, and Oliver found, to his chagrin, that he couldn't even face the thought of that.

* * *

The next birthday to be celebrated was Julia's own, in the middle of October, and not at all fancying the idea of another dinner party — which seemed unlikely to be anything other than twice as bad as the last one — she suggested they have a little tea party instead.

The days were getting short now, and the weather chilly and unfriendly. No one worked on the vegetables very often, there wasn't much left to work on anyway, and no one sat on the terrace much, either. Most of the bottling and preserving was done, and a store of apples had been laid down for the winter. It was time to leave summer behind.

She mentioned the tea party one morning at breakfast and, as she glanced around, everyone seemed to look very pleased at the idea.

'That should be nice,' Sophie said as she spread a piece of toast with butter and marmalade for Edward. Annie was sharply reminded of that first summer at Tremar, when Julia had fed her copious quantities of toast and marmalade. 'Mrs Collins can make us some treats, and we'll ask the old girls in the shop to get us some ice-cream!'

Everybody burst out laughing and then, briefly, they thought about ice-cream with a yearning delight and wondered if they would ever taste it again.

'Well, at least you can wear your black dress,' Annie said to Julia. 'You know, the one you bought for that first birthday party. An' we'll ask Miss Vincent, too, 'cos we ent seen 'er in a long time.'

Julia smiled.

'It sounds like great fun,' she replied. 'And what would you like especially, children, if we can get it.'

Alice and Edward looked up from their breakfasts.

'Could we have balloons?' Alice asked shyly. 'Only I found some in the desk drawer in the library.'

Julia looked amazed.

'Did you really?' she said. 'I suppose if they haven't perished, yes, we'll blow them up. Good Lord, they must have been there for years! Anything you'd like especially, Edward?'

'Some of Mrs Collins's chocolatey fings,' replied the little boy, licking marmalade off his fingers. 'An' can we ask Doreen? 'Cos she's ever so helpful, you know. I'm not sure if she didn't c'lect the eggs an' feed the chickens with me that I'd get it all done sometimes, it's *dreadfully* hard work.'

Edward had inherited the imperiousness of his grandmother, and it sat close against his need to impress Matt. He was not a particularly sociable little boy, but his loyalty was unwavering and, despite having been back at school long enough now to have made any number of friends, he came home every afternoon and went straight to Five Elms to do his job. After that he would hunt for Matt, and Matt never failed him. He rewarded his loyalty with firm loyalty of his own. Theirs was a binding friendship.

He looked up grandly at the assembled company as he finished his little speech. He had a tiny piece of orange peel stuck to his nose, and there was not a single adult at the table, except for Minnie, who didn't ache with suppressed laughter.

Julia kept a perfectly straight face; it was masterful, and learned as a small child in the exalted company of her oddly distant parents.

'Of course we shall ask Doreen,' she said placidly. 'And Annie's mother.'

'And Daddy?' Alice whispered, looking faintly scared.

Julia touched her silky dark head affectionately and deliberately kept her eyes away from Sophie.

'Naturally your daddy, darling,' she answered. 'Along with Patrick and Guy and probably some of the others. We'll have a *lovely* party.'

Alice and Edward finished their breakfasts and then went off to get their coats for school. When they had gone, Sophie looked up at Julia.

'Thank you,' she said quietly, 'for not laughing. He is funny, I know, but it's not all bravado. He really does seem to think it's his business to be the man of the house at the moment, to help his daddy out. Would that Oliver had as much consideration towards other people.'

Julia didn't want to get into a discussion about Oliver.

'I don't think you'll find he'll repeat his performance of the night of Guy's birthday,' she said quietly. 'Not with his children there. When did you last speak to him, Sophie?'

Sophie shrugged.

'When did you?' she enquired defensively.

Julia looked down at her empty plate.

'I try to speak to him most days,' she answered with great care, trying very hard not to sound critical. 'After all, I see him most days, don't I? He spends pretty much all his time with Patrick and Guy.'

Sophie smiled, but it was a brittle, meaningless movement of her mouth, and it was only just polite. Julia hunched her shoulders slightly, waiting for a sharp retort, but then Alice and Edward appeared in the doorway, which served to curb their mother's tongue.

'Yes,' she said. 'He'll be much happier with that arrangement, I'm sure, and I am busy with my teaching, you know. As his mother was always so quick to point out, we all have our war work to do, don't we? Goodbye then, have a good day.'

'She's a cow,' Annie said to no one in particular as they heard the front door close a few moments later.

'She's a scorned woman,' Julia replied softly, 'which is why I forgive her for pretty much everything. I won't forgive her, though, if she allows Rory to make her pregnant.'

Annie's head came up quickly and her eyes were wide with disbelief.

'Is she 'aving an affair with Mr Nelson?' she exclaimed. 'I didn't know that!'

'I don't know it either,' Julia answered, 'not for sure, but the way they behave with each other doesn't leave much room for doubt, I'd say. Rory's desperately in love with her, you can see it every time he looks at her — and I have to say I think she's in love with him, too, which is lovely for them, but leaves Oliver in an entirely untenable position.'

'Well I ent going to feel sorry for 'im,' Annie declared, beginning to gather up the breakfast things. 'He wouldn't never 'ave given it a thought if he'd spoiled things for me and Patrick.'

Julia smiled and then hugged her fondly.

'But he didn't, Annie,' she whispered, 'so try and have a little compassion for him. I don't know what's going to happen in the end, you know, but I'm beginning to wish I'd never put myself in the middle of it.'

She was gathering up the dishes with Annie when Mrs Collins swept into the room. She carried a huge silver and ebony tray, and as she plonked it down on the table and then touched Minnie's cheek with great affection, Minnie smiled at her adoringly.

Anyone, Julia thought fondly, who can make Minnie smile like that is all right by me.

'Mrs Collins, did you know that Mrs Crompton and Mr Nelson is 'aving an affair?' Annie said as she helped to load the tray.

'*Annie!*' Julia hissed, appalled, but Mrs Collins didn't look affronted or surprised, and anyway Julia knew she would never tittle-tattle about the village. It was just, she thought wryly, that old habits died hard. In her parents' day, absolutely *no one* would have said such a thing in front of a servant.

'Well, you can't miss it, can you, really?' the housekeeper replied cheerfully. 'I mean they'm gazing at each other like they'm young lovers. Course it ent none of my business, but I do feel a bit sorry for the doctor — 'cept, if you'll pardon me saying, he didn't do much to help his marriage along when they were 'ere before. An' that's not,' she declared, staring boldly at Julia, 'a criticism.'

Julia chuckled.

'You have my full permission to criticize, Mrs Collins,' she said. 'I was wrong and I know I was. I also admit I was extremely naïve when I asked them all to come here to live, and I richly deserve what I'm getting now. Tell me,' she carefully piled delicate bone-china cups and saucers on to the tray, 'is it common knowledge in the village?'

'Well, not 'zac'ly common knowledge,' Mrs Collins answered truthfully, 'but them two old witches in the shop is talking about it. Although what they thinks they knows, I can't imagine. They ent never seen nothin', 'cept

Mr Nelson and Mrs Crompton going in there after school occasionally. And why not? They both lives up here and they both teaches at the school; stands to reason they'd be together a lot of the time. Don't make no difference to them two, though. They'd cause trouble in an empty 'ouse, given half a chance!'

Julia smiled grimly.

'I'm taking them that blackberry and apple pie this morning, so I'll see what they have to say, I think,' she observed. Mrs Collins's face sharpened.

'T'ent none of my business,' she snapped, 'but I don't know why you'm so generous with them, frankly. Though I 'as to say you'm about the only person they don't claw to bits anymore. An' I should think not, too!'

Julia touched Minnie's grey head with great affection and Minnie instantly nestled against her like a loving child. It was an automatic reaction, she knew that, but they had been touching each other lovingly for pretty much all their lives, and Julia's love for Minnie was deep and fierce.

'I wouldn't give them the time of day if they didn't get me those sugared fruits for Minnie,' she whispered. 'But all the while they go on doing that, I'll be as generous to them as I possibly can be.' She looked up at

Annie. 'Have you got time to walk into the village with me, darling?' she asked. 'Or are you out with Matt?'

'I'm late already!' Annie replied regretfully and planted a hard kiss on Julia's cheek before rushing out of the room.

Julia touched her face for a long time, smiling as she rubbed the spot where the kiss had landed, then she glanced at Mrs Collins.

'In the midst of this war, and bearing in mind that I seem to get it wrong far more often than I get it right most of the time, what on earth did I do to deserve such happiness?' she asked, and Mrs Collins uttered a short laugh and began easing Minnie out of her chair, to take her into the drawing-room and the warmth of the fire.

'I'll tell you sometime,' she retorted, 'when you got a couple of hours to spare.'

10

As Julia walked down the narrow road to the village half an hour later, a keen wind with angry spits of rain tugged at her hair and nipped at her fingers. The air smelled of autumn that would very soon be winter. The 'mist and mellow fruitfulness' period was pretty much a distant memory already, and it had been early this year, she thought. She had few birthdays to compare it to, most of hers had passed unmentioned and unnoticed, but she did recall the day she had stood on the cliffs with Gladys, when she had known she was pregnant, and Arthur was hundreds of miles away in France — and she'd been bitterly cold then.

Winter had its compensations: she saw much more of Matt and Annie in the cold months, but unfortunately it had its drawbacks, too, for Minnie fared badly in the winter, no matter how much care Julia took to keep her warm.

Certainly Tremar was a lot warmer than Blackridge had ever been, but then Julia had long since accepted that Minnie would have been dead by now if they hadn't been rescued when they were. These days, however, Minnie's one-dimensional world was filled with joy, and Guy would be remembered forever for the happiness he had given her.

In her shopping basket, along with the pie she had brought four fresh eggs. There wouldn't be eggs for much longer, because the chickens weren't so ready to lay during the dark months, so sparing four for the ladies in the shop was a bit of a sacrifice. However, if they were really going to have a party for her birthday, then it was a good idea to keep them sweet, and fresh eggs would certainly do that. They were a greedy pair, they never said no to anything. They were fair, though, and they did at least return the compliment when they could.

Nevertheless, Julia wasn't stupid enough to imagine that they did it out of affection. They were like far too many people in Polwean, hidebound by class consciousness: she had no doubt that she would not have done so well from Miss Penrose and Miss Hewlett if she had lived in Pinch Street!

The bell over the shop door jangled tunelessly as she went in, and as she looked around her, she was aware that the small emporium became barer each time she saw it these days. The ladies had done their best to keep the shelves from showing nothing but wood, but everyone knew the boxes so carefully displayed on them were all empty. Most of them shouted items that had been unavailable now for so long they were nothing more than a vague memory.

She said, 'Ladies, good morning,' and put her basket down on the counter, carefully lifting out the pie and the eggs.

Miss Penrose's eyes gleamed greedily.

'Well, I never did!' she exclaimed. 'That's a proper 'andsome pie, and no mistake, ma dear. Did you make it yourself?'

'Oh, I did indeed,' Julia replied with a smile. 'There is no end to my talents. And to think my mother knew nothing more about food than in which order she should use her cutlery at the table. Nice to know not all the Drakes are entirely decorative but useless, isn't it?'

Miss Penrose wagged her finger in disapproval.

'Now you oughtn't to go saying things like that 'bout your mother,' she observed. 'She were a very gracious lady. Things was different in them days.'

Gracious lady indeed! Lady Florence had been withering when she had spoken of these two. Julia smiled to herself, but outwardly her face remained impassive.

'There will be fewer eggs from now on, I'm

afraid,' she said, 'with the winter coming, but I promise you shall have some whenever I have a couple to spare . . . if you continue to be so kind as to get me the sugared fruits for Minnie.'

Miss Hewlett bustled out to the back of the shop at that and returned a moment later with two boxes of crystallized fruits which she pushed across the counter towards Julia rather as if they were a deadly secret and there was a shop full of people watching.

'There you are, ma dear,' she muttered conspiratorially, sucking her teeth in her strange fashion. 'We'm just so glad we can help your friend, that's all. That nice young officer, the one — you know — with the sad accident to his legs; 'e comes in here from time to time and 'e do talk very fondly of her, says how she gives him so much pleasure with her funny ways.'

The idea of Guy talking about Minnie's misfortunes as 'funny ways' was ridiculous, but the euphemistic 'sad accident to his legs' was just as ridiculous in its way. Guy had gone to war and his legs had been crushed like matchsticks. He would one day walk proudly on his tin legs, when the problems he still experienced with his stumps had been overcome, but it was man's inhumanity to man that had robbed Guy of his legs; it was no 'sad accident'.

Julia smiled politely as she tucked the boxes of sweets into her basket.

'Who does Guy mostly come down to the village with?' she asked conversationally and with no intention of dropping a stone into the pond.

The two old women looked at each other quickly, and instantly Julia knew she had said something that was going to bring forth some vitriol. Cautiously she waited.

'Well, he do come with the doctor an' the blind boy, actually,' Miss Penrose replied. 'That lad who's so fond of Annie Paynter. He don't never stop talking about her when he's in here, neither. Proper head-over-heels in love that one is.'

You say *anything* about that, Julia thought savagely, and I'll make you sorry you opened your foul old mouth. But it wasn't Annie and Patrick the old girls wanted to gossip about, it was evidently Oliver and Sophie.

'Course we do feel *very* sorry for the doctor,' Miss Hewlett stated, turning to look at her partner in crime. 'He was al'ys such a gentleman when they was 'ere before, an' we used to like that little Mrs Crompton so very much. Al'ys felt so sorry for her, you know . . . ?'

Yes, Julia knew, and she felt a jolt under her diaphragm. It really was extremely hard to keep an impassive face in front of these two. Her mother would have been proud of her, she thought wryly as she leaned on the counter and gazed at them.

'So what's changed, ladies?' she enquired. 'I'm happily married now, you know, and Oliver is a patient in the dower. I do see him fleetingly each day, but only ever in company.'

'Oh, t'ent you, ma dear,' Miss Penrose replied hastily. 'Well, we knows you was 'aving trouble adjusting, when you come home from Blackridge, that's all. And the nice little Mrs Crompton, well we see'd her standing up to Arthur Paynter and his mob on the green that day, so we knows there weren't no animosity 'tween the two of you by then. It's the way she'm behaving now, with that schoolmaster. We'm *very* surprised at her. *An'* when they'm both lucky enough to be under your roof, an' all. They should know better!'

No animosity between her and Sophie? If they only knew! Julia decided she'd better let that one go by. However, she had arrived at her goal, and they had very kindly led her there themselves.

'Sophie and Rory?' she said, mystified.

The two old ladies glanced at each other

again, and Julia realized she was beginning to find the gesture really quite disturbing. How was it possible, she wondered, that they had been so persistently spiteful all their lives and yet seemed to have managed always to get away with it? Everyone was terrified of them, but everyone apparently told them everything, almost as if it were some kind of ghastly ritual.

'Huh!' exclaimed Miss Penrose with relish. 'They comes in 'ere an' they'm like young lovers the way they behaves. They do walk down from the school and I sees them comin' across the green together, with her 'anging on his every word; 'anging on 'is arm, an' all, 'alf the time. She smiles and simpers, and he do 'old the shop door open for 'er like she'm bleddy royalty. They should be ashamed — an' *you* should stop it. After all, they'm living in *your* house!'

So, if there was anything to know, they knew nothing, Julia thought, relieved. She gazed placidly at the little, fat, black-clad shopkeeper and categorized her in her mind. Crow? No, too fat. Slug then? Yes, possibly; slug.

'You've got it all wrong, you know,' she observed with a smile. 'And poor Sophie would be appalled if she knew what was being said. Sophie lost her mother last year, and her father went to live in Scotland, leaving her to cope with Oliver's terrible injuries all alone. That was why Rory and I were so insistent she should come to live at Tremar. You see, Sophie looks upon Rory as another father. It's *very* touching. It helps her to be strong for the children, with their father being the way he is. You know, sometimes in the evenings when the children have gone to bed, she will sit and weep with despair and Rory mops her tears and comforts her, gives her good advice — Matt and I are *so* touched by his fatherly concern for her. Rory told me once she's like the daughter he never had, and I know how that feels, because Annie's the daughter I never had. The difference is . . . ' she leaned forward conspiratorially, 'between you and me, I think he's the father *she* never had.'

The demeanour of the two old ladies changed in an instant, and with a silent little crow of triumph, Julia thought, *got you!*

'Well, that's *so* sweet,' Miss Hewlett said, and really looked as if she might pull forth a hanky and dab her eyes. 'An' we did find it 'ard to believe, you know; they'm *such* a lovely pair, the two of them. You can be sure, ma dear, that if anyone else comes in 'ere spreading nasty rumours about them any more, we'll soon put them straight.'

270

'Oh, I would be grateful,' Julia replied seriously. 'How kind of you, thank you. Sophie is very delicate, you know. She shouldn't be hurt by evil gossip, she's not at all strong. That's why I'm so glad she's at Tremar, so that we can keep an eye on her. Now I think I should be on my way home. So much to do; Tremar never sleeps.'

She put her hand on her boxes of sugared fruits, as much as anything to calm her rage, and managed a wide, friendly smile.

As she reached the door, however, Miss Penrose said, 'Oh, one more thing afore you go, Julia, ma dear, I almost forgot. The shop'll be closed tomorrow for the day, I'm afraid, so if you could just tell anyone at Tremar that if they needs anythin' they must come in afore five tonight, I'd be most grateful.'

Julia frowned. This was most unusual. The shop was *never* closed, except on Sundays.

'Are you going away?' she enquired in surprise, and for probably the first time ever she saw a genuine expression in the old Penrose's face.

'It's ma sister,' she explained. 'She'm goin' downhill rapidly, an' Miss Hewlett an' me is goin' to Plymouth for the weekend to see 'er. It'll be the last time; my niece is certain of that.'

'Plymouth?' Julia repeated. 'Oh dear, I

271

understand the bombing's very bad in Plymouth at the moment. Wouldn't you be better to leave it for a while, perhaps?'

Miss Penrose smiled.

'Of course I would if I could,' she replied, 'but I'm afraid it just won't wait. Anyway, us'll be back Sunday evenin', so the shop'll be open Monday as usual.'

'Then have a pleasant time, ladies,' Julia said and left the shop, walking across the green towards the church.

Her mind was full of Sophie and Rory, and she was furious with them. Hopefully, she thought, she'd nipped any trouble in the bud. She doubted there would be any more vitriol coming from those two now; in fact, she fully expected that by Monday they would be singing Sophie's praises, but for all that Sophie and Rory were undoubtedly being careless — and what the old ladies had seen, the mothers of the children in school would have seen as well.

She went back to Tremar, and when Sophie and Rory came in from school that afternoon she was sharp in her admonition of them. She told them that if they knew what was good for them they would be very careful in the shop for the next few weeks, and though Sophie's eyes were cold with resentment at being spoken to in such a way, Julia knew Rory had taken it on board.

'If I were you,' she advised, 'I should start going in there separately for a while because, believe me, those two can make your lives a misery if they choose to.'

But Sophie and Rory never got a chance to find out, for when Mrs Collins came into the dining-room at breakfast time on Monday morning, her face was white and grim, and heavily she passed on the news she had been given on her way.

Miss Penrose and Miss Hewlett had died on Saturday night in the middle of a savage bombing raid, when the shelter they were in had taken a direct hit. They had died together with Miss Penrose's niece and her two great-nephews, one of whom was only a few months older than Edward. The only person left was Miss Penrose's ailing sister, lying in hospital robbed of everyone in her life.

Two little boys with all their lives ahead of them, their mother only in her early thirties and the two old shopkeepers whose relationship with each other had always been an unasked question, and who had spent the best part of their lives poking their noses into other people's business. Julia had been five years old when Miss Penrose had inherited the shop from her father, and Miss Penrose had been thirty. But feared and mistrusted as they might have been by most people in Polwean, their sudden, violent deaths ripped a hole in the fabric of the village. Everyone had heard the bombers going over on Saturday night. The familiar, uneven drone of the heavy planes coming in from the sea, heading north. Probably no one had even remarked on it and now, somehow, that seemed so dreadfully remiss.

Julia and Rory stared at each other uncomfortably across the breakfast table.

'I feel awful,' she sighed. 'We've just spent the weekend tearing them to rags, and they've been dead for half that time.'

'Me too,' he replied quietly, and glanced at Sophie.

Sophie said nothing. It had been a stormy weekend, and she had been angry ever since Friday evening at having incurred Julia's wrath, for she didn't consider Julia had any right to disapprove of her relationship with Rory. She had been further annoyed by Julia's dire warnings of what would happen if she became pregnant. They had assured her they were being careful, but they were in the first unthinking passion of this affair, and were hungry for each other all the time. They were not careful and they knew it; sometimes they thought seriously about it, but never when they were in bed. In bed they thought only about each other . . . and the old ladies being dead was likely to make them even more careless, rather than less.

Julia got up from the table. Alice and Edward had already gone upstairs to get ready for the walk to school, and she decided she would walk down to the village with them all. Somehow she felt that she needed to do penance in some obscure sort of way; if nothing else, to stand for a moment outside the shop door and say goodbye.

When they reached the school she went briefly into Rory's office, and the three of them stood for a moment looking wretchedly at each other. They had hardly been able to speak on the way down from Tremar, there just wasn't anything to say, and now it seemed no one knew what to do; what they were supposed to do or say.

'I couldn't bear them, spiteful old witches,' Rory said at last, 'but, dear God, it brings it all home, doesn't it? I think we've been guilty of being somewhat complacent in Polwean since the beginning of the war.'

Julia nodded.

'Well, let's face it,' she replied. 'We hear the planes, but they're never coming for us so we've learned to ignore them.' She shivered. 'It doesn't seem quite so obscure now, does it, when you're faced with the blunt reality of where they were going?'

For a moment no one said anything, and all three of them knew that each, in his or her own mind, was forming an unwilling picture of Miss Penrose and Miss Hewlett lying horribly mutilated and dead amongst the rubble. Then suddenly Rory glanced up at Julia and his eyes were full of guilt.

'I suppose now at least the village won't abound with spiteful rumours quite so much,' he observed and then winced at himself. 'Oh God, I shouldn't have said that, should I?'

'I think you should,' Julia replied quietly. 'It won't bring them back to life if we sanitize them. They *were* horrible old women — but I still can't believe they're dead.'

As she left the office and went out across the playground towards the village, it seemed to her that the children were muted; they were not running and playing as usual, but simply standing in little groups, talking to each other. Obviously the news had gone all round the village now and this was their first real taste of the horror of war.

Rory would say prayers for the two women in Assembly, and there would be questions asked in many homes this evening; questions about death, which the children had not asked when their fathers went away in uniform because 'Daddy gone to war' was not quite real, not like Miss Penrose and Miss Hewlett never being in the village shop again.

As she crossed the green she suddenly stopped short, for to her bewilderment the shop was open. Finding that her hands were trembling slightly, she reached out for the door handle and as the door swung open the familiar bell clanked above her head.

Behind the counter was Mr Dawkins, the butcher.

'Good Lord, what are you doing in here?' she asked, slightly breathless. 'I'm sorry, I . . . I was almost frightened to come in.'

Dawkins, a big man in his early seventies who had known Julia since she was a child and had spent most of his working life buying and selling poached game from the Tremar estate — until Matt's arrival on the scene — gave her a rather tight smile.

'I'm sorry, Mrs Logan,' he replied. 'I seems to 'ave frightened rather a lot of people this mornin', but on the rare occasions the old girls went away, they al'ys left their keys with me, see. Just in case there was an emergency. Well, we know they ent comin' back now, but the fact is there's people relying on this shop; there's deliveries comin' in an' so forth, an' somebody's got to keep it open, till we find out what's to 'appen to it. So I thought it 'ad better be me.'

Julia regarded in horror the empty boxes on the shelves, seeing Miss Hewlett, in her mind's eye, carefully rearranging them as she had been wont to do recently.

'So who's running your shop?' she asked, rubbing her cold hands together.

He rested on the counter for a moment and he seemed to see, as she did, the emptiness of the shop which, before the war, had always been a sort of bursting fullness.

'I just come in to open up,' he replied. 'My wife's going to be servin' in 'ere for now; she'd rather leave the butcherin' to me. You know . . . ' His eyes suddenly filled with tears and he stared at Julia as if he was indignantly angry at the outrage of war poking its skeletal finger into the calm complacency that was Polwean. His voice was trembling. 'When I went out the back first thing,' he whispered, 'they'd laid out their supper, for when they come 'ome yesterday evening. There was plates an' knives and spoons on the kitchen table, an' on the side there was a little saucepan with a wooden spoon an' two fresh eggs. Then in the larder there was this lovely blackberry and apple pie. Someone must 'ave given it to them as a treat . . . '

He uttered a sob and a couple of tears trickled down his big red face. Julia thought she was going to be sick.

'I'll — um — I'll make sure I tell everyone, you know, at Tremar,' she muttered almost hysterically, feeling the colour drain from her face. 'I'll — I'll pass on the word, and if there's anything I can do . . . '

'Thanks, Mrs Logan,' he said, but she barely heard him, and as she stumbled blindly across the green tears were streaming down her cheeks.

Half an hour later, alone with Minnie in the drawing-room at Tremar, she was huddled by the fireplace, shivering and wiping her nose on her sleeve, when Gladys came quietly into the room.

'Julia?' she whispered and Julia began to cry again. 'Mrs Collins is bringin' some coffee. She come into the dower an' said she thought you needed a spot of company for a few minutes. They said to take as much time as I needed.'

'But I hated them, Gladys!' Julia burst out. 'Why do I feel like this? Is it guilt? Was I not supposed to hate them because they were going to be blown to bits by a bomb?'

'Of course not,' Gladys replied softly, sitting down beside her. 'It's shock, that's all. They *was* poisonous, it's true, but some'ow none of us ever thought to see the village without 'em. Now we just got to face the fact that they'm not comin' back.'

Julia sniffed and searched around in her sleeves for a handkerchief, finding one eventually and scrubbing at her nose with it.

'I gave them four eggs and a fruit pie, to say thank you for Minnie's little treats,' she mumbled. 'They were going to have them for supper when they got back last night . . . ' She uttered a little sob and gazed up at Gladys, and suddenly the pain of the past seemed to sweep over her like a huge wave. 'Do you remember the boys, Gladys?' she said in a voice full of pain. 'That time the musketeers and Sandro found some way of making that damned shop bell ring when there wasn't anyone in there? When eventually old Hewlett discovered what they were doing, she chased them across the green, and she caught one of your brothers and threatened to box his ears. Sandro stood there in front of her like Lord Muck and told her that if she hit him, Papa would shut the shop. The fact was Papa would have thrashed him till he couldn't sit down . . . '

Gladys chuckled. 'Old Hewlett let 'em go anyway,' she said, and reached across gently to take Julia's hands. 'An' that's what you'm mourning for, my love,' she whispered. 'The past.'

Julia drew a small, sobbing breath and looked down at their hands, linked together in their everlasting friendship.

'I think you're probably right,' she said. 'I want it back, Gladys, so that I can do it differently. I want it back so that I can just *have* it, I suppose . . . ' She broke off and then, frowning, she raised her eyes to Gladys's face. 'You would say if you minded, wouldn't you?' she whispered. 'I mean I know I've said it before, but I do worry.'

'Minded what?' Gladys asked, puzzled; then the penny dropped. 'Oh, 'bout Annie, you mean?' She smiled and squeezed Julia's hands tightly. 'Julia, Annie missed out on most of 'er childhood. She got nowt from Arthur at all, an' not a lot from me either, 'cos I was so bleddy frightened of 'is reprisals as much as anythin'. She loves bein' a daughter to you an' Matt, but she don't never forget me, you know. She got Patrick to come an' ask me first if 'e could marry 'er. I don't mind. There ent nothin' *to* mind. Far as I'm concerned she'm a very lucky girl, an' I'm mostly pleased to see she don't take it for granted.'

'It's what she deserves,' Julia said, wiping her nose on her hanky again. 'She deserves to be happy, Gladys, and with my last breath I'll see to it that she is, I promise you.'

★ ★ ★

281

They brought the remains of the two elderly shopkeepers home in two identical coffins, and they were buried together in the same grave. The church was almost full for the funeral and, in an effort to uphold the tradition that so many people in the village were still used to, Julia and Matt, with the other adult members of Tremar, led the mourners. No one from outside came for them. Evidently neither of them had anyone to come.

Fanny Penrose and Cecille Hewlett; Julia thought she had never heard their Christian names before. As the vicar droned his eulogy, and her mind wandered, she remembered them when they had been much, much younger. Miss Penrose still plump, with pink cheeks, and Miss Hewlett the taller, stronger-looking one who was always marginally less spiteful, probably because the shop did not actually belong to her. It was hard to imagine that they might ever have been intimate with each other. It was hard to imagine them even calling one another by their Christian names. It was incredible to think that they were dead.

Julia knew she would bring flowers for them sometimes, when she was bringing them for Sandro; she would have to, to make amends. Though what she had to make amends *for* was unfathomable, so she left it alone.

★   ★   ★

In the end she didn't have a party on her birthday, because it didn't seem appropriate, but on the afternoon of her birthday Matt took her to Blackridge, to have tea with Ilona Vincent.

Matt understood Julia's bond with the asylum in which she had spent half her life and recognized, probably better than she did, her need to return there on occasions so that she could put her life into perspective. The death of the old ladies in the shop had disturbed the fabric of her past, thrown her into disarray, and she needed the comfort of the woman whom she had once described as the nearest thing to a proper mother she had ever had.

Ilona Vincent had a small, self-contained flat on the top floor of one of the Blackridge buildings and from the window the view across the moors was breathtaking. Matt had walked Julia up to the distant plateau of lonely rocks during their first summer together, to allow her to look down on her prison and sense the freedom of the world that she had only ever seen through bars; but there was always something faintly uncomfortable about seeing the view in the familiar way, something that usually made her keep her eyes away from it.

'You know, Julia, my dear, this hasn't got so much to do with those old ladies from the shop as the other things in your life,' Ilona Vincent said quietly, as Matt and Julia sat in her cosy little sitting-room drinking tea. 'It's hard for you to understand, but I think you'll find this is about Dr Crompton, mostly.'

Julia kept dabbing at her eyes with her handkerchief as a seemingly non-stop stream of tears trickled down her cheeks, and the mention of Oliver made them worse. The thought of him overwhelmed her with grief, and being here, remembering him so handsome and beautifully dressed that first time she had ever seen him, threw everything into sharp relief.

'I shouldn't condemn Sophie and Rory, should I?' she sobbed miserably. 'I shouldn't interfere, I should just let them get on and sort it out for themselves ... God, and they're not even going to get talked about in the village any more, let's face it.'

Ilona Vincent smiled calmly.

'That may be so, but it's not easy when they're doing it right under your nose,' she observed. 'Only it isn't your fault, Julia, and you really must stop punishing yourself for it. The pain Dr Crompton is suffering is not of your making any more. He may think it is, but it isn't. What's more you cannot force Mrs Crompton to feel the same way about him as you do. You have a great deal of compassion for him, which I'm not sure he fully deserves, but which the circumstances of your background create in you, and she has no concept of it, I'm afraid. She never will be happy with him again, you know, and the best you can do is soften the blow.'

Soften the blow? Surely it was more than that, wasn't it? Heavens, Julia knew better than most how callous and indifferent Oliver could be at times and how jealous and obsessive he was too, but was this really the moment, when he faced such a shaky future, to deliver the death thrust?

'It just seems so cruel,' Julia complained and Miss Vincent nodded.

'But it is *not* your affair,' she replied firmly. 'So, now tell me about everything else. Tell me about Annie and her beau.'

'Oh, Annie . . . ' Julia said and frowned very slightly. 'Annie's madly, passionately in love. In fact, I would have said blindly, but it's not appropriate.'

Outside, the doleful bell on the Blackridge clock tower suddenly tolled out the hour of five, and the dying embers of the afternoon showed grey against the windows. That sound filled her with nightmarish memories. The onset of winter with the cold to come and the miserable, dark, lonely evenings. The sense of despair, and sometimes fear, in the draughty stinking corridors, the knowledge that Christmas was coming again, but would not touch this place.

'If you want the truth,' she whispered, 'I'm frightened for Annie and Patrick. They're so young — at least she is, anyway. Do you really think she knows what it's going to be like, tied to a blind man for the rest of her life? He won't get better as the years go on, and I sometimes don't think she's really thought about it. He'll never see their children. She'll never hold a fence post for him, whilst he knocks in nails ... Well you know what I mean; I could go on forever.'

Ilona Vincent smiled enigmatically. 'And she could marry a handsome, golden boy with two eyes and complete independence who beats her mercilessly, Julia, my dear,' she said. 'Trust Patrick. He's not after her fortune; he neither wants to cheat her nor steal from her — which is more than can have been said for Dr Crompton in 1938, if you remember. He was most anxious for you to sell Tremar so that he could have what he wanted in life, and although that included you, never lose sight of the fact that it would have been on *his* terms, will you? My impression of Patrick is that more than anything he wants to be loved — as badly as Annie wanted to be loved when she fell out of your cedar tree that afternoon — and surely you have some to spare for him, don't you?'

Julia gazed at her, and not for the first time she acknowledged how much strength she drew from this woman. She was the only person in the world to have looked beyond Julia's regulation blue asylum dress and blank expression, and found the sane and suffering woman inside.

'They're getting engaged on Annie's birthday,' she said. 'At the party. I know it's Minnie's day as well, but Minnie won't mind a bit. Just as long as there's someone to make a fuss of her, and lots of sweet things to eat, she'll be as happy as a sand boy. Will you come and spend Christmas with us this year, Ilona?' but Miss Vincent smiled and shook her head, despite Julia's begging.

'Not Christmas,' she replied. 'I need to be here for Christmas, and besides, you have Matt and Annie at Christmas now, so you're not on your own, are you? I'll come for the party, though. Whatever happens, I'm not missing the big engagement, I can assure you.'

Julia's face darkened as unwelcome memories intruded suddenly.

'Before you came here,' she whispered, 'there was no such thing as Christmas, but then you arrived and you had a tree brought in. You hung decorations on it, and you made sure everyone had sweets or chocolate on Christmas Day . . . It was awful, like having my nose rubbed in it . . . I'm sorry, I didn't mean to say that, it sounds so ungrateful.'

Miss Vincent touched her gently.

'You were never ungrateful, Julia,' she answered gently. 'I think I knew how Christmas hurt you, but you see it wasn't meant for you. You weren't supposed to be here at all. My ladies don't understand the concept of Christmas, but they like the tree, it's something different to look at, and one or two of them can dimly remember 'O Come All Ye Faithful' from childhood, those who have any recollection of childhood. It isn't supposed to be painful, it's supposed to be a tiny spark of brightness in their lives. You make sure you enjoy Christmas, and never mind what the Cromptons are doing to each other, we'll have a lovely party two days later, and you never know, it might all have resolved itself by then.'

But the Cromptons' situation wasn't going to resolve itself, it was too personal and they were all too close. It was going to get worse, and then one day it would come to a head, because one day they would tell Oliver in the dower that they weren't going to keep him any more. What then, if he told his wife and children to pack their belongings and Sophie refused? Everyone was going to have to start taking sides, and Julia truly didn't know on whose side she was likely to come down.

11

On 7 December 1941, the Japanese sneaked into Pearl Harbor without warning and bombed the American fleet. It came completely out of the blue and cost a great many lives, for the ships were at anchor and sitting ducks for the bombers. The carnage was appalling. On 11 December the Americans finally came roaring into action in fury, and the war entered another phase.

'With any luck this'll be a turning point,' Matt remarked at breakfast the next morning. 'They're a nation of great resources, the Americans, apart from anything else.'

Alice, who was busy with her bowl of porridge, suddenly looked up nervously. The talk of races she knew little about and places she knew nothing at all about was confusing. Her small world revolved around Polwean; she was happy. Talk of change brought into her mind the nagging fear that it might somehow result in her being forced to return to live with her grandmother again, and Alice would have been ready to do just about anything to prevent that. What was worse, she had heard her parents shouting at each other about it, and any mention of Granny, for Alice, was enough to send her into a frenzy of terror.

Christmas was just around the corner and despite the fact that most of the shops around the country were empty, and life, after over two years of war, was getting bleaker by the day, Julia had promised Alice and Edward a splendid Christmas. Then there was going to be the party on Annie's birthday. Alice felt her heart twinge in her chest with fear.

'We will still have Christmas, though, won't we?' she asked, her brow furrowing in alarm. Julia touched her cheek fondly.

'Of course we will, sweetheart,' she replied, 'and we'll have a splendid Christmas, too, like I promised, with a very special party for Annie and Minnie two days later.'

Alice blushed with relief and went back to her breakfast. If Julia said it was going to be all right, then it was. Julia never told her lies.

Christmas was always a special time at Tremar; Julia's father had loved it and spared no expense to celebrate it, and he had passed on his love to his daughter. Since her return from Blackridge, Julia had been anxious to make up for all the Christmases of which she had been robbed, and even with the austerity of wartime, no expense was spared to see to it that everyone had a wonderful time.

When Matt cut two magnificent trees and brought them up two weeks before the day, one for the manor and one for the dower, Julia crawled about in the attic finding the carefully stored decorations. They were exquisitely coloured and frosted glass baubles, very old indeed and made in Germany — though no one mentioned that. There were birds with real tail feathers; lanterns and bells, and enough for two trees because there had always been two trees in Julia's childhood.

'Goodness, aren't they wonderful!' Sophie exclaimed when they had finished decorating the manor tree that evening. 'I'm surprised you're prepared to risk them, with so many people about.'

Julia shrugged.

'If they get broken, they get broken,' she replied. 'Nothing lasts forever. The little white goose-feather trees, which Mama always stood in that stone window in the hall, are pretty moth-eaten now if you look closely, but no one will of course. I shall put them there with a candle between them, just as she did, and we shall light the candle each evening from Christmas Eve to Twelfth Night.' She chuckled. 'I don't think one candle will have us up in court for showing a light, do you?'

Sophie smiled and Julia was alarmed at how thin and wan she was looking. She still powdered her face and painted her mouth when she was going out, but since cosmetics, like everything else, were in short supply nowadays, she didn't do it so much when she was at home any more. There was something wrong with Sophie and Julia wondered if it was simply the strain of her crumbling relationship with Oliver, or whether it was something more than that.

Sophie didn't wonder, she knew exactly what was wrong with her and she felt like a rat in a trap. There was no escape. Each morning, in the cold bathroom at the end of her corridor, retching painfully, with her eyes and nose running and her skin breaking into goose bumps, she wondered in panic what she was going to do.

Sometimes she remembered that she wasn't the first person at Tremar to be facing the terror of an unplanned pregnancy, and just once she even contemplated, briefly, throwing herself on Julia's mercy, but she had no more real an idea of doing that than Julia had ever had of throwing herself on the mercy of her parents. Julia had made it clear at the beginning that if Sophie got herself pregnant she would be furious — and the thought of being turned out of Tremar was as frightening to Sophie as it was to Alice.

It would be a long time before it showed,

she knew. She wasn't quite sure why, but neither with Alice nor with Edward had anyone outside the family known she was pregnant until well over halfway through. But there would be no hiding it from Oliver. Oliver always knew when she was pregnant, and very early on, and as a consequence she began to avoid him even more than usual. She stopped coming to breakfast, she yawned a lot in the evenings, she went to bed early, and Julia began to be really quite alarmed.

So did Rory. Sophie looked as if she was fading away, and Rory couldn't get the picture of Penny out of his head. In the beginning she had been hollow-eyed and fragile, too, until the disease had really taken hold. Surely it wasn't going to happen again, he thought in panic? He'd never be able to bear it, not again! He asked her numerous times if she was all right and each time she smiled at him and assured him she was just a bit tired, but she was snappy with the children and evidently unhappy, and Rory began to feel strangely isolated from her.

She finally told him, lying beside him in bed, on the night when the newly decorated tree glittered with its wonderful glass ornaments in the drawing-room, and the sky outside was a myriad of stars as the temperature plummeted. It was not a night to be out and about, not a night to be facing the fact that they might well have no home shortly.

'*Pregnant?*' he whispered in horror and at once she burst into tears.

Immediately he took her into his arms, holding her tightly, soothing her as he promised her that everything would be all right, but in truth he was as much at sea as she was.

'I will look after you, no matter what, my love,' he promised as her tears soaked his face and her distress frightened him. 'You know I will.'

'I don't just want you to look after me!' she retorted. 'I want you to love me!'

'God, I *do* love you!' he cried. 'I love you more than anything in the world, you should know that by now. I'm just not sure what we ought to do next.'

'What will Julia do, do you think?' she whispered in a frightened little voice. 'Will she throw us out, Rory? We've got nowhere to go. We can't go back to Cliff House and there isn't anywhere else.'

Rory frowned.

'Well, she won't throw us on to the street,' he replied immediately. 'Heavens, Julia of all people won't do that — and particularly not with the welfare of Alice and Edward to think of.'

'Alice and Edward!' A fresh wave of tears flooded down Sophie's face. 'When Oliver finds out, he'll take them back to Arundel to punish me; you see if he doesn't!' She began to sob brokenly. 'I *can't* let them go back there, Rory, it's just not fair!'

Rory hugged her close to him in the darkness.

'We won't,' he promised. 'Anyway, that's looking too far ahead. Oliver doesn't know yet, and we won't tell him before we have to. Look, Sophie, I know how reluctant you are to ally yourself to Julia, but don't you perhaps think this might be a good time? I mean, it isn't as if she's a stranger to this situation . . . '

Sophie hunched her shoulders against him. It seemed a dreadfully bleak gesture, as if although she could share the words with him, she was completely unable to share her pain and fear.

'And then have her tell me that she's going to tell Oliver,' she answered bitterly, 'because it's the only fair and honest thing to do? No, I don't think so, thanks. I don't want to tell anyone at the moment, I only told you because . . . I needed to know if you were going to reject me. I don't know what I'd have done if you had.'

'*Reject you?*' He stared at her in

bewilderment. 'Sophie, as if I would! I'm going to be a father; that's an extraordinary new experience for me.'

'You're also going to be reviled as a wife-stealer,' she muttered sourly, 'and I'm going to be branded a whore — in fact, worse than that. I'll be that dreadful painted tart who betrayed that nice handsome doctor when he most needed her. You wait.'

There was an undeniable truth in her words, but Rory didn't think he could let his mind wander through the minefield of that; not yet.

'We'll face that if we come to it, my love,' he promised her, trying to sound positive, 'and perhaps it might not be quite so bad now that those two old cats in the shop have gone.'

Sophie pressed her face into his neck and her soft hair brushed against him. Rory stroked her to comfort her, and knew he must be strong for her.

'Be thankful for small mercies, then?' she whispered miserably. Rory kissed her.

'Maybe one day we'll be thankful for great mercies, my darling,' he replied seriously. 'Sophie, if I haven't said so before, after the war I intend to make you my wife, and that's a promise.'

She squeezed her eyes shut, breathing in

the familiar scent of him. Little Sophie, the shrinking violet who had ultimately become the worm that turned. It was easy to paint one's mouth and fingernails red, and pretend to be modern and hard, but she was discovering it wasn't actually that easy to change one's basic personality.

'After the war,' she repeated very softly. 'Oh God, will there ever *be* an after the war? I'm sick of living in limbo, Rory.'

He sighed. 'Aren't we all, my sweet?' he said and they lay in silence for a while, remembering.

One day, he supposed, he could go back to Cliff House — if the army hadn't completely destroyed it — and one day there would be soap and toothpaste whenever they wanted it, and coffee, and bananas . . . And one day Sophie would be his wife and they would have a child of their own, but he didn't allow himself to dwell on the pain they would have to endure before that day.

Christmas week arrived, the run up to the great day, and any number of presents began pouring into the manor for Edward and Alice, for they were extremely popular at Tremar. They were nice children, whose obvious love for their daddy touched everyone's hearts and whose devotion to duty on the estate was much appreciated. Patients and Land Girls alike had all remembered the Crompton children this Christmas.

Julia had made Alice her first ever long dress, and re-costumed all the china-headed figures who peopled her dolls' house, for they were a bit moth-eaten after having spent so many years in the attic. Matt had lovingly restored Alexander Drake's magnificent rocking-horse for Edward, and Julia had made him a little uniform.

'They've never had so many presents in their lives!' Sophie exclaimed as the gifts kept arriving. 'What a Christmas this is going to be for them! Better than last year when bloody Harriet gave them a new pair of school socks each, and a diary — which they were supposed to keep faithfully each day, and then let her read, if you please! Absolutely pointless, since Edward could only just write his name then.'

Julia smiled. 'I had to do that as a child,' she said, 'keep a diary and give it to my father to read on Sundays. It was supposed to be a test of my observation skills. I found it in one of the trunks when I was looking for material for Edward's uniform.' Suddenly she uttered a bitter little laugh. 'No one offered me pen and paper in Blackridge; if they had, I could have kept quite a tidy diary. Observation was the only thing I had left.' She gazed into the fire. 'I lost that in the end, too, of course.'

For a moment Sophie stared at her and longed to tell her she now knew exactly how she must have felt when she was desperately trying to stave off the inevitable discovery of her pregnancy, but the words stuck in her throat. Instead she said, 'I'm glad you like Christmas so much. When I was a child our Christmases were rather quiet because my mother was delicate, and Christmas at Arundel always had more to do with how many times we could be dragged into church than anything else. I'm sure this one is going to be like something out of a dream.'

Julia grinned. 'And very special,' she said, 'for Annie and Patrick.'

On Christmas Eve Annie, Alice and Edward solemnly hung their stockings by the huge fireplace in the drawing-room, with the firm conviction that Santa Claus would find his way around war-torn Europe to fill them in the traditional way. At least Alice and Edward believed that anyway. Julia was enormously touched that Annie wanted a stocking, for she knew there had been nothing like that in Annie's childhood, but it seemed to prove her generosity that she should wish to perpetuate the myth for children luckier than she had ever been.

The children left a mince pie and a glass of

punch for Father Christmas before bed, and when they, and Minnie, were fast asleep, all their lovely presents were brought out of hiding and placed under and around the tree, with each stocking being lovingly filled for the next morning.

Minnie had no real idea what was going on; she didn't properly understand the concept of Christmas, but people were kind and kissed her a lot, and the tree was fascinating. The children sang some carols before they went to bed, which delighted her, and she was told she would have a present in the morning. That was enough for Minnie.

Oliver came in with Guy and Patrick for a while and was touched to see everything displayed with such care for his children. Julia caught him looking hard at Sophie — and she hadn't missed the fact that Sophie had put powder, rouge and lipstick on her face. She didn't miss, either, that Sophie suddenly seemed to become the life and soul of the party; sparkling and enchanting, and looking quite beautiful. But for all that she couldn't hide her tiredness, and it sat oddly against her extraordinary struggle to be scintillating. Oliver watched her for a while, then he stopped looking at her and became involved with something else. When he did so, Sophie seemed to switch off like an electric light bulb

— and Rory appeared to be peculiarly agitated the entire evening.

And you're very tired and seeing ghosts where there aren't any, Julia told herself severely. You were told not to get involved, so don't!

Annie and Patrick went off on their own at about ten o'clock, and Guy excused himself and said he had to go and write home before bed. Matt took the dogs and went out for his regular last walk of the night around the buildings, Sophie went to bed and Rory insisted it was his turn to clear everything away to the kitchen. It left Julia and Oliver alone together in the drawing-room.

Oliver sat and gazed into the fragrant wood-smelling fire; the room was warm and the glass decorations on the tree winked and sparkled in the firelight. He wore a black patch over his empty eye socket nowadays, and the full extent of the burns on his face were there for all to see. When he had first appeared like that he had been extremely nervous of the reaction of the children, but Alice hadn't even seemed to notice much and Edward now delighted in calling him Blackbeard the Pirate. They had both been amazingly brave about it; in fact, it sometimes seemed as if they were actually rather proud of his injuries.

'Thank you so much,' he said after a while, 'for all the trouble you've gone to on behalf of my children. Tomorrow is going to be beyond their wildest dreams, I think.'

'It's no trouble, Oliver,' Julia replied softly. 'Everyone is very fond of your children; they're an important part of life at Tremar now.'

He nodded.

'So, apparently, is Sophie,' he muttered and absently touched the damaged side of his face with his good hand. Julia looked at the black silk glove with padded fingers that he wore on the other one; it was hard to believe it wasn't a normal hand, until you saw its stilted movements. 'My time here is almost up, by the way,' he went on suddenly. 'I don't know whether they've told you, but all three of us, Patrick, Guy and myself, we're nearing the end of our stay, only that won't matter to Patrick, of course, and Guy will be here a bit longer, because he's still having problems with his stumps. I shall have to move on soon, however, only Sophie says she doesn't want to come with me.'

Julia stared at him and felt an uncomfortable pang of guilt. It made her want to squirm.

'If Sophie doesn't want to go, you don't have to either, Oliver,' she said recklessly.

'You know that. You're as welcome to move into the manor as Patrick will be.'

He threw her a slightly cynical look and Julia remembered why she didn't like to be trapped in corners by Oliver; he always managed to make her regret the things she said. Surely, she thought crossly, after all this time I can stop feeling that because you saved my life and I rejected you, everything is somehow all my fault!

'I don't think Matt would be terribly happy at having me as a long-term bedfellow, do you?' he said, arching the eyebrow above his good eye. 'It doesn't seem terribly tactful. Besides, I'm due for some surgery to give me a new eyelid, so I'm told. That way I will be able to wear a glass eye instead of this black patch, although I don't think it'll make me look vastly different. When I told Sophie, she informed me that she and the children would be staying in Polwean for the foreseeable future; and if *you* didn't like the idea, she said, she would find herself somewhere else to live. She's afraid I want her to move back to Arundel.'

'And do you?' Julia asked.

He shrugged.

'Well, I've got nowhere else to go, and she *is* my wife. Oh, I know Mother can be difficult, but Edward and Alice are older now, things should be better.'

'Six months older,' Julia pointed out very quietly. 'Nothing is going to have changed, Oliver, and however you look at it, Alice and Edward are very happy here. Surely they can stay until the end of the war? Perhaps you could go and have your surgery and, whilst you're away, we could find somewhere in the village for all of you to live as a family?'

Oliver climbed to his feet. Julia saw his depression, and remembered how handsome he had once been. She felt desperately sorry for him, for he was simply not able to cope with what was happening to him now. He had no control over anything any more, not even his own life. Sophie was deeply in love with Rory, Julia knew that, and if, to spite her, Oliver left Tremar and took the children with him, the situation would be dreadful, and Alice and Edward would suffer terribly. Slowly she got up and went to stand beside him, and very gently she touched his arm.

He looked up and then his mouth twisted into his familiarly crooked smile.

'We're under the mistletoe,' he said. 'May I kiss you, for old times' sake?'

'You may kiss me for Christmas if you like,' Julia replied. 'I'm not sure old times' sake is any good to anyone, Oliver.'

He put his arms round her and then

suddenly it was not a Christmas kiss, but a hard, hungry kiss full of pain and yearning. He held her tightly and though she knew she could easily enough have pulled away from him, to do so would have bluntly and cruelly displayed his physical inadequacies. When she could she turned her head, arching her neck away from him.

'No, Oliver,' she said, and he pawed at her.

'Oh please, please,' he begged. 'I love you so much, Julia!'

'Oliver, don't!' she snapped firmly, stepping back from him. 'You're hurting yourself and there isn't any point. I won't be your mistress again, but I want to be your friend. Please don't spoil it.'

'My friend,' he said, and to her horror she saw a tear splash down his cheek.

The horror was worse because on the other side he had no eye to cry with.

'My *friend?*' he repeated bitterly, and brushed his cheek angrily with his fingers. 'I would die for you, Julia, in fact you can't imagine how many times I've wished you'd broken *my* neck on the beach at the same time as you broke Arthur Paynter's!'

Julia shook her head furiously.

'No,' she protested. 'you don't mean that, and you know you don't. This isn't fair what you're doing; I don't deserve it!'

There was a soft cough behind them and they both turned to find Matt standing in the doorway. His face was completely impassive and the dogs sat one either side of him, their eyes bright from the cold night, their pink tongues lolling. Julia was aware that they were so well trained they would have taken Oliver down if Matt had told them to, but this didn't seem the moment to mention it, somehow.

'Is everything all right?' he asked and Julia went to him immediately.

'Everything's fine, darling,' she replied, touching his face and feeling the cold on his skin. 'Oliver was just going, weren't you, Oliver?'

Oliver gazed at them for a few seconds, then his mouth briefly curled in contempt, and he swung away towards the library.

'Goodnight to you,' he called back, 'and a Happy Christmas.'

'Goodnight,' Julia replied, knowing he couldn't hear her because he had gone. 'And a Happy Christmas to you, too ... I suppose.'

Matt asked quietly, 'What was all that about?' and Julia looked at him wretchedly.

'Oliver wants to die,' she replied. 'But you know Oliver, he doesn't want to die for himself, he wants me to take the blame.'

Matt nodded.

'Aye,' he said darkly. 'Well, hopefully he doesnae have the courage to be more than wantin' to die, for the sake of those two little bairns. He really doesnae think about anyone but himself, does he? Mind you, neither does little Sophie, most of the time. Still, it'll be Christmas Day in a short while, and I refuse to worry about them any more until I've had ma Christmas lunch, opened ma presents and celebrated Annie's birthday. So there!'

Julia chuckled and slid her arms about his neck, and they were lost in each other, their lips touching with great pleasure.

'I love you, Matt,' she whispered after an age, and he held her close to him.

'Aye, and I love you, too, Julia,' he replied.

★ ★ ★

Alice and Edward on Christmas morning were a joy to behold when they were found, in their dressing-gowns, sitting under the Christmas tree surrounded by their presents. Sophie was cross at first, because she thought for a moment Julia might be. When she realized that Julia was simply enchanted by their excitement, she sat herself down in an armchair and watched them.

Sophie was wrapped in her dressing-gown, and shivering, despite the fact that the fire had stayed in all night and the drawing-room was not that cold, and she was ghostly pale — but Christmas morning was not the time to ask awkward questions, so Julia carefully ignored it.

Annie and Matt came in from the morning chores, full of good wishes from the Land Girls and the other farms. Matt brought in logs for the fire, and Alice and Edward were finally bullied into bathing and dressing.

Julia was just putting the finishing touches to the lunch table when Gladys arrived, carrying a cake tin and fresh from supervising a splendid Christmas lunch for the patients in the dower. As she greeted Julia she was grinning all over her face, and it was obviously not just Christmas that had made her so happy this morning.

'What?' Julia demanded, staring at her. 'You look just like all your Christmases have come at once. What's happened?'

'Jed an' Jethro's comin' 'ome tomorrow,' Gladys replied with a light in her eyes that no one had seen for a very long time. 'They'm got ten days leave, an' they rang us this mornin', early. Annie, your brothers is goin' to be at your engagement party!'

Annie went dashing off to tell Patrick and, for a moment, Julia and Gladys gazed after her lovingly, then together they went to the

French windows in the drawing-room and stood looking out at the wintry day. It was cold, but bright, and the cedar tree bobbed its great branches in the breeze.

Beautiful Tremar; the enchanted place.

'Do you remember Christmas when we were small?' Julia whispered with a faint longing in her voice. 'When we all wriggled and fidgeted in church because we wanted to be away to our presents, but stopped fidgeting when we sang 'Away in a Manger' and 'Once in Royal David's City' because we liked them so much? We had brothers then, too, Gladys.'

Gladys smiled sadly.

'I'd like to think Annie might still 'ave 'er brothers when all this is over,' she replied. 'I don't let meself dream too much, 'cos it's painful, but dear God, my boys *earned* Rectory Farm when they was kiddies, 'aving to work so bleddy 'ard 'cos Arthur was al'ys drunk. It'll not be fair if thanks to Hitler they dies afore they gets it.'

Julia stared out of the window, and with a complicated mixture of pleasure and great pain, she let her memories roll in unchecked.

'Please God, Gladys,' she whispered eventually. 'Please, God.'

The engagement party was a truly splendid affair, to which pretty well everyone on the estate came at some point during the evening. Land Girls, patients, doctors, nurses and tenants: sometimes the drawing-room was packed! And throughout it all Mrs Collins marshalled her girls from the manor, and Gladys's girls from the dower, like a sergeant-major so that food and drink arrived, and empty plates and glasses left, quite seamlessly.

And war-time it might have been, but here there was a sufficiency of everything.

There was dancing, there were games and a lot of singing of popular songs, and all the time Julia watched the beautiful Annie and couldn't believe that the little girl she had inherited only three years ago was suddenly a woman.

Minnie fell asleep quite early during the proceedings, but Annie looked as if she would never sleep again. She glowed, sparkled like a diamond, and she wore Patrick's ring with such pride. To see her with her brothers was very touching, for they were inherently nice boys who had never enjoyed their little sister's suffering and were not remotely envious of the luck which had fallen into her lap since the return of the 'mad woman from Blackridge'.

To see her with Patrick was heart-warming. Julia knew just by looking at them that whatever her fears might have been, and might still be for that matter, their love for each other was honest and generous. In this depth of winter, and depth of war, when no one could get what they wanted and most people were weary of looking for an ending that never seemed to come any closer, this was a bright moment; an unexpected day of sunshine amid a week of rain.

At last, when the party broke up and the last diehards finally went on their way, Annie stood before Matt and Julia in the wreckage of the drawing-room and looked as if she might burst with happiness.

'I ent never 'ad such a wonderful time in all my life!' she declared, and then flung herself into their arms, kissing and hugging them frantically.

A moment later she floated away up the stairs to bed, and as they were switching out the lights they heard her singing joyously on the landing.

'Well, I'll no get anything out of *her* tomorrow,' Matt declared, glaring up the dark staircase towards the music. 'She'll be fit for nothing; you see if she's not. In fact, I might as well give her the day off now and have done wi' it!'

Julia chuckled at him warmly.

'Old grouch,' she retorted and then added,

kissing him, '*lovely* old grouch!'

Sleep completely eluded her as the manor sank into the silence of night. She thought about the evening, turning the events over and over in her mind, thinking about being right on the brink of another year. There would be the wedding at some point, of course, but what else, she wondered? How much more suffering for Oliver and Sophie before they resolved their differences? How much sorrow at losing Guy, who would certainly be going home in the new year?

After more than half an hour, with Matt sleeping peacefully beside her, she slid very quietly from the bed and padded along the almost dark landing to a normally empty bedroom. Tonight Ilona Vincent slept in it, and, unlike Julia, she was fathoms deep in a lake of dreams.

As Julia softly pushed the door open she awoke immediately, as was her way when there was the slightest noise, and reached out to switch on the bedside lamp. The two women blinked at each other in the sudden light, and Julia noted with a slight shock that Ilona's long hair, brushed out of its tight bun at night, was grey as it hung about her shoulders. Beneath it, the rather sharp little face, which belied the gentle woman within, was free of any make-up and growing old.

She looked vulnerable, shaken roughly from sleep, and Julia loved her.

'What is it?' she gasped. 'Has something happened to Minnie?'

Julia crept in and sat on the bed, feeling guilty.

'No! I'm sorry,' she mumbled, 'I just wanted to talk. Oh God, I'm ever so sorry. I'll go.'

'Oh, don't be ridiculous,' Ilona replied. 'I'm awake now and happy to talk. So what do you want to talk about?'

'All of it,' Julia admitted, gazing at the beautifully appointed bedroom with its rich, dark furniture and long velvet curtains, at the huge bed and gilt mirror above the mantelpiece. 'If it hadn't been for you,' she whispered, 'Minnie would be dead by now, Tremar would belong to someone else, Annie would have been bundled away to Falmouth to be a kitchen maid and would be involved in some sort of very menial war work by now no doubt, and I would have been entirely forgotten, by everyone.'

Ilona Vincent smiled gently.

'And that's keeping you awake?' she asked.

Julia glanced at her sheepishly.

'Well no, not exactly,' she answered. 'But sometimes I fear I'm way out of my depth with all this. Not for a moment do I believe

Lady Thornby is going to accept this engagement without putting up a fight. Guy showed me the letters Patrick has written to his mother and his so-called fiancée, and whilst I have to admit they're charming, thoughtfully written and gentle — well, at least the one to Miss Baines-Morton is anyway — I just don't believe it's over. Am I strong enough to fight their battles for them if I have to, Ilona, or am I just kidding myself?'

Miss Vincent uttered a low chuckle and lay back on her pillows.

'You know, in the convalescent home you're known as the tigress,' she observed with a little twinkle in her eyes. 'I'm told even Matron doesn't frighten them as much as you do, when Annie's involved. Yes, when you came home from Blackridge in 1938 you were foolish with Dr Crompton; it's true, but for heaven's sake, you'd been deprived of every sort of human right for over twenty-three years! Frankly your dalliance with the doctor was mild in comparison to what you *might* have done. You've adjusted to real life magnificently if you really want to know, and I see you having no problem whatsoever fending off Patrick's awful family if you have to.'

She reached out a small hand and touched Julia's arm, and in some strange way her white flannelette nightgown, buttoned tightly at the neck and the wrists, was comfortingly no-nonsense. Julia thought for the umpteenth time how fortunate she had been that this sometimes sharp-tongued, sometimes blunt, but always compassionate woman had chosen to take the position she had at Blackridge.

'There is,' Miss Vincent suddenly added, 'one more thing I should like to talk to you about, Julia, my dear, since you're here. I would have spoken to you before I left in the morning, but now seems like a good time. Little Sophie isn't very well, but no doubt you've noticed that. Anyway, whatever is the matter with her, and I have my suspicions, Dr Crompton acknowledged it in the middle of the party this evening. I saw him look at her and their eyes met. I saw great fear pass across her face and I saw an emotion I can only describe as furious despair pass across his. I watched them after that and they never spoke to each other once. Dr Crompton danced with his pretty daughter and played a couple of games with his little boy, and at the end of the evening he spoke to them privately, but I didn't hear what he said. Whatever it was, however, they went to bed looking like a couple of frightened rabbits.'

Julia looked greatly alarmed.

'What do you think he said to them?' she

asked and Miss Vincent pursed her lips.

'I shouldn't be surprised if he told them he was planning to take them away with him,' she replied quietly. 'I fear that Dr Crompton has formed an idea in his tortured mind that he can get his own back on the world. He wants to hurt his wife and he loathes your husband with an unhealthy passion. By using his children as pawns he plans to win himself a victory — and the real sufferers will be those two young things who deserve less than anyone to be hurt. I may be wrong, of course, but I don't think I am.'

She wasn't.

In the darkness of their bedroom, Alice and Edward slept, for the excitement of the party had exhausted them. But they slept in the same bed, wrapped in each other's arms, and they had gone to bed in an agony of uncertainty.

Oliver had been cruelly vague when he had spoken to them; he had told them just enough to scare them half to death. He had said they would *probably* be leaving before the end of January, and *probably* be going back to Arundel, but he hadn't said their mother would be coming with them, in fact he'd rather suggested she might not, and both Edward and Alice knew that their mother would rather die than go back to Arundel.

In the darkness before they had fallen asleep, Alice had wept, and Edward, who got angry rather than tearful, had boiled with indignant rage and railed against his father. In the end, warm and sleepy and comforted by each other, they had made tentative plans to run away.

They had talked about living in the woods and stealing food — they knew enough of Annie's background to know that she had survived her childhood by stealing food. But not having experienced it they had no concept at all of what Annie had suffered, of the biting cold and the pain of starvation. They knew nothing of the fear of being locked out on freezing nights and of digging into piles of straw in the barn to keep from dying of cold.

And they had none of the skills required to do it.

They knew only that in one short conversation with their father, their Christmas had been ruined.

12

Just as Ilona Vincent had been right about the Cromptons, Julia had been quite right about Patrick's family. In the self-absorbed life that Lady Thornby lived, she made the rules and her family were expected to obey them, and when they didn't, revenge was swift.

When she had made the arrangements for Patrick to marry Mona Baines-Morton, she had thought it was almost certainly going to be the easiest one to engineer. Patrick had always been compliant, because he had spent his life struggling to please, but he could never have pleased his mother, however hard he tried. The one way he might have earned at least some gratitude from her would have been to have died a hero, and he hadn't even been able to do that properly. Now she had no desire to see him, blind and disfigured, and worried about him only in as far as what he might be doing — to cause her problems — now he was beyond her control.

She was about to find out.

His letter arrived on the table at breakfast time on New Year's Day and sat on top of a neat pile of other letters, the first to come to hand. Robert Thornby was away on business, so only his wife and his two sisters were at the breakfast table with Lady Thornby, and they were all familiar with Guy's rather distinctive handwriting.

They were familiar with their mother's reaction to letters from Patrick as well, but they were in no way prepared for this one.

She picked up the envelope, sliced the flap neatly and took out the letter. As Susan and Cecily chatted over their eggs and bacon, and Kate found herself for the most part ignored, Lady Thornby read the letter . . . and very slowly her never very colourful face became white with anger. Her family weren't watching her, they were busy amongst themselves, and their attention was grabbed only by the sound of paper being scrunched furiously in her hand.

She spat, 'How *dare* he?' Her hands shook with rage, and her daughters stopped their conversation and stared at her.

'What is it, Mother?' Cecily asked. 'What on earth has Patrick done now?'

Lady Thornby's fine nostrils flared and her once beautiful, but now ageing face looked as if it had been cut from stone. In the cold, blue-and-white Adam dining-room of Chawston Hall, its chatelaine was a Fury, simmering on the edge of control.

'Your brother,' she hissed, 'informs me that he has become engaged to be married. He has written to Mona, breaking off their understanding, and is planning to marry the heir to Tremar instead. He says that he and Miss Paynter have enjoyed a romance for some months now and that on her eighteenth birthday they celebrated their engagement with a party. They plan to get married in the local village in June, and we are all invited to the wedding.' She shot a look at Kate, narrowing her eyes to thin slits. 'And now tell me you and Robert didn't know anything about this,' she snarled.

Kate gazed at her steadily.

'Nothing,' she replied. She had become an accomplished liar in the years she had been a Thornby. 'He never said anything to Robert when he was in hospital, I'm sure.'

Susan, the younger of Robert's sisters and marginally the better looking of the two, suddenly put down her knife and fork and knitted her brows thoughtfully. She was an unimaginative woman and running to fat after two children, but she had a gift for spite, which attracted her swiftly to others of her ilk. She and her husband, Jack, had been notables among the smart set, before the war.

'Miss Paynter, the heir to Tremar?' she said. 'That would be Annie Paynter, I suppose. Yes, it must be. Good God, *Annie Paynter!*' She glanced at her sister, with a spiteful gleam in her eyes. 'Annie Paynter, *what* a bloody turn up for the books!'

'What?' Lady Thornby demanded. 'What do you know about Annie Paynter?'

Kate Thornby went quietly back to her breakfast as she waited for the cruel assassination of this girl who had written so beautifully to Robert. There were times when she actively hated her sisters-in-law, and now was one of them.

'Remember I told you about the Markhams?' Susan asked of her sister and her mother. 'We met them in Singapore in '37? Well, as it happens they have a daughter, Charlotte, who goes to school at St Margaret's Academy in Bodmin. Lives with her grandparents somewhere near Falmouth during holiday times, I gather. Anyway, Lottie must be coming up to eighteen now, and I remember her telling Jack and me, just before the war started, that Annie Paynter had arrived at St Margaret's after Christmas in '39. She was absolutely appalled by the girl; I mean completely overtaken by her awfulness. She said you couldn't understand a *single* word she said, and apparently she was nicknamed 'The Milkmaid' because the other girls said even if you scrubbed her with carbolic soap, she still

322

reeked of the cowshed! Positively frightful, and totally despised by everyone in the place. She only stayed a couple of terms, then vanished off the scene, much to everyone's relief!'

Lady Thornby sneered unpleasantly.

'And this is what your brother wants to marry?' she whispered. 'Dear God in Heaven!'

Kate sipped her tea and thought of Robert telling her of Patrick's adoration as he spoke of Annie, of the hope and delight in his voice. She knew she had to creep away and ring her husband as soon as she could, but first some indication of what her mother-in-law planned to do would be good.

'I suppose that's what half a lifetime in an asylum does for you,' Cecily observed as she poured herself another cup of tea. 'Julia Logan, I mean. Why else would she have willed Tremar to an oik? She's married to one, too, so I'm told; some bushy-haired Scottish gamekeeper. God, Tremar must be an awful place, it really must.'

'And Robert wouldn't allow me to take Patrick away when I wanted to,' Lady Thornby replied coldly, throwing Kate a significant look. 'None of this would have happened if he hadn't interfered. And now *I'm* left to sort out the mess.'

'So what do you plan to do, Mother?' Susan enquired, looking — Kate thought in disgust — as if she couldn't wait. 'Are you going to send Barrington down to fetch him? Might be better if you went yourself, perhaps. After all, they can't refuse to hand him over to you, but they could refuse to hand him over to the chauffeur.'

Not a word, Kate noticed, about Patrick's rights. He was twenty-six years old, way beyond the age of consent. He was a fighter-pilot, a hero, and neither his mother nor the family chauffeur had any right to be interfering in his life at all.

She waited with interest to see what Lady Thornby would say, and in the end was faintly surprised by her mother-in-law's reaction. But Lady Thornby was viewing this situation from a standpoint none of the girls knew anything about, and her chance to once and for all bury her awful secret loomed large on her horizon.

This could be just what she had been waiting for. With any luck, Patrick could be humiliated, abandoned and forgotten about, and when the time came no one would ever ask any awkward questions.

'No,' she said slowly and apparently with great thought. 'I'm not sending anyone anywhere at the moment. I have another idea entirely. I think perhaps we need to employ legal means in this situation. I have no wish to be humiliated at Tremar, and no intention of submitting Barrington to such a fate. One doesn't treat one's servants in such a fashion — not if one expects any loyalty from them.'

Loyalty! Kate thought sourly as she watched her mother-in-law pat her lips with her napkin, throw it on to her empty plate and rise to leave the room. You wouldn't recognize loyalty if it rose up and hit you in the face.

Half an hour later, in his Whitehall office, Robert Thornby listened to his wife's voice over the phone and tried to estimate his pile of work at the same time.

'Oh Lord, darling,' he said. 'I'm so sorry. And I'm about to be even sorrier, too, because I'm going to ask you to do something I know you hate doing. But it's the only way, I'm afraid.'

Kate sat in her drawing-room and looked out at Chawston's great park, frosted and glittering in cold sunshine, and she longed for London. She was a city girl, born and bred, and this particularly cold corner of the country bored her witless. She knew that one day Chawston would be her permanent home, that one day she would be its châtelaine, but she had already promised herself years ago that things would change a great deal once she was.

'You want me to listen at doors, I suppose,' she muttered wearily. 'All right, but I wouldn't do it for anyone but Patrick, Robert, and that's a fact!'

Robert chuckled, and the sound made her feel strangely warm and yet terribly lonely at the same time.

'And if you could telephone me back before four this afternoon, my most precious darling,' he said, 'I would be so grateful.'

★ ★ ★

She phoned him back at three, enormously pleased to speak to him and drop the ball firmly in his court. She had done her share, and hated it. She had spent all day hovering where she couldn't be seen but could hear what was happening; and as her mother-in-law never closed doors when she was on the telephone, her greatest fear had been running into Cecily or Susan at an inopportune moment.

She knew exactly what Lady Thornby was planning for Patrick now, and she was furious. But she hadn't failed to notice that as her mother-in-law carefully made her plans and dictated her wishes, Lord Thornby had been mentioned often enough, but apparently not informed of her intentions.

'Robert, she's making arrangements to disinherit your little brother and basically erase him from the family,' she said disgustedly to her husband over the phone, 'unless he agrees to do precisely as she says. In other words, in front of Miss Paynter and Mrs Logan she's going to wipe the damn floor with him!'

At the other end of the line there was an astonished silence for a few seconds, then Robert Thornby echoed, '*Disinherit* him? What's the point of that? He's marrying the heir to Tremar, so any paltry offering he might have received from the Chawston fortune won't mean a thing. In fact, I'm given to understand that Tremar is a very wealthy estate.'

'Well, that's what she's doing,' Kate assured him. 'I heard her speaking to a firm of solicitors in Bodmin, dictating a letter that must be read out loud to him, setting out precisely her instructions It's really nasty, Robert. She says unless he returns home immediately and does as he's told, not only will he be disinherited, but he will no longer be acknowledged as a Thornby. No one from the family will attend the wedding, the marriage will not be recognized, and if for any reason it should fail, he will not be permitted to return to Chawston.'

In his drearily painted cream-and-brown Whitehall office, with its bomb-damaged ceiling and its brown paper taped across the windows, Robert gazed out across battered rooftops as in his mind he skipped through his childhood memories.

'There's something wrong with all of this,' he said at last. 'I smell a rat, Kate, and that marble monument of a mother of mine is going to get away with it, if I don't find out the truth. I need to talk to Pa.'

From her window Kate Thornby watched their two sons coming back from Home Farm. Goodness knows what they'd been doing, but they were incredibly dirty. Another excuse for her mother-in-law to moan, no doubt.

'Then you'd better hurry,' she replied, reaching for her cigarettes, 'because it won't be more than a day or two before Patrick gets a visit from a solicitor at Tremar.'

Robert made a quick, firm decision.

'You're quite right,' he agreed. 'It must be sooner rather than later. Look, darling, I'm leaving now and I'll drive straight home. I'll be very late arriving, but that'll be so much the better because I'd rather talk to Pa without Mother knowing I'm at Chawston at all. Can you wait up for me, do you think?'

'Of course I can,' Kate promised and heard the door in the corridor swing open as the boys, quarrelling cheerfully, came banging into the apartments. 'Oh Lord,' she sighed wearily. 'If the boys came up the white staircase in the state they're in, I'll probably still be getting my telling off by the time you arrive home!'

Robert Thornby laughed indulgently as he shrugged his shoulders at his cluttered desk, broke the telephone connection with his wife and collected his hat and coat from the stand beside his office door. It would take him hours to drive home to Chawston in the dark, and then it would be morning before he could speak to his father. So it would probably be twenty-four hours or more before he could do anything to lessen the impact of his mother's actions.

But it didn't matter as it happened.

Lady Thornby had arranged to do business with the oldest and most reputable firm of solicitors in Bodmin, and Mr Cruikshank, of Cruikshank and Scattergood had unemotionally taken down on paper the exact words she had dictated to him over the phone, assuring her politely that he would carry out her wishes precisely. Mr Cruikshank, however, had been at Annie and Patrick's engagement party, Julia Logan was his most valued client; and he had no intention of invading the happiness of the young couple at Tremar without first giving them some days to enjoy it.

He had given Lady Thornby's instructions to his secretary to type up for him, but he had told her that there was no hurry for it. No hurry at all.

★   ★   ★

The following morning, when snow was floating in the air around Chawston Hall, the skies were grey and the cold of the house was abysmal, Robert Thornby wound his way through rooms he barely saw from one year to the next, and finally let himself into the first of the great hothouses that sprawled along the back of the building.

The damp heat hit him like a wet blanket.

He began picking his way through the great variety of potted plants that were like a jungle in this extraordinary hot, wet place, and finally came upon Sykes, Lord Thornby's long-time devoted servant, who was entirely responsible for banking up the stoves and regulating the heat in this fantasy world of rare and exotic plants. He, like Lord Thornby, cared not a jot for Government appeals to conserve fuel in these hard times. In fact, like his master, he was probably only vaguely aware of the war at all. The little cast iron stoves, dotted about amongst the vast acreage of glass, were bouncing with heat, and he was levering off red-hot lids and dropping in logs.

'Master Robert!' he exclaimed in his Bristol accent, which hadn't lessened the smallest amount in all the years he had lived at Chawston. 'We don't often see you in 'ere. Your father's in the propagation room, if you'm looking for 'im.'

Robert thanked him and ploughed on through the humidity, already aware of his shirt sticking to his back, and finally there was his father, in an old shirt, loose trousers and a worn-out cardigan, gazing with total adoration at a formidable bloom, stood alone on a long trestle table and glorious in its isolation. Robert stared at it, too, and although he was ashamed to say he didn't even know the species, the vibrant red blossom, sharp against the iron-grey of winter beyond the glass, was indeed remarkable.

'My word, Pa . . . ' he whispered, and Lord Thornby turned and blinked at his son with pale, vague eyes that gleamed with pride.

Robert regarded him and felt a deep affection in his heart. He was old, vulnerable and scruffy, and his son loved him dearly.

'Good, eh?' he exclaimed. 'I'm going to win an award with this one, me boy, and all me own work, too. Just look at her; ever seen anything so beautiful?'

'No, never,' Robert replied seriously. 'You are very talented, Pa.'

Lord Thornby turned back to his bloom, and appeared to forget about his son for some moments as he turned it this way and that, touching perfect red petals with delicate fingers. Then his head jerked up and he spun round on his heels.

'Robert!' he cried brightly, as if he had only just recognized his visitor. 'Don't see you in here very often. Welcome, dear boy. What can I do for you?'

Robert drew in a long, deep breath as he honestly wondered if Lord Thornby was actually going to be of any help whatsoever.

Finally he replied, 'I'd like to talk to you about Patrick, Pa.' At once, something in the vague blue eyes that perused him seemed to close down; almost like window shutters.

Gerald Thornby shook his head.

'Domestic issues are y'mother's domain, son,' he observed. 'Always have been. Better that way, you understand. Don't interfere, never have done.'

Robert put his hand on his father's arm in

332

a gentle gesture of affection and with the faint hope of drawing him back on to the subject.

'It isn't a domestic issue, Pa,' he said slowly. 'It's Patrick. I need to talk to you about him, *really* talk to you. I need you to tell me about him, you understand?'

For a moment he thought he saw a dreadful betrayal in his father's eyes and he seemed to glance at his prize blossom as if it had in some way lost its lustre. Then he turned his back on it and gazed around his impressive domain, this place of which he was lord and master, and for the most part free of his awful family.

'Ah . . . Patrick,' he muttered, and Robert knew he had been right to do this.

★ ★ ★

It was on the morning of 5 January, cruelly cold and with a spiteful wind hooting in the chimneys, that Julia received a surprise visitor at Tremar. She was just in the throes of helping Minnie with a warm drink when Mrs Collins bustled into the room

'Mr Cruikshank from Cruikshank and Scattergood 'as called to see you, madam,' she announced proudly, and Julia brightened at once.

'Oh lovely,' she replied. 'How nice! Show

him in, Mrs Collins if you would, please, and then make us some coffee, will you? Whatever that stuff is that passes for coffee these days, anyway.'

As always, her housekeeper wore a black dress with a sparkling white apron across her ample bosom, a sort of self-imposed uniform, and Julia was suddenly impressed that, even with the difficulties of wartime, Mrs Collins never looked any different. Evidently she was a highly disciplined woman.

Mrs Collins, the no-nonsense, often bluntly outspoken housekeeper who had once said Annie Paynter was a thief — and now thought the sun rose and set over her. Mrs Collins, whom once Julia had thoroughly disliked and now looked upon as a dear friend, without whom she would never manage.

She went away in a rustle of starched garments, and a moment later the tall, thin, quaintly Victorian Mr Cruikshank was shown into the drawing-room.

He went straight away and spoke gently to Minnie, finding a sweet for her in his pocket. Julia watched him in great admiration, aware that she liked him quite disproportionately for a mere family solicitor, and remembering, as she always did, that he had been the person who had sent Matt to her door in the

334

beginning. They exchanged small talk for a few moments as he thanked her for the lovely party and she asked about his elderly father, then Mrs Collins brought the coffee and Mr Cruikshank sat down.

'So, what can I do for you?' Julia asked, pouring the coffee and watching Minnie snoring softly. 'We don't see each other in months, and then it's twice in less than a fortnight. This is a rare treat and no mistake.'

He glanced up at her quickly, and then away again. He was like an intelligent bird, she thought; watching and waiting. With great care he moved his coffee cup and spread some papers out on the table in front of him, then he coughed and looked up again.

'I'm very sorry, Mrs Logan, but this is extremely embarrassing and you're not going to like it, I'm afraid,' he began, and then immediately corrected himself. 'I mean, there are two reasons I've called, as it happens, and one of them you're not going to like. On 1 January, I had a phonecall from one Lady Thornby of Chawston Hall, mother of the charming Patrick. Of course, she doesn't know I'm your family solicitor, and I certainly didn't advise her of the fact, but I'm greatly distressed to say that she has asked me to draw up an official letter, which I am to read to him out loud. It advises him that unless he

335

agrees to break off all contact with young Annie, leave Tremar immediately and go straight away to Ireland to fulfil his obligations to Miss Mona Baines-Morton, he will not only be disinherited, but no longer acknowledged as a Thornby.'

Julia stared at him and her brown furrowed in alarm.

'*What*?' she whispered after a moment. 'Dear God! Well, you've got to hand it to her, she's certainly built of ruthless stuff, isn't she? Her son is a blind, disfigured war-hero, and she plans to cast him out like a black sheep. *What* a monster!'

Mr Cruikshank pushed his spectacles up his nose and peered benignly across the table at his client.

'From a purely monetary point of view, it couldn't matter less,' he observed. 'The Tremar fortune is quite sufficient to support Annie and her husband, and she *is* your sole heir. However, I am obliged to read the letter to him, I'm afraid, and you and Annie are to be present when I do, to give, as she put it on the telephone, *him* a chance to come to his senses, and you and Miss Paynter a firm understanding of the fact that he is not going to be your way into the Chawston fortune. In other words, she wants you standing there like naughty children while she casts out her

336

son . . . ' he paused and then looked over the top of his glasses. 'Painful memories for you, I fear — which seems to indicate that the woman has done her homework!'

Julia chuckled.

'Into my background, certainly,' she replied, 'but not into my nature if she thinks it's going to matter a jot to me. Ah well, I'll get Mrs Collins to find Patrick and send someone out for Annie. Might as well get it out of the way, I suppose. In the meantime you can tell me the other reason for your visit.'

Mrs Collins was outraged when Julia told her why Patrick and Annie were needed. She muttered to herself furiously, banging out of the room as if it was Julia or Mr Cruikshank who had personally slighted those in her care, and when she had gone Julia smiled in amusement.

'I love her so much,' she stated fondly. 'Her loyalty is way above and beyond the call of duty. I bet she's down in the kitchens even now yelling at the girls as if it's their fault.' She suddenly paused and glanced quickly at Mr Cruikshank. 'If I'm honest,' she said, 'she was the only good thing Oliver Crompton ever did for me — apart from coming to see me at Blackridge in the first place. I wish I could deal with his problems as easily.'

Mr Cruikshank raised his eyebrows. He was a very careful man, had been brought up to be, and the rule of any solicitor was never to say anything that might be used in evidence, so he always thought carefully about the words that came out of his mouth.

After a moment he said, 'Certainly I have to say I didn't feel Dr. Crompton was as happy as he might have been when I saw him at the party, that's true, but then it must be very difficult for him to adjust to his injuries. A doctor, robbed of his profession — it's very disheartening.' Then he smiled. 'How extremely lucky for him, though, to have come here to Tremar to convalesce. Surely being amongst friends is a great bonus?'

Oh, if only *that* were true! Julia thought wryly, and smiled.

'One would think so, certainly,' she replied non-committally. 'And now, Mr Cruikshank, let's have your other reason for coming to see me, before Annie and Patrick arrive.'

'Ah yes, the other reason,' he said, bobbing his head at her as he prepared to pass on formal news. 'Right then, whether you're going to be pleased or not, I can't say,' he informed her in his dustiest, most professional tone, 'but I am obliged to inform you that after all the necessary searches have been done, it transpires that the village shop on the corner of The Green and Pinch Street, formerly the property of Miss Fanny Penrose, is now your property. Or, to be exact, the property of the Tremar estate. It therefore falls to you, I'm afraid, to draw up instructions for its welfare, which must, I fear, be done sooner rather than later.'

Julia stared at him in stunned silence; it was the very last thing she had expected. She had begun to wonder, certainly, with Mrs Dawkins still serving behind the counter and no one apparently interested in the place, but this was incredible.

'Miss Penrose left the shop to *me*?' she asked eventually. 'Why?'

'Oh no, she didn't *leave* it to you, Mrs Logan,' Mr Cruikshank answered. 'You inherit it by default so to speak, and I was rather hoping that when you and Annie and poor young Patrick have finished with this silly business, you would accompany me down to the village for a meeting with Mr and Mrs Dawkins, and a look at the property. Do you think you would be able to do that today?'

Julia shrugged, still reeling from the news.

'Yes, certainly,' she replied. 'I'd be happy to, but ... ' Before she could finish, the drawing-room door opened admitting Patrick, who looked oddly nervous. She put the shop out of her head for a while.

As he was invited to sit down, he said in a slightly shaky voice, 'Mrs Collins is in a foul temper, isn't she? Have I done something unforgivable?'

Julia felt her heart wrench in her breast and at that moment she thought she would have liked nothing more in the world than to give Lady Thornby a piece of her mind.

'You've done nothing wrong at all, Patrick,' she replied firmly. 'Mr Cruikshank is here on your mother's behalf, I'm greatly sorry to say, but that doesn't mean anything either, and once we get it out of the way we need never talk about it again.'

She saw him press his lips together hard and knew he was frightened.

'I'm not leaving!' he declared firmly. 'If that's what she wants, the answer is no.'

'It is, I'm afraid,' Mr Cruikshank said. 'That's exactly what she wants. I'm here to read you a letter formally advising you that unless you instantly obey her orders, you are disinherited — amongst other things. However, you and Annie are never going to go short, I can assure you, so if you have no desire to return to Chawston — and I can conceive of no reason why you should have, you have no need to worry.'

Julia saw the hurt on Patrick's sensitive,

scarred face. She saw the cruel betrayal, and she knew precisely how he felt. Either Lady Thornby had done her homework extremely well and knew exactly how this moment would feel, or else she had struck lucky, but either way she had failed if she thought it would change anybody's mind.

'It couldn't matter less, Patrick,' she whispered, watching as his eyes filled with tears. 'Remember what happened to me, and look at me now. Just tell yourself that it takes more than cruel parents to destroy the likes of us. It certainly takes a lot more than that to put the likes of Annie down, I promise you.'

'But it means I'll be a dependant,' he replied miserably. 'A charity case living off a fortune I can't in any way contribute to.'

'Oh no, it doesn't,' she assured him firmly. 'Unless that's how you see Matt. Once you and Annie are married, you *will* be contributing to Tremar, just like everyone else does, you know that, we've already talked about it. So please, don't let that worry you.'

Patrick lowered his eyes and it seemed to Julia and the poker-backed Mr Cruikshank that he suddenly slumped in defeat, as if his pain ran much deeper than his mother's actions, as if the betrayal was closer to his heart somehow.

'I'm surprised I haven't heard from

Robert,' he said dully. 'I wonder if he knows? Maybe he'll write and . . . He was so happy for me, you know, when I was in hospital.'

Or maybe he couldn't care any more than the rest of your bloody family, Julia thought bitterly.

The reading of the letter might have been unpleasant but for Mr Cruikshank, who read it so fast and so matter-of-factly that it sounded like no more than a laundry list. As instructed, Annie, Julia and — at Mr Cruikshank's request — Mrs Collins were present in the room when Patrick heard that he was no longer to be acknowledged as a Thornby and would be cut off without a penny. Dimly, and briefly, as Mr Cruikshank was droning on, Patrick wondered about what his mother was doing and felt faintly surprised that it was the best she could come up with. In his heart he had expected much worse, but he didn't go into it deeply and obediently nodded his full understanding when it was over.

'An' it don't matter a scrap, young man!' Mrs Collins declared ferociously, giving him a firm kiss on his cheek. ''Cos you'm *family* 'ere; you'm loved an' wanted, an' your mother don't deserve lovin' children if she treats them like this!'

'I couldn't agree more,' Julia said with a

smile, and then the three adults watched as Annie pressed her lips to Patrick's, holding him tightly in her arms.

'You'm all mine now,' she observed. 'So I 'ope you ent goin' to change your mind, 'cos I'm not lettin' you go if you do!'

'Oh, I'm not changing my mind, my darling,' he replied, cupping her face in his hands and kissing her again. 'And I don't give a damn about my bloody mother, or the money, either.'

But though he might not have cared about the money, he *did* care about his mother, the hurt on his face said so painfully.

13

Julia was glad of a lift to the village shop in Mr Cruikshank's enormous black car once the gloomy business of Patrick's inheritance had been dealt with, for it was a wickedly cold morning with the remains of last autumn's leaves blowing about the drive and skeletal trees rubbing their bare branches together making tuneless music. She would not have chosen such a day to wander down into the village on her own; in fact, given the chance she would have lurked by the fire all day, and so she was surprised when, halfway down the lane, they saw someone walking ahead of them with a rather ungainly gait.

'It's Dr Crompton,' Mr Cruikshank said cheerfully, sliding to a gentle halt. 'How nice.' He wound down his window and stuck his head out. 'Good morning, Doctor! Are you going to the village? Hop in and we'll give you a ride.'

Oliver glanced into the back seat of the car and straightened up again swiftly.

'No, I don't think so, thanks,' he replied. 'I'm quite happy to walk.' But Julia was having none of it.

'Come on, get in, Oliver,' she said. 'It's absolutely freezing out there. Be grateful for the offer of a lift.'

He climbed into the worn leather seat beside her and the car slid smoothly on towards the village. Julia moved closer, so that she could touch the black silk glove on his mangled hand, and did not ask him why he did not wear a leather one over it, for it seemed likely that pulling one on and off would be too painful.

'Your hand must get cold in this weather,' she said gently. 'I imagine it aches a lot, doesn't it?'

He nodded.

'Very much, but I still like to get out each day. Besides, it's my turn to buy the cigarettes this morning. I was going to ask Guy to come with me, but he's working with his legs.'

'We're going to the shop,' Julia said. 'I have just, to my extreme amazement, discovered that it has become estate property since the death of the old girls, and Mr Cruikshank is going to tell me why in a minute. So why don't you come along with us and then we'll walk back together? Unless there are any awful family skeletons to be exposed, Mr Cruikshank?'

The solicitor chuckled, shaking his head. The road widened as they reached the green with the pub, bare of creeper at this time of year, the church, grey and weathered with age, and the familiar row of six showhouses along the edge, one of which, the one on the corner, was the village shop.

Julia grinned at Oliver.

'So, how do you fancy being a shopkeeper?' she asked and at once wished she hadn't.

His mouth tightened perceptibly.

'What, so that I can have the pleasure of serving my teacher wife every day?' he asked sarcastically. 'I don't think so, thanks, Julia. Four years ago I was the respected doctor in this village, if you remember. I'm not sure I want to be the cripple reduced to shop-keeping whilst his wife holds the position of responsibility instead.'

'I'm sorry . . . ' she whispered and she felt his body stiffen against her. It was as if he struggled all the time to build a wall around him with which to repel all comers and regularly reinforced it, to ensure they stayed out. She licked her lips and found them dry. 'No, of course not,' she murmured. 'I'm sorry, I wasn't thinking . . . '

Mr Cruikshank had parked, and Julia was glad, for it meant their conversation was obliged to finish, at least for the time being. Collecting her thoughts then, she looked up at the facia board above the shop door and shuddered. 'J. Penrose. Grocer and Purveyor of Quality Goods.' Unchanged in anyone's living memory and always carefully repainted in exactly the same way.

J. Penrose had been dead for years, and it had been much more than just a grocer's shop for a long time, too. J. Penrose had died before the 12th baronet of Tremar had incarcerated his daughter in the asylum, but Julia remembered him vaguely from her childhood. A florid, portly little man with a handlebar moustache, who had always worn a big white apron and a straw hat.

What, she wondered, had he made of his daughter Fanny and her friend Cecille? Had he understood that they weren't the sort of women who got married; was that why he had left her his shop? And where did Tremar fit into the story?

Only Mr Cruikshank was going to tell her that.

The harsh little bell jangled as she pushed open the door and she made a mental note to get rid of it as soon as possible. Whomever she found to run her little shop eventually, she was not going to be brought up short every time she came through the door as that nasty little metal bell stirred up a flood of memories.

'Good mornin', Mrs Logan,' said Mrs

Dawkins somewhat curtly from behind the counter. 'I see you 'as your solicitor with you. I do 'opes as 'ow you'll tell me what you decide, when you comes down.'

She opened the big wooden flap to let them all through and only just avoided banging it behind them. She was evidently expecting to be given her marching orders and Julia sensed waves of hostility washing from her.

With an idea of smoothing things down a bit, Julia gave her what she hoped was a friendly smile.

'Of course I will,' she replied. 'After all, you're an integral part of the shop, Mrs Dawkins.' She, Oliver and Mr Cruikshank then went through into the small dark hallway beyond the shop, with its flight of steep, very dark stairs.

Julia had never been upstairs before, in fact she had never been beyond the customer area of the shop, and it had never occurred to her that it was such a big building. In size it was equivalent to Lamplighter House and the other properties on the green. The show-piece dwellings of the village; a fact that Oliver recognized before she did and quietly remarked upon.

As they observed this inner sanctum, into which few, if any, of the villagers had ever been, Julia didn't think she had ever wondered how the old ladies had lived during their lifetime, but thought she hadn't imagined it would be in surroundings so depressingly old-fashioned, amid cream-and-brown paint and heavy Edwardian furniture. There were four big rooms and a kitchen upstairs, all extremely neat and tidy, but no bathroom or inside toilet. The ladies had evidently heated their water on the gas stove and washed with jugs and basins in their rooms, but been obliged to go down the dark staircase and out into the concrete yard to a privy to fulfil their other personal duties.

Downstairs, behind the shop, there was another kitchen, with a big porcelain sink, a wooden draining board, a copper, and a gas ring for boiling a kettle. The other rooms were used for storage — though they were pretty much empty now. Lamplighter House had been fairly well modernized in 1935, but this place had stood still in time.

Julia gazed in silence at the neatly made beds in the two bedrooms. For certain no one had disturbed the beds since the old ladies had died, and they would still carry the sheets they had slept in for the last time, before they went away to Plymouth for the weekend. One quick peep in the wardrobe in Miss Hewlett's room was enough to tell her that no one had moved any of their clothes, but then why should anyone have done so? There was no one to do it.

Tight-lipped and uncomfortable, Julia went back into the sitting-room, the windows of which looked out across the green, and saw that the only thing to have been thoroughly gone through was the Davenport which stood in the corner. Mr Cruikshank stood by it now.

'Miss Penrose,' he said, 'was a very neat woman; there was not a paper out of place. It's made my job a great deal easier, I'm pleased to say. Were they popular, Mrs Logan? You know, the heart of the village sort of thing?'

'*Popular?*' Julia cried, glancing at Oliver who actually grinned at her in reply. 'They were universally hated and feared, Mr Cruikshank. They were spiteful old spinsters who spread gossip with relish, no matter how untrue it might have been. And yet everyone came in here and told them everything; it was almost as if they felt obliged to. I think the only person who was absolutely truthful about their deaths is my housekeeper — and she said they died not a moment too soon. Mind you, Mrs Collins has got more courage than most!'

Mr Cruikshank chuckled and cast his gaze about the aggressively tidy room. Not for an instant could it be called cosy; it was big and over-furnished, but not remotely homely.

'I think I could tell that they weren't sweet old ladies by the awful neatness of the place,' he observed, looking quickly at the fireplace. 'Two last war bayonets, in a polished brass shell case, used for poking the fire. Grim. Right, shall we all sit down and I'll tell you how the Tremar estate comes to inherit the property? Mr J. Penrose, Christian name, Joseph, died in 1908; you might just remember him.'

Julia nodded. 'Oh I do, very well,' she replied. 'At least, I remember what he looked like. I've no idea what he was like as a person — but if his daughter was anything to go by . . . what can I say?'

Mr Cruikshank smiled broadly. He had a charming face with owl-like spectacles. Julia thought he would probably make a benign and gentle husband, but the thought of him courting a young lady was beyond her imagination!

'He certainly suited one member of your family,' he said. 'He was your grandfather's batman in the Boer War, which is how the Penrose family came by the shop. It would appear he did a first-class job, in fact one that was above and beyond the call of duty, and when they returned home your grandfather

351

made him a gift of the emporium and the building that housed it, in recognition of his services. The only entail that was stipulated at the time was that succeeding generations of Penroses might leave it to suitable family members, but they might not sell it on, and if there should come a time when there weren't any family members to inherit, or they didn't want it any more, it would go back to the estate.'

Julia bit her lip, she felt thoroughly uncomfortable. She hated allowing her imagination free rein over that shattered air-raid shelter in Plymouth, it conjured up such dreadful pictures.

'It was left to Miss Penrose's niece then?' she enquired, slightly shakily.

'And if the niece should fail to outlive her aunt, to the great-nephew,' he answered. 'However, of course, both the children died with their mother and her aunt. The only surviving member was Miss Penrose's sister, and she's dead now too. The niece's husband is still alive, but he doesn't come into the equation; he cannot inherit, I'm afraid. The premises are now officially part of the Tremar estate again.'

Julia stared at the cream-and-brown mottled carpet, noticing tiny burn marks around the edge of the grate where hot coals or logs had spat sparks over a succession of winters. She looked at the blackout curtains and the well-worn, dark suite of furniture, the small bow-fronted cabinet that held what she supposed to be family heirlooms — cups and saucers, little dishes, some glassware, a couple of rather dusty-looking dolls in foreign costume, and a hideous silver-plated tea-set — and her heart sank into her boots. It was she who would have to make decisions about all of this now, she who must toss it out if no one wanted it — and it had all been someone's treasures once.

'And so, what now?' she enquired.

Mr Cruikshank shrugged his shoulders.

'Of course, you could sell it, if you wanted to,' he replied. 'There are no restrictions on what you do with it, but I would advise you not to. You remember we had this discussion once before about selling off bits of the estate. If I were you I would find someone to run it for you, until after the war anyway, and then you and your husband could take some time to decide its future. I certainly get the impression there is a need for a shop in the village.'

She looked miserably about the room for a moment, suddenly aware of its coldness. A shiver crept across her back.

'Mr Cruikshank,' she asked uncomfortably,

'must I come down here and — you know — sort through their things? I truly cannot contemplate rooting about amongst their underwear drawers, or taking the sheets off the beds.'

Mr Cruikshank smiled. He had a very comforting smile; it always made her feel better, and it did that now.

'I'll arrange all of that,' he promised. 'Leave the keys with me and I'll have everything removed, and I promise to have it done sensitively. Nothing will be tossed down into the street, or anything awful like that. Perhaps if you just speak to Mrs Dawkins on the way out, then it can be forgotten about for a while, all right?'

She smiled at him gratefully and then they made their way down the dark staircase again and out into the shop. Mrs Dawkins, a forceful woman in her late sixties and evidently prepared for dismissal, drew her mouth into a thin line when she saw them and picked up the bunch of keys from the counter.

Julia approached her with extreme politeness, as she did with all the inhabitants of the village who remembered her as a child. They all knew why she had been sent to Blackridge, and they were all ready to condemn her if she so much as breathed improperly. It was a narrow path full of pitfalls she trod as owner of Tremar, but surprisingly enough her choice of husband had been a bonus, for Matt was extremely popular amongst the villagers. He was universally liked — except by the poachers.

'You'll be wantin' these back then, no doubt,' Mrs Dawkins snapped. 'I got 'em here for you to take, 'cept someone will have to lock up tonight.'

'Actually,' Julia replied diffidently, 'I was rather hoping I might persuade you to continue to run the shop for me, Mrs Dawkins. You're doing such a grand job, and you know all the suppliers and so forth. I thought we might put it on an official basis — unless of course you'd rather not.'

The butcher's wife looked faintly suspicious.

'Wot, you mean you'd pay me, an' that?' she enquired, as if she fully expected to be laughed at.

Julia nodded.

'I thought twenty-five shillings a week — unless that's not enough?'

She knew by the raised eyebrows on Mr Cruikshank's face that it was a great deal more than enough, but twenty-five shillings a week to ensure there were no worries seemed a fair price to pay.

Mrs Dawkins's face softened and took on a whole new expression. She beamed at Julia in delight.

'Well, I must say that's *right* generous, Mrs Logan,' she said proudly, 'an' I do be very 'appy to accept, 'cos I likes working 'ere very much as it happens. I shall do me best for you, I promise, though I think I should warn you that after the war me an' Mr Dawkins was thinking 'bout retiring — whenever that should be of course — so it'd not be a permanent thing, you understand. However, if you'm 'appy with that, well it'd suit us grandly.'

'If you can just give me a breathing space, I would be *most* grateful,' Julia replied, smiling at the woman warmly. 'And of course I shall cover all your expenses, right back from the Monday morning after Miss Penrose and Miss Hewlett . . . '

No one finished the sentence, no one could have done even if they'd wanted to.

Finally, at the door, she turned back once more.

'Mrs Dawkins,' she said, 'I believe you and your husband were quite friendly with Miss Penrose and Miss Hewlett. Upstairs in their sitting-room there are many of their treasures, in a glass-fronted cabinet. Perhaps in recognition of your kindness you would like to have them? It would be lovely to think they had found a home where they might be appreciated.'

Mrs Dawkins actually blushed and made Julia feel thoroughly guilty by thanking her as if she had been given the crown jewels, not a few odds and ends of china and silver-plate that Julia wouldn't have known what to do with. With a final, uncomfortable wave, she hurried outside on to the pavement.

'Was it all right to do that?' she asked her solicitor in some embarrassment. 'I — I mean, they weren't mine to give away, really, but . . .'

Mr Cruikshank smiled at her cheerfully. 'It was a lovely idea, Mrs Logan,' he assured her, 'and much kinder than piling them in boxes and sending them to a second-hand shop. Mr and Mrs Dawkins shall take whatever they would like.'

He offered her and Oliver a lift back to Tremar, which they politely refused, and so, with a charming farewell, he climbed into his big car and purred out of the village towards the main road to Bodmin.

'Such a nice man,' Julia observed, waving one last time at the disappearing car, and then starting across the green towards the church with Oliver. 'I consider myself very lucky to have him, both as a solicitor and as a friend, you know.'

He glanced at her cynically.

'I think I might have liked him better if he hadn't been the one who sent Matt to your door,' he replied, and saw her mouth tighten.

'Not again, Oliver,' she said wearily. 'No more, I beg of you. Why can't you understand that Matt is not the issue? He simply isn't. You didn't want what I wanted, you didn't want Tremar, and I would *never* have given up Tremar for you. If just once you could try to see it from my standpoint, I can't help thinking it might make you feel better.'

He saw her put her hand in the pocket of her coat and draw out a pale blue, heavy silk square, which she folded neatly into a triangle and tied around her head. It was a present he had given her back in her days in Truro, and he wondered if she remembered. Then she tugged on black leather gloves and glanced at him in the icy air.

'No more talk about what might have been, all right?' she said firmly. 'Now, I'm going into the church first and then into the graveyard, and after that back to Tremar. But if you bully me, I shall send you on your way, and that's a promise!'

He watched her as in the cold, grey church she dusted Alexander Drake's memorial,

358

touching it delicately, as if she thought she might wake him if she rubbed too hard. There were no flowers at this time of year, but she had woven him a wreath of holly and fir branches at Christmas time, and he would get the first snowdrops when they appeared, which would be quite soon now. The statue was ghostly white in the dim interior of the church, smooth and polished, and utterly serene. Oliver remembered old Miss Higgins laying her floral tribute upon it at Lady Florence Drake's funeral, and remembered, too, how he had loved Julia in those days.

The days before his love, his jealousy and the crumbling of his marriage had thrown his life into total disarray.

When Julia had finished in the church, she went outside and Oliver continued to watch her as she cleared away the winter rubbish from Miss Penrose and Miss Hewlett's grave. They would get some snowdrops, too, when they bloomed. When it was done she stood up and brushed the dirt from her hands, and a gust of icy wind moved the bare branches of the Albertine rose that grew against the wall of the Drake family mausoleum, causing them to scrape against the stone. Moles had been digging around the door, piling up the earth, which would prevent it from opening at the moment.

'Someone should dig that away,' Oliver commented.

Julia looked surprised.

'Why?' she asked. 'No one's ever going to need to open it again. I hope it rusts shut for all time. I'm not going in there, if that's what you were thinking. I'm going in a nice cosy grave with Matt and Minnie. Dear God, fancy spending eternity with my damn father. What a dreadful thought!'

She straightened the empty flower tub on the grave of the two old shopkeepers and then searched in her pockets for her gloves again, smiling brightly at Oliver.

'Right then,' she said briskly, 'all done.'

Oliver stared around the little churchyard for a moment. Many of the older tombstones were covered in ivy and some leaned at an odd angle. No one maintained Arthur Paynter's grave; it had had no Christmas offering, and in the summer it grew high with weeds — which were usually pulled out by the vicar, who felt it was his duty to do a little tidying when he could. Julia had given him a headstone, but nowhere upon it were the words 'beloved husband of . . . ' or beloved father of . . . ', and she had done it for the sake of the twins, not for Gladys or Annie.

'Tell me,' he asked as he watched her turn from the old ladies' grave, 'why do you tend the grave of two spiteful old spinsters when you never touch Arthur's or the Drake family tomb?'

Julia shrugged. 'I suppose I feel someone should at least care about them in passing,' she replied. 'After all, they did die in the most awful way. As for Arthur — well, you don't really expect me to put flowers on his grave, do you? And you know how I feel about the family tomb.'

He smiled wryly and was pleased to follow her out on to the green, for his hand was aching very badly in the cold.

'Would you feel the need to care about my grave in passing, do you think?' he asked. 'Put flowers on it in the summer and clear the debris away when it's cold?'

Julia swallowed uncomfortably. She didn't like the question and particularly didn't like the implication behind it.

'Oliver, you are six years younger than me,' she pointed out, 'so if you live your full lifespan, as you should, I'll be rather old to be putting flowers on your grave, don't you think? Oh, come on, I'm happy to remember Sandro and I feel duty-bound to care for the old ladies, but I don't want to make a career out of tending graves. Anyway, you won't die here, will you? You once told me you hated the country, so surely you'll be heading back to town eventually?'

They began to walk up the road towards Tremar, stepping out smartly because it was extremely cold. The hedgerows were bare and did nothing to keep the wind out.

After a moment he said, 'I'm being officially discharged on 20 January, by the way.'

'And then what?' she enquired with a smile. 'Will you be taking up my offer of a bed in the manor?'

She was stunned by what he said next.

'And which bed would that be?' he enquired sardonically. 'The one my wife is supposed to occupy, or the one she spends most of her nights in? No, probably not that one; be a bit squashed with three of us in it, wouldn't it? So hers then. Going to cramp her style a bit.'

'Oliver!' Julia exclaimed, stopping and turning to face him. 'What a thing to say!'

Oliver stared at her in a kind of weary defeat. 'Oh, please,' he retorted sourly. 'Don't humiliate me by pretending you don't know. If it's my feelings you're struggling to spare, don't bother; I know the truth, the same as everyone else does. You've only got to look at them — and besides, in case you haven't spotted it, Sophie's pregnant. And that doesn't have anything to do with me!'

A cold, merciless blast of wind suddenly whipped down the lane, blowing grit at them spitefully. Julia felt it squeeze her heart with its sharp, painful fingers and she stared at his disfigured face in deep sorrow. So it was true then, what Ilona Vincent had hinted at, and it left him teetering out on a limb, alone and stripped bare.

'Oh God, I'm so sorry,' she whispered, hugging him. 'I'm so, so sorry, Oliver.'

Oliver hugged her back, putting his arms about her and closing his good eye, to remember how she had once so willingly come to his arms. The headscarf smelled subtly of her perfume, and brought the past flooding back into his mind. He wanted to cry, but it was so much more than that. He wanted to hurt as well, to hurt the people he saw as his betrayers; to hurt them all.

Except Julia.

'I've had to come to a decision, of course,' he said, as they stood still with their arms about each other. 'It hasn't been easy, but I have no other course that I can see. I shall be leaving Tremar on the twentieth, with the children. We shall be going back to Arundel. As for Sophie — well, that's up to you. You can throw her out for the whore that she is, or you can let her stay and condone what she's done. Either way it won't make any difference to me in the long run.'

Julia heard his words and her stomach knotted with fear. She stared at him, aghast.

'You can't!' she whispered. 'Not the children; you can't!'

'They're *my* children.'

'So they might be, but you know how unhappy they were in Arundel. Oh, Oliver, *please*! It isn't fair.'

He shrugged and brusquely put her away from him, and Julia realized he was expecting her to be on his side. Either that, or he was subtly trying to blackmail her into turning Rory and Sophie out. Whichever, it was unacceptable.

'They're older now,' he said. 'Things will be better.'

'We've talked about this before,' she retorted. 'As I told you last time, they're only six months older and nothing will have changed, as well you know. So that was what you said to them at the party, was it, that you were going to take them away? If you do that, Oliver, I will forever know you for the selfish, self-centred man you are, I warn you. And, more than that, you will condemn two lovely, delightful children to a life of misery. They're too young to be taken from their mother. I'm sorry, but they are, whatever you might think!'

She saw a bitter sneer creep across his face, and at the same moment they arrived at the gateposts of Tremar. A Land Girl crossed the front of the building and waved to them, and the house looked warm and cosy. Safe. A safe and happy place for two children to grow and flourish.

'So I must give up my wife *and* my children, must I?' he growled. 'It's right, is it, that I give again? I have no profession any more, my wife couldn't care less if I live or die, you don't want me, and now you think it's acceptable for me to go away without my children? My God, what a victory for your bloody grizzly bear!'

It was not the moment to lose her temper, Julia knew, and afterwards she was furious with herself, but all she had ever tried to do was help, and she was sick and tired of the Cromptons blaming everything on her and Matt.

'This has got nothing to do with my husband!' she shouted at him. 'He is not trying to steal your son any more than I'm condoning what your wife is doing. You're both adults, and you're supposed to be grown up enough to make your own choices. So do me a favour, will you? Compromise! But don't you *dare* take your children away from here simply as an act of revenge. You have no right to do that, whatever you think!'

Oliver watched her, suddenly noticing the first signs of grey in her beautiful chestnut hair, held down against the wind by *his* headscarf. He knew she was right, but he hated her for saying it, and her condemnation of what he wanted seemed to leave him standing alone in the world.

She capitulated first, felt herself flood with guilt, and opened her mouth to say sorry, but he gave her no chance.

'Well . . . thank you for your advice,' he said, curling his lip. 'It's important to know where you stand when you've been betrayed, isn't it? To know who your friends are? Quite obviously I have none, so I'll bid you good day!' And turning on his heels he strode away from her towards the dower.

She took a couple of steps after him, but instinctively she knew he wasn't going to come back, so she let him go, but as she went into the manor she flung down her scarf and gloves and went on the hunt for Rory and Sophie as fast as she could. She was boiling with rage because, once again, she had been humiliated, and it wasn't fair.

They were in the drawing-room, where Rory was talking to Minnie, and Sophie was standing at the French windows, watching Alice and her friend Peggy

Jackson outside on the lawns.

The two little girls were playing at being mothers, dressed in long skirts and fancy hats from the vast dressing-up box Julia had provided for them, and pretending to be elegant ladies pushing their prams towards the rhododendron walk.

Just how much more unfair can this get? Julia thought savagely, glaring furiously at her house guests.

'Right,' she said sharply, 'since you're both here I might as well say my piece. I've just walked back from the village with Oliver, and guess what he told me? Frankly, I would have thought at least you owed me the courtesy of telling me yourself, not leaving it to someone else. This is *my* house you're living in, you know!'

Sophie swung round quickly, and if Julia hadn't quite believed it before, she certainly did now. Sophie looked frightened out of her life; but then, there'd been all those uneaten breakfasts in November, and the white, pinched look that had at times been quite alarming. Julia couldn't imagine why she hadn't thought of it herself — except that she had no experience of pregnant women. People hadn't given birth at Blackridge; there was no renewal of life there.

'So he knows then?' Sophie sounded

forlorn. Julia raised her eyebrows.

'Of course he does!' she replied. 'Did you think he wouldn't spot it? He's not only your husband; he's a doctor as well, in case you've forgotten. And he now wants to take Edward and Alice away with him in the middle of January, back to Arundel, would you believe? And I seem to remember I begged you to be careful — well, what a pity you couldn't even have done that for me!'

Quickly Rory was on his feet, stumbling slightly in his haste to protect his love.

'It was my fault, Julia,' he exclaimed, and she glanced at him cynically.

'It takes two to make a baby, Rory,' she observed. 'It always has done, with one notable exception. So, why didn't you tell me? Did you think I was going to throw you out into the cold of winter without so much as a blanket between you?'

Sophie's face was as hard as flint, but her eyes were filling with tears and her hands were trembling as she squeezed them into fists. This was the thing she had dreaded for so long, and she had to resort to spite because she was so frightened.

'Well, aren't you?' she snorted defensively. 'I can't believe your Lady Bountiful act extends to letting us stay!'

The moment she'd said it, she could have

bitten her tongue off, for Julia was not able to keep her face under control, and though Sophie already knew that many of her barbs had hurt in the past, this one had quite obviously shot home savagely. Julia's eyes filled with tears and she turned away, fighting to control herself.

'If I throw you out,' she said eventually, 'what does that make me, exactly? My father's daughter, perhaps? You think about it. No, I'm not going to throw you out. If you choose to *leave*, I shan't stop you, either of you, but I will not be turning you out. If at any time, however, you feel you might like to talk to me about your predicament, I shall be happy to listen, and it would at least be nice to know when the baby is due.' She paused, briefly exhausted by the pain of her wounds, and she looked out of the window at Alice and Peggy, pushing their prams back towards the house and nodding to each other like ladies. Finally, drawing a deep breath, she added, 'If you let Oliver take Alice and Edward away with him to save your own skin, then I will never forgive you, I promise. Up until now I've let you punish me because I knew I deserved it, but we're even now. You *will* go and talk to him, and you *will* reach a compromise, or so heaven help me I'll banish the lot of you!'

14

Today hadn't been a good day, Julia reflected sourly, as the cold January night crept in and freezing draughts sneaked under doors to pounce on the unwary. First with Patrick being discarded by his family like so much unwanted rubbish, and then the ever worsening problems between Oliver and Sophie. It really hadn't been a good day at all.

At just after seven, with Minnie already tucked up in bed, she was alone in the drawing-room banking up the fire for the evening and dreading the arrival of Sophie and Rory and the subsequent stilted dinner conversation, when out in the hall the telephone rang.

She knew she wasn't in a particularly friendly mood, but as she snapped 'Tremar!' into the receiver, it seemed to come out excessively hostile.

There was a short pause at the other end of the line, then a cultured male voice said, 'Good evening. I wonder if I might speak to Mrs Julia Logan, please?'

'Speaking,' replied Julia, only marginally

less sharply, and again there was a little pause.

Finally the voice at the other end said, with extreme politeness, 'Mrs Logan, this is Robert Thornby, Patrick's brother.'

It was all she needed, an encounter with the bloody Thornbys; ringing up to ensure sufficient humiliation had been meted out, so that they might eat their dinner basking in the glow of victory, no doubt. Oh God, she wasn't up to this tonight, she simply wasn't! As she spoke, her voice was as cold as the temperature outside.

'Ah, Sir Robert,' she said with biting sarcasm. '*What* a surprise — or perhaps not, eh? Well, if you've telephoned to check that the deed has been done, I give you my word that your *more* than charming young brother has been suitably humiliated, and his humiliation witnessed, as ordered, by Annie and myself. All executed according to the decree; done and dusted. We are suitably cowed, we know *exactly* where we stand, and if there's nothing else we were about to sit down to dinner.'

Robert Thornby thought, Crikey! I wouldn't want to make an enemy of this one, and hastened to speak again before the receiver was put down on him.

'Please, Mrs Logan,' he said, 'do let me

explain. That bloody letter was nothing whatsoever to do with me, I promise you. In fact, that's why I'm ringing now, because I've only just managed to sort it all out. It was a ridiculous act of spite on my mother's part, a last-ditch attempt to get Pat to do what she wanted, and it has well and truly backfired on her as it happens. Believe me, I'm on his side, I always have been. I love my little brother very much, and I'm most anxious to tell him the truth.'

Julia was silent for a little while. Sir Robert certainly *sounded* genuine enough, and Patrick had always maintained that his brother was his friend.

Eventually, albeit slightly grudgingly, she said, 'Well, all right then, I'll fetch him for you if you like, though it will take a little while. He doesn't live in the manor, you know, he lives in the convalescent home.'

'Oh no, please wait,' her caller said hastily. 'I don't actually want to speak to him on the phone, what I have to tell him is much too important for that. Mrs Logan, I was rather hoping I could shamefully impose on your hospitality, and ask if it would be all right if my wife and I called at Tremar the day after tomorrow for a few hours, to spend a little time with Patrick? I'm anxious to see him, and I'm most anxious to meet his wife-to-be.

I read all her letters to him when he was in hospital in Salisbury, and she sounds quite delightful.'

'She *is* quite delightful, Sir Robert,' Julia assured him, her voice as sharp as a knife edge. 'She is honest, beautiful, hard-working and extremely clever. She loves Patrick devotedly, and she will make him a wonderful wife. Of course, she's a local farmer's daughter with a Cornish accent, but she doesn't drink from the horse trough; she takes a bath every day, and she knows how to use a knife and fork — and in what order to use them, as well.'

Robert Thornby thought he could feel her tongue cutting through his flesh. He also thought that if he hadn't been told differently, he wouldn't have wanted this woman as a mother-in-law any more than he would have wanted his own mother. But Patrick had talked with great affection of Julia, and particularly of her love for Annie. This was an adult fiercely protecting its young — something his mother knew nothing about.

'I take your point, Mrs Logan, and I fully understand your meaning,' he observed quietly, and then he chuckled. 'And she writes a mighty readable letter as well, I might say, even if you're not into farming. I found her *most* entertaining. So might we trespass on your time, do you think? And, if so, could you recommend a hotel where we could stay? Somewhere not too far away.'

Julia looked up. Matt was at the top of the stairs with Annie beside him. They were dressed for dinner and chatting between themselves. Annie was talking about a new feeding regime at one of the farms, and Matt was saying 'Well you're in charge there, so if it's what you want, do it.'

Julia made her decision quickly, and it wasn't too difficult because they were offering to come to her lair, she wasn't going to theirs. Besides, she was very interested to meet this brother of whom Patrick spoke so fondly.

Into the telephone she said in a much warmer voice, 'Of course you and your wife may come to Tremar, Sir Robert, you'll be most welcome I assure you. And please, don't think about a hotel. Naturally, you will be our guests. Oh, and please, do us the honour of staying for two or three days, otherwise you won't get a clear picture of Patrick's new home. We're not quite the size of Chawston, but Tremar is a big enough estate, I assure you, and I do want you to see for yourself that we love Patrick very much.'

'You're very kind, Mrs Logan,' Robert replied with much relief, 'and we should love to stay for a couple of days. That's most generous of you. Give my love to Pat, will you, and tell him we're looking forward to seeing him. Thanks so much.'

Julia replaced the receiver and turned towards the stairs as Matt and Annie reached the bottom.

'Who was that?' Matt asked. Julia smiled like a tigress.

'It was Patrick's brother,' she replied smoothly. 'He and his wife are coming to stay the day after tomorrow. It seems he wants to tell Patrick something very important. He wants to apologize for that bloody letter, and he wants to meet Patrick's intended. And *we* don't have to go to *him*, he's coming here to us. So chalk that one up as a victory!'

Matt chuckled, but to his great surprise Annie's eyes opened wide in alarm.

'*What?*' she cried. 'They're comin' the day after tomorrow? But . . . but that don't give me any time to prepare! I mean . . . I ent got time to do anythin'.'

Matt opened his mouth, closed it again and then gazed at her in bewilderment.

'Prepare for what?' he demanded. 'Annie, what on earth is the matter with you?'

But Annie had started something that wasn't going to stop for two days — and it didn't matter what *anybody* said.

'But s'pose they don't like me!' she exclaimed to Guy, wringing her hands in despair. 'S'posing they thinks I'm common an' cheap, like Patrick's mother does? What d'you think I should wear? Should I put lipstick on, d'you think? *C'mon*, Guy! Tell me, they'm goin' to be 'ere in a couple of hours!'

They were in the drawing-room, where Guy was making his daily visit to Minnie. She had begun to cough badly in the last few days, and he was very much aware that the light had gone out in her eyes since her birthday party. However, Julia seemed to think Minnie would rally when the better weather came, and for now, anyway, she certainly showed pleasure at his visits, even if she didn't talk to him much.

Holding her hands between his and stroking them gently, he glanced up at Annie and began to laugh.

'For Lord's sake, Annie!' he retorted. 'I've never seen you like this. Patrick's brother is going to *love* you, just the same as Patrick does. Now do, please, stop. You're driving us up the wall!'

'Oh, you ent any 'elp,' Annie snapped rattily. 'I'm goin' to find someone else.'

She hurried away and a moment later Julia

came into the room. She stood for a while watching Guy and Minnie, realizing that Guy was unaware of her presence. She saw him take a sweet from his jacket pocket and pop it into Minnie's mouth and then put his finger very softly against her lips.

'Our secret, eh?' he whispered. 'Don't tell the others, or they'll all want one.'

For a short while Julia was completely transfixed as her heart seemed to pour out in gratitude, then she cleared her throat to let him know she was there, and came to sit on the arm of Minnie's chair.

'She doesn't look so good, you know,' he murmured and Julia smiled sadly.

'Every day is a bonus for Minnie,' she replied, 'and I think that each morning when I find her still alive. If she'd been left at Blackridge she would have been long since dead by now, even with Ilona Vincent's love and care. Can you understand, Guy, a man who gets so drunk he breaks his little daughter's arms and legs, and then throws her against a wall to make her be quiet?'

Guy pursed his lips, gazing into Minnie's not quite focused eyes.

'I'm told Annie's father treated her a bit like that,' he said. 'Bloody awful, isn't it? I love my little Edwin more than life itself. Oh, by the way, Annie is fussing like a girl on her first date.'

Julia burst out laughing.

'I know,' she retorted. 'I'm avoiding her like the plague. And Matt's fed up to the back teeth with her. He says please God the Thornbys will come and go and she will finally remember that she's supposed to be a farmer! Poor Annie.'

A log settled with a comfortable crackle in the huge fireplace and sent an army of sparks marching up the back of the chimney breast. The drawing-room was warm, except over by the windows, and outside, even though it was afternoon and the sun had been shining, the frost had not melted in the shaded areas. There were a couple of hardy servicemen taking a walk on the lawns, the smoke from their cigarettes drifting upwards in the still air, and on days like this it was possible to hear the sea rumbling against the cliffs, such was the stillness.

Both Guy and Julia were lost in their thoughts, but had they been able to read each other's they would have found that they were not so very different. Both, for the umpteenth time, were appreciating the placid beauty of Tremar, but Guy was acknowledging that he would soon have to give it up, and each time he remembered that he found himself a little bit sadder.

Suddenly he kissed his fingers and touched Minnie's cheek softly.

'I've got to go, lovely girl,' he said. 'Got to get myself all poshed up for dinner because we're eating in here tonight. Shall I sit next to you?'

Julia smiled.

'She won't be at dinner tonight,' she said. 'She's not well enough. I'll give her some soup at about six o'clock and then put her to bed, but it was so nice of you to offer.' He smiled and then backed his wheelchair away from the fireplace, but before he could wheel himself into the library Julia said quietly, 'Guy, I know your time is almost over here. What are you going to do when you leave?'

He looked up at her from his chair, and then shrugged his shoulders cheerfully.

'I haven't got a clue, Julia,' he answered. 'I was brought up to be 'something in the city', which was what I was until the beginning of the war. But, you know, I wasn't awfully good at it, and I don't really want to go back and do it again. In fact, the only things I was ever really quite good at were cricket and soldiering — and I can't do either of those any more.'

Julia licked her lips. She had been forming an idea about Guy for a couple of days now, but to her surprise her heartbeat quickened as she planned to voice it. She was nervous, frightened of offending him.

'Look, I've got a proposition to put to you,' she said, 'and I'd really like you to go away and think about it — but you must say, right away, if the idea is offensive to you. Do you promise me to do that?'

Guy chuckled.

'Julia, I can't imagine you ever saying anything offensive, to anyone,' he observed. 'You are patently obviously not the offensive type — no matter how much you might like to be. So come on then, out with it. What would you like me to do for you?'

'No, it's what I'd like to do for you,' she replied. 'No doubt Oliver told you about the village shop, so in recognition of your endless kindness to Minnie, and to say thank you for all you've done to help Annie and Patrick, I was wondering whether you and your family might like to take it on? I mean, of course, the estate will fully modernise it, put in a bathroom and so forth upstairs, and a decent kitchen. We'll look into installing a small lift, as well; the building should be strong enough to take it, and it's certainly big enough. What do you say? Do you think you and your wife would like a life in Polwean?'

Guy didn't know what he had expected,

but it certainly wasn't this, and he was speechless. He was also overwhelmed with a rush of excitement, for he could think of nothing in the world he would like more than to stay permanently close to Tremar, to count Patrick and Annie as friends he could see whenever he liked — and Matt and Julia, too.

After a long pause he exclaimed, 'Julia, I'm — I'm astonished,' and saw her eyes widen in alarm.

'You hate the idea!' she cried.

'On the contrary, I love it,' he replied firmly. 'I'm just not certain we could afford it. Pam and I don't have much money, you know. She and Edwin are in rented accommodation at the moment.'

Instantly Julia's face lit up with a smile of relief.

'Guy, I want to *give* you the shop,' she explained. 'On precisely the same basis as my grandfather gave it to Miss Penrose's father. It still belongs to the estate, but you don't pay any rent or anything; effectively it's yours, and it continues to be yours for as long as you or your descendants want it, but you can't sell it on to anyone else. It is the estate's job to effect any and all repairs and modernization work now, but once we've signed contracts and so forth, all maintenance falls to you. If you run it into the ground, of course, the estate will claim it back — but I think you're highly unlikely to do that, don't you?'

For a long time Guy sat in his wheelchair and stared at nothing in particular as what Julia had said sank in. He tried to work out whether he was being offered charity, but it didn't feel like that. It felt like an honest offer, honestly made — and it also felt like his fairy godmother had just waved her wand over him!

Eventually he looked up at Julia, and for a moment they simply regarded each other, then he smiled and squeezed her hands in his.

'I don't need to think about it, Julia,' he said very quietly. 'I can give you an answer right this minute. I can't think of *anything* I would like more, and I promise you faithfully we will run your little shop for you extremely professionally.'

Julia laughed, and then swallowed as she found a lump in her throat and thought she might cry. She bent and kissed him on the cheek, and then turned to open the door and let him into the library.

'There are just two things I would like you to do for me,' she said as he began to negotiate the chair through the doorway. 'The first is to get rid of that bloody little bell over the shop door, and the second is to promise that it will once again be the centre of gossip in the village, but this time honest gossip.'

Guy grinned happily. 'I swear not to frighten a single soul,' he replied with a chuckle. 'And I swear to be the one who spreads the news of your first grandchild faster than you can say knife!'

* * *

It had been a long drive from Chawston, on icy roads a lot of the time, and as Robert Thornby turned his car in between the gateposts at Tremar he was much relieved to have arrived, for he was cold and weary. Ahead of him he saw a charming old grey manor, and heard his wife give a little gasp of delight, but before he was able to say anything to her, a lady he took at once to be Julia Logan came out of the front door and walked towards them with a welcoming smile.

'Good Lord,' he observed softly. 'Can you imagine Mother actually walking down the steps at Chawston to greet anyone? I say, she's rather beautiful, Julia Logan, isn't she?'

Julia opened the car door herself for Kate to step out; the Thornbys could see no sign of a butler anywhere and they were beginning to like it here already, before they'd even entered the house. They introduced themselves, shook hands warmly with Julia and then went to get their luggage from the boot.

'Oh, don't struggle with your cases,' Julia said. 'I'm sure my husband Matt will bring them in for you, he won't mind a bit. It is good of you to come, you know. Patrick is so looking forward to seeing you.'

'You say 'seeing' us . . . ?' Robert observed thoughtfully, and Julia chuckled.

'We don't try to find ways around people's handicaps here, Sir Robert,' she assured him. 'Patrick is Patrick. The fact that he can't see makes very little difference. Guy has no legs, but he's going to be running our village shop by this time next year.'

Robert Thornby stared at her, and he couldn't remember when he had last been so impressed. This woman, whom his mother had delighted in telling him had been thrown into an asylum in 1915 for committing nothing more than the sin of desire — she was remarkable!

It was dark now, so Kate knew she would have to wait until the next day before she could see the view from the windows, but as she stood in the drawing-room, which was warmed by a roaring fire, and gazed about her at its graceful comfort, a dozen different emotions chased across her face.

In the end Robert put his arm around her shoulders and chuckled softly.

'My wife came from a home a little like this, Mrs Logan,' he said, 'and to come into another one reminds her strongly of what she lost, I think.'

'Lost?' Julia echoed. 'But Patrick tells me Chawston is exquisite.'

'Absolutely exquisite,' he agreed with a sort of amused cynicism, 'and one feels it should be covered everywhere in 'Please Do Not Touch' notices. Chawston is huge, magnificent, and freezing. Nothing is ever out of place and my mother forbids her six grandchildren to use the main staircase because it is built of white stone and is in danger of being — heaven forbid — marred by dirty finger marks. I doubt the children here are refused entry to anywhere, are they?'

Julia smiled at him and suddenly liked him very much indeed.

'Absolutely not, Sir Robert,' she answered happily. 'Please, make yourselves at home. My housekeeper is about to bring in some tea and a most delicious cake — and Patrick and Annie should be along in just a moment. You seemed to imply that you had something important to tell him, when we spoke on the phone, so if you'd like to be alone with him after tea, you have only to tip us the wink.'

Robert shook his head slightly and for a

few seconds he allowed his eyes to wander about the room, then he smiled at his hostess and Julia saw the gentleness in him that his lovely Kate must have seen in the beginning.

'I'm actually not planning to tell him until the evening before we go,' he said quietly, 'because he will probably need a little time to adjust to it. He will certainly need those he loves around him, and it's much the best that we leave that to you and Miss Paynter. I will say only that you will have a better understanding than most.'

Julia nodded and glanced for a moment at Minnie. She thought of Annie, of Arthur, of Blackridge . . . and without any sense of shock she thought she knew what Robert Thornby was going to tell his brother.

★　★　★

In the next forty-eight hours, Robert and Kate Thornby were allowed a glimpse into the lives of people who lived for each other, not for a perceived set of rules that were unwritten and meaningless, and they loved what they saw.

Robert hadn't known what he had expected upon meeting Annie, but he didn't think it had been quite such a beautiful, highly intelligent girl. As an art lover he thought she had the most exquisite Titian hair he had ever seen, and her gentle, Cornish lilt was charming. He hadn't known quite how it would be to see his brother again, either, for when Patrick had been in hospital his face had been entirely obscured by bandages. But if anyone at Tremar thought his face oddly crooked they certainly didn't show it, and Robert couldn't remember ever seeing Patrick so happy and contented in his life — which seemed ironic, when one considered his handicaps.

Dinner on their first night was a leisurely affair in the panelled, subtly lit dining-room, which might have been half the size of the one at Chawston, but was surprisingly warm and comfortable. The ladies sat with bare shoulders — not something you could do at Chawston if you wanted to survive — and the conversation was amusing and relaxed. They met Patrick's room-mates, Guy and Oliver, and they also met Gladys, Annie's mother.

Julia had deliberately sat Gladys next to Robert, and the purpose of that little exercise was not lost to him. It took him less than five minutes to discover that Annie's mother was a phenomenally clever woman, and looking across the table at the sparkling Annie he realized that even he, who thought himself pretty much a man of the world, still had an awful lot to learn about inbred prejudices.

The following morning after breakfast, he went with Matt to see the estate, interested to compare it to Chawston's Home Farm. What he saw greatly impressed him, and as they came back to Home Farm from a tour out round Five Elms and the two farms beyond, he stopped and narrowed his eyes, surveying the regiment of fields.

'Was the estate working this well when you took it over in 1938?' he asked. Matt chuckled softly.

'Home Farm was derelict,' he replied. 'The land had either been poached or left fallow, and it took a wee while to sort out the boundaries, I can tell you. But I've kept ma eye on that during these war years; there'll be no disputes when we split into tenanted farms again.'

Robert gazed at Matt and bit back the comment he was going to make; then he decided to make it anyway, and smiled warmly at the huge, benign Scotsman.

'I'm inclined to say I wish you'd come to Chawston instead of Tremar,' he said. 'Our estate manager is good, there's no doubt about that, but he's not in the same league as you. Mind you, my father's no help to anyone. He knows nothing about anything but flowers, and cares even less. What happens to Home Farm when the war's over? I mean, it's full of Land Girls now, but having pulled it back from the edge, you must have plans for it.'

'Oh, aye,' Matt answered calmly, watching two of the girls, in their familiar baggy trousers and green sweaters, driving one of the tractors across to Five Elms. 'Annie and Patrick plan to run Home Farm when the war's over.'

Robert Thornby gaped at him, amazed.

'Annie and Patrick! But, come on, Patrick's going to be pretty limited as a farmer, surely?'

Matt smiled and, shielding a match between his hands, lit his pipe before resuming their journey back towards Tremar. Some of the girls were working in the pine copse between the orchard and the bay, and the delicious scent of pinewood smoke assailed their nostrils, making them pause to breathe appreciatively.

'Aye,' he agreed. 'There'll be things Patrick can't do, of course there will. There'll also be any amount of things he can. Patrick's blind, so which is best then, that he lives a comfortable, useful life within his scope, or that he sits in a chair and is fed soup and sweets, like Minnie? Minnie cannae help herself now, but for twenty-three-and-a-half years she was all that kept Julia alive. Patrick is Annie's future and, like Minnie, he has an important role to play. Do ye ken what I'm saying?'

Robert stared at him and after a moment he smiled gently.

'Yes, I do,' he replied, 'and I can't begin to tell you how happy I am that Patrick has been lucky enough to find you.'

They had been at Tremar for two days and were leaving for Ireland in the morning. When they began to gather in the drawing-room for tea, he and Kate found themselves part of a smaller group than usual, for Rory and Sophie had been told the Thornbys had something rather personal to tell Patrick and had taken the children to the morning-room ostensibly to play a board game; only Matt, Julia and Minnie kept Annie and Patrick company.

Julia poured the tea, Minnie snored gently in front of the fire, and Robert gazed at the comfortable gathering as he carefully worded his opening in his head. Patrick sat on the other end of the sofa with his arms around Annie, and as Robert watched them he realized that there wasn't any real need to tell Patrick what he'd discovered at all; it wasn't going to make the slightest difference to his life. He would tell him, though, because he deserved to know why he had always been treated so indifferently at Chawston, but if he had any sense he wouldn't let it matter.

It made Robert feel a whole lot better.

'Pat, old man,' he began, taking his tea from Julia and sipping it gratefully, 'since we're only a small group this afternoon, and Kate and I are off tomorrow, there's something I want to tell you, if you've got a moment or two to lend an ear, so to speak. It's nothing too awful, in fact you might be quite pleased when you come to think about it, but it makes a complete nonsense of that bloody letter of Mother's, and because of her spite you've a right to know. First of all let me ask you something: have you any recollection of when you last saw Pa?'

Patrick frowned slightly and pushed his fingers upwards through his curly blond hair. Julia watched him, sitting beside his brother, and she knew she would have guessed the truth anyway, even if she'd never been told it, because except that they were both charming men, Robert and Patrick couldn't have been more different. Pity he was about to lose the *wrong* parent though, she thought cynically.

'It must have been before I went to Cranwell, I suppose,' Patrick replied at last. 'In my last school holiday at home. I went into the glasshouses to admire his flowers — is he still growing flowers?'

'He doesn't grow anything else,' Robert answered. 'As far as he's concerned, war or no war, it's not his job to grow vegetables. Besides, he's only vaguely aware of the war at the best of times. It doesn't mean anything to him, other than that Cecily and Susan are resident at Chawston. What I want to tell you, however, is why Pa has always treated you the way he has, why he didn't come to your Passing Out Parade or to any of your prizegiving days at school, because you must have wondered. He isn't a bad chap, you know, not really. Actually, despite the disinterest he's always shown towards you, he's a surprisingly good man, and when I spoke to him the other day he told me he'd always cared about your welfare very much.'

Patrick smiled and it seemed rather sad somehow, then he kissed Annie's hair, as if she were a talisman and he must keep her with him for luck.

It wasn't hard to see that Patrick had been systematically starved of love.

'Oh, I've always liked Pa,' he said. 'I suppose I just thought I was a disappointment, that's all. I mean, I've always known I was a disappointment to Mother, because she regularly told me so, but Pa just ignored me. Sometimes he seemed to look right through me, as if he didn't know who the hell I was.'

Robert Thornby sighed heavily and then glanced at his wife. He wondered, angrily, if he could have done better in the past, been a better brother, a better guardian for his highly sensitive sibling — but he'd been too young to understand what was going on himself then.

'Yes . . . ' he muttered. 'I'm so sorry. The simple fact is, old man, that Pa doesn't acknowledge you, and because of that he's pushed you out of his mind, but he does know who you are; perfectly well, if you ask him, only of course Mother never does. It all began the summer before you were born, I'm afraid. As usual we were in Ireland, and as usual I celebrated my birthday; my thirteenth, as it happens, not that it matters. Anyway, Mother decided on a party — but not a children's party of course, well, this *is* Mother we're talking about — and she invited the Baines-Mortons, plus our other neighbours, the Wards, with no thought of me, needless to say. Anyway, the Wards had a brilliant young concert pianist staying with them at the time, convalescing from a bout of TB. He was an enormously good-looking young man with the most brilliant blue eyes and remarkable blond hair you've ever seen, and for the only time in her tightly corseted life, our mother looked in another direction.'

The room suddenly went very still. Nobody clattered teacups or plates, everyone watched Patrick as different emotions came and went from his face, and everyone was a lot further along the road to enlightenment than he was.

'You mean she had an *affair*?' he asked at last with a hint of amusement in his voice. '*Mother* did? Good Lord! I somehow can't picture her frolicking naked in the long grass.'

Robert chuckled softly.

'Oh, I'm not sure she went that far,' he replied. 'Mother's a silk sheets person, affair or no affair. But be that as it may, she had a short summer of glory with this delicate young man and then — because as far as she's concerned, if she doesn't want something it won't happen — she didn't pay attention to what was happening to her, come the autumn.'

Patrick put his hand up to his mouth and very slowly ran his fingers around his lips. In their heads everyone else in the room had already arrived, but it wasn't so surprising he took longer to get there, it was a fairly shattering moment in his life.

Eventually he raised his head and looked in Robert's direction. Oh, those blue eyes, they were so brilliant in their colour, like the sky.

'Are you saying . . . ' he whispered at last, 'that this concert pianist was my father?'

'Yes, old man,' Robert murmured, 'he was.'

There was a definite, if very soft, sigh from the whole room, as if everyone suddenly let their tension slip just a little.

Robert went on, 'By the time Mother acknowledged that she was pregnant it was far too late for her to fudge it; she and Pa didn't sleep in the same room, let alone the same bed, and Mother hadn't made the journey to his room for years. She was obliged to come clean — well, it isn't something you can hide forever, is it? — and Pa tells me he told her very firmly that with family honour and so on in mind he would accept you as his son; that he would feed, clothe and educate you, but that he drew the line at your inheriting any part of the Chawston fortune. Actually, I think Mother was damned lucky . . . ' he paused and glanced at Julia, receiving an unequivocal answer from her eyes. 'And you would have thought that bearing *and* being allowed to keep, the child of her lover would have secured for you a happy and indulged childhood . . . '

'But who knows better than me that it didn't?' Patrick finished bitterly. 'So I've not been disinherited then, I've been summarily thrown out of a family I've never belonged to anyway! God, no wonder Mother was so angry with me for not dying when my plane came down; what a perfect opportunity missed! She must have been spitting bits of broken glass! Tell me, do I have a name? A real name?'

Robert reached across and touched him gently. Julia saw Patrick clasp his hand and hold it so tightly his knuckles showed white. The neglected, sensitive little boy was suddenly finding that his whole life had been a lie, that he was not part of an ancient lineage at all; he was a mistake, a bastard, and his mother had spent twenty-six years desperately trying to ensure that no one ever found out.

'Your name's Thornby,' Robert replied quietly. 'It's on your birth certificate. Your father, however, was called Lawrence Blake — and if you're wondering why you've never heard about his career, it's because he never recovered from the TB. He died eighteen months after you were born. You look exactly like him, Patrick; your hair, your eyes, everything. Fortunately, though, you inherited Mother's constitution; I predict that you and Annie will have a very long and happy married life.'

Patrick grew very still suddenly and everyone in the room saw his head drop. Julia wanted to grab him and kiss him, to tell him that they all loved him like mad and none of this mattered, but that was Annie's job, not hers.

He put his hand out and touched Annie's cheek, and if he could have seen the love in her eyes he wouldn't have needed to ask, but he was confused and frightened.

'Will you still have me?' he asked miserably. 'I'm not the person you thought I was, Annie. I'm not the person you thought you knew ten minutes ago.'

Annie stared at him indignantly for a second, then she cupped his face in her hands and kissed him hard on the lips, in front of everyone.

' 'Course you'm the same person!' she retorted. 'How can you 'ave changed? So the father you thought you 'ad grows flowers, an' the father you *really* 'ad played the piano — don't make no difference to you, do it? It don't make no difference to me, I can assure you!'

Robert Thornby grinned cheerfully.

'Well said, Miss Paynter,' he observed. 'You're quite right, it makes no difference at all. The only reason I wanted Patrick to know was to relieve him of any more worry about our ghastly mother. Kate and I will away to Ireland tomorrow to explain things to the egregious Mona and, despite that foul letter of Mother's, *we* are extremely anxious to come to your wedding, if you'll have us.'

Suddenly Patrick said, 'I never did propose to Mona, you know. I never asked her to marry me, I never would have. I suppose that was Mother's final revenge.'

'She planned for it to be,' Robert replied, 'mostly in the hope that when you got nothing from the Thornby fortune no one would notice because of the fortune Mona would get from her family; but I've planned a little revenge of my own, and Mother knows now that if she tries to stir up any trouble, if she starts egging Mona on to a breach-of-promise suit or whatever, I shall take great pleasure in telling our awful sisters what I've just told you. So be happy, little brother, you had a very worthy father and you've landed yourself a wife in a million. I know that for a fact because I've got one too.'

'As have I,' said Matt placidly. 'And, young Patrick, you're about to gain a *new* father in your life, one who pays a great deal of attention to what you're about. You ask Annie: I'm no' the kind of father who lets anyone get away with anything.'

Annie turned her head to look at him and a wide grin lit up her face. 'Rubbish!' she cried. 'You'm a big old softie!'

15

The Thornbys left Tremar early the next morning and Julia saw them off alone. Annie and Matt had gone to work and it was too early for Patrick, who still lived by the dower rules; so just Robert, Kate and Julia stood in the half-dark on the drive outside the front door, bundled up against the cold.

'Thank you so much for coming,' Julia said as Robert slid their suitcases into the boot of his sleek black car. 'You can see for yourselves what a difference it's made to Patrick and Annie.'

Robert smiled and found the ignition key on his ring.

'She does fully understand what she's taking on, doesn't she?' he asked, glancing across at Julia as his eyes watered with the cold and his breath steamed. 'Believe me, Patrick is the best of all of us, truly he is, but I can't help wondering what I'd be like if I'd just been blinded.'

Julia smiled gently. 'Annie teaches him to see with his fingers,' she replied. 'She is wonderfully patient, but at the same time she doesn't allow him a moment of self-pity. Next we're planning to teach him to find his way round the village. It will be nice for him to be able to pop down to the shop and spend time with Guy whenever he feels like it; they've become very close friends.'

Robert gave her an almost wistful smile and then climbed into the car and started the engine. It coughed into life rather unwillingly and then grumbled for a bit whilst Julia and Kate stood together in the cold.

'When we come to the wedding,' Kate said, 'may we bring the children, do you think?'

'Of course you may,' Julia replied. 'I'm sure they'll love seeing their Uncle Patrick get married, besides, it'll be quite an occasion — Tremar weddings always are. One way or another pretty well the entire village gets involved.'

Kate Thornby suddenly looked sad, and then, Julia thought, slightly resentful.

'It sounds wonderful,' she said, her rich, dark hair contrasting sharply with the light grey fur of her coat in the gloom of the winter's morning. 'My wedding to Robert was strictly an invitation-only occasion — and I didn't have a say in any of it. My mother-in-law even organized my dress and shoes. I think if I hadn't loved Robert as much as I did I would have run screaming from the whole thing.'

Julia frowned.

'Life must be very difficult for you sometimes,' she observed and Kate chuckled mirthlessly.

'Oh, you don't know the half,' she said. 'When my mother-in-law is feeling particularly spiteful, she refers to me as the 'chorus girl'.'

'Chorus girl?' Julia gave her a puzzled stare. 'Were you on the stage then, before you married Robert? Somehow I thought you must have been a beautiful but useless debutante — like I was supposed to be.'

Kate smiled sadly.

'Oh no, I don't come from your sort of world,' she replied. 'I was an opera singer, and had I stayed with my career I would almost certainly have been a great diva by now. My place in that world was secured, but I chose to marry Robert instead.'

Julia stared at her in amazement.

'And you gave that up for him?' she asked. 'But surely he didn't ask you to do that? You could have been both, couldn't you, his wife *and* a great singer?'

'I could,' Kate answered simply, 'but I chose not to be. I love Robert with all my heart, because he is a good, honest man; a true gentleman. I chose to be the wife of the Master of Chawston, with all the obscure ties and titles that go with it — which for the most part lie dormant because Pa has forgotten all about them — and I don't regret the decision for a moment. But I was not my mother-in-law's choice by a long stretch, and she never fails to remind me of that on a depressingly regular basis. Still, one day Chawston will be Robert's, and then, with any luck, we can set about turning it into a home. Then, too, I hope you and Matt and Annie and Patrick will come to visit. Annie and Matt can talk estate management to their heart's content, and you can enjoy a chuckle at the museum piece that is Chawston.'

'We'd love to,' Julia said truthfully, and as she held the car door open for her, found herself both touched and deeply impressed by this lovely woman who was about Sophie's age and faultless in her chosen lifestyle.

Waving in the freezing air, she watched the car slide away gracefully between the gateposts and turn left down towards the village. They had a long drive ahead of them to Holyhead, and then a long boat trip to Ireland after that. She was pleased to return to the warmth and security of Tremar.

She went upstairs to the bedroom next to her own and found Mrs Collins getting Minnie ready for the day. She had lifted her on to a clean towel and was talking to her peacefully as she did her job. Minnie looked dreadfully old and vulnerable lying there naked, but her eyes were on Mrs Collins all the time, and from time to time she smiled. It was very touching.

'Nice bit of lavender soap, my lover,' Mrs Collins said. 'Make you feel a whole lot better, an' then we'll put a bit of talcum in places; stop 'em getting sore.'

Julia said, 'Mrs Collins, you're such a dear to do this for Minnie.' The housekeeper smiled kindly.

'T'ent no bother,' she replied. 'I'll do the bed when I'm finished. They seemed a nice pair, that brother an' sister-in-law of young Patrick. Ever so polite — '

Julia grinned and lifted Minnie so that she could be well powdered.

' — which you didn't expect,' she observed, and received a sharp look for her pains.

'No, I didn't, frankly, with the sort of mother the poor lad's got,' Mrs Collins retorted sourly. 'Who does she think she is, I'd like to know!'

'She thinks,' Julia replied, 'that she's better than the rest of us. She thinks that because she has a title and has enjoyed a privileged childhood it somehow gives her rights over her children's lives. And she's just discovered that it doesn't, I'm pleased to say. So, two out of three, then.'

Mrs Collins dressed Minnie with a deftness and gentleness that might not have been expected from someone normally so brisk and efficient. Minnie had to be carried up and down stairs now, and Julia and Mrs Collins had found that they could manage it between them, so when she was ready they carefully lifted her and made sure she was safe.

'Two out of three what?' Mrs Collins asked on the stairs.

'Happy endings,' Julia answered, moving slowly forwards, step by step. 'Guy is to have the shop, and Patrick and Annie are to have each other. Now there's just Oliver.'

Edward and Alice ran across the bottom of the staircase as they were coming down, heading for the back kitchen door, and when Minnie was finally settled in her chair by the fire, Mrs Collins straightened up and glanced out of the French windows. Oliver and Guy were walking together through the vegetable garden, whilst the children, who had obviously shouted a greeting to their father as they went, were heading for the rhododendron walk yelling their freedom to the cold, bright sky.

'You'm left the 'ardest one till last, I see,' she observed. 'I'm afraid I dunno what you'm goin' to do about that one, 'cos he'm a very unhappy man.'

'Oh, thank you,' Julia answered grimly. 'You think I don't know that? Frankly there isn't an answer to Oliver and Sophie, but if I could only find a compromise.'

Mrs Collins chuckled. 'Good luck,' she said cheerfully. 'I'm away to do the beds.'

It was a splendid morning with bright, sharp sunshine after the early gloom, though it was mighty cold. Guy had strapped on his artificial legs, grasped his sticks with determination and set off for a stroll with Oliver, because suddenly he had a purpose in his life, and something to work for.

He had telephoned his wife and told her of Julia's offer the day before, and she had reacted with great excitement. Now she was talking of giving up their little rented house and moving down to Cornwall as soon as possible, and Guy wanted to meet her and Edwin on his feet when they came.

He did not yet walk with confidence on his legs, nor with any degree of grace, but whereas up until now Tremar had been only a staging post on the journey back to real life, from hereon in it had a whole new purpose; it had presented him with a challenge, and he was going to make quite sure he was up to it.

As they strolled together around the

vegetable beds Guy said, 'What about young Patrick's face this morning then, eh? Looks like he lost sixpence and found a shilling! Oh, God bless Annie for the splendid girl she is.'

Oliver slid his damaged hand into the pocket of his overcoat and stared up at the cloudless sky. Tremar showed signs of the end of winter. New daffodil shoots were just poking through the soil and the suggestion of buds on some of the trees whispered that spring was not far away now. Another year of war, he supposed, that would not be allowed to touch Tremar more than was absolutely necessary.

'Do you know,' he said slowly, 'when I first met Annie I thought she was simple. She was half-starved and dressed in rags, she flitted about the village stealing or cadging food where she could, she was completely indecipherable when she opened her mouth, and she had a nice line in stupid stares. I thought she would finish up in Blackridge one day, I really did. Everyone in the village did. It took Julia to see how clever she was.'

Guy negotiated the edge of a vegetable bed with care, knowing that if his foot slipped he would be incapable of stopping himself falling over. When he was comfortable again he glanced at Oliver and saw him gazing up at the manor.

'Look, old man,' he said quietly, 'tell me to mind my own business if you like, but isn't there some way you could stop being in love with Julia? You're hurting yourself so much.'

Oliver's head shot sideways and Guy knew he had touched a raw nerve.

'Is it so obvious?' he demanded, and then pressed his lips together. 'Yes, of course it is. Everyone knows I'm still in love with Julia; well Matt certainly does, and Sophie. I've made a fine mess of it, one way or another, haven't I? The thing is, she was in love with me once, till that bloody Scotsman turned up . . . and I would have given her everything in the world that she could ever have wanted, if she'd only had the courage to go with me.'

Guy was careful not to look at him as in his mind's eye he saw very clearly the way Julia and Matt looked at each other when they were together. They never touched intimately or kissed in front of other people, but Matt laid claim to her every time he set eyes on her, and she acknowledged it comfortably.

'If you ask me,' he said, 'she's got everything in the world she wants right here. I don't know what your relationship was, but I do know what I see around me, and . . . well, to be absolutely blunt, the only person you're hurting now is yourself. Couldn't you try and right things a bit between you and Sophie?

After all, you have the two most adorable children in the world. Couldn't you leave Tremar, the four of you, and start again somewhere new?'

Oliver smiled bitterly and thought of Sophie and Rory, then he thought of Julia and Matt, and then of Annie and Patrick, and in the cold stillness of the winter morning, with the beauty of the sky above him and the promise of renewal all about, he thought he had never felt quite so alone in all his life.

'I wish it were that simple,' he replied softly, and they turned and began to walk across the formal lawns towards the orchard. 'And I wish I had time to think about it, too, but I'm about to be discharged. Then the choices have to be made, and my choices are different from my wife's, I'm afraid.'

'Oh, for goodness sake,' Guy observed roundly, 'being discharged won't make any difference. You know perfectly well Julia is happy for you to move into the manor; I've heard her say so. You never know, old man, but this might turn out to be just the opportunity you were looking for.'

And it might not, Oliver thought bitterly; but strangely, as the strings that held his life together seemed to get looser every day, he was growing less and less inclined to talk about it. He looked at the open-faced Guy and was suddenly very glad that Julia had offered him the shop. He would be good for the village, someone always ready with a smile.

He said, changing the subject, 'I found Robert Thornby a nice chap, you know, and I have to be honest, I wasn't expecting to.'

'After his awful mother, you mean?' Guy agreed. 'I was fast reaching the point where I was beginning to think some of the stories you hear are true.'

Oliver chuckled, and watched his breath rise from his lips into the still air.

'About our noble aristocracy, you mean?' he said. 'They're probably not all so bad, but remember Julia's lot didn't have much to recommend them — as parents, I mean. I don't know, maybe it's just that they don't have to worry about the real world, so they've got time to worry about the things that don't matter. Anyway, once this war is over I wouldn't be surprised if things change quite considerably.'

Guy's eyes twinkled.

'Oh Lord!' he exclaimed. 'Not thinking of voting Labour next time we have a General Election, are you? I had you down as firmly Conservative!'

They had reached the railings around the orchard. Oliver leaned against them and fished in his pocket for a packet of cigarettes. They would smoke one apiece and then go back slowly; it was as much as Guy could manage as yet.

Oliver gazed at Tremar, watching the smoke rising from the chimneys, and he thought he already knew what his plans were, and he thought he probably wouldn't be voting at all in the next General Election, whenever that might be.

★ ★ ★

The following Saturday morning, Alice awoke with a start of excitement. It was Peggy Jackson's birthday, and Alice was guest of honour at the party. What was more, Uncle Matt had made a wonderful set of dining-room furniture for Peggy's dolls' house; a Welsh dresser and everything. Of course, Peggy's dolls' house wasn't anything like as splendid as the one Julia had given her, but it was starting to become nice, with all the things she was collecting in it, and she was going to *love* Alice's gift.

'Peggy says you can come to her party, you know,' she said to Edward as they hopped out of bed and began their usual morning play with their toys, before anyone else was about. 'She says she'd really like you to.'

410

'Well, it's very kind of her, but I'm afraid I can't,' Edward replied with six-year-old pomposity, as he re-arranged his fleet of planes. 'I've absolutely *promised* Doreen I'll go across to Five Elms this afternoon. She says there'll be heaps for me to do, an' I can't possibly let her down, can I? Not just for a party.' He paused and picked up his favourite little Spitfire, gazing at it fondly. 'She can come to mine, though, if she wants,' he added. 'Aunt Julia says I can have a party for my birthday an' invite Doreen and everything . . . '

Suddenly he stopped and they stared at each other uncomfortably, as the same thought crept into both their heads.

'Unless they make us go back to Granny's first,' he said in a whisper. 'I'll *die* if I have to go back there, Alice. I won't do it. I just *won't*! But Mummy hasn't packed our cases, so maybe we're not . . . '

They hadn't seen much of their father since the engagement party; it hadn't been meant unkindly, it was simply that logic dictated they might avoid going back to Arundel if they gave him time to forget his threats.

Oliver was aware that they were avoiding him, and it seemed to add to his isolation. He knew he couldn't really take them back to

411

Arundel, he loved them too much for that, but to be forced to leave them, to let Sophie's be the final victory — it just seemed so unfair. Certainly he had been the one to be unfaithful first, but did that really mean she could get away with flaunting her lover in his face *and* stealing his children? And that he should have no redress whatsoever? It rankled, and it was getting worse by the day.

He wasn't particularly looking for Julia when he went into the old stables at eleven o'clock that morning; either he or Guy made a cursory check for eggs every morning, though they rarely found any at this time of year, and she didn't normally clean and straw the chickens on a Saturday.

He watched her from the doorway for a moment as she shook out new straw and the dust from it danced in a shaft of sunlight creeping in through the window above, and he remembered vividly her first morning back at Tremar; how beautiful she had been in trousers and a hacking jacket, and how much he had loved her. Then she turned, as if she sensed he was behind her, and though she looked quite different now, heart still leapt in his breast at the sight of her.

'Hullo,' she said, smiling at him. 'Not a single egg from any of them at the moment, but they still expect clean straw and plenty to eat. Damn cheek, I call it!' And she laughed softly.

Oliver walked across the wooden floor towards her and suddenly she remembered that first morning, too. It seemed a thousand years ago now, and the memory of it made cruel mockery of his uneven gait, black-gloved, ruined hand and burned, twisted face.

His eye was cold as he looked at her.

'Don't you ever get bored with this life?' he asked. 'Laying fresh straw for the chickens and growing vegetables with a clutch of mutilated servicemen? Surely you must.'

Julia shrugged her shoulders, determined not to bite.

'I haven't been living it long enough to be bored with it,' she replied and stood quite still as he raised his hand and touched her hair.

'You have no concept of the war here at Tremar, do you?' he observed. 'It doesn't touch you at all, really. Oh, the bombers come and go and drone overhead, and some of those the conflict has blinded and maimed sit about on your terraces or dig in your vegetable plot, but life here is cocooned, sliding along gently without touching the sides. Dressing for dinner and observing all the politenesses of life; the lady of the manor thing; God, Julia, how can you be happy with it?'

She watched him, there was a lot of anger beneath his self-pity this morning, a great deal more than usual, so she struggled to keep the encounter calm.

'I'm very happy with it,' she answered. 'It's what I was brought up to, if you remember. I know you think you could have offered me so much more, Oliver, but you would have wanted so much from me in return, and in the end I wouldn't have lived up to your expectations. To be honest, I didn't have a chance.'

He was very close to her and he could smell perfumed soap on her skin. She stood quite still, and she knew exactly what he was going to do, but she made no attempt to pull away because she knew if she did he would be spiteful. As his lips touched hers he meant for the kiss to be violent, for he was certain she would try to fend him off, but she didn't. Instead she parted her lips very slightly, so that he could taste the fresh dampness of her mouth, and she let him kiss her for a long time.

When finally he released her, he stepped back and his mouth grew thin and bitter, as tears welled up in his eye. He was furious and oddly humiliated. What was it? Pity? Was she showing him how gracious she could be when they both knew how easily she could hurt him, if she chose to, simply by squeezing his mutilated hand? Julia put her fingers against his lips, determined to stop him from speaking.

'Don't spoil it,' she whispered. 'It wasn't an act of charity; I didn't kiss you because I feel sorry for you, I kissed you because I knew quite well that we were full of the same memories just then, but it doesn't alter the fact that I'm married to Matt and I love him dearly; I can't change that, however much you might like me to. I wouldn't leave him for anything in the world and I wouldn't leave Tremar, either. But you were the man who saved my life, Oliver, and for that I will always be grateful beyond words. Can't you let that be enough?'

He touched her once more, brushing a couple of stray hairs from her forehead as he seemed to scrutinize her so closely she wondered if he was trying to find a way into her soul. Then he withdrew his hand and gave her a bitter, twisted little smile.

'I don't want your gratitude,' he said. 'But thanks, anyway, for the shared memories. I haven't forgotten any of it. It's nice to know you remember at least a bit.'

And without another word he turned and went, with his uneven steps, across the wooden floor to the door and the cold morning. Julia watched the empty doorway for a long time after he had gone and wondered at the significance of the encounter. She wouldn't have to wait long to find out.

* * *

Oliver saw Edward playing on the lawns as he looked out from one of the dower windows at about 2.30. The little boy had his fleet of tiny planes with him and was happily re-creating the Battle of Britain, ducking and weaving as he ran about. Oliver watched him for a long time.

When eventually he went out on to the terrace and began to make his way down to join his son, he wasn't absolutely clear about anything, but he did glance back at the manor once, as if he half expected not to see it again.

'Hullo, Edward,' he said, and the battle stopped. The handsome, blond child looked up at his father and smiled.

'Hullo, Daddy,' he replied fondly. 'I went an' helped Doreen at Five Elms after lunch, but the work's all done now. She said she wouldn't have got it done in *half* the time if it hadn't been for me. Good, isn't it?'

'Very good,' Oliver agreed and put his hand on his son's curly hair. 'Where's your sister?'

'Oh, gone to Peggy Jackson's party,' Edward answered scornfully. 'They said I could go, but I hate girls' parties. They play silly games and fings, an' I'm much too old for all that now. After all, I'm going to be a farmer.'

He said the words so proudly that Oliver felt a stab of pain in his heart. His son wanted to be a farmer — like his bloody, precious Uncle Matt. Not a doctor, like his battered and useless father!

'How would you like to go for a walk with me, Edward?' he asked, looking down at the little boy-Sophie, remembering, for no apparent reason, that they had been happy when he was born, that she had presented him with his son so proudly and he had been enchanted by how much like his mother the tiny baby looked.

Edward shrugged and glanced with a moment of longing at his planes. He'd been really enjoying his game and he was reluctant to stop it, but Uncle Matt had told him regularly that he must always be kind and helpful towards his father.

'Well, OK then,' he said after a little pause, 'but can I bring my favourite Spitfire?'

'Of course you can,' Oliver replied, putting his hand on the child's shoulders.

They walked away together, leaving the rest

of Edward's little fleet of planes parked carefully on the grass. From a window in the dower, a nurse saw them together and thought it a touching sight. She watched them go through the little iron gate into the orchard, smiling to herself, before she went on with her work.

No one else saw them at all.

The pine copse was cold, because the winter sun had failed to penetrate most of it, but there were signs of recent forestry activity, and Edward spotted a piece of wood that would make a lovely plane. He picked it up carefully, examined it and then stood it on a tree stump. He would collect it on his way back.

He said, chatting cheerfully to his daddy, 'Uncle Matt'll fink that's a really good find. He's always telling me that I have to keep my eyes open. He says a good farmer doesn't miss anyfing. I'll make a good farmer,' he looked up at Oliver, 'won't I, Daddy?'

'You'll make a wonderful farmer,' Oliver replied and ruffled his hair. 'Let's walk to the top of the cliff path, where that stone bench is. I could just about manage that.'

Edward wasn't allowed on the cliff path on his own, not particularly because it was dangerous, generations of children had roamed those cliff paths quite safely in the past. Julia's strict rule was because of the army training going on around there — ever since she had heard of a small boy in Devon being killed by a piece of equipment coming crashing through a hedge — so to Edward this was quite an adventure.

He did just briefly wonder if he ought to say that they weren't allowed to come up here, but he thought that the rule probably didn't apply where his Daddy was concerned, so he said nothing.

Before they climbed the cliff path they spent a few moments in the bay. The tide was going down, and there was enough newly uncovered sand to run about on, so Edward set off with his Spitfire, swooping it through the air making machine gun noises. Oliver stared at the place where the boat shed had once stood, blown away on the night of Arthur Paynter's death. He watched the tiny waves lapping on to the shore and he remembered Julia jumping about in the water in her bare feet, as a balmy summer's night closed cunningly around them.

He called to his son and glanced back at the yellow sand and shiny, dark rocks once more, but as Edward came to stand beside him and slipped his little hand into his father's good one, Oliver realized that he was running out of things to say.

He didn't allow himself to think ahead; he climbed the path with his bright little boy, and once or twice stopped for breath, but he wanted Julia there with him as he walked away from Tremar, and he didn't turn and look back once.

The stone bench was cold and deserted. It was after three now and still so early in the year that it would be dark by five at the latest. To herald the coming night, the temperature was dropping and everywhere was breathlessly still. The sky to the west was beginning to show the first signs of evening.

'We ought to go back soon, Daddy,' Edward said. 'Otherwise it'll be dark an' we won't see the way.'

The little boy wore short trousers, wellington boots, a grey coat and a pair of gloves that from time to time he took off and stuffed in his pockets. He clutched his beloved Spitfire to him closely and his bare little knees were pink with cold. Oliver stood by the bench and stared out to sea, and after a longish silence, Edward shuffled uncomfortably.

'I'm cold, Daddy,' he said plaintively.

'Come here,' Oliver murmured gently, putting his arm around his son's shoulders. 'Come to the edge and look down. Look at that: what a lovely sight, eh?'

Edward stood on the edge and obediently looked down. They were at a point on the path where a small section of cliff had dropped away at some time, and looked as though a giant had taken a bite out of it. The drop to the rocks was sheer, and below them, yet high above the ground, a fulmar hung on a current of air. On either side the cliff face was rough and dotted with tufts of grass and hardy plants that would blossom into little pink and blue flowers in the summer, and right down at the bottom, just before the jagged rocks, there were some grey, flat stones and a bed of pebbles. There was nothing between the cliff top and the rocks but the remains of a bush that had slid with the cliff and now clung tenaciously, growing at an angle of ninety degrees.

'Will you come with me, Edward?' Oliver asked his son, tightening his grip slightly on the child's shoulders. 'It won't take any time at all.'

'Go where?' the little boy enquired in some alarm. 'I don't want to go back to Granny's, Daddy. Please don't make me.'

Oliver smiled down at him peacefully.

'We're not going back to Granny's,' he said. 'We're going to a much better place than that; somewhere lovely, where we'll be happy all the time. All you have to do is shut your eyes and lean forward. It won't take any time at all, I promise. No time at all.'

Edward opened his eyes wide in fright. 'No!' he exclaimed, but it was too late. He felt his father's body sway forwards and the instinct of self-preservation kicked in. He ducked, so that Oliver lost his grip on his shoulders, but he couldn't stop himself falling, because the momentum of his father's body carried him with it.

Oliver fell outwards without a sound. He bounced off the cliff face only once before he hit the rocks and landed on his back. Clattering down the rock face behind him went Edward's little Spitfire, smashing to smithereens below, but Edward had slid, not fallen, and his descent had been halted by the bush. For what seemed like an age he just hung there in wordless terror, waiting to fall, but the bush was strongly rooted and so, in as much as he could be, he was safe. He didn't fall and he was still alive.

Finally he turned his head slightly to look, and as he did so he clawed at the little bush in panic. His father lay flat on the rocks below with his arms thrown out and his body twisted inelegantly. It was a very long way down and it was hard to see, but there seemed to be blood coming from his head and his eye patch had been wrenched off somewhere in the fall. He was completely still. Lifeless.

Edward clung frantically to the bush, though it scratched and pricked his bare legs. With a strength born of fear he actually managed to drag himself up a bit and get a foothold, but there wasn't any way he could get back up to the cliff path; it was at least four feet above him, and without a handhold anywhere.

Desperately he clung on and closed his eyes.

'Daddy . . . ' he whimpered. 'Daddy, I don't like it . . . ' and he began to sob quietly as evening came ever closer and no one came.

★ ★ ★

Matt came back along the rhododendron walk at 4.30 and the dying embers of the day burned a cold, dark red in the sky. It was twilight, the brief time when the manor and the trees were sharply silhouetted, picked out as if cut from black paper. He was looking down as he crossed the lawn, which was just as well for he very nearly stepped on Edward's carefully parked little fleet of aircraft, and as he saw them there he was a bit cross. It wasn't like Edward to abandon his toys, but he'd tell him off all the same when

423

he found him. He gathered them all up and carried them into the house.

It was blissfully warm in the kitchen; dinner was underway and smelled good. Julia was always careful to grow plenty of onions in the summer and store them carefully, and they bottled everything that was remotely edible at harvest time so that winter meals could be looked forward to.

Matt washed his hands then picked up the little planes and went up to the drawing-room.

Annie was there with Patrick and Guy. She looked up as Matt came in.

'Have you seen wee Edward?' he enquired. Annie shook her head.

'I thought he'd gone to Peggy Jackson's party,' she replied. 'That's where Sophie an' Rory are; down the village collectin' 'em, or so I thought.'

Matt nodded.

'Aye, well I'll have a word to say to him when he gets home,' he declared and went upstairs to find Julia, first depositing the little air force in Edward and Alice's room. He noticed that Edward's favourite Spitfire wasn't there, and he hoped he hadn't missed it on the way in, but he didn't think he had.

Julia was tucking Minnie into bed, despite it being so early. Her cough was getting worse, and bed was now the only place they could keep her warm. For a while they stood beside the bed, watching her together, then Matt slipped his arm around his wife and bent to kiss her softly before going to bath and change, and at the same time, Rory, Sophie and Alice returned from the village.

Alice was full of excitement, hopping about from foot to foot as she told the occupants of the drawing-room all about the party, whether they were interested or not.

Annie listened carefully, and when at last Alice paused for breath, she asked, 'Where's Edward then? Did 'e 'ave as good a time as you?'

Alice looked a bit baffled.

'Edward didn't go,' she replied, and Sophie told her to go upstairs and change.

When Matt came down some while later, he was still looking for Edward and Annie was slightly puzzled.

'Well if 'e'm not in 'is room, then 'e must be in the dower with Dr Crompton,' she said. ''E can't be no place else. P'raps they said 'e could stay and 'ave tea . . . ' She broke off and frowned. ''E wouldn't still be at Five Elms, would 'e? I mean, Doreen would 'ave sent 'im 'ome long since.'

'He's no' at Five Elms,' Matt replied, 'because I was there on ma way home. I think

I'll just go in the dower and see if he's wi' his father.'

Matt didn't know why he felt unsettled, there really wasn't any need. Everyone at Tremar was safe, always. The worst thing that could happen to Edward if he was out in the dark was that he should trip over something and graze his knees, but deep inside him his adrenalin was pumping. There was something wrong, he just knew there was.

He was only halfway across the library when he met a nurse coming the other way. She looked vaguely harassed.

'Oh, Mr Logan,' she said, 'is Dr Crompton with you? He is naughty, you know, he didn't say he wouldn't be in for tea and you know Matron doesn't like having a patient adrift, even if the chances are he's just next door. One of our nurses saw him and his little boy going for a walk through the orchard much earlier this afternoon, but no one seems to have seen him since.'

Matt turned with a swiftness that belied his size and strength and ran back into the drawing-room. Julia and Rory were there now, and as he burst in through the door, everyone gaped at him. Annie rose from her seat. She had never seen Matt look like this before.

'Get your coat and boots!' he ordered her

quietly. 'Bring the dogs and meet me at the back door as quick as you can. Oh, and Annie, bring a torch. Edward and the doctor are adrift somewhere.'

'Matt . . . ' Julia cried in horror, but he shook his head.

'There's no time,' he replied. 'I'm taking Annie because she's as fast as I am in the dark, and Julia,' he wiped his hand across his face and his eyes seemed to tremble with alarm. 'Would you ring the girls at Home Farm and tell them I might be needing them, please? And would you no' tell Sophie anything at all for the time being?'

Julia felt the blood drain from her face.

'It'll be all right though, Matt,' she whispered. 'It will, won't it?'

Matt shook his head. 'I'm no' counting on it,' he answered softly.

16

Edward could no longer see his father's body, but he'd watched him until it got too dark in the faint hope that he might move. Clinging to the bush he saw darkness close silently around him, and as his hopes of rescue faded, so the cold ate spitefully into his flesh.

His hands were hurting, but of course, he couldn't put his gloves on, as they had fallen out of reach. His feet were painful, too, and threatening to slip all the time, because it was hardly a ledge he clung to, more a small outcrop of soil, and the unyielding branches of the bush, which had thorns to add to Edward's discomfort, dug into his stomach and ribcage.

He had stopped crying some time ago and now he concentrated on trying to ease the bits that hurt most. He couldn't breathe comfortably and so he tried to edge upwards a little, just to get the gnarled branches sticking into some other bit of him for a change; and all the time he listened to the silence. He was beginning to feel sleepy, and that frightened him a lot because although it seemed like a really nice idea to go to sleep and not wake up again until daylight, he knew that if he did so he would almost certainly lose his grip and fall.

Miserably Edward fought to stay awake, along with struggling to hang on to the bush, keep his feet on the ledge and inch about to ease his suffering. It really wasn't fair and he felt like crying again.

In the darkness, led only by torches adjusted to meet blackout regulations, Matt and Annie, with the dogs at their heels, hurried through the orchard into the pine copse, listening all the time for any sound and occasionally calling out. The copse was still and silent, and they were both reminded of the night of Arthur's death. That night the noise of the wind and rain had been deafening; now there weren't even the rustlings of night animals foraging. It was as if the frost held everything in an iron grip and the very air seemed almost solid with the cold.

When they reached the gate in the wall, they found it open. Matt knew immediately that none of the Land Girls would have come this way tonight, for there was a dance on in the village hall, and anyway, almost certainly they were all waiting at Home Farm to see if they were going to be needed first. Besides, though everyone came and went this way in the summer, few chanced it at this time of year; it was not quite such a friendly walk in the depths of winter.

Stepping out on to the path, he shone his torch carefully over the sand in the bay. The tide was beginning to come up now, but it only covered the soft sand by the steps in stormy weather, and since no one came here much these days, footprints were rare. Very soon he saw what he was looking for: a line of child's prints.

At the same moment, Jasper, the male collie of the pair Annie had stolen from her brother in the summer of 1938, pricked up his ears and then bounded away up the path, barking shrilly. He came back seconds later and the bitch, Daisy, sprinted to join him. Then they were away, their urgent barks filling the air.

Jasper and Daisy were very fond of Edward and Alice. Matt knew they had heard something he hadn't, and he knew time was short, as well, for their barking was desperate.

'Come on!' he yelled, and he and Annie began pounding up the cliff path.

It was iron-hard with frost underfoot, and extremely dark, but they were both quite used to the path. Annie knew where every blemish and pothole was with her eyes shut, she'd been coming this way all her life, and though

Matt rarely drank in The Smugglers' Inn any more, he still checked the condition of the cliff path regularly because it was part of the estate.

They were fit and moved fast, though the bitter air clawed at their lungs as they ran. They climbed the steep path and the atmosphere seemed to get colder as the air from the sea touched their faces. Then they were at the stone bench, gasping to get air into their lungs, and Jasper and Daisy were at the cliff edge, crouched as if they were herding sheep.

Edward's foot slipped and it jerked him awake. He whimpered and tried to close his frozen hands tighter around a rough branch as he searched for a hold with his numb foot, but the desire for sleep was becoming overwhelming now and he thought he wouldn't be afraid of falling for much longer. His body was beginning to feel strangely warm and comfortable, and his hands were slowly hurting less and less. He'd be all right till morning, he thought vaguely, and then, when it was light, maybe he could find a way up on to the path. But he had to sleep now ... he must sleep ... He looked up just once more and couldn't believe his eyes: looking down at him with their bright eyes and their black-and-white muzzles were Jasper and Daisy.

For a moment he thought he was dreaming, but just in case he wasn't he tried to cry out. Nothing came out and he panted, rocking slightly to try and make a noise.

'Help!' he whispered and at once the dogs had gone.

'Edward!' Matt said with great gentleness. He was right above him, gazing down on him. He was saved!

Matt turned to Annie and sloughed off the length of rope he had been carrying over his shoulder. Carefully he tied it around her waist and shoulders in such a fashion that he would always have complete control of her movements.

'Are you strong enough to hold him?' he asked, and she nodded, peeling off her gloves and flexing her fingers. 'Then get hold of his wrists, not his hands, and don't let go for anything. He'll no' be able to hang on to you, his hands'll be too cold.'

Annie inched her way down the cliff towards the bush face first, but without any fear. She trusted Matt completely; she knew he wouldn't let her drop.

'Don't wriggle,' she said to Edward. 'Don't do nothin'. I'm going to grab your wrists an' Matt's goin' to pull us up, but you mustn't struggle, all right?'

The little boy nodded and in the darkness his face was fearfully white, his eyes large and luminous with terror. He let Annie take hold of his wrists in a tight grip, and then he prized his own fingers open to let go of the bush, wailing with the pain as he did so.

He knew he was suspended in mid-air, and if Annie let him go he would fall straight to the rocks without hitting anything on his way down. Annie hung on grimly; it felt as if he was going to yank her arms right out of their sockets.

'Don't struggle! Don't struggle!' she cried frantically. 'Matt! Hurry! I've got him, but I can't 'ang on for long!'

Matt began to haul them up as quickly and safely as he could, but they were heavy, the two of them together, and his purchase on the cliff path was slippery with the frost. Edward felt himself sliding from Annie's grip, as his freezing legs were being clawed by the branches and thorns of the bush. He screamed and began frantically to tread air as his head fell backwards and his hands clawed at Annie's wrists, and then, to his utter shame, he lost control of his bladder.

'No!' he wailed, and at last he was high enough for Matt to grab him.

Pulling Annie back on to the safety of the

path, Matt snatched the child into his arms, tearing off his thick coat to wrap the boy in it. Edward began to cry and then, as his terror and suffering seemed to swamp down over him like a waterfall he began to wail.

'I'm wet!' he howled, wriggling with misery. 'I've wet myself!'

Matt sat on the bench with him, rocking him gently and soothing him as he rubbed some life back into Edward's blue little hands. Either side of him Jasper and Daisy crowded in, wagging their tails and greeting him lovingly, and as he wept Matt comforted him patiently.

'It's no matter that you're wet,' he said. 'It's the cold, that's all; it'd happen to anyone, so don't you worry yoursel'. Edward, you're a brave wee boy and I'm very proud of you; you did everything that was right. You're going to make a fine countryman one of these days. So where's your father, laddie, did he go for help or did he fall?'

Edward's face crumpled and a fresh tide of misery welled up inside him. All that time he had been clinging to the bush, all the cold and agony he'd suffered; it was all his father's fault!

'He fell!' he sobbed indignantly. 'But he tried to make me go with him . . . ' He scrubbed his runny nose on the sleeve of

Matt's coat, furious and at the same time devastated. He was angry with Oliver for what he had done, but he was suddenly, agonisingly aware that his father had gone forever, that he would never come back. 'He said we were going to a better place,' he wept, 'but I didn't want to go. I don't want to be dead. I don't care if it *is* a better place, I don't want to be dead!'

Annie saw Matt's face become hard and grim, and she watched as he lifted the little boy in his arms and held him tenderly. They both knew there was no point in looking down, it was far too dark to see the rocks at the bottom, but they also knew that they must recover the body tonight or high tide would wash it away.

Annie gathered up the rope, slinging it over her shoulder, and swiftly they started back down the cliff path in silence, Edward cocooned in Matt's huge coat and sobbing quietly to himself as they went. The cold was savage and they needed to keep moving, but Annie knew it was more than the cold that kept Matt so silent. He was angry and disgusted. It was his way; Matt despised anyone who put a child's life at risk, and particularly if that person was the child's own father.

They went back through the gate into the

pine copse, and only when they were emerging into the orchard did he finally speak. Edward was quiet now, Annie thought he might be dozing as Matt cradled him safely in his arms.

Eventually, as they came out from under the pine trees, Matt said softly, 'Would you go to Home Farm for me, Annie, please? Tell 'em what's happened, and what has to be done, but that I only want volunteers. It's no' a nice job, and it's no' what they're paid for, I know, but I must get him back tonight. I'll take the lad up to the house and then I'll join as many as can make it at the gate into the orchard. We're going to need a stretcher to bring him home, some extra light and more good, strong rope.'

Annie nodded, and at the gate to the orchard they parted and she sprinted away towards Home Farm.

As he entered the manor with the child held tightly in his arms, Julia was in the kitchen, and he had an idea she'd been there for some time. She saw the expression on his face and he saw hers lose its colour.

'Oliver?' she whispered and he shook his head.

'By accident or on purpose?' she asked.

'On purpose,' Matt replied as he sat the child on the edge of the table, so that he could retrieve his coat. 'Annie and I have to go back for the body, else the tide'll take it. The lad needs a hot bath, a hot sweet drink and lots of comfort. He's had a wee accident as well because of the cold. I'll come back for him as soon as we've done the job.'

Julia stared at him wretchedly.

'Do I tell Sophie? She knows something's amiss; it wasn't possible to keep it from her. Apart from anything else she knew that Edward was missing.'

She saw Matt narrow his eyes very slightly, and she wondered what thoughts were going through his head, though she knew he wouldn't voice them.

'Well, she has to know sometime,' he said, and gave Edward a final hug. 'I'm away to fetch your Daddy now, lad,' he said softly to the child, 'but it'll no' take long, and when I'm back I'll no' leave you again, I promise.'

Edward's small body shuddered pitifully and his head was lolling about as if he couldn't control it properly. He wasn't cold any more, at least he didn't think he was, but he felt terribly sleepy and very sick, and his head thumped with pain. He concentrated on Matt, knowing he needed to tell him something important.

'I lost my best Spitfire,' he muttered thickly. 'My favourite one. It fell when Daddy

437

fell, and it smashed, 'cos I heard it . . . ' He uttered a couple of forlorn sobs.

'That's no matter,' said the gentle Matt, cupping the little face in his hands and gazing slightly doubtfully into the little boy's befuddled eyes. 'We'll find a perfect piece of wood to make another one, and it'll be just as good.' He glanced up at Julia, frowning. 'He's in shock,' he whispered. 'I think he might be ill. He needs dealing with quickly.'

'Should I get a doctor?' she asked, but he shook his head.

'Not at the moment,' he replied, 'but he shouldnae be left alone. Someone must stay with him all the time until I come back.'

They watched him go back out to the scullery, pulling on his thick coat as he went, and Julia lifted Edward down from the table. The moment she set him on the floor his legs folded under him and he collapsed in a heap, vomiting everywhere. For a moment he stared in bewilderment at what he had done, then he moaned softly and began to rock, and Julia scooped him up in her arms.

'Come on, sweetheart,' she whispered. 'Let's go and find Mummy.'

As she carried him into the drawing-room she saw every face in the room turn anxiously towards her. Guy, Patrick, Rory, and together, wrapped in each other's arms, Alice and Sophie, their eyes alert with fear and ringed with shadows.

'*Edward!*' Sophie yelped lurching to her feet and staggering towards him. Julia didn't want to hand him over to her; he was a big boy now and Sophie was worringly delicate in her pregnancy.

'He's very shocked and a bit sick,' she said quietly, 'and in need of a warm bath. I'm going to take him up straight away, if you want to come. I'll carry him.'

Sophie's face had gone as white as a sheet, which darkened her already shadowed eyes even more. She looked as though she might faint, and all the muscles in her face were taut and stretched.

'Oliver . . . ?' she breathed.

Julia sketched a tiny shake of her head, but it was enough. Enough for Alice as well, unfortunately. Her face crumpled in torment and disbelief.

'I want my Daddy . . . ' She chewed her lips as her sobs rose like a fountain inside, threatening to choke her. '*I want my Daddy!*' she screamed, throwing herself at Sophie in a passion of agonized weeping.

Julia saw Guy put a hand on Patrick's arm and both men quietly lowered their eyes. Patrick didn't even ask about Annie, a fact that Julia found touchingly considerate. Rory stumbled rather unsteadily to his feet, grabbing clumsily for his stick.

'Is there anything I can do?' he asked in a tone that begged her to say there was, so Julia offered him a gentle acknowledgement.

'Yes, I would think so, Rory,' she replied. 'Almost certainly.'

★ ★ ★

Six girls from Home Farm and Annie had gathered at the end of the rhododendron walk, waiting for Matt. They had a stretcher with them, borrowed from the dower — where they had already broken the news — and a blanket with which to cover the body, plus another stout length of rope. They were subdued; they'd been looking forward to the dance in the village hall and the last thing they had expected was to be outside in the dark, retrieving a body.

There had been offers of help from the staff in the dower, but Matt had specifically asked for the girls, and so they had elected to go themselves, but it had certainly been tempting to hand over the responsibility to someone else.

Matt gathered the Land Girls around him. They seemed rather wide-eyed and white-faced in the torchlight, and he was grateful to them, for this would not be pleasant.

'I'll go round the point on ma own,' he told them, 'but I'll need a rope around ma waist in case I slip, and another one to pull him back with. I dinnae know what state he's in, but you've to bear in mind that he fell from the top of the cliff, so it'll no' be pretty. Edward says he's on his back.'

One of the girls from Home Farm touched him on the arm.

'Is Edward all right, Mr Logan?' she asked. 'Oh God, if only I'd known. I could have kept him at Five Elms all afternoon, you know, there was always something he could be doing.'

Matt returned her touch reassuringly.

'You're no' to blame, Doreen,' he replied. 'No one's to blame, probably not even Dr Crompton himself. We cannae know what was in his head; it might have been a spur of the moment thing. And,' he added grimly, 'we're no' going to find out now, so we best get going, before the tide washes him away.'

It was a thick, black night in the pine copse, but when they came out on to the cliff path, the sky shimmered with thousands of stars. It was breathtaking. Somehow the spectacular beauty of the icy night seemed to make their job twice as dreadful, and as they all picked their way round the first of the rocks in the bay, they were completely silent.

Eventually it got too dangerous for them to go on, so they grouped beneath an overhang of cliff as Annie secured a rope around Matt's waist. The two of them would go on until they were at the point, then Matt would cover the last bit alone.

The path was treacherous; the rocks sharp, uneven and slippery with seaweed, the incoming tide splashing ever closer. As they inched their way towards Oliver's body they skidded and slid, bumping and bruising themselves painfully, and all Matt could think of was that the misery of this would have been insupportable if he'd been struggling to reach Edward's little body as well as his father's. Finally, as he slipped for the umpteenth time and cracked his knee on a sharp piece of rock, he let forth a stream of abuse, and for a brief second he and Annie glanced at each other and shared a tiny smile. He was so grateful to have her there; he couldn't have begun to voice how he felt, so he didn't try. But he didn't have to anyway — she knew.

Matt left her on the edge of the point, scrambled over an inlet, which was already full of water, and risked a couple of small jumps in the dark. Getting the body back over this would be a nightmare, but it would have to be done. It felt as if he had been slithering about on these damn rocks for hours. He was tired and stretched to the limit, and the cold was beginning to bite into him. He remembered little Edward, hanging from the bush with his bare hands and bare legs, and he cursed with anger under his breath: he could remember few occasions in his life when he had not wanted to be somewhere as much as he didn't want to be here now.

When he finally reached the body he paused for a moment, resting on his haunches as the freezing air scoured his lungs and his wet clothes stung his grazed legs, then he switched on his torch again and took a close look.

Oliver, lying on his back with his arms flung out and his head towards Matt, was cold and stiff and wet right through from the splashing of the incoming tide against the rocks. His face was waxy; his one good eye open but unfocused as it stared upwards in death, his other an empty, lidless socket with water collected in it. There was a considerable amount of dark substance on the rocks beneath him, which Matt knew to be blood, but he had stopped bleeding long ago, and with no heartbeat to pump it out, what hadn't spilled on to the rocks had sunk back into his body, pooling uselessly. Matt pushed a couple of exploratory fingers under the dark hair and then drew them back quickly, for the skull was smashed like an eggshell and soft to the touch.

'God have mercy on you, you stupid bastard,' he muttered as he began to haul the body unceremoniously and found when the head was moved that there were tiny bone fragments scattered on the rock beneath it. 'Could ye no' have considered your children over yourself just once?'

He bound the rope around Oliver's legs, tossed it accurately to Annie, whom he could just make out standing on the point, and then waited as he saw her toss it back yet again. The rope became taut and then the body moved: they had started the awful return journey.

Matt's main concern on the most dangerous part of the journey was to keep Oliver's head together, and it wasn't easy. He inched his way forward, very often up to his thighs in water, feeling the current snatching at his feet, as he held the head tightly between his huge hands. To tie a rope around it would cause dreadful post-mortem injuries, and there was just a chance that Sophie might want to say goodbye to her husband.

Yard by ghastly yard, Oliver returned to the bay. There would be only one more journey left for him now — the one to his grave.

When they finally got him on to the stretcher, it was unlikely that anyone could have spoken, even if they'd wanted to. The exquisite night was tainted, flawed by the grossness of what they did. They covered him completely with the blanket they had brought for the purpose, and then between them they lifted him and began to carry him back to Tremar. He was a dead weight, and Matt had been forced to perform a gruesome service to ensure that his arms could be folded on his chest. It had been sickeningly noisy.

Finally they deposited him, still covered by the blanket, on a trestle table in the old stables, and left him with the chickens, because there wasn't anywhere else to put him.

Matt gave the six Land Girls five shillings each and thanked them gratefully for their assistance; a doctor from the dower officially pronounced life extinct and then went back inside because there wasn't anything further anyone could do at this time of night. Matt and Annie stood in the darkness of the stables and stared at each other.

'I never liked 'im,' Annie whispered, finding herself more disturbed than she had expected, because she was no stranger to death. 'But this? I never wanted this.'

Matt took her in his arms and held her close to him. Both of them were wet and very cold, and appalled by what they had been forced to do on this dark, sparkling night.

'I cannae imagine anyone would have wanted it, Annie,' he said, hugging her. 'But I think, mebbe, it'll no' come as such a shock to everyone. Still, it's no' our place to speculate. We've just to be there for those bairns now, to help them through it, so come on, let's go and get warm and have a dram. Oh, and tomorrow, if I could leave you in charge, I'd be most grateful. I'm thinking I'd like to spend the day with the lad, and maybe wi' his sister too, if she'd like that.'

Annie kissed him in the darkness.

'You'm such a good man, Matt,' she said softly, 'an' I love you so much.'

*　*　*

Edward lay curled up in bed after his bath, and with the gas fire popping comfortably in his room he was warm, but he was still trembling uncontrollably and could do nothing whatsoever to stop it. Guy and Patrick were in the children's bedroom, and Alice was curled up in Patrick's arms, sobbing her heart out as he soothed her gently, their faces touching as her tears soaked his collar. Guy talked softly to Edward and held his hand, but he longed for Matt to come back, for the little boy was pitifully disturbed.

Next door, in her own room, their mother lay, white and silent in the darkness, as Rory sat on the bed beside her. She clutched and twisted a lace handkerchief between her fingers, staring wretchedly up at the ceiling, but though she searched deep inside herself, she could not find any tears. She suffered fear and great anger, but no sorrow.

She was now a widow — just over a year after she should have been; that was all she could think, and her stomach turned over in revulsion against herself, but she couldn't shake the thought. It seemed to have branded itself into her brain.

Matt, Annie and Julia stood together in the drawing-room, and they all shared the same thoughts. They all remembered a violent November night in 1938, when Tremar had creaked and groaned under the onslaught from outside and someone else had died on the rocks. But they had left *his* body splashing about in the surf.

Oliver had come to the manor at eight o'clock the next morning, pale and tense and looking for someone to blame. Who was to blame now? Oliver, who had chosen death as the answer to his problems, but unforgiveably tried to take his little son with him?

'Edward is terribly distressed,' Julia observed as she watched Matt and Annie drink a hot toddy, and noted that they were both bruised and dirty. 'He shakes all the time and he's running a temperature. I thought I might ask someone from next door to take a look at him.'

'I'll go to him first,' Matt replied gently. 'If he's still poorly in the morning, then we'll get a doctor. Where's Sophie, by the way?'

'In her room with Rory,' Julia said. 'She hasn't even had so much as a cup of tea. I wish to God she would.'

'Not with 'er children, then?' Annie remarked sarcastically. 'Poor Sophie not up to that?'

'Annie don't, please,' Julia begged. 'I know you get angry with her because she doesn't always behave very well, but Oliver was her husband, when all is said and done. I think as much as anything she's in a state of shock.'

Annie sneered.

'He wouldn't 'ave killed 'isself if she 'adn't made it so obvious she was carryin' on behind 'is back,' she snapped. 'I didn't 'ave any time for 'im, you know that, but I ent got a lot of time for 'er, either. I think they was both plain selfish, an' so wrapped up in their bitterness towards each other that them kiddies didn't 'ave nothin' like the love they deserved. And,' she added, as Matt and Julia simply stood gawping at her in silence, 'you'm never going to change the way I feel, because you don't come to it from the same direction as I do. She'm got a second chance now, just like my ma 'ad when Pa died, an' let's see if she makes half as good a fist at it as Ma's done. I'll lay odds she don't!'

Julia swallowed uncomfortably and for something to do she stood the guard in front of the fire.

'She hasn't quite got the tenacity of your mother, Annie,' she said quietly. 'But in defence of her, she does love those children, you know, and I think she loves Rory, too. He's completely besotted with her.'

Annie sniffed.

'Clearly there's no accountin' for taste then, is there?' she retorted. 'So far as I can see, the only good goin' to come out of all this is that that little boy's goin' to be able to stay 'ere in Polwean an' 'ave a *real* man to learn 'is lessons in life from!'

And so saying she huffed out of the room, leaving Matt and Julia staring after her.

'Did she mean me?' he asked at length.

'Well, who else?' she replied simply.

Matt kissed her and she watched him go

449

upstairs to get out of his wet clothes and have a bath. He said nothing about how he felt, but she knew well enough that he had hated what he had had to do, and that whilst Oliver taking his own life might have elicited some sympathy, trying to take Edward with him would forever condemn him in Matt's eyes.

'Oh, Oliver,' she whispered to the empty drawing-room, 'how could you have done this? How could you have been such a fool?' And a couple of tears trickled down her cheeks as she switched out the lights and prepared to go upstairs.

★ ★ ★

On climbing out of the bath, Matt found that he was extremely bruised and grazed from falling down so many times on the rocks and was showing signs of swelling around his right knee, but things like that were of little importance to him.

Many years ago now, in a time he fought very hard not to think about, he had spent weeks in a mud-filled trench, fighting an enemy who occupied another mud-filled trench. He had stepped over and manhandled his dead comrades-in-arms, had seen and smelled their flesh rotting on their bones, had endured the heart-stopping terror of going

450

over the top, only to kill mindlessly when he had somehow survived the hail of bullets, and had coped, amid the horror and gore of it all, with festering, swollen wounds and appalling trench foot. Any wounds he received now were always subconsciously measured against that time in his life, and so his only acknowledgement of his knee was to put a bandage around it.

He found Annie and Julia in the children's room when he arrived. Guy and Patrick were still there, and he noticed that the two single beds in the room had been pushed together. Alice was still being comforted by Patrick, and now by Annie too, but Julia's concern was for Edward, and she was much relieved to see him turn as the door opened, to see who had come into the room. A moment later he was up and out like a jack-in-the-box. They watched him skim across the floor with his feet hardly touching it; they saw him throw himself into Matt's arms, and then they saw him attach himself like a limpet to a rock.

Matt held him tightly, feeling his small body rigid against his chest, their hearts beating together in secret. He didn't say anything at all, he just climbed into the middle of the bed and propped his back against the headboard, settling in for the

451

night; and moments later he was like a huge rock to which two fragile empires clung unsteadily. Alice was in his right arm, her head pressed into his neck; Edward was in his left, curled like a foetus, vulnerable, terrified, shocked, but — for the moment — safe.

'I think we'll have the lights off now, please,' he whispered, when Annie, Guy and Julia had made sure they were settled, turned the fire down and spread an eiderdown over them. 'We're all needing some sleep.'

Outside in the corridor, Julia wanted desperately to cry. Taking a deep breath she thanked Guy and Patrick very fondly for what they had done and then, suddenly losing strength, she put her hands over her face and uttered a bitter sob.

'I'm sorry . . . ' she whispered, and Annie squeezed her hard.

'D'you want me to stay with you?' she asked. 'Like you stayed with me that night, you know?'

Little bruised and battered Annie, sprawled in her bed, eyes bright with fever. Oh, she remembered, *how* she remembered, and Julia knew that what Annie asked for now was what *she* wanted, not just what Julia herself might want.

452

'Yes, please,' she murmured. 'Say good-night to the lads and come back, Annie. I need you.'

Her voice broke wretchedly and she hurried away, not wanting to break down in front of Guy and Patrick. Annie came back to her less than ten minutes later, and then they were both in their nightdresses. For a while they stood and looked at each other, and Julia's face was awash with tears: they streamed uncontrollably down her face.

Everything reminded her of Oliver: of his bringing her home to Tremar; and then of him finding his way, naked, into that very bed with her; of all the things that he had thought bound them to each other, all those same, suffocating things about him that she had rejected. But surely she'd done the wrong thing, hadn't she?

'It's all my fault, isn't it?' she wept. 'He was obsessed with me, and if I hadn't rejected him it wouldn't have ended like this. I left him for someone else, and he couldn't forgive me.'

Annie's green eyes gazed at her, affronted.

''Course it ent your fault!' she retorted crossly. 'You can't be 'eld responsible for someone else's obsession. An' you never left 'im; you wasn't 'is to start with.'

Julia sat on the edge of the bed. She was

cold and shivery, and appalled at the thought of what Oliver had done. She had never tried to kill herself at Blackridge, not even when escape had ceased to be even so much as a dream. She had stayed alive for Minnie; there was *always* a reason to live; and Oliver had not only killed himself, but tried to take Edward with him.

Annie said, 'Tell me something, if Matt 'adn't've come into our lives when 'e did, would you 'ave married Dr Crompton in the end, d'you think?'

'No!' Julia replied at once, and was shocked by how instinctive her answer had been. It had required no thought at all. 'No,' she said again, more softly, 'because I could never have been what he wanted. No one could live up to Oliver's expectations. When he married Sophie she was everything he thought he wanted, but she couldn't keep it up because he kept wanting her to be something different. It would have been exactly the same with me.'

The gas fire was hissing softly in the bedroom, and Annie bent to turn it off. Julia was grey with shock and exhaustion, and Annie had aching muscles and stinging cuts and bruises. It was time they went to bed.

'I saw you making love once, you know,' she said quietly, as she folded back the sheets and blankets to sleep where Matt normally slept. 'I was up in the attic, 'iding behind all them boxes an' trunks. Actually, I was up there in the first place 'cos I was readin' stuff you wouldn't 'ave approved of, so when you an' 'e come up, I crawled away bleddy fast, 'cos I thought you was goin' to catch me. Then, of course I couldn't go anywhere, so I watched you both.'

Julia felt a hot stinging blush rise like a fire from her neck and she stared at Annie in dismay.

'For God's sake!' she whispered awkwardly, and Annie chuckled and climbed into the bed, which smelled familiarly of Matt and made her feel safe.

'I didn't tell you 'cos I wanted to embarrass you,' she explained. 'I told you 'cos I wanted you to know what that moment meant to me. See, that was when you told 'im that you wasn't goin' away with 'im; that you was stayin' 'ere, for me an' Minnie. No one had ever loved me like that before — well, Ma might 'ave done I s'pose, but she weren't never allowed to show it — an' it was the most wonderful thing that 'ad ever happened to me in my life. I just wanted you to know, 'cos I know you feel guilty 'bout 'is dying, an' you shouldn't. What 'e's done, 'e chose to do; t'ent no fault of yours. Now come 'ere to bed and get some sleep. Things'll start to look better in the morning.'

Julia crawled into bed beside her and they switched out the lights. At once tears welled into her eyes again and she stared up into the darkness, as she became congested with her misery.

'Things'll get better for whom?' she asked thickly. 'Not for Oliver, certainly, and not for those poor children.'

In the darkness Annie touched her softly.

'I think you'll find things'll get better for them fairly quickly,' she observed. 'Their lives are goin' to be settled from now on. They'm not pawns in a grown-ups' game no more, an' they'm goin' to be livin' with grown-ups who ent tryin' to score points off them all the time. They'm goin' to be just fine, you'll see.'

Julia rolled on to her back and focused at the ceiling, and suddenly she realized, with a tiny jolt of surprise, that Annie was growing into a very wise woman. What was more, she was almost certainly quite correct — and, after all, she should know: she was the one with first-hand experience of coming to Tremar as a broken, frightened child.

17

Julia woke early, disturbed by Annie creeping from the bed, and it took her a few seconds to remember why Annie and not Matt was in bed with her. Instantly her heart sank and the pain poured in. She uttered an involuntary gasp and Annie turned towards her.

'I'm sorry, I didn't mean to wake you,' she whispered, 'only I got to get out early this morning. Matt asked me to take charge; 'e wants to stay with the children.'

'Go with me to their room, first, will you?' Julia asked.

Annie smiled.

''Course I will,' she replied gently. 'Oh, Julia, you don't look like you slept at all.'

Julia crawled from the bed, searching around for her dressing-gown. The room was cold, but she didn't notice it particularly: twenty-three and a half years in the towering dormitories of Blackridge had taught her not to notice.

'I think I did,' she mumbled. 'I must have done, because I had some awful dreams.'

They pushed open the door to Alice and Edward's bedroom cautiously. This room was

457

warm because the fire had been left on low all night, and it was semi-dark, with a shaded lamp burning. On the bed Matt was dozing, with his back still against the headboard, but the two children slept peacefully in his arms and all of them were covered by a rumple of eiderdown. Matt awoke instantly when the door opened; as was his way.

'Matt?' Julia whispered, and he smiled at her. 'Did any of you get any rest?'

'Oh aye,' he replied. 'They settled quite well in the end; they've been asleep for hours. I tell you what, hen, I think we could all do wi' a hot drink. Would you mind?'

'It'll be a pleasure,' she answered, loving him. 'I'll be as quick as I can.'

When she came back up from the kitchen with the tray, Alice and Edward were awake, but Edward seemed to have regressed into babyhood. He sat hunched on Matt's knee with his thumb in his mouth and stared dully at Julia, doing no more than tighten his grip on Matt's shoulder when she offered him one of the mugs of cocoa she had made for him and his sister.

Matt watched him for a moment, then gently released his grip.

'Come on, laddie,' he said softly. 'you've got to have a drink, and so do I, so let go, there's a good boy. I'm no' planning on going anywhere, I promise.'

Alice took her mug of cocoa and went to her dolls' house in silence. Matt and Julia watched her for a moment as she began to rearrange the china-headed figures that peopled her tiny world, putting them into different rooms. Then to their deep distress, she took the little father doll from the sofa in the drawing-room, stood him on the edge of the table and watched him fall with a tiny thud on to the floor.

After that, Alice sat cross-legged and hugged her drink, as tears spilled silently down her cheeks.

'Alice,' Julia whispered, holding out her arms.

Alice turned to look at her and her pretty little face crumpled in misery.

'I want my daddy,' she sobbed.

⋆　⋆　⋆

Sophie looked dreadful when Julia took some tea into her room; her hair was unkempt and tangled, and her face blanched and hollow. She was crouched on the bed with her arms wrapped around her knees, and she was rocking, as Rory, evidently beyond trying to comfort her, simply sat and watched her.

'Where are the children?' she demanded

459

hoarsely as Julia put two cups of tea carefully on to the table beside the bed.

'With Matt,' she replied quietly. 'He's been with them all night, but they are at least having some cocoa now, and I really think you should have some tea.'

Sophie hunched her shoulders as if she was trying to keep everyone out.

'I want to see him,' she declared, her voice hard with anger. 'Oliver. Before they take him away — or whatever they're going to do with him. I want to see him. Will I be allowed to?'

'Of course you will,' Julia answered. 'Someone will take you when you're ready.'

'No, *you'll* take me!' Sophie snapped, glaring at her. 'You will. I want *you* to take me!' and she whined, and put her head on Rory's shoulder as she dissolved into tears.

Julia crept out of the room.

Matt began to dress Alice and Edward because Julia had to go and see to Minnie. It was Sunday, and Mrs Collins's day off, but by 8.30 the news had obviously filtered down into the village, because Mrs Collins arrived, looking shaken but determined — and Julia was reminded of the fact that she had been Oliver's particular choice as housekeeper at Tremar. He had promoted her from newcomer to important member of the community, and in the ensuing years she had

460

come to love and respect Julia. She was fiercely loyal.

'This is your day off, Mrs Collins,' Julia said, but Mrs Collins sniffed indignantly.

'An' they two girls from the village will be rushing about like frightened virgins, breaking plates for a pastime!' she declared. 'No, I'm sorry, Mrs Logan, but you needs me to keep things runnin' smoothly, an' that's what I'm 'ere for.'

Indeed, Julia had to admit that was true. They were very sweet, the two young girls from the village who came in alone on Sundays, but to be truthful they were only any good at lighting fires, peeling vegetables and washing up. In an emergency they would be hopeless.

And this was definitely an emergency.

Mrs Collins organized breakfast and insisted that it was attended. Matt came in with Alice and Edward — they were like two frightened little mice, clinging to him. Julia somehow coaxed Rory down, and with Rory came Sophie. She looked terrible and sat at the table in silence, picking at a piece of toast with hands that trembled.

Matt insisted that Alice and Edward have a bowl of porridge, and he promised them a trip to the workshop when they'd eaten it, but as Edward ate, tears began to trickle down his cheeks until suddenly he uttered a despairing howl and slid off his chair on to the floor, clutching at his legs.

'They hurt!' he sobbed. 'They hurt and they itch . . . '

His legs were terribly scratched and bruised from his experiences of the day before and he was a forlorn little creature, crouched under the table. Sophie, however, didn't seem to notice — or if she did, she simply didn't have room beside her own misery and rage to accommodate her son. Whichever, she simply watched in silence, as Matt lifted him gently into his arms.

'Do we have some cream upstairs?' he asked Julia. 'Something to give him a wee bit of relief?'

Mrs Collins was in the room and at once she smiled.

'I know just the thing,' she declared. 'We've some special cream we use for Minnie sometimes, an' it 'elps her no end. C'mon, my lad, let's go and see if we can find it.'

Edward looked at her dully, but she swept him up into her big arms and carried him away, and since he didn't start yelling, it seemed he was happy enough to be with her. Sophie finally pushed her nibbled piece of toast away, and Matt moved his chair back and offered his hand to Alice.

'Shall we go and find your brother?' he suggested fondly. 'And then, mebbe, take a trip to the workshop? I'm thinking your kitchen in the dolls' house could do wi' a nice Welsh dresser, like the one I made for wee Peggy . . . ' He smiled. 'Time to do a spot of re-decorating and modernizing, what do you think?'

Alice paused, frowning at her mother in great concern.

'Mummy . . . ?' she whispered and Sophie, to everyone's surprise, put her hands up in front of her face, in a gesture as if to ward her daughter off. For a dreadful moment Julia thought she was going to shout but she didn't, she simply darted her eyes away and bit her lips.

'Not now, Alice,' she muttered unsteadily. 'Not now, darling, please . . . '

Matt led Alice away without another word — but Julia did not miss the expression on his face, and even through his beard she could see how tight his mouth was. He disapproved, and it was black and white to him.

Matt had scant respect for people who didn't come up to his expectations. Julia had realized years ago that if she had become stuck in time on her release from Blackridge, if she had sat around and done nothing but complain about her lot in life, Matt would have left her employ very quickly. He hadn't liked Oliver from the first time he had met him, but he had been the children's father, and Matt considered their needs at the moment were of paramount importance.

From the drawing-room windows, some moments later, Rory and Julia watched Matt and the children head off in the direction of the pine copse and Julia supposed he had decided to take them for a walk, to blow some fresh air through their shocked little bodies. In fact, Edward had remembered the chunk of wood he had found when he had gone that way with his daddy the day before, and that was to be the chunk that would replace his favourite Spitfire.

His little eyes filled with tears when he found it and he clutched it to him, before offering it to Matt for his approval. Matt said it was perfect and then asked them to go on with him for a while, and they agreed.

He finished up taking them to the bay, and there, sitting on the rocks close to the steps, with the tide going down and the waves no more than tiny ripples on the sand, they talked about their daddy and they asked God to take care of him. A herring gull called above them, looking down, eagle-eyed, as it swooped in the brilliant blue sky.

'Is Daddy in Heaven now?' Alice asked, gazing upwards.

'Of course,' Matt replied immediately. 'He's in Heaven, watching the two of you with love, and what's more, because he's in Heaven he'll no' have his scars any more, either. When you next see him, he'll be just like he was before he went away in his uniform. But you have to understand that it'll be a long time before you do see him; you've many, many years of life yet, the both of you.'

Edward stared at the cold, quiet sea and his bottom lip trembled as his eyes yet again filled with tears.

'Do you *promise* he can see us?' he whispered, and Matt hugged him close, his heart aching as the little six-year-old's arms clung to his neck.

'He's going to watch over you all the time,' he replied softly. 'He's going to see you grow up and be the farmer you want to be, and he's going to be so proud of you, so proud of you both. Whatever happens to you in life from now on, always remember that your daddy loved you more than anything in the world.'

★ ★ ★

For Julia, the service she was obliged to offer was not quite such a gentle one; she had been detailed to take Sophie to see her husband for one last time. Oliver's body was to remain in a carefully cordoned-off area of the old stables until the undertakers came to collect him, but he had been nicely laid out on a long table and was covered with a white sheet, his head resting on a pillow. The nurses who had done the job had found a spare eye patch in his locker and been thoughtful enough to place it over his empty, shrivelled socket. They had also dressed him in his uniform, and he looked a great deal better than he had when Annie and Matt had left him there the night before.

When Julia asked Sophie if she was ready to go and see him, Sophie stared wildly at Rory and he took her hand.

'I'll go with you,' he said, and she nodded, but her face was full of fear, and as they entered the stables she hung back, showing the whites of her eyes and shaking noticeably.

A few moments later, Julia found out why.

'I've never seen a dead body before,' she whispered, finally approaching the table in terror, as if she half expected Oliver to leap at her.

Julia had to remind herself that her own life had been different from everybody else's. At

Blackridge she had regularly been asked to lay-out over the years, and the dead were no strangers to her. In fact, she could remember sometimes feeling slightly envious of a patient for whom she was performing these last kindnesses; the body was going to a grave, but the spirit was free. The restricted, handicapped, half-formed mockery of a human being, whom she washed and dressed as best she could, was whole and complete again somewhere else, Julia had always believed that. She didn't think she could have endured Blackridge if she hadn't believed her spirit would one day be free.

It was all very different with Oliver, though.

With his eye closed in death and his hands folded neatly on his breast, he reminded Julia of the white marble effigy of Sandro in the church. His face was completely without colour, waxy white in contrast to his dark-blue uniform and dark hair. She gazed at the hair, that soft, shiny hair he had passed on to his lovely daughter, and tried not to think about what Matt had told her the back of his skull looked like. She thought it was just as well Sophie couldn't see it.

The stables were cold and the silence was punctuated only by the gentle scratching and clucking of the hens. Julia gazed at Oliver's face and remembered him in life, finding

467

herself keenly aware of the uncanny emptiness that death left behind once the spirit had departed. She watched him for a long time, and then suddenly looked up because the silence had become vaguely uncomfortable. What she saw made her draw in her breath sharply, for Sophie was staring at Oliver with flinty anger in her eyes and something resembling a sneer on her lips: nowhere in her expression was there a shred of sorrow or regret.

Eventually she put out her hand and touched his face with one finger, and then she drew it back hastily and wiped it surreptitiously on her skirt. Julia was appalled and struggled to keep her face impassive. She cleared her throat.

'Sophie, I'd like to ask you a favour, if you wouldn't mind,' she said. 'I was very much hoping that you could see your way clear to Oliver being buried here in Polwean rather than having him taken back to Arundel to be buried. After all, it would seem likely that you will make your home here now, with Rory, and at least it would mean Oliver would always be close by for Alice and Edward, for them to give him flowers and such like on his birthday and at Christmas. It would also mean you wouldn't have to travel, which has got to be an advantage at the moment.'

Sophie's head shot up swiftly and she blinked at Julia a couple of times, as if she had said something completely outrageous. She looked savage, and after a moment she uttered a little noise of disgust in the back of her throat and her face flushed an ugly red. Julia saw Rory put out his hand rather nervously, but it was much too late; Sophie was ready to explode.

'*Buried?*' she echoed at last. 'What, all of us sit there in church thanking God for his life and all that? You can dig a hole and shovel him in it for all I care! He tried to murder my son, and as far as I'm concerned that doesn't entitle him to a Christian burial — not one I'm going to have anything to do with, anyway!'

Julia pressed her lips together tightly as indignation threatened to choke her. She knew she should have been used to it by now; Sophie had been at Tremar for just over six months, and the pace of her bitter, unremitting resentment towards Oliver had not slowed once. But for all that he was dead, lying here ruined and wasted. She could at least have shown a little basic forgiveness.

'Remarks like that don't help anyone,' she pointed out, struggling to keep her voice calm. 'I'm prepared to do my best to make it as easy as I can for you; I'll make all the arrangements if you want me to, speak to your in-laws, arrange for them to be collected from the station and so on, but you must at least co-operate with me. He *was* your husband, Sophie; you owe him a certain respect, if nothing else.'

To Julia's utter dismay Sophie's eyes suddenly blazed in fury.

'*Respect!*' she snorted. 'He tried to kill his own child, and you want me to respect his memory, to care what happens to him now he's dead? Do you think his children will care? The only person who cares, Your Ladyship, is you. And don't think I don't know what all the rest of it's about, either: get his parents down here as quickly as you can, so that you can bundle us off back with them, out of your hair. After all, why should you want us here now? Your lover's dead, isn't he?'

Julia was so taken aback by the outburst that she just stood there, her mouth gaping. However, Rory — he of the gentle nature and amazingly even temper — was almost poleaxed with embarrassment. Rounding on Sophie he glared at her, his cheeks red with anger.

'That's enough, Sophie!' he barked. 'What do you think you're doing? How dare you speak to Julia like that, when she's been

470

nothing but kind to you? I think perhaps you should go back to bed for a while, my dear, you are obviously not at all well, and I think you should apologize, before you go, as well.'

Sophie stared at him, her eyes glittering with fury. She looked really quite unhinged and threatening enough for him to feel the need to take a small step backwards.

'*Apologize!*' she screamed at him. 'To *her*? From the first moment he laid eyes on her she was the only thing he ever thought about again. He didn't give a damn what happened to the children or me; he didn't care one jot how much we suffered. She used him; she lured him into her bed, made him all sorts of promises that she never intended to keep, and then, when she'd had enough of him, she threw him back at us. And you want me to apologize to her? When hell freezes over, Rory. *When hell freezes over!*' and she fled from the stables, sobbing uncontrollably.

The silence in the cold presence of Oliver's body was deafening as Rory and Julia stood opposite each other, rigid with discomfort. They looked anywhere but at each other, and Rory was blushing deeply.

'Oh God, I'm *so* sorry,' he whispered at last. 'I really am, Julia. She's dreadfully overwrought. She'll be devastated when she calms down, I know she will.'

471

'That's as maybe,' Julia retorted coldly, 'but to be honest with you, Rory, I'm coming very close to the edge as far as Sophie's concerned. Frankly I've had enough of being constantly blamed for her failed marriage. If she really thought of me as such a flagrant husband-stealer, what did she come here for in the first place? Let's face it, on her own admission Oliver could have gone somewhere else to convalesce; anywhere else. *She* chose Tremar, not his doctors; and now she's wandering about pregnant with *your* child, but somehow it's still all my fault!'

Rory winced. He was miles out of his depth. He had come to Tremar in all good faith at the beginning of the war, promising himself that he would be the most accommodating companion they could ever wish for. Now he felt he had disgraced himself, and he would have given just about anything to have had somewhere else to go.

'So this time,' he said, 'we are definitely under notice to leave, then?'

Julia's eyes filled with tears and she touched Oliver's icy skin, stroking his cheek with her fingers. Her heart ached for him; he'd been her saviour and she was going to miss him and bitterly she acknowledged that she was on her own with her feelings. It was hard.

472

'You would be,' she replied bluntly, 'if it weren't for the children. But Alice and Edward have become very precious to us; particularly Edward, he and Matt adore each other and in many ways he's the son Matt will never have.' A couple of angry tears trickled down her cheeks and she used her hands to rub them away. 'But I've had enough, Rory,' she continued. 'This is *my* house and I'm sick of walking about on eggshells all the time. If you don't sort Sophie out and make damn sure she behaves herself when Oliver's parents arrive, I might just harden my heart and send them all packing back to Arundel!'

Rory gaped at her as his heart jolted in his chest.

'You wouldn't?' he whispered, and she narrowed her eyes.

'You watch me!' she snarled.

★ ★ ★

Harriet Crompton came back from the telephone and sat herself heavily in the armchair across from her husband. It had been cold in the dark, empty hall, and it was still cold in the sitting-room. Cautiously, she shuffled her feet a little nearer to the grate in which burned a carefully controlled 'wartime' fire: a miserable blaze that did nothing to cheer.

'That was Mrs Logan from Tremar,' she said, her mouth set hard. 'It seems Sophie has chosen that Oliver should be buried in Cornwall, rather than come home to be close to us, and the funeral is to be next Friday. Actually, she was very charming. She has kindly invited us to stay at the manor, and will send a car to meet us at the station. The painted doll didn't speak to me, needless to say. Couldn't be bothered, probably, or more likely she's gloating because she can dictate where our son is to be buried, knowing there isn't anything we can do about it!'

Charles Crompton glanced up at his wife wearily. The news of Oliver's suicide had hit her hard, for Harriet was a woman who would soldier on against any odds, no matter what, and that her beloved son should have simply given up and dashed himself on to the rocks was, in her eyes, a terrible betrayal.

He knew she wanted someone to blame, and almost certainly it would be Sophie. She had been waiting for them to come creeping back unwillingly from Cornwall with Oliver's body in tow, and for sure she had been planning a spectacularly awful welcome. Now Mrs Logan at Tremar had robbed her of it. Now they must go to Cornwall instead, and

Harriet wouldn't find it nearly so easy to vent her spleen on her daughter-in-law in someone else's house.

'Did she give you any more reasons, than the doctors I mean, as to why Oliver should have killed himself, my dear?' he asked, and she flared her nostrils at him contemptuously.

'I don't need reasons,' she retorted. 'He killed himself because he was a coward; what other reason could there be? Because he was too much like you and not enough like me!' she blew a stream of air from her nostrils and her lips trembled slightly as she stared, unseeing, into the struggling fire. 'Francesca isn't able to come to her brother's funeral, by the way. I spoke to her on the phone this afternoon. She has no one with whom she can leave the children, apparently; but then I didn't really expect anything else.'

Charles sighed and thought he might have suggested they phone their daughter back to tell her the funeral was now going to be in Cornwall, but as he looked at his wife, at her blunt, uncompromising face, he was as always painfully conscious that, like a lot of opinionated bullies, she somehow managed to elicit sympathy. No one liked her, but everyone avoided blatantly hurting her. It was how she got away with so much, how the women on her many committees, though they couldn't stand the sight of her, persistently did what she wanted. It was why Francesca wouldn't come to Oliver's funeral no matter where it was held, for she didn't want to be in her mother's company. Francesca knew she would be criticized and belittled whilst everyone else would feel sorry for Oliver's grieving mother, and would creep away afterwards to lick her wounds, and acknowledge yet another victory for Harriet.

So instead he muttered, 'I'll make the arrangements tomorrow then, shall I, for us to travel to Cornwall and so forth? Then I can perhaps ring Tremar and tell them what time we'll be arriving.'

'If you think you're capable of doing it properly,' his wife snapped back. 'I do not want to find myself on the wrong train, or worse still, on the wrong platform somewhere waiting for someone who is never going to arrive.'

'I'll double-check it all with you, my dear,' he promised soothingly, and then, as the cheap coal in the fireplace spat angrily and a burning ember landed on the rug, he reached to put it out with his foot and decided to risk her wrath and say his piece. 'Harriet,' he said, 'I wonder if you would do me a favour?'

Her eyes appraised him suspiciously.

'Favour?' she repeated. 'What favour?'

He watched her. He so rarely criticized her, or even hinted that anything she did might be unacceptable, that most people didn't think he was capable of such a thing. He was though, when pushed hard enough.

'I want you to promise me that you will be careful what you say to Sophie,' he said quietly. 'In front of the Logans I really don't care to have our dirty linen aired, and we're all overwrought and hurt by Oliver's death. Please don't let Mr and Mrs Logan hear you shouting at Sophie or the children. Tremar is not our home.'

An indignant sneer formed itself on Harriet Crompton's face, lifting one corner of her mouth unpleasantly.

'If you think I am going to attend my son's funeral and not find out exactly why he died,' she told him, 'you are much mistaken. I know as well as you do that there was some trouble with this Logan woman when they were in Polwean before the war, and I intend to find out exactly what drove him to kill himself.'

'Has it ever occurred to you that it might simply have been his injuries?' her husband asked sadly. 'Have you considered that, Harriet?'

She turned her head away swiftly and for a moment her eyes roamed about the room. This room, hardly changed at all over the years, where Oliver had grown up, had told them that he planned to be a doctor, had introduced them to the shy little Sophie the first time, and had said goodbye as he went away to war in his uniform. Her son, whom she had tried to teach correctly. The boy not allowed to cry, because real men didn't cry; the boy taught that he was clever, and therefore had more right to the things he wanted than people who were not so clever; the boy who had almost beggared them financially so that he could have a public school education.

It was wasted. All of it. There was nothing left but bitter memories and two children whom Harriet doubted she would see more than once in a blue moon now, and didn't greatly care for anyway.

'What I find most extraordinary,' Charles said suddenly, when their silence had hung for so long it was too heavy to bear any longer, 'is why he should have tried to take Edward with him. That's the thing I find hardest to understand. Why take a little boy.'

'If Edward is still as unpleasant as he was when he was staying here,' Harriet opined coldly, 'then I'm not surprised Oliver tried to push him off the cliff!'

The moment she'd said it she experienced a very rare acknowledgement that she had made a very nasty remark, and wished she could have bitten off her tongue.

Charles Crompton stared at her in shocked silence — but he didn't say anything, and she didn't apologize.

* * *

Oliver was coffined on Monday morning and Julia insisted that the lid be screwed down. She did not want the children going into the stables and seeing him; they had been kept away until now and everyone agreed that it would do neither of them any service to look on their dead father. It was enough that Edward had nightmare memories of looking down, as he clung desperately to the cliff, at his looking down, as he clung desperately to the cliff, at his father spread on the rocks beneath him, and enough that Alice should have shown her full understanding of the situation, when she had dropped her little doll from the table in front of everybody in the bedroom.

Guy and Patrick, finding comfort in each other's company, and both extremely upset at their room-mate's death, had spent some time with Oliver when he was laid out on the table, and spent some more beside his coffin during the week, where they stood with their hands on the lid and quietly wished him luck. Julia wove a wreath of evergreen and laid it on his breast: she had ordered flowers, such as there were available in January, from a florist in the town for the funeral, but the wreath was from her, and she mourned him very privately.

Matt didn't go anywhere near Oliver at all, but he spent a lot of time with Alice and Edward, and between him and Mrs Collins, who spent hours making them tasty little goodies to eat, they began to climb out of their bewilderment a little.

Alice picked up her father-doll and put him back into the house eventually, but Julia spotted immediately that she had put him in the attic, lying on a little pillow, and asked her why.

'Because he's dead,' the child replied simply, 'and he's gone to Heaven. I thought I might dip him in some white paint and then lay him on a grey box — 'cept that I haven't got a church to put him in. He'll be like your brother then, and he's in Heaven, isn't he?'

'Yes, he is, sweetheart,' Julia said, 'and watching over us all the time. Your daddy will be with him now, and I promise Sandro will look after him.'

Alice nodded and stared broodily at the doll for a moment, then she carefully closed the front of the house.

'I didn't believe in Heaven, I don't think,' she said quietly, 'not before, only Uncle Matt told us Daddy was definitely in Heaven, and Uncle Matt wouldn't tell us a lie, would he?'

'No,' Julia replied firmly. 'He wouldn't, ever.'

The new Spitfire took shape in the workshop and every time he went in there, Edward touched it reverently with his small fingers.

'It will be my *really* favourite,' he announced. 'I shall keep it forever an' it'll always remind me of . . . ' he stopped abruptly and his eyes swam with tears.

Matt bent and kissed his corn-coloured head very gently.

'Remind you of your daddy?' he asked. 'It's all right. After a while the pain will go away, laddie, I promise, and then you'll be proud to look at your Spitfire and remember that your daddy was a hero.'

Edward looked up at him as the tears splashed down his face, because he couldn't hold them back yet, no matter how hard he tried.

'Will we win this war, Uncle Matt?' he asked in a trembling voice. 'We will won't we?'

Matt cupped his face in his hands, and gazed into his tear-drenched eyes.

'Aye, we will,' he said firmly.

Edward sniffed loudly.

'Promise?' he whispered, and Matt thought about the state of the world, the fearful news that clamoured in the headlines every day, the awful sense of standing alone and having nowhere to go and nothing much to fall back on other than the indomitable British spirit. He thought of the bombers droning overhead in the night, and the hours and hours worked in the fields until every muscle ached and the weariness was almost unbearable. And he thought of the millions he knew nothing about, who suffered in ways those in the comfort of Tremar couldn't begin to envisage.

'I promise!' he replied, and he meant to keep his promise.

18

On Thursday morning at breakfast, Matt watched the children quietly, and it seemed that in small ways they were already beginning to slip back to normal, except that they had yet to face their grandparents and bury their father, which would be a big hurdle for them.

Fortunately they had no black clothes, and Julia had been most unwilling to provide them with any, though Sophie didn't appear to be too worried. Julia remembered when her irascible old grandfather had died and she and Sandro, swathed in dreary black which was much too warm for the time of year, had been expected to wade through the funeral looking suitably distressed — when they'd cared not one jot that the old boy was dead.

Alice and Edward wore their everyday clothes. At the funeral the next day, Alice would wear her best dress and her winter coat, and Edward the grey shorts and blazer that he wore to school. After the funeral they were going to Five Elms to spend some time doing jobs for Doreen, predominantly to get them right out of the way in case one or other

Mrs Crompton decided to lose her temper.

As they finished eating Matt said, 'I was wondering if one or both of you would care to come to the station with me in the big car after lunch to meet your grandparents from the train? I thought it might be nice for them to see familiar faces.'

Edward didn't even look up, but his bottom jaw shot out firmly.

'Not me!' he growled. 'I don't want to see *her* at all!' He began to wriggle sullenly in his chair.

Matt smiled benignly.

'D'you no' want her to see what a man you've become since you came to Tremar, then?' he enquired. 'I think that's a wee bit sad, when the work you're doing towards the war effort is so valuable.'

Julia watched the children from under her brow, but said nothing, simply went on with her breakfast. Annie, however, glanced at Alice and grinned.

'I bet Alice'll want to go,' she declared. 'I would, if it were me. I didn't know 'alf as much 'bout farmin' when I was 'er age, an' look at me now.'

That was patently untrue: Annie had been born with an affinity to animals, and had known the importance of the seasons probably before she was even out of nappies;

her brothers had never talked about anything else, they still didn't. When they had come home on leave at Christmas, they had been out inspecting Rectory Farm almost before they'd had time to shed their uniforms. But the little lure drew Alice in tidily.

'I'd like to go with you, Uncle Matt,' she said shyly and at once Edward threw her a sharp glance.

'Well, if you're going then I s'pose I'll *have* to,' he declared in his 'girls are such a trial' sort of voice. 'But I tell you what, if she hits me with a hairbrush even once while she's here, then I'm going to bite her till she bleeds!'

'She won't,' Julia assured him calmly. 'In my house no one hits anyone with a hairbrush, or anything else.'

★ ★ ★

The Cromptons had been travelling since very early in the day, and felt sooty and creased when they finally stepped out of the train. A sharp, unforgiving wind blew along the platform and Charles, having climbed down first to take the suitcase and other odd assorted bits of hand luggage, found it quite painful.

Matt approached them and politely offered

his assistance, and then a couple of awkward minutes later they were all on the platform and the guard's shrill whistle was announcing the train's departure.

'You're very kind, sir,' Charles said turning to Matt and rubbing his hands together in an effort to keep them warm. 'Your help was much appreciated. We are expecting to be collected, but we're not altogether sure by whom.'

At once Alice and Edward, who had stood well back during their grandparents' struggle, came shyly forward and Edward took it upon himself to perform the introductions.

'This is Uncle Matt,' he said in his most lordly way. 'Uncle Matt, this is our Granny and Grandpa. We've come to collect you, and the car is waiting outside.'

Anyone else but Matt might have been tempted to laugh, but he shook hands with Oliver's parents without so much as a hint of a smile and then handed the lighter of the hand luggage to Edward to carry. The Cromptons had brought very little with them, but then they weren't staying for very long; just long enough for a brief, painful glimpse into the life and death of their only son.

Harriet Crompton peered down at Edward, who stared boldly back.

'My, how you've grown!' she observed in a

tone that seemed mostly to be disapproving. 'And you too, Alice. The country air must agree with you.'

'We've grown because we work,' Edward replied proudly, leading them through the booking hall and out into the station yard. 'We do very valuable work towards the war effort now, me and Alice. Good, isn't it?'

Charles Crompton, who had frankly been dreading their arrival in Cornwall and their encounter with their grandchildren, was both surprised and delighted at what appeared to have been a remarkable transformation in his grandson. Harriet, however, looked at the little boy sharply.

'And what valuable work towards the war effort could *you* possibly be doing?' she enquired doubtfully.

Before he could answer, Matt broke into the conversation.

'They work very hard, Mrs Crompton,' he said in his matter-of-fact way, opening the boot of the great, blue Lagonda. 'Everyone at Tremar works; ours is a huge acreage and we need a full team to farm it. Alice and Edward are very much appreciated at Five Elms Farm; it's time-consuming, working with two hundred chickens that have to be fed and watered twice a day and regularly strawed down, and their effort frees up my Land Girl

487

there to do something else.'

When the luggage was safely stored, Edward politely held open the back door for Harriet and Charles to climb in, then he and Alice squeezed into the big leather front seat beside Matt. They had simply not been able to agree on which of them would go in the back with Granny and Grandpa, and both had agreed that an uncomfortable journey back to Tremar, squashed together in a seat meant for one, would be infinitely preferable.

Matt simply let them get on with it.

It was warm in the car, but as they travelled along narrow lanes between winter hedgerows and past sleeping fields, the Cromptons were not treated to the real beauty of Cornwall. As they came into the village, the green looked dull beneath the leaden January sky, there was no creeper on the front of the pub, and the church was coldly grey. Matt swung the car up the road leading to Tremar and turned in between the weathered old gateposts. As the car came to a halt on the drive, the front door opened and Julia emerged.

Harriet Crompton had never seen Julia, or even a photograph of her, but she remembered Oliver telling her about the heir to Tremar. He'd been very proud of himself for rescuing her, and he had talked about her a lot. Rather more, Harriet had always thought, than evidently pleased Sophie. She certainly was a splendid-looking woman, this refugee from an insane asylum, that much was true, and it appeared, as Alice and Edward piled out of the front seat and both very willingly gave her a kiss, that she had a close affinity with Oliver's children.

'Run inside,' Julia whispered to them. 'It's almost tea-time and Mrs Collins has baked a cake. You've got about ten minutes to do what you want to do, then make it snappy into the drawing-room, all right?' They needed no second bidding, and when they were gone she straightened up and opened the car door for Harriet and Charles. 'Mr and Mrs Crompton, welcome to Tremar,' she said, holding out her hand to them. 'I'm just so sorry we have to meet under these very sad circumstances. Do, please, come in and get warm.'

There was no doubt that they were impressed with Tremar — it wasn't possible not to be. The beautiful, understated opulence was a long way removed from their normal surroundings, and despite the fact that Tremar was a great deal larger than their home in Arundel, it was also a great deal warmer. Charles Crompton wondered how they managed that, but of course he didn't ask.

When Julia had relieved them of their

coats, she took them into the drawing-room where they found a huge fire dancing in the grate. They also found their daughter-in-law, looking pale and haggard, and when she stood up they saw immediately part of the reason why.

Harriet Crompton's mouth fell open in horror.

'Good God, you're pregnant!' she exclaimed. 'I don't believe it.' She narrowed her eyes. 'Or perhaps I do,' she said icily. 'So *that's* why Oliver killed himself, is it? Because you've rewarded his heroism by sleeping with someone else? I should have known . . . '

Julia saw Sophie's face flush an ugly red, and she also saw Rory's blanch, but she allowed no one time to speak.

'The child is Oliver's, Mrs Crompton,' she said smoothly,' 'and he knew he was going to be a father again when he died. It had nothing to do with his death, I'm afraid.'

Harriet Crompton swung round and stared at Julia with her small, beady eyes. Stood there, bulky in her heavy, grey costume and her solid black shoes, she was a formidable figure, and Julia thought she knew why Edward and Alice had feared her so much. She looked most uncompromising, and her husband looked suitably cowed, standing beside her.

'I thought this was supposed to be a convalescent home!' she snorted indignantly. 'What sort of place is it, that men and women are allowed to share beds with each other?'

Julia could see that Sophie was building up to shout, and with calm determination she set about preventing it. She did not wish to begin this encounter with an immediate breakdown in communications, and she did not wish for Minnie, who dozed as yet unseen in a chair by the fire, to be frightened out of her life. Minnie had become very sensitive to ill-feeling since she had become ill, as if locked in her now static little world she was able to dredge up horrible memories from the past.

'This is not a convalescent home, Mrs Crompton,' she said quietly. 'The convalescent home is next door, in the dower. But nobody does anything to stop the officers coming into the manor; we all share the library for a start, and we regularly socialize. One of Oliver's room-mates, Patrick, is marrying our ward, Annie, in June, and the other, Guy, is going to be taking on the running of our village shop with his wife in a few months' time. So you see, it's a very comfortable arrangement, and no one minded when Oliver came into the house to see Sophie and the children.'

Harriet Crompton tightened her mouth.

'I find it a touch unorthodox, nevertheless,' she remarked.

'But not improper,' Julia answered, smiling benignly. 'They *were* married to each other, after all. And now, please, do sit down; my housekeeper will be bringing tea any minute. After that I'll take you up to your room.'

'And after that we'd like to spend a little time with our son, if it's at all possible,' Charles Crompton said almost apologetically. 'We don't want to put anybody out but . . . '

'I'll take you to see him, Daddy,' Sophie said, to Julia's surprise. 'Of course I will, but if you're going to ask me, either of you, why he killed himself then I don't know . . . ' Her eyes filled with tears and she seemed almost to glare at them. 'I don't know why he tried to take Edward with him, either,' she snapped, 'and I find it rather hard to forgive him for that.'

Harriet Crompton looked away quickly, but Charles went across to his daughter-in-law, touched her hands softly and sat down beside her. Sophie introduced him to Rory and he continued to sit by her during tea, which Mrs Collins had served in the huge silver teapot always used when guests came. The conversation eased and small talk flowed quite readily for half an hour or so, then

492

approaching darkness necessitated the pulling of the curtains, and the Crompton children, who had crept in for tea but stayed very close to Matt, asked permission to go to their room.

Harriet and Charles Crompton watched the interplay between the regular residents of Tremar with interest. Annie came in for tea, and they found her charming when she was introduced; they saw Julia gently feeding Minnie tea and cake; and intentionally or not, they realized that they were being made aware of how calmly and quietly life flowed at Tremar. When they came downstairs from their room a while later, to go and see Oliver, they found only Sophie and Julia waiting for them in the drawing-room, and it suddenly occurred to Charles that Julia was acting like a bodyguard.

When Harriet, looking her daughter-in-law up and down in her usual disapproving fashion enquired, 'Are you and the children expecting to return to Arundel with us after the funeral?', it was, as always, Julia who answered.

'No, Mrs Crompton,' she said, smiling. 'That's why Oliver is to be buried here in Polwean, because Sophie and the children want to make their home here. It was the last place they were all together as a family, and so they want to stay. Besides, Edward and Alice are doing wonderfully at school, and Edward seems to have made up his mind that he's going to be a farmer — so start him early, is Matt's philosophy.'

Charles Crompton studied Sophie's face closely, and he didn't miss the look she gave Julia. It was a mixture of relief and gratitude, and it made him wonder how things had really been here before Oliver died. He felt very sad that his son had killed himself, but he had always been much more aware of Oliver's shortcomings than Harriet had — and he thought he remembered now, too, what the trouble had been when Oliver had been in practice here: he'd been in love with the beautiful Julia, this aristocratic lady who now protected Sophie so carefully.

On the surface it was all very charming, but for all that, and because he was much more perceptive than his wife, he had an idea that they were seeing only what they were being permitted to see.

And he felt certain, though he knew he would never be told, that Sophie was *not* carrying Oliver's child.

★ ★ ★

The familiar glass hearse, drawn by the two great horses, that had taken Lady Florence to her grave in 1938, came at ten o'clock the next morning to take Oliver to his. It was a cold day with a dull sky, but at least it was dry, for the funeral party were to walk down to the church behind it.

Sophie had found herself something black to wear and she looked awful, the black accentuating her strained, white face alarmingly. Julia also wore black, but Annie, like the children, had no black and Julia was quite happy about that. Annie was young and beautiful and much too fresh for mourning clothes.

Julia escorted Sophie, walking with her directly behind the wheels of the hearse. The Cromptons followed, and behind them Matt hung on tightly to Edward's hand and Annie to Alice's, though Patrick stood on the other side of Alice and made her feel as if she wasn't just being comforted, but guiding him at the same time, which cheered her somewhat.

Other officers and staff from the dower came behind the group, including Guy, who would very much have liked to walk but didn't trust himself on his legs for such a long time. He was grateful for Rory's company on the journey, but not half so much as Rory was for his. Guy knew Sophie's baby was Rory's; he knew Rory would marry Sophie one day, and it seemed a small relief from the great big lie Rory found himself living these days to at least be alongside someone who knew the truth.

In the church, Alexander Drake lay white and shadowy in the north aisle. No bell tolled Oliver's departing, for the church bells across England had been silent for a long time now, and though a lot of people from the village had turned out for the funeral, because they remembered Oliver with pleasure, the church itself felt like an icehouse.

Throughout the service Edward clung to Matt, clenching his teeth so hard it was a wonder he didn't break some. When he allowed tears to well into his eyes he blinked them away hastily and his rigid little body swayed. Alice did not fare so well and collapsed sobbing on to the pew eventually, at which point Patrick gathered her up into his arms and held her against him tightly, allowing her to wrap her arms and legs about him and weep into his neck.

Julia tried to imagine what this would have been like for them had they not been here at Tremar, and had they had no choice but to return home afterwards to the house in Arundel where they had been so unhappy, where life for them would have been twice as bad now, with their father gone forever. She closed her eyes and thought about it, and found herself with the same agony of spirit she suffered when she thought of Blackridge.

So there were many different prisons then, but all as painful as each other. Oliver had rescued her from hers: perhaps she was now returning the compliment.

After the service they went through the west door of the church out into the cold, colourless graveyard, and Julia gritted her teeth, for this was the bit she hated most of all. She remembered standing here in swirling sleet, watching Arthur's coffin being lowered into the earth, and she remembered Oliver standing close by her, like a guard. Their affair had been over by then, and he had been driven to spite by her rejection of him. She hadn't known for certain whether he was going to take his suspicions to the police, and yet at that moment her life had been overwhelmed by her newly acknowledged love for Matt.

Now that gloriously handsome man in the flannels and sports jacket, whom she and Minnie had first seen from a barred window in Blackridge and not acknowledged because he came from a world they knew nothing about, was sliding into the earth, to rot in the darkness forever.

She saw Matt and Annie making certain that they kept Edward and Alice away from the edge of the grave, and was grateful to them. She saw Sophie and Harriet each throw a handful of dirt, and she heard it patter against the coffin lid, then she turned away as her heart seemed to tear in her breast.

Oh, Oliver! she cried out silently. Why? What have you gained by doing this? You were much too young to die, and you had far too much to live for!

And on the breath of the icy breeze that was just enough to chill her to the bone, she heard Oliver's voice, ghostly in her mind: 'Will you feel the need to tend my grave in passing, do you think?'

Had he known then, she wondered, that death would eventually be his way out of the mess?

Of course she would tend his grave, and encourage his children to do the same thing, but they shouldn't have to, she thought bitterly. If he'd gone down with his ship, that would have been different. This was simply an ignominious death, and both he and the children deserved better.

★　★　★

They ate lunch in the company of Guy and Patrick who had been such good friends to Oliver in his last months. It was a subdued occasion, and immediately afterwards Sophie asked if anyone minded if she went to bed for a while, which Julia thought was the best thing possible, since she had eaten next to nothing and looked on the verge of collapse.

Alice and Edward asked if they could go to Five Elms, and Matt said he would walk them across and then go on to his work. Annie kissed Patrick and excused herself, heading back out on to the land, and Guy and Patrick went back to the dower. It left the Cromptons and Rory alone with Julia.

Charles had found himself sitting next to Rory at lunch and they had struck up a conversation, discovering that they shared quite a number of interests. They left the dining-room and settled comfortably in the drawing-room, chatting quietly, but Harriet went slowly to the French windows and gazed out across the estate, noting the silent fountain on the terrace and the sleeping vegetable beds beneath it, the formal lawns and winter-skeletal orchard. Beyond them, and beyond the distant pine trees, lay the sea, so she had been told. The bay and the cliffs . . . the last place Oliver had drawn breath.

'Mrs Logan,' she said at last, turning to

look at Julia who was hovering close to the door. 'I would like to see the place where my son died. Would that be possible, do you think?'

For a second Julia considered demurring, then she acknowledged that the woman not only had a right to see it if she so wished, but was more than capable of making the journey. Perhaps they could walk together, and perhaps Julia could patch a few holes along the way? These two lonely people were, when all was said and done, Alice and Edward's grandparents, and it seemed not just fair, but correct that they should not be denied contact with them in the years to come.

'Of course, Mrs Crompton,' she replied with a gentle smile. 'You'll need your coat and your flat shoes. It's quite a walk, but we'll take it reasonably slowly.'

Julia didn't miss the fact that Harriet didn't even bother to ask her husband if he would like to go with them; she simply fetched her coat and gloves, changed her shoes and then met Julia again in the drawing-room.

Charles Crompton watched his wife go, then he turned his attention back to Rory, and Julia and Harriet stood on the terrace together in the cold afternoon air.

The sea smelled sharp and very salty today. At the bottom of the terrace steps they picked their way through the vegetable beds and Julia explained about the officers working outside in the spring and summer sunshine. They crossed the lawns and went through the orchard, and met Annie with three of the Land Girls in the pine copse. They were coppicing, and burning the rubbish on a fragrant-smelling bonfire. It crackled as dead pine needles spurted flame and turned to ash within it, and Harriet watched them for a long time, completely silent.

Finally they went on to the bay and then up to the stone bench, to the place where Oliver had decided to die. Harriet did not huff and puff on the steep climb, she was obviously much fitter than she looked, but when they reached the top she sat down first and simply stared at the ocean, which bore the reflected grey of the sky. No waves crashed on to the rocks beneath, the weather had been still for days now. No sound at all invaded the silence but the gulls, and it was a peaceful place today.

'Was it a beautiful day when he died?' she asked eventually.

'As a matter of fact it was,' Julia replied. 'It had been lovely here all day; sunny, but very cold. That was the worst problem for Edward, he was very sick and confused for a while when Matt finally found him and brought him home.'

Harriet Crompton stood up and seemed to take the three of four steps to the edge of the cliff very deliberately. She gazed down at the brown, shiny rocks where Oliver had smashed his skull, and then, broodily, she stared at the hardy little bush, hanging out from the cliff, which had saved Edward's life.

She stared for ages, as if it were possible to stare long enough to bring the day back and replay it differently. She fished in the pocket of her coat and found a handkerchief, and wiped her eyes roughly, as if she felt to be seen crying was a sign of weakness.

'Why did he kill himself, Mrs Logan?' she asked, finally turning away from the cliff edge. 'Please tell me why. I trust you to be truthful.'

Julia moved to stand beside her and for a moment they listened to the sea splashing lazily against the rocks below them. The air was clear and, for Julia, the place was beautiful. She looked about her and knew she could never come here and dash herself to death, because this was a place of renewal, but if Harriet had only asked why *here*, she could have answered the question quite truthfully. As it was she must lie, because the truth was simply too painful.

'I don't know, Mrs Crompton,' she said at last. 'I wish I did. I do know, though, that his injuries were painful and debilitating.'

Harriet's mouth tightened slightly.

'Captain Taylor has no legs,' she pointed out. 'Squadron Leader Thornby has been blinded. Oliver was hardly alone in his suffering.'

'No, but neither Guy nor Patrick is a qualified doctor,' Julia replied sadly. 'What's more, Guy will have a splendid life with his wife and small son in the village shop, and Patrick and Annie will live at Tremar. Oliver was a dedicated professional and his career was in ruins. He was a handsome, charming man whose facial injuries were enough to make most people avert their eyes. He couldn't even cut his own food properly.' She pushed her hands into the pockets of her coat and they began to walk back down towards the bay as it threatened to be evening soon, and darkness would come early on this dull day. 'People have different ways of coping, I'm afraid,' she added eventually, 'and Oliver simply wasn't very good at coping. He felt, rightly or wrongly, that his children thought less of him than they did of Matt, because Matt was whole and strong.'

'He killed himself because of your husband?' Harriet exclaimed in astonishment, but Julia shook her head.

'No,' she replied. 'Matt was just one of his problems.'

In the copse they passed the girls again and Harriet was grateful for the words of kindness she received from them. As they came again into the orchard, Julia thought about how wonderful it looked in late summer, so leafy and laden with ripening apples, and she remembered Oliver walking amongst the trees with her.

At the gate to the formal lawns they stopped, and Harriet leaned on the railings, staring first at the house and then at Julia. Julia was getting used to her now and had no trouble understanding Sophie's abhorrence of her. Sophie would simply have no touching point with her; Julia had met many women of Harriet Crompton's ilk in the course of growing up — first and foremost her own nanny.

'I think my son was in love with you,' she stated at last.' 'Am I right?'

Julia swallowed. There was no point in being anything but truthful about that.

'Yes, I'm afraid he was,' she answered, 'and in my own way I loved him back. I shall miss him dreadfully, he was a dear friend and the man who saved my life . . . but I couldn't love him in the way he wanted.'

'He had no right to want it,' his mother snorted. 'He was a married man with two children. But then maybe if the painted doll had been a bit more accommodating . . . '

Julia pressed her lips together, and then dampened them with her tongue as she tried to pick the right words with great care.

'Mrs Crompton, please don't blame Sophie,' she said eventually. 'Oliver was very obvious in his love for me and it was humiliating for her. It was the reason he closed up their London flat and pushed her and the children on to you at the beginning of the war; he was punishing her because I'd rejected him. And it wasn't going to change anything, he knew that.'

They began to cross the last of the formal lawns, walking slowly side by side, and as Julia glanced up she saw Sophie at her bedroom window, staring down at them. As their eyes met Sophie sneered and turned away swiftly, and Julia was very pleased Harriet hadn't seen her.

Finally they were at the foot of the terrace steps.

'Your home is very beautiful, Mrs Logan,' the tough Harriet remarked, her sharp little eyes briefly appraising Julia's face. 'You are a lucky woman, though I have an idea you are fully aware of how lucky you are. I would like to ask you a favour, if I might.'

Julia smiled.

'Ask away,' she replied, and saw one of Harriet's big, brown-gloved hands grasp the terrace wall firmly.

'Left to her own devices my daughter-in-law will have nothing further to do with Oliver's father and me,' she said, 'and it may be that I was harsh with the children when they lived with me, but I thought it was what Oliver wanted. Here they have much more freedom than they ever could have done in Arundel, of course, and they have regular jobs to do, which is good, character-building stuff and keeps potentially idle hands busy. However, Charles and I would be very sad if we never saw or heard anything of them again. Would you be kind enough to send me a snapshot of them now and again, and perhaps one of the baby? I would be most grateful.'

Julia touched her quickly, a tiny gesture of understanding.

'I'll not only send you snapshots,' she promised, 'I'll get them to write as well, and then maybe, when the war is over, you might like to come back to Tremar for a visit, or something?'

Harriet Crompton laughed softly.

'Yes, who knows?' she said, meaninglessly.

* ★ ★

Matt drove them to the station the following morning, their brief visit to Oliver's last world over. Alice and Edward went with them in the car, but it didn't go unnoticed by anyone that Sophie didn't even make an appearance before they left.

When she finally did come down to the drawing-room, Julia was in there alone, feeding Minnie, and Sophie seemed to slide in, almost like a thief, glancing all around her as she came.

'They've gone then?' she asked. 'Thank God for that . . . or perhaps not, eh? You and the old witch seemed to be getting on wonderfully well yesterday. No doubt she's gone away kicking herself that you are not, after all, her daughter-in-law.'

Sophie's hostility had grown so much since Oliver's death that Julia was beginning to find it unbearable, and actually found herself occasionally hiding when she saw her coming. There certainly didn't appear to be any ending to this war yet, and the army, as far as she could gather, was destroying Cliff House enthusiastically, so even when the war did finally cease it would still be a long time before Rory could go home. The idea was depressing.

507

'She asked to see where Oliver killed himself,' she told her quietly, wiping Minnie's chin with a napkin, 'so I took her. She also asked me if Oliver had been in love with me, and when I told her yes she was angry with him. She never expressed any desire to have me as a daughter-in-law, I assure you, but she did ask that she and her husband should not simply be forgotten. So I said we would send snapshots of the children from time to time, and of the baby, too.'

Sophie's mouth, which was painted bright red this morning, tightened and her lip curled.

'Whatever for?' she demanded. 'It's not Oliver's child!'

Julia turned and glared at her, and she would have *loved* to shout she realized, struggling hard not to.

'Well, *they* don't know that, nor ever will,' she said evenly. 'And let me give you a piece of advice: if you intend to stay in Polwean forever, I should make sure that nobody who doesn't already know ever finds out the truth, either. This isn't London, people don't live free and easy lives down here, and they *do* pay a lot of attention to what everyone else is doing. Immorality goes down very poorly, and I should know. Pretty much everyone in the village knew why my parents had me thrown into Blackridge — but no one ever did anything about it. So long as you and Rory know whose baby it is, it doesn't really matter what everyone else thinks.'

Sophie wandered to the window and gazed out at the grim, January day. This winter seemed to be taking so long and she hated it. As she watched she saw Gladys coming back from Home Farm with a net of swedes in one hand and a net of cabbages in the other. Dumpy, plain Gladys who, as she got older, compared less and less favourably to Julia.

The fact that such a thing mattered not in the least to either Gladys or Julia now made no difference to Sophie.

'You know,' she observed, watching Gladys's progress across the lawns, 'I sometimes think Annie's mother and I have a lot in common. It isn't easy to be anyone's second choice, and we were both second choice . . . to you.'

'You were Oliver's first choice,' Julia replied coldly, and Sophie uttered a mirthless chuckle.

'Until he met you,' she said.

19

Spring finally drove winter away and at last
the weather grew warmer. The days lengthened and snowdrops were followed by
daffodils and primroses, and then apple-
blossom. Soon there would be bluebells in
the orchard and the blossom would snow on
them as it did every year. Soon, Julia thought,
it would be a year since Mrs Collins had first
told her that the Cromptons were coming
back to Cornwall.

She remembered the day clearly, remembered sitting in the housekeeper's room with
the windows open, listening to Guy teasing
Minnie out by the vegetable beds.

So much had changed in one year.

Guy was gone from the dower now; he
and his wife and little son were living at
Rectory Farm with Gladys. Although they
had been offered a home at Tremar, Guy
had not been able to manage the stairs,
which were polished wood and lethal for
him, so Matt had organized a downstairs
bedroom for them at the farm, from where
every day they made their way to the shop
to learn the ropes of shopkeeping from an

extremely helpful Mrs Dawkins.

Patrick had gone from the dower, too, and was living in the manor, but branching out boldly and could walk to the village and back by himself now. He was meticulously preparing for his wedding, and in a few weeks Annie would be a married woman.

Oliver was simply gone.

Julia put flowers on his grave each week, along with flowers for her other charges, and sometimes took the children, though to her knowledge Sophie had not been again since the day of the funeral. Julia had paid for a headstone, and whether Sophie liked it or not, it described him as 'beloved husband of Sophie and beloved father of Alice and Edward'. In the village, his death was officially spoken of as a tragic accident, though what people said behind closed doors Julia could do nothing about.

It was May: only three weeks until Sophie's baby was due, and a mere seven weeks to Annie and Patrick's wedding, but before both of those things there was going to be another funeral, for Minnie was gently but inexorably fading away.

She had never recovered from her winter cough and her breath now rattled painfully in her clogged lungs. She no longer spoke, nor did she eat. Julia and Mrs Collins spent hours of each day patiently feeding her sips of rich beef tea, chicken soup or hot milk, and when they lifted her into and out of her bed she was skeletally thin. Yet she grimly hung on to life.

'Maybe she'm waiting for the young ones' weddin'?' Mrs Collins suggested one morning as she lovingly changed Minnie's improvised nappy and carefully washed and powdered her, in the constant fight against painful bedsores. 'She'm certainly 'anging on for some-thin'.'

Julia gazed bleakly at the tiny, wizened, twisted body on the bed, and ached with her memories of their lifetime together.

'She won't live another seven weeks,' she replied quietly. 'She can't. I've had to explain that to Annie and she's absolutely distraught, but I don't see how she can possibly live another week, to be honest. Ilona's coming tomorrow, by the way, Mrs Collins; if you remember I told you she promised she would be here at the end, and she seems to think it will be any day now.'

Mrs Collins smiled and then lifted Minnie with great gentleness, dressed her in a clean nightdress and warm dressing-gown, and sat her in the big armchair beside her bed. She barely made a dent in the seat any longer.

'I'm glad about Miss Vincent, ma dear,' she said, glancing up at Julia. 'I do know what this must mean to you, an' it ent made any easier with Mrs Crompton be'aving so badly. I'm sure I don't know what's got into 'er, I really don't. You'd think as 'ow she'd be grateful for bein' allowed to stay an' that, but she don't seem like it, do she?'

Sophie's hostility was an ever-present running sore nowadays and Julia was fast reaching the end of her tether. She no longer ate at the table with everyone else, either at breakfast time or in the evening. She'd made a sarcastic remark about not having anything to wear to dinner in the beginning, but it hadn't been anything to do with that and everyone knew it quite well.

The fact was she had heaped up guilt and resentment since Oliver's death and closed herself in with her suffering until there wasn't even any room for Rory. She lived an isolated existence, barely communicating with anyone, wandering the paths of the estate in her heavily pregnant state for some part of every day, and lying on her bed the rest of the time; and if she even so much as came upon Julia accidentally she would immediately turn round and walk away.

Julia looked at her housekeeper wretchedly and shook her head.

'I never meant for it to be like this,' she complained. 'All I was ever trying to do was help, you know. Help, and make amends.'

Mrs Collins shrugged her shoulders and there was a resentful gleam in her eyes as she began stripping Minnie's bed and rolling up everything that had to be taken down to the laundry room.

'Some people,' she replied, 'don't know when they'm well off, I'm afraid . . . an' even some people who ought to know better. Well you got enough to worry about, ma dear, so you leave 'er be. Maybe she'll come round when she sees them lovely kiddies in their finery for the weddin'. At least *they'm* making an effort; in fact they'm doing remarkably well, I think, for 'aving lost their father so recently.'

It was true, Alice and Edward were coping splendidly, but that was in no small way thanks to the inhabitants of Tremar, for despite everything else they had to do, they were never too busy to give them time. Edward wanted to spend most of his time with Matt, but Alice needed more than making model aeroplanes and mending farming tools; she needed to be needed — and Patrick had stepped brilliantly into that particular role. He had chosen her as his teacher, and with Alice for company he had learned his way about the manor, about the estate and about the village. Alice and Patrick were perfect for each other.

Annie had chosen Edward and Alice to be her pageboy and bridesmaid on her big day, and Julia, on yet another forage through the attics, had found a wonderful evening gown of her mother's made of blue silk and cream lace, which she had pulled apart and then made into a perfect bridesmaid's dress for Alice, with a little matching hat. Edward was to be dressed exactly the same as his adored Uncle Matt.

From a bolt of Logan tartan, which Matt had carried with him ever since he left Scotland, he was having a dress kilt made for the child and Julia was making him a tiny black velvet jacket. With it all underway, Matt, in a solemn ceremony, had made the little boy an honorary Logan and presented him with a silver and amethyst brooch to hold his plaid in place across his shoulder, and Edward was completely enchanted. Now he leaped out of bed every morning to see if his beard was growing yet!

It was all getting closer and closer; Julia's wedding gown had been carefully unpacked and was hanging ready for Annie, with a diamond tiara dug out of the family jewels and a crisp white veil, and Julia was busy with her sewing-machine for both Gladys and herself. But Sophie was detached from all of it: left out, uncaring, closed tightly in her misery, and beginning to feel desperately ill.

★ ★ ★

Ilona Vincent gazed down at Minnie and shook her head sadly. She had been at Tremar for three days now, and she and Julia were taking it in turns to keep a vigil at her bedside, for the presence of death seemed to hover in the room all the time, and yet Minnie never quite gave in to it. Her breathing would slow and she would seem to be fading away and then with no bidding from anyone she would rally. She would even open her eyes sometimes and it seemed to Julia that she was waiting for something ... listening ... and then drifting back to sleep because, whatever it was, she couldn't hear it yet.

It was nine in the morning on a gorgeous May day. All over the manor the windows were open letting in the fragrant warmth; down amongst the vegetables servicemen chatted peacefully as they worked; out in the fields tractors ploughed up and down, but unaware of any of it, Sophie slept soundly in her bed.

Alice, Edward and Rory had long since gone to school, and this morning she hadn't even been awake to say goodbye to them. She had awoken much earlier, at about five o'clock, and needed to pad along the corridor to the bathroom, and on the way back she had felt excessively unwell. Falling back into bed she had found herself wet with sweat, and crawled under the covers, wrapping her arms about herself in despair; and in that position she had drifted back to sleep. Now she was fathoms deep in a lake of troubled dreams, and the first, sharp labour pain brought her swiftly to the surface, blinking in surprise. It was not yet time!

She was leaning against the wall opposite the staircase when Julia came up with a cup of tea for Ilona some twenty minutes later. She had staggered from her bed and stumbled down the corridor in the hopes of meeting someone . . . anyone . . . and as she saw Julia coming up towards her, another contraction seized her and her waters broke.

As Julia reached the top step, Sophie had collapsed against the wall, groaning in pain, lying in a pool of water, her nightgown plastered to her legs.

'It's coming . . . ' she whispered, blinking at Julia in terror. 'And it's three weeks early. Get the doctor . . . please!'

Both the midwife and the doctor in the

village were out on separate calls, for no one had been expecting the baby yet. Julia slammed the phone down desperately.

'Wouldn't you just know it!' she cried angrily, and ran upstairs again to find that Ilona, with her nurse's training and exceptional calm, had organized the bedroom for the delivery and helped Sophie into bed.

Mrs Collins was there as well, and she also seemed to know what to do — for which Julia was extremely grateful — but as they murmured amongst themselves, Julia began to realize that neither of them was particularly happy. They whispered about Sophie's unhealthy colour and her evident lack of strength, and they seemed most unsettled about the fact that the child would be three weeks premature.

Julia watched Sophie in alarm, then she went to the bed and sat down, taking her hand and squeezing it softly.

'I'm no good at anything like this,' she said softly. 'I have no experience, but don't be frightened. They'll help you, I promise they will.'

She didn't know whether it was the right thing to say or not, or even if it sounded utterly stupid, but Sophie didn't appear to think so, for she hung on to Julia's hand grimly.

'Don't leave me,' she begged. 'Please don't leave me . . . Please stay with me . . . ' and she dissolved into tears.

Julia forgot all their troubles in an instant.

'Of course I'll stay,' she promised firmly. 'Of course I will.'

The hopes that the confinement might be smooth and trouble-free faded quickly. Morning became afternoon as Sophie's contractions increased in their intensity, but nothing moved. She began to weaken, for she was already short of resources, and as she lay propped on the pillows wailing in agony, the baby rested against a nerve in her back and the pain became excruciating. Sweat-soaked and exhausted, she clutched the edges of the bed so hard that her knuckles showed white, and she began to look so bad that Miss Vincent's concern grew considerably.

By four in the afternoon a string of messages had been left at the surgery and still the doctor didn't come. Sophie lay like a limp ragdoll as her strength ebbed away and now Ilona's concern was for Julia as well, for she, of everyone, knew what memories this must be dredging up. She had been many times into the room where the frightened seventeen-year-old had given birth all those years ago, and she knew it for what it was: a mortuary. They had never expected Julia's child to live. Now it seemed less and less likely that Sophie's baby would live either, and Ilona wasn't sure she wanted Julia to see that.

'God, I wish that damn doctor would get here,' she whispered, frowning at the failing Sophie. 'I can't believe they can't find him.'

Julia glanced at her, seeing the strain on her face and fearing it.

'Or the midwife?' she replied hopefully, and Ilona shook her head.

'I doubt there's any more she can do than I can,' she answered. 'Frankly, the child is stuck and somehow we have to move it, otherwise they'll both die.'

Julia tried not to think about Alice and Edward. The prospect of them losing their mother so soon after their father's death was unspeakable. She tried not to think about Rory, either, for this was his wonderful second chance in life. He was to be a father, to be a husband again when he had expected to grow old alone, and she wanted it for Rory so much.

She sat on the bed close to Sophie's head and began to wipe her forehead with a cool cloth. Sophie moaned and then her eyes opened and in terror she grasped at Julia's hands, hanging on as blood from a torn fingernail smeared Julia's fingers.

'If I die . . . ' she wheezed breathlessly, 'if I die . . . promise me you'll look after my children. *Promise me!*'

'You're not going to die!' Julia retorted firmly, squeezing the damp hands. 'It's going to be all right.'

Sophie began to sob, but there were no tears, it was pure exhaustion.

'*Promise me!*' she hissed. '*Promise* . . . ' and Julia bent to kiss her.

'Of course I promise you,' she whispered. 'We would love them as our own and never let any harm come to them, you know that.'

Sophie sank back with a sigh and then immediately was wracked with another contraction that thrust her body upwards in agony and brought screams tearing from her lungs.

Ilona Vincent drew in her breath sharply.

'Right, that's it,' she said, 'I'm going to try and move the baby. I have to or else her heart will simply give out. It will hurt, and she will scream and try to stop me, Julia, so hang on to her very tightly, please.'

She did what she had to do and Sophie screeched in agony, fighting as Julia struggled to hold her down. When the contraction passed, her head fell back on to the pillow and she sobbed dryly, her eyes wide with fear and pain.

'No more, no more ... ' she begged pitifully. 'I can't stand it, I can't!'

Ilona touched her with gentle, compassionate fingers.

'I'm sorry, my dear, but I *must* do it,' she whispered. 'Please try to be brave, you're doing so well, but your baby will die if I don't move him.'

Sophie shook her head in panic, ineffectually trying to push herself up the bed to escape, but there was nothing she could do to stop her contractions. Three more times Ilona struggled to move the child, until Sophie screamed unmercifully for her to stop; and during the break, to her great relief, both the doctor and the midwife, who had met on the doorstep, came into the room.

She stood back immediately, not wishing to trespass on their territory, but the new doctor in Polwean was young, like Oliver had been, and not afraid to ask for help, nor to acknowledge efficiency. For some moments the three of them conferred, then the doctor removed his jacket and rolled up his sleeves.

Day drifted into evening, and then into night. Rory and the Crompton children returned from school, and Mrs Collins fed them, along with Matt and Annie. After dinner, Matt took over the job of keeping the children occupied whilst Rory fretted in the drawing-room and Annie sat with Minnie. At nine o'clock Matt put Edward and Alice to bed — in a room as far away as possible from the one in which their mother agonized — and firmly read them to sleep, then he took a turn with Minnie, and this time found himself comforting Annie.

In the confinement room, Sophie had reached the end of her strength. The doctor listened to her heart a couple of times and then shook his head slowly, pursing his lips.

'We'll have to cut her,' he whispered. 'She's dying. In fact, we may already have left it too late, and I fear there isn't anything we can do for the baby. One more attempt to get it moving, and if that doesn't work we'll prepare her, all right?'

The midwife and Miss Vincent nodded grimly, and Julia clutched Sophie desperately as the memory of her own tiny, dead baby sliding into the world, never to draw breath, flooded her mind.

'Oh please, Sophie,' she begged softly. '*Please*! I know you can do it, I *know* you can.'

Sophie stared at her, but there was nothing in her eyes any more, just glassy emptiness; yet as another contraction began to tense her body, she clutched at Julia's hand urgently.

'I want to . . . push,' she whispered almost inaudibly.

'Oh, thank *God!*' the doctor muttered and they positioned her legs.

Sophie bore down, grunting with the effort. It was nearly midnight and her child was at last about to be born. Julia hung on to her, whispering encouragement as once again Sophie pushed with all her might. Then she cried out in her final agony. Hands reached for the little head that at last appeared; strong hands that grasped it and gently eased it into the world; and with the tiny, wrinkled, grey and lifeless infant came spurts of bright red blood, flooding the bed.

'She's haemorrhaging,' the doctor cried. 'Nurse, I need a hand!'

The midwife cast the baby aside in her hurry to assist the doctor, and he lay where he landed, crumpled and still. Julia stared at him in terrible grief, and then watched Miss Vincent carefully lift him in her arms and carry him to the chest of drawers in the corner, where there were blankets and warm water.

Her first efforts at reviving him were useless; he responded to nothing. Julia could do no more for Sophie now, and so went to stand beside Ilona, willing the tiny baby boy to live. Miss Vincent poked her finger into his mouth, clearing mucus and fluids as best she could, then she tried again to make him breathe. She smacked him hard and this time his little body jerked, his fists clenched, he drew an unsteady little breath and uttered a thin wail of protest.

Julia burst into tears.

They paid no more attention to what was happening on the bed, for they could do nothing whatsoever to help. Miss Vincent washed the child, wrapped him warmly in soft blankets and motioned to Julia to leave the room with her. On the landing they stared at each other, and each wondered if she looked as tired and drawn as the other.

'Will he live?' Julia whispered.

Ilona Vincent looked serious.

'I very much doubt it,' she answered honestly. 'I'll be surprised if he survives the night, and I'll be surprised if she does, either.'

'Oh God!' Julia whimpered. 'There's got to be something I can do. Please, Ilona, tell me what to do!'

Miss Vincent glanced down at the unhealthily coloured infant in her arms and then looked broodily at Julia for a moment.

Eventually she said, 'Well, there might be something you could try, if you felt you were strong enough, but you will need to be strong, because if it doesn't work it won't be your fault. As you know, my mother was a midwife in a Cornish tin-mining village at the turn of the century, and, frankly, in those days of no money and no medical treatment to speak of, there was a pretty poor survival rate. If she delivered an ailing one like this she used to suggest to the mother that she take the child into bed with her, lie him on her breast so that he could feel her warmth and her heart beating against his own, and keep him there all night. Obviously Sophie can't do that, but . . . you could. I know it's asking a lot, I know how much you yearn for a child of your own, but at least you would be doing everything humanly possible to help this little one to live.'

Julia stared at the child and her heart ached for him. She didn't have to make a choice, it was instinctive.

'I'll do it,' she said immediately, 'but . . . ' She looked away uncomfortably, ' . . . but I didn't want to leave Minnie to die without me . . . Oh God, that sounds so selfish, doesn't it?'

Ilona shook her head.

'Julia, you are the least selfish person I know,' she told her. 'But, you know, Minnie knows exactly how much you love her; she's *always* known that; it was the mainstay of her life. There isn't anything you can do for her any more, except keep a vigil by her bedside, and I can do that just as well as you can. Don't you think she would have wanted you to struggle to save a new life, rather than sit and watch an old one slip away?'

Julia bit back her tears and nodded firmly.

'Come and help me,' she begged, and they hurried away to her bedroom.

She stripped herself naked and climbed into bed as Ilona unwrapped the tiny child and placed him on his front, between Julia's breasts, then she put a soft blanket over him and pulled up the bedclothes, so that she could just see his wrinkled little face. Skin against skin, this tiny, precious thing . . . that wasn't hers. He needed the warmth from her body and she gave it willingly.

'Talk to him,' Ilona suggested gently. 'Encourage him, it can't do any harm. Will I fetch Matt for you before I go?'

Julia smiled at her and could not have begun to describe, even to Ilona, how it felt to have this tiny vulnerable little thing against her heart. Her little daughter had been much more premature, of course; she had had no chance of life at all, but even had she lived a few moments, the callous officials at Blackridge would not have cared. They would not even have shown her to her mother, let alone allowed them any contact with each other.

'Tell Matt,' she said, slightly shakily, 'to make sure Rory is all right first, please. And Ilona, I want to know *immediately* if Minnie goes . . . or, God forbid, if Sophie does.'

Miss Vincent bent and kissed her.

'I promise,' she replied and as she went away, Julia closed her eyes and sobbed as if her heart would break.

She dozed as she nursed her precious burden, and he became warm with her body heat though he did not stir and only just breathed. At about 1.30 in the morning, Matt tiptoed into the room and sat beside her on the bed, resting his back against the huge, polished mahogany headboard. He touched the baby's cheek softly with his fingers, and then bent and kissed his wife. He knew as well as she did what this meant to her, and so he didn't talk about it.

At exactly two o'clock they both heard the rich Westminster chimes ring from the grandfather clock in the hall, and Rory and Sophie's little son jerked. He drew a deep, shuddering breath and clenched his little fists and as he relaxed again against Julia's warm skin, some colour appeared in his wrinkled little face.

Julia put her finger against one of his hands and he grasped it loosely. His tiny mouth make a sort of sucking motion and he breathed deeply again.

'He's coming back,' Julia whispered. 'I thought he was going to die, but he's not, he's coming back. Oh, Matt . . . '

Then the bedroom door opened very quietly and Ilona Vincent crept into the room. By the dim light of the bedside lamp they had kept burning, Julia saw the sadness in her eyes and knew without needing to be told.

'Minnie's gone?' she whispered.

Miss Vincent nodded.

'She slipped away peacefully and quietly, my dear,' she replied. 'At exactly two o'clock as it happens. It was as the chimes were dying away. Annie's desperately upset, but I think she understands it was the only kind thing. Minnie was suffering and it was time for it to end.'

'Exactly two o'clock!' Julia repeated in astonishment. 'It was at exactly two o'clock that this little chap drew his first deep breath and moved his hands. It was as if new life suddenly flowed into him.'

Ilona Vincent's face suddenly lit with a beautiful smile, and she nodded in delight.

'So *that* was what she was waiting for,' she murmured. 'Of course, I should have known.'

'Waiting for?' Julia echoed and Ilona grinned.

'Fanciful old wives' tales, my dear,' she

replied, 'but my mother firmly believed that a loving, departing spirit would sometimes find a place for itself in an ailing baby whose spirit was too weak for it to live. So maybe our lovely Minnie will live again, in this little chap. It would be nice to think she could; nice to think she would be loved this time, be allowed to be strong and run about and have a carefree childhood.'

Matt gazed at her warmly.

'Aye,' he said softly, 'My mother believed precisely the same thing. One out, one in, she always used to say, and would spend years pointing out the likenesses. And they were there sometimes, too. Or maybe it was just a fancy. Either way, I'm happy with the idea. D'you know the news of Sophie, by the way?'

Ilona nodded.

'I looked in at the door, briefly,' she replied. 'She's alive and sleeping peacefully, though she's very weak. She did lose a lot of blood I fear, but thankfully they managed to stop it. Mr Nelson is with her now, the doctor and the midwife have gone.'

Julia closed her eyes and for a moment she allowed herself to wander through her memories of Minnie. Her gentle, nervous, doglike devotion in those nightmarish early days at Blackridge; her struggle to learn the days of the week and months of the year; her devotion to Matt and then to Annie. She had touched so many lives and had no idea she had ever done so, and by those who had loved her she would be long remembered, yet she had lived for most of her life with no name and no birthday, and if she had died at Blackridge she would have been buried in an unmarked grave and forgotten.

'Give Minnie a kiss goodbye for me,' she said, as Miss Vincent prepared to leave the room. 'And tomorrow we'll administer to her ourselves. She's to be buried in her favourite dress, and I want it to be perfect.'

Ilona nodded and then crept away.

When the dark hours finally passed and the sun climbed early into the heavens, everyone slept late. Mrs Collins was first into Julia's bedroom, and found, to her relief, Matt asleep sitting up, Julia asleep on her back, and the tiny baby Nelson stirring in his warm cocoon.

He was getting hungry.

Ten minutes later Julia carried him quietly into Sophie's darkened bedroom, that still smelled of yesterday's struggle and pain. Rory, crumpled on a chair by the bed, his head resting on one of Sophie's hands awoke with a start and sat up, grimacing at stiff bones and muscles. Sophie turned her head with a little moan and then opened her eyes.

Mrs Collins was pulling the curtains, letting in the morning.

'He . . . lived . . . ' Sophie whispered, trying and failing to pull herself up. 'You saved his life.'

Mrs Collins and Rory pulled her up gently between them, plumped and turned her pillows and then allowed her to sink back against them. She was as white as a sheet, with big dark circles beneath her eyes and cracked, colourless lips, but she held out her arms and received her child with a deep sigh of pleasure.

'Thank you . . . ' she murmured unsteadily, and Julia and Mrs Collins went away quietly, to leave Rory and Sophie together, with their son.

★ ★ ★

One week later, on a perfect afternoon with the air heady with the scents of summer and the sky a clear, burnished blue above them, they laid Minnie's earthly remains to rest in a sunny corner of the churchyard. She wore her most colourful summer dress, the one she had always loved the best, and round her neck the string of pearls that Matt had presented her with on his wedding day. On her headstone she would be remembered as

Minnie Logan, with her birthday the same day as Annie's. Only the people who had loved her came to her funeral, and at Julia's insistence, nobody wore black.

Annie wept quietly into a handkerchief as the coffin slid slowly into the earth, but Julia found no reason to cry. All that was going to the grave here was a body that had served its owner poorly. The soul, the spirit that was the girl who had latched herself to the abandoned Julia and given her unwavering loyalty for a quarter of a century, was free. Maybe she lived in Sophie's baby son, or maybe she roamed Tremar unseen, but all-seeing — either way, Julia knew Minnie would always be close by them, and was contented.

Julia and Matt each threw a handful of earth on to the coffin as the undertakers pulled away their ropes, and then in a gesture of great fondness that touched her heart, she saw Guy throw in a handful of sweets.

Afterwards the small party walked back to Tremar in the glorious sunshine and found that Mrs Collins had baked a special cake for tea — in which she had put fresh eggs, sugar and all sorts of goodies normally so carefully guarded in this time of war.

'A cake especially for Minnie,' she announced, 'to celebrate her life.'

It promised to be the best cake anyone had tasted for months and months!

Rory was sitting on the terrace as they returned to the manor, rocking his baby son in a lovely pre-war pram borrowed from someone in the village. Even in one week the infant had filled out and was no longer too small for his skin; he was growing into it nicely.

'I should take him upstairs,' Julia said, hearing that he was uttering slightly fretful noises. 'It must be almost time for his feed.'

'And I would be most grateful,' Rory replied, smiling at her, 'because those stairs frighten me to death when I'm carrying him. Did it all go all right?'

Julia kissed his forehead and then lifted the baby in her arms. He smelled warm and milky, and he tugged at her heart with nails as sharp as claws — but she never said so.

'It was lovely,' she said softly. 'Just right for my darling Minnie. She was the gentlest soul I ever met in my life, and I feel very privileged to have known her. She made me live when all I wanted was to die. She made me live so that in the end I was rewarded with all this. She certainly earned her place in Paradise! Just make sure they save Sophie and me a piece of cake, Rory, won't you?'

Rory chuckled.

'I'll be sure,' he replied, and as she was walking away he added, 'Oh, and by the way, Sophie has something she would like to tell you when you go up; something *we* would like to tell you.'

Julia took the baby upstairs, whispering to him softly as she went. Sophie's room was so freshly aired and orderly now, it was hard to believe it had been such a battlefield of pain and fear only a week before. Next door, Alice and Edward were safely back in their room, and though Edward pretended he was much too busy to care, Alice was enchanted with her baby brother.

Sophie looked much better, but she still had a way to go, though lots of sweet, rich milk sent up regularly by Doreen was doing her all the good in the world. She was no longer even remotely in danger of dying, but she knew she would never have any more children: it was far too dangerous. She and Rory had no choice but to be happy with their one son — even though they could never publicly acknowledge him.

She was dozing and awoke with a start when Julia entered the room. In her weakened state, the day after her son was delivered, she had begged Julia's forgiveness for everything, and asked if they might be friends. She had still been half expecting to die then, and Julia had wondered how long the truce would last once she knew for certain she would live, but it seemed that the dark world Sophie had inhabited for so long had finally spat her out. She was alive, she was in love and she was a mother again. It was enough.

She asked about the funeral and then, as she took her baby in her arms ready for his feed, she said, 'Julia, can you stay for just a minute? There's something I want to say.'

Julia sat on the edge of the bed.

For a moment Sophie looked at her, and then briefly a bright blush rose on her cheeks. It made her look heaps better, Julia thought, though she didn't say so.

'I've been talking to Rory,' she began, 'and we're both of one mind. We would like it very much indeed if you and Matt would agree to be godparents to our son.' Her corn-coloured hair, newly washed now, brushed her shoulders and touched her baby's face as she looked down at him. 'And, unless you have any violent objections,' she added shyly, 'we plan to call him Oliver Julian, to be known as Julian. You saved his life, Julia, despite all the awful things I've said and done in the past months, and despite the fact that you can't . . . you know . . . You saved him, when everyone else thought he didn't have a chance. I remember when I started to bleed, I saw the midwife just move him out of the way. She wasn't even going to try . . . and . . . well . . . '

Julia reached out and touched her arm very gently.

'Ilona managed to get him to breathe,' she told her.

'Yes, but you took him to bed with you and you nursed him all night,' Sophie said. 'Miss Vincent told me what you did.' Suddenly her face looked very vulnerable and her eyes grew big with tears. 'I hated and resented you,' she whispered unsteadily. 'I thought it was all your fault what happened, but it wasn't. I needed someone to blame and you were there. I can't begin to explain all that I felt, but I promise it's over now, and I so much want you to be a part of Julian's life.'

Julia smiled, and for a while she watched the baby in his mother's arms. Oh yes, she wanted so badly to be a part of his life.

'Matt and I would be honoured to be Julian's godparents,' she replied warmly, 'and honoured to be a part of his life, as well.' Suddenly she laughed softly. 'Only I don't quite know how Edward's going to feel about it.'

Sophie sighed and raised her eyes to the ceiling.

'Oh God, isn't he boring about his beloved Uncle Matt?' she muttered. 'It's enough to drive you frantic! Anyway, with any luck, he'll have grown up a bit by the time Julian is demanding attention, otherwise there'll be hell to pay! He's asking at the moment if he can have his surname changed to Logan.'

'I'm afraid Matt won't allow that,' Julia said. 'He has very strict ideas about honouring thy father and thy mother — except in my case, of course — but he'll be hugely flattered I promise you.' Then she slipped out of the room. She was not able to watch Sophie feed her son; it was more than she could bear.

As she went out on to the terrace a few moments later, she found Matt sitting on the edge of the fountain basin smoking his pipe and enjoying the sunshine. The little fat boy in the fountain and his fantastical fish were shiny with the splashing water, and goldfish flashed and glittered in the basin.

'They want us to be godparents,' she said, sitting down beside him. 'We have a godchild, Matt.'

He nodded, and for a little while they were silent as the murmur of voices drifted up to them from the vegetable beds beneath the terrace and a breeze moved the branches of the cedar tree above their heads. Then Gladys came out of the French windows and beyond her, in the drawing-room, Julia could see Annie and Patrick, deep in conversation.

Tremar; the enchanted place. In her mind Sandro and the three musketeers played at sword-fighting on the lawns whilst she and little Gladys sat on the terrace wall, their legs dangling, eating apples they had scrumped from the orchard; and all the suffering between then and now slid quietly into its place to become one piece of Tremar's huge and varied jigsaw.

She joined Gladys by the wall and they watched the blossom falling in the orchard.

After a moment she said, 'What are you thinking?' and Gladys laughed softly.

'All fer one and one fer all,' she replied. 'The musketeers an' your brother fightin' it out down there, an' your father clickin' 'is tongue, an gettin' all angry 'cos we was makin' so much noise. You know, if Annie was to 'ave twins one day, we might start up the musketeers all over again!'

Julia glanced over her shoulder at Annie who was leading Patrick out into the sunshine. Her heart was so full it felt as if it might burst.

'Yes, but only if they let us join this time!' she declared. 'You've got to back me up on that one, Gladys. They've got to let you and me into the gang; none of this silly 'boys only' stuff, and only using us to drag around when they needed a damsel in distress. Damn cheek, I called it!'

Gladys chuckled heartily.

'Oh, quite right,' she agreed. 'This time they let us join!'

THE END

HOT POPPIES

Reggie Nadelson

A murder in New York's diamond district. A dead Chinese girl with a photograph in her pocket. A plastic bag of irradiated heroin in an empty apartment. A fire in a Chinatown sweatshop. The worst blizzard in New York's history. These events conspire to bring ex-cop Artie Cohen out of retirement and back into the obsessive world of murder and politics that nearly killed him. The terrifying plot uncoils first in New York — in Artie's own back yard — then in Hong Kong, where everything — and everyone — is for sale.

COME HOME TO DANGER

Estelle Thompson

Charles Waring has come home to Queensland to attend his mother's funeral and his remark, intended only for a family friend to hear, is inadvertently overheard by several other people. The chain of events which follows convinces Charles that his mother was murdered because she knew a terrible secret from someone's past, and he finds himself in a deadly game of cat-and-mouse as he tries to unravel the mystery. Meanwhile, he must face the certainty that someone among those he has come to care about poses a cruel threat.

SUMMER OF SECRETS

Grace Thompson

When Bettrys Hopkyns' alcoholic sister Eirlys committed suicide, Bettrys was determined that Eirlys's baby daughter Cheryl — the result of Eirlys's secretive summer love affair — would stay with her. Still yearning for Brett, her former lover, Bettrys sets herself a challenge: to find Cheryl's father. Her search takes her and Cheryl to a small seaside village in west Wales; to a close-knit community seething with secrets. Befriended by the cheerful Gordon, who falls in love with her, Bettrys is quickly drawn into a web of deceit and is forced to face the terrifying possibility that Brett might be a murderer . . .

A MORTAL AFFAIR

Stella Allan

Frances Parry seemed to have it made. She was married to a Harley Street consultant, she had a beautiful home, wealthy friends — including the fascinating Bernard, her husband's friend since undergraduate days — and a creative job. But suddenly Frances's world was turned upside down; her home was sold, her sideline job became a vital means of livelihood, and Bernard, who had become her lover, was exposed as a criminal. And then Frances found that she herself was indulging in criminal activities in a deadly duel with the law.